RACHELLE ATALLA

# The Pharmacist

HODDER

First published in Great Britain in 2022 by Hodder & Stoughton
An Hachette UK company

This paperback edition published in 2022

2

A CIP catalogue record for this title is
available from the British Library

Paperback ISBN 978 1 529 34214 7

Typeset in Plantin Light by Hewer Text UK Ltd, Edinburgh
Printed and bound in Great Britain by Clays Ltd, Elcograf S.p.A.

Hodder & Stoughton policy is to use papers that are
natural, renewable and recyclable products and made
from wood grown in sustainable forests. The logging and
manufacturing processes are expected to conform to the
environmental regulations of the country of origin.

Hodder & Stoughton Ltd
Carmelite House
50 Victoria Embankment
London EC4Y 0DZ

www.hodder.co.uk

Praise for *The Pharmacist*

'Atalla nails the atmosphere of claustrophobia and brings this world to life convincingly, as well as fostering sympathy for her protagonist, despite her flaws. This debut author is one to watch'
*Sunday Times*

'Reminiscent of Orwell's *Nineteen Eighty-Four*, this unsettling story is a nightmare for our times of end-of-the-world prepping, increased nuclear insecurity and political inequality'
*Guardian*

'A compulsive, claustrophobic but wonderfully compassionate read, beautifully written and set within a brilliantly realised world. Rachelle Atalla is a major talent and I can't wait to see where her mind goes next'
Kirstin Innes, author of *Scabby Queen*

'Sitting somewhere on the spectrum between Paul Auster's heart-rending *In the Country of Last Things* and Bong Joon-ho's pulse-thumping film *Snowpiercer*, *The Pharmacist* is a slow-burn nightmare about how ordinary human decency gets eroded – and also how it perseveres'
*The Times*

'An unflinching portrayal of what we might all be capable of, Atalla's stunning debut is essential reading for our times'
Helen Sedgwick, author of *Where the Missing Gather*

'There are shades of George Orwell in this stunning writing debut, but Rachelle Atalla's voice is highly original. And wholly her own'
*The Herald*

'Atalla's speculative literary thriller debut draws you in with its mounting sense of tension, disquiet and desperation'
CultureFly

'This horrendously claustrophobic, utterly absorbing debut. The fiercely controlled narrative beautifully translates the horrendous grip of dismal routines and tiny, stolen pleasures'
*Daily Mail*

## About the Author

Rachelle Atalla is a Scottish-Egyptian novelist,
short story writer and screenwriter based in
Glasgow, who previously worked as a community
pharmacist for a decade. Thankfully she has yet to
be locked in a bunker, but there is still time.

Her short stories have been published widely in literary
anthologies; she is the recipient of a Scottish Book
Trust New Writers Award and co-edits New Writing
Scotland. Her first short film screenplay *Trifle* was
commissioned by the Scottish Film & Talent Network,
and most recently Rachelle was selected to participate
in the 2021 Young Films Foundation Skye residency
programme, developing her first feature length screenplay
with BBC Films. *The Pharmacist* was her first novel.

For Angus

*I should like to end gloriously and greatly like a Shakespearean hero; it is shocking to think that as the bomb bursts I shall be wondering how to find the money for next month's bills.*
Bertrand Russell

# I

In the recreation room a man was lying on the concrete floor.
He was gripping his stomach, while his grey boiler suit, identical to the ones we all wore, hung loosely from his body.
Some of the Velcro strips had come undone and you could
see the hairs on his chest, the growth thickening towards his
groin. I didn't know his name, nor did I recognise him. But
there were so many faces in here, and I tried not to linger on
any of them for too long.

Some of the kids who had been playing a board game
surrounded him, and the adults who had bothered to follow
the noise stood perplexed. The doctor on duty was Stirling
and he was kneeling beside the man. What's your name?

Templeton, he managed through gritted teeth.

Can you stand?

Templeton let out a slow and stifled howl before he thrust
his fingers into his mouth. He bit down and dots of bright
red moistened his lips. For a brief moment I would perhaps
have done anything for red meat.

Stirling turned to us. Help me get him to my surgery, he
said, and four men flocked forward, desperate to exercise
some of their fading and wasting muscles.

What happened? I asked.

A boy of maybe thirteen years old replied. We were just
playing Monopoly and he came in and ate the houses.

He swallowed most of them, and the hotels too, one of the girls chimed in.

I glanced at the Monopoly board. The little metal dog was on its side and the top hat upturned. When did he eat the pieces? I asked.

They looked at each other.

He swallowed them maybe thirty, forty minutes ago, the girl said.

And you didn't think to do anything?

They shrugged in unison. He wouldn't let us leave, the boy said. Kept talking about little fish.

Fish?

Yeah, the fish that eat the dead skin off your feet.

It made him feel clean, the girl added. Said he wasn't clean in here.

Go back to your bunks, I said. Let your parents know you're OK.

I turned and looked at one of the bookcases behind me. The literature had been carefully censored: children's books, light romance, travel and craft magazines made up the bulk. I picked up a book called *Upper Fourth at Malory Towers* and on scanning the blurb wondered if anyone actually read this. The spine of the book had snapped in the middle and was only really held together by its cover. I opened the book randomly and my eyes traced over a few lines but I couldn't concentrate. There was no shock left in watching someone attempt a suicide but I was struck by Templeton's originality, impressed even. I doubted it would be something I was capable of. My whole life had been made up of these moments – envious of other people's convictions. I felt feeble in comparison.

I made my way to the bathroom blocks. The only segregated space in the bunker – male and female, any hint of inclusivity from our previous world completely eradicated. Fluorescent lights shone brightly regardless of the hour, and the toilet and shower cubicles were hidden behind plastic curtains so it was difficult to determine if anyone was behind them. It was only during the night and very early in the mornings that I found the bathroom blocks bearable. Sometimes I fantasised about creeping over the bunker's boundary line and using the opposite side's blocks just to break routine. Perhaps I'd discover something different, like more toilet paper or better water pressure.

Trying my best not to let my thoughts linger on Templeton any more, I sat down on the toilet seat and stared at my knees. They were hairy. Everything was hairy – coarse and itchy, and I enjoyed clawing at my skin, opening up buried follicles, forcing ingrowing hairs back through the surface.

There was the noise of my urine hitting the pan but nothing more and I decided I was alone. When I wiped I imagined there was a glow of light rising up from the seat. Like when my husband Daniel and I had been on a train in Malaysia and the toilets were only holes that opened out on to the tracks below. There was something liberating about urinating across the land, as though somehow you were fertilising it and hoping it would pros-per. The flush was weak. It cleared my urine but the toilet paper stuck.

Placing my toothbrush under the toothpaste dispenser, I waited for the white blob to slither out. I found myself wondering if you could overdose on fluoride. My brother used to worry my niece was receiving too much in her toddler toothpaste, fretted over the white milk spots that might appear. The ritual of brushing enamel was still strong with me. The strongest substance in my body – I challenged myself to keep them healthy. Many seemed to have given up their brushing, perhaps acknowledging it as the chore it had always been, but I considered that short-sighted, since extractions were being carried out now without proper anaesthetic.

After spitting I brought my face close to the metallic sheets screwed to the walls that offered me something of a reflection, but I was blurred and distorted, like in mirrors at a funfair. Peering at this image of myself, I could make out the bushiness of my eyebrows and the growth above my lip. I could see the mass of white that covered my scalp.

I used to think I had nice hair – black with a natural wave – but I'd started going grey young, maybe even as early as seventeen, eighteen. At thirty, I was dyeing it every six to eight weeks to hide the colourless strands. And now at thirty-four I thought I looked older than I was. I'd been granted a small hairband and I tied my hair up in a knot, scraping strands back from my face. I considered booking an appointment with one of the supervised hairdressers and getting my head shaved, but, as I ran my fingers across my scalp, I decided I didn't have the right shape of head. Too lumpy and asymmetrical.

The sensible thing would have been to go to bed, but, as I looked at the clocks displayed in the main chamber, I knew Stirling had a long night ahead of him. The lights above flickered then, the generators surging with power and the bulbs momentarily brightening before returning to normal. I was aware of footsteps in the distance, slow across the concrete with nowhere really to go. Our leader's young wife had made exercise videos in her previous life, and when we'd first arrived she'd wanted everyone to join in with her boot-camp-style regime, but it hadn't lasted long. There weren't enough calories to sustain everyone who was running around the bunker. One of the inhabitants had a heart attack while she was marching and died on the spot. She was the first to go and it had only dawned on us then that we had nowhere to put dead bodies. She was wrapped in a black bag and placed in one of the two exiting airlock chambers. I suppose the logic was that she'd hopefully be nothing but bones by the time we were due to leave. But both airlock chambers held bodies in them now. I was already wondering where this potential new one would go.

The door to the doctors' surgery was closed and I stood, staring and hesitating before knocking.

What? said the voice of one of the nurses.

It's the pharmacist.

The door opened and a small woman inspected me with a tilted head. Dr Stirling is busy.

I've come to help.

Beyond the waiting room I could hear Templeton's cries of pain in Stirling's examination room. I'd witnessed a man jump in front of a moving train once while I waited on the platform and could still remember the noise of bone and flesh meeting metal and momentum. It had felt like a great inconvenience at the time, to be burdened by a stranger's pain. So why was I here now?

Stirling emerged from his examination room and stood at the threshold. His stethoscope was still hanging from around his neck and he forced his hands into the pockets of his lab coat. He was the son of the health secretary and appeared to benefit from the privilege. But even so there was something likeable about him – right from the start, when we'd worked together in the military hospital, I had been drawn to his kindness. He was only twenty-eight years old but he'd visibly aged since arriving in the bunker. The smile was still there, though, honest and warm.

Fuck, he said, looking from me to his nurse, before glancing back to his patient. He gestured for me to follow him and I entered. Templeton was spread out across the examination bed, his boiler suit opened to the waist. Stirling stopped beside him, crouching so that their faces were nearly touching.

Did you do this to die? Stirling said.

Templeton opened his mouth but only a piercing noise escaped.

Stirling pressed closer towards him. Nod your head if you want to die. I need to know this is what you wanted . . .

I moved forward too, peering from behind Stirling. Templeton's head did something of an involuntary jolt forward but it didn't seem definitive enough.

Stirling looked at me and I stared back.

What did the other doctors say?

A laugh escaped from his lips. What do you think? I asked Nurse Appleby to go and get some of them but they just said it was a lost cause and I was the one on duty. I was to make an *executive decision*.

What does that mean?

What do you think it means?

We both turned back to look at Templeton. The noise of his agony was slowly beginning to lose its effect on me. Was it merging into background noise, like the television or radio? What I would have given then to hear an advert or even a song – my niece humming *The Wheels on the Bus*.

Stirling took me by the elbow and led me out into the waiting room, where his nurse was sitting, checking stock. She was licking her index finger and filing through a wad of sealed dressing pads, seemingly unaffected by what was taking place in the room next door.

Appleby, you can go, Stirling said.

She glanced at the small clock that ticked above our heads. But I still have two hours left on my shift . . .

Luckily this isn't a real hospital – and the man in there isn't a real patient. He's a figment of your imagination. No one else has noticed him.

But there's nothing for me to do out there.

It's better out there than in here, Stirling said.

Appleby placed the dressing packs back inside a green first-aid box. She closed the lid over and pulled the plastic tongues down until there was a click. She rose to her feet and was almost at the door when she stopped and turned towards me. I've got a sore throat, she said. Dr Stirling was kind enough to check my tonsils and there's no infection but it is very painful. Do you think you could offer me a throat spray or lozenge?

Of course, I said. I'll be back in the pharmacy tomorrow morning. I'll give you something then.

You couldn't just give it to me now? It would only take a minute . . .

Appleby, is this an emergency? Stirling said.

Well, no, I don't suppose it is.

Then Wolfe will be happy to deal with your request when she starts her shift tomorrow.

Stirling closed and locked the door behind Appleby. He managed a smile but it was awkward and not a happy one. He's got a perforation, he said. Suffers from ulcerative colitis. I'd need to open him up to see the true damage.

I was in Appleby's seat and it was still warm. I had a growing urge to unclip the plastic hooks of her first-aid box just to hear that clicking noise again.

But can he be treated? I said.

He ate too many.

I was hoping he'd just be able to shit the little houses out and go back to normal.

They're too sharp to pass through his gut now. Judging by the pain he's in, it has to be a bad perforation, and then it'll be blood poisoning and we can't go back from that.

Quick or slow?

It'll be slow. Really pretty slow.

I wish this hadn't fallen on you.

Stirling was quiet for a moment. The other doctors have done it before but not me. They say it's like putting the family pet down. That it's cruel to prolong the suffering . . . His hands began to shake and he forced them back into his pockets.

I'll stay with you, I said.

I can't ask you to do that.

You didn't ask.

There was silence in the other room and it stayed like that.

Maybe it's already over? I whispered.

Stirling shook his head.

Will you give him an injection or something?

Stirling shook his head again.

What should *I* do when I get in there?

Maybe just hold his hand . . .

Stirling walked back in first. Templeton had rolled on to his side and was facing us. He didn't blink, and hope started to stir within me. I was praying for him not to blink, for his eyes to already be glazed and cold, but then I caught the motion of his eyelashes flickering. He blinked again. I thought he looked peaceful, perhaps even grateful.

Stirling lifted Templeton's head slightly and removed a pillow from behind. Templeton's breathing quickened, his nostrils flaring, and I came closer, clasping his hand as Stirling had suggested. He gripped my hand tightly and it hurt but it didn't matter. I wondered who this man had been and why I hadn't noticed him before. It was difficult to gauge his age. I thought he was maybe in his early forties – staring blue eyes, and handsome before coming here. He started moving his lips, tracing silent words, but I couldn't determine what they were. Maybe he was trying to tell me his first name, letting me know who he really was. It was probably something simple – perhaps Peter or John.

I inched closer towards his body. Everything's going to be OK, I said, but I didn't know for whose benefit I was saying it.

Templeton blinked and tears started to slide down his face.

Stirling cleared his throat. Try not to struggle. It'll all be over soon. And suddenly he thrust the pillow down on to Templeton's face and was forcing his own body weight on to the frame of the examination bed. I looked at Stirling's hands, gripping either side of the pillow, then at the arch of his back; I couldn't equate this with the person who treated his patients with such care and sensitivity.

Templeton started to resist and fight. The balls of his feet rolled from side to side, his toes too curled inwards, but I refused to release his flapping hand from my grip, all the while whispering words I couldn't remember. Stirling pinned him down harder, as though his own life depended on it, using the whole weight of his body. And he was crying too, letting the tears stream down his face, begging with Templeton for it to be over.

And finally it was.

Stirling fell to the ground but I just stood there, gripping Templeton's hand for what felt like a long time, his fingers still warm from life. When I eventually prised my hand free, it was throbbing, and it occurred to me that he might have broken some of my bones. His hand fell away and I saw a wart on his index finger, next to the nail bed. I imagined him as a patient in my previous life. I would have given him Salactol lacquer and told him to be persistent. I would have told him to keep going until he'd reached the blood vessels of the wart and not to stop until they were dead and eradicated.

When Stirling got to his feet his eyes were dry. There was a change: something professional had come to life within him. He was pulling a fresh sheet over Templeton, running it gently along his body, letting it float for a second before it rested across his face, the projection of his nose visible and prominent. Stirling took a step back and observed the scene.

Your hand, he finally said. I need to give it the once-over.

I cupped it in my other hand, shielding it from him. It's fine.

No, it's not. He came to where I was standing and paused, perhaps contemplating whether he should touch me. Let's go back through to the waiting room, he said.

I followed him and he closed the door behind us, leaving Templeton alone. Stirling's hands wouldn't settle as he moved, running them up and down the chest of his lab coat. He pulled a seat out for me and then sat down opposite so we were facing one another.

I carefully offered my throbbing hand up to him.

Does this hurt? he said, lightly applying pressure to my fingers.

I flinched but managed to straighten them.

What happens now with the body?

He focused on my hand, his touch soft and gentle, as a doctor's should be. I'll write a death certificate and the soldiers will take him away. That should be it.

What will you say is the cause of death?

He hesitated. I'll write perforation, organ failure. No one else will check.

I think you should take his boiler suit, I said. It's about your size and it's only going to get colder.

He nodded. That's probably a good idea.

# 2

It was early but already there was a queue for food. The pouches of puréed strawberries and raspberries were always the first to go, followed by the blueberries and apples. Think of it as space food, our leader had said when we'd first entered the bunker – when he'd still circulated among us. We are blessed, he had added. Nutritionists from NASA designed these meal plans to ensure we receive enough of what we need for the duration of our stay.

We shuffled forward, the area cramped and at risk of over-crowding. In front of me a mother was carrying her child, his head resting against her shoulder. His eyes drooped, opening and closing before opening again. As we took another step forward, the boy pressed further up against his mother and thrust his hand out towards me.

I hesitated, glancing at his fingers before reaching out to take his hand. His childish touch was foreign to me.

Mummy, he said, and the mother half-turned and noticed our connection. Flustered, she made to pull away, already apologising.

It's OK, I replied.

He just loves holding hands.

Me too.

They're clean, she said. We just sanitised our hands, so you don't need to worry.

I shook my head. I'm not worried.

It's Baxter. That's our name.

That's a nice name, I said, my eyes focusing on the child. It seemed easier to focus on him than to look at her. His fingers were damp and soft with saliva and I gripped them a little tighter. I'm Wolfe, I added.

I know. You gave him medicine once when he had a fever.

Ah, right, yes. I remember, I said, knowing this to be a lie. How old is he?

Nearly four.

The bones of his little body were small, stunted and perhaps easy to break. There were no babies – no place for the elderly either – because what use were the truly vulnerable in here? Little Baxter didn't know how close he had come to not making the cut, but I imagined his mother was all too aware. I could barely remember what a child under the age of two looked like, let alone what they were capable of. And to be old – who defined those parameters? The ages of the men in the bunker varied, possibly into their mid, even late sixties, but never the women – certainly not the female patients I encountered in the pharmacy. None of them had the aged and dignified hands of my late grandmother, or the life experience to see history repeating itself.

As we reached the front of the queue I was forced to release my grip from Baxter's hand. They were given their ration of pouches for the day and the mother tried to plant the boy down on the ground but he clung to her leg, wrapping his arms around her thigh. Her nostrils flared and she hoisted him back up, balancing their pouches between elbow, arm and torso. One of his pouches faced me – it was miniature in size and had a caricature of an elephant printed on the front. As the mother turned to leave she ever so slightly lowered her head and bowed to the kitchen porter before offering the same gesture to the soldier keeping watch, his rifle dangling like a satchel over his shoulder. The porter was oblivious, already thrusting my three pouches across the stainless steel counter. I gathered my quota and turned away, inspecting my puréed options as I walked: there was a mango fruit pouch, a sweet potato one, and finally something described as chicken casserole. Somehow it reminded me of being on an all-inclusive holiday. Initially, I had felt liberated by the concept of not having to carry money. But then there was something vulgar in the way I started to behave, in my frantic consumption, as though I didn't trust the process, was anxious that it could all be taken away at a moment's notice. No one questioned what happened to the rations of those who died – but there seemed to be no redistribution, no opportunity to ask for more. Perhaps the soldiers kept them for themselves, considered their nutritional needs superior, although I had nothing to back this speculation up with.

The bunker was intricately designed – the North side a supposed mirror image to the South. In the sleeping quarters there was nothing but narrow rows of bunks, stacked in columns of four. Each row was identified by a letter, each bedframe stamped with a number. I used to associate bunk beds with children – wooden frames and ladders, or cosy duvets with desks and drawers underneath for storing treasure. But these bunks were suspended rectangular metal frames, shrink-wrapped in canvas, like a stretcher hinged to the walls. The blankets were a similar shade of grey to the boiler suits and made of bobbled wool, coarse to the touch. Despite this I clung to mine; took my blankets and spare boiler suit everywhere for fear of them being stolen. Along with a toothbrush, a set of underwear and our laceless gym shoes, we possessed little else. And, like an unspoken rule, if items were left unattended then they were game for anyone's taking.

Mr and Mrs Foer were sleeping on the bottom two bunks below me and Canavan snored above. He was a giant – too big and broad for the bunks, his feet overhanging and encroaching on my space – I'd often stare at his discoloured toenails, thick and brittle with fungus. His body sagged through the canvas and I feared that one day it would give way, crushing me and in turn Foer and Foer. I had thought about asking him to switch but for some reason I could never muster the energy. The thought of having to climb further up was almost more overwhelming than the thought of him crushing me.

I slowly ascended on to my bed, trying not to wake the Foers. Once I was lying flat with my blankets brought close to my chin I broke the seal of the mango pouch. It was thick and gloopy, and sweet enough not to make me want to gag. The pouches were nothing more than glorified baby food with added calories, designed to be consumed cold. And I wondered how babies had endured this for so long. Why hadn't they rebelled against their mothers? Surely it should have been considered some form of child abuse.

Canavan was moving above, turning and pulling at his blankets. I closed my eyes, not yet ready to face him, but as I focused on the floaters gliding across my eyelids I started picturing Templeton and the white sheet that had settled over his body. It had been more than a week but still I was struggling with sleep. The insomnia felt like jetlag – a fuzziness settling in, like drinking too much caffeine to compensate. I had imagined Templeton in every male patient who had visited the pharmacy since.

I sensed Canavan with his dishevelled brown hair looking down on me and I opened my eyes.

Morning, he said, smiling.

Morning.

Have you checked the forecast? I hear it's going to be a beautiful day outside.

I could feel my mouth curling into a smile. Unfortunately, some of us have to sit inside and work today.

You never seem to catch a break, he said, before he swung his legs past my bunk and began to ease himself down, the weight of him landing with a thud. The hems of his boiler suit had ridden up to his calves and he bent to pull the fabric down. If I could have gifted him anything it would have been socks to bridge the gap of skin between gym shoe and boiler suit. I'd never been able to place Canavan's age – like a chameleon he morphed from thirty-something into his fifties. Most of us had been gifted roles and jobs to fill our time but he appeared to have no purpose and I wondered why he had made the cut. The soldiers never came and forced him into menial jobs the way they did with the others. And he didn't seem to be here on the merit of family members. I was under the impression he was like me – alone. We were thrown together like misfits, slotted into spare bunks between existing families.

Canavan stretched his arms out and proceeded to do a few lunges in front of little Mrs Foer and I smirked, sensing she was awake. The Foers kept themselves to themselves, full of polite nods and pleasantries but not much else.

Don't worry, Wolfe, Canavan said looking back up at me.
I'll have dinner all ready for you when you get home tonight.

I stared at the three time-zoned clocks that hung from a wall
on our side of the main chamber. The middle clock was the
one around which I centred my bearings, the others seeming
like a hangover from days on the stock market. But I liked the
idea of there being other nuclear bunkers across the world –
like an alternative universe – lots of people wondering why
they needed to know the time in a place that probably didn't
exist any more. I brought myself close to the wall, my nose
nearly touching the concrete, and tried to listen for the clock's
tick, but there was nothing. Was it possible for a clock to not
tick? I stepped back and looked up at its face again. I was
starting my shift in ten minutes. And right on cue there was
the noise of a xylophone scale sound effect, immediately
followed by the same overly cheery female voice:

Good morning. We hope that you have woken well rested
and ready to tackle another day. Adult French lessons will
be taking place in the North bunker's recreation room from
7.30 p.m. this evening. Places are limited so please do let the
librarians know if you wish to attend. The doctors would
like me to remind all inhabitants that the weekly temperature checks are non-optional. Water pressure on the South
side is currently being addressed. Please do bear with
Maintenance. We appreciate your patience. Finally for our
quote of the day: *Coming together is a beginning. Keeping
together is progress. Working together is success.* Have a produc-
tive day, one and all.

The pharmacy's opening hours were 9 a.m. to 9 p.m. but I
always worked the morning shift until 3 p.m. I had to scan

my fingerprint to unlock the door and, inside, the shop floor resembled something of a retail unit: the shelves were stocked with empty medicine boxes, like artefacts from a museum, and posters depicting migraines and flu remedies hung from the walls. There was a cardboard cutout of a woman holding a bottle of oil for stretch marks, except no one ever asked me about stretch marks any more. The image only served to highlight how many things had since become redundant. The whole pharmacy reminded me of the fake dispensaries with their out-of-date tablets we used to practise in at university, offering us an insight into our futures. I reasoned that it was like working for one of the supermarket pharmacies – long hours in a windowless box. And to think I had toyed with the idea of becoming a teacher. The teachers had it worse than me – it was nothing but crowd control in a place with nowhere to go. What education could they offer? What history could they teach, aside from token anecdotes of imperialism?

Towards the back of the shop floor stood the dispensary, protected by a door and a Perspex partition. I had to scan my fingerprint again to open it before quickly closing and locking myself inside, the same fearful way I used to run and climb into my car at night. Valentine, the other pharmacist, had left the dispensary spotless as he always did. I opened some of the metal medicine drawers then ran the tap in the sink, washing my hands, its lukewarm temperature warming the tips of my fingers.

Facing the shop floor and cut out from the Perspex was a hatch. Beside it, Valentine had left a stack of plastic measuring cups and paper cones for water. I liked the fact that, for most of the time, I didn't have to touch anyone. I had been forced to touch too many strangers in the real world. My heart sank even now when I was asked to step out for a private consultation.

There was a calendar in one of the drawers and I flicked through its pages. Each month was a different breed of dog, and I paused on one of my favourites, a white and tan Jack Russell terrier. This calendar was my only means of distinguishing days and seasons, of being able to associate memories with a particular time of year. When conversations about nuclear fallout and isotopic half-lives appeared to be endless, it proved to me that time was indeed passing – seven months of a supposed thirty-six in total, to be precise. However, nothing appeared to be set in stone, only the vagueness of being told we were on the right trajectory. To have existed like this for any real length of time seemed ridiculous to me but here we were, the days scored out in permanent marker.

Two plastic chairs had been brought into the dispensary and I contemplated why Valentine needed two. I sat on one and pulled the other forward to rest my feet on. I was staring at the cutout figure for stretch marks, convinced the eyes were following me, when my first patient arrived: female, possibly early forties. Her eyes were brown and there were a few skin tags sitting on the curve of her right cheek. Perhaps I had served her the day before, but her face brought no recognition.

ID number and surname . . . please. The *please* seemed to roll around my mouth as if I were testing it out for the first time. I thought people were so predictable – a dog always looked like its owner; now the drugs told me everything I needed to know about a person. I was already guessing what she was on before I'd even opened up her drug chart. There was a sullen expression across her face and the eyes continuously shifted. My gut instinct was telling me anxiety and I could feel a smile surfacing as I collected the 40mg strength of propranolol from the drawer. It was fluorescent pink – comically cheerful and a smack in the face to her worries. I placed the tablet in a plastic measuring cup and handed it to her through the hatch.

She looked down at it. Do you think it makes a difference?

I shrugged.

She took her time, placing the tablet on the back of her tongue, and I stared on, my arms crossed.

She took a sip of water and made a few heaving noises before eventually swallowing the tablet and opening her mouth for my inspection. I nodded. Her eyes fixed on the permanent marker I held in my hand ready to score off her dose for the day. I wondered then how far she would go to get her hands on a pen or marker. What would she write? Probably her name again and again, a thousand times over. I signed her drug chart, acknowledging with surprise my signature on the previous day's dose.

There was a steady stream of patients throughout the morning and I stacked their drug charts in a pile, running my thumb up the paper spines, pausing to feel the coolness of the staples that bound them together. I tried to visualise the damage those little pointed Monopoly houses must have done to Templeton's already ulcerated stomach. I suspected staples would have done similar damage.

Around lunchtime there was a lull in footfall and I retrieved my food pouches. I held the sweet potato in one hand and the chicken casserole in the other. I took a deep breath and forced myself to break the seal on the puréed chicken. I had the idea to sit the pouch in a cup of lukewarm water, thinking that might make it more tolerable. Hadn't I seen a mother do that for her baby once in a café? I'd tried to eat a beef stroganoff pouch cold a few days before, but was sick after forcing down only three mouthfuls.

I was listening to the rattle of pipes above when my next patient arrived. He walked with purpose, bringing his face closer to the Perspex.

Can I show you something? he said. It's kind of delicate.

Sorry?

He pointed to the consultation cubicle. I just want to know if it's serious. If it's something I should bother the doctors with.

I tried to hide the disdain from my face. OK, give me a minute, I said, already removing some disposable gloves from under the counter. I'll be round in a second.

He led me to the cubicle, entering and waiting.

What is it you want me to look at? I said.

Can you close the curtain . . . ? Please.

I did as he asked, aware of a kink in the rail as I pulled the curtain across.

It's probably nothing, he said, already yanking apart the Velcro on his suit. But I've got this pubic rash . . .

Wow, wow, wait, I said, raising my hands up in protest. I'll need to call for a chaperone.

I reached for the curtain but he grabbed my wrist, his fingernails digging into my skin. Just touch it, he whispered, pulling my hand into his suit.

Let. Go. Of. Me, I said, trying but failing to free myself.

His breathing grew heavy. Is it true you were there? With Templeton . . .

My body prickled with fear. Please, I'm asking you to let me go. I visualised the panic button in real pharmacies, imagined my fingers reaching for it. There wasn't meant to be the need for a panic button any more. And I wanted to laugh, as though this was all some ridiculous misunderstanding because the reality couldn't possibly be true. But it was true, and it was remarkable that I hadn't seen it coming.

Tell me . . . Did you see Templeton take his last breath? He was panting now, trying to force my hand further. Silly fucker couldn't cope with his eye for the young girls . . . He gripped me then from the back of my neck and tried to force me into a kneeling position. It's better not to resist, he said.

I heard the door to the pharmacy opening but he showed little concern; many of the soldiers were already known for turning a blind eye.

Excuse me . . . a woman's voice said. Hello? Is anyone here? And before he could stop me I was screaming Yes, yes in response. It was enough to break his confidence and he bolted from the consultation cubicle and out of the door with his boiler suit still undone.

The woman stared at me. Are you OK?

I closed my eyes, placed a hand on my chest. Eventually I nodded. I'm OK . . .

I'm in for my meds, but I can come back another time if it doesn't suit?

No, it's fine, I said, slowly making my way back to the dispensary.

She told me her surname and ID number without me asking and I pulled out her drug chart, my hands shaking, before retrieving the medication: tramadol for pain and ramipril for high blood pressure. She threw them into her mouth and took one short sip of water. With her mouth open wide for inspection I could see several rotting teeth, like a row of condemned houses.

The plastic cup and crumpled paper cone were pushed back through. Thank you, she said.

You're welcome, I replied, but I couldn't quite meet her eye.

I started scoring off her doses with my marker, the ink blotching slightly from the persistent shake in my hand, when I realised she wasn't moving.

I'm sorry, she said. You'd think in here we'd finally be safe. She paused. Many of us will only come to you now, did you know that? Some women have stopped taking their night meds altogether because they hate dealing with that man Valentine.

They really shouldn't stop taking their medication, I said.

You're not listening to me. We women – we need to look after each other.

I took a step back from my side of the counter and she stared at me. You don't have anyone in here, do you? She glanced over her shoulder, acknowledged another patient walking in. If I were you, I wouldn't be working in here on my own, she whispered.

For the rest of my shift I tried to compartmentalise what had happened and remain professional, because in the world of pharmacy I was still accountable for errors. But I kept placing my hand on the back of my neck where I'd been held. And my breathing was off; like a short-circuit, there was something wrong with its rhythm. I could hardly concentrate as a man tried to explain to me that the doctor was starting him on a water tablet for the fluid retention in his legs. I nodded, glancing down at the prescription he'd slipped through the hatch and focused on Stirling's signature, comforted by seeing his name in ink.

When Valentine arrived for handover he was a few minutes

late. He was small, with an impressive head of grey hair and a pointed nose. It occurred to me that we knew very little about one another, having hardly spoken about life outside the dispensary's walls. But there was still something familiar about him; I felt as if I'd worked with carbon copies of him in my previous life.

More women come when I'm on shift, I said. Did you know that?

What do you want me to do, force them to come? He glanced at me then, his eyes narrowing. What's wrong with you?

I swallowed, a jagged sensation moving down my throat. Nothing . . . I replied.

He watched as I gathered my blankets and spare suit. If I'm quiet I'll tidy the drawers and check the expiry dates, he said, as though he was doing me a favour. And I nodded because I didn't have it in me not to look grateful.

Canavan was lying on his bunk sucking on a food pouch when I returned. I suspected he'd been there all day. Aside from the fear of him crushing me, I also considered the realistic possibility that one day he might piss himself and in turn piss on me.

He heard me and lowered his head. Welcome home, honey!

Ignoring him, I started climbing up on to my bunk, sprawling out flat on my back.

Hard day at the office?

You've no idea, I whispered, focusing on the bulging canvas, practically willing it to give way.

I cooked us spaghetti bolognese but you were late and now it's cold, he said, holding his pouch out for me to inspect.

Did I miss anything? I said.

The woman three bunks along from here, he said pointing left. Well, she accused her bunkmate below of stealing her blankets. You should have seen the fallout, Wolfe. Shit got wild . . . Biting and everything.

I tried to sit up, forcing my shoulders back in the cramped space.

Canavan, if you wanted something around here, who would you have to speak to?

The frame of our bunks shook as he turned on to his belly. The arms dropped first, dangling in the air before a face appeared. Are we still role-playing?

No, I'm serious. I need to speak to someone about security . . . About maybe getting a soldier to guard the pharmacy. Like they do for the kitchens.

Did something happen?

Can you just answer the question?

I do know someone in Human Resources.

Are we still role-playing? I said.

He smirked. I'm not as useless as you think I am.

I stared at him. You could talk to someone with authority? I said, trying to disguise my scepticism.

It'll cost you.

I have nothing to trade.

He had this strange, almost sinister expression on his face. There's always something that can be traded.

I shifted, acid rising up my throat. What do you want?

Why do you want a soldier for the pharmacy?

I was quiet for a moment. I just want to feel safe.

You bunk with me.

My mouth wrinkled into a smile. You can't always be where I need you to be.

He paused. OK, but I want one of your little magic marker pens.

Why?

His face changed – a sadness that was real and painful. A poet needs a pen, he said.

# 3

I was in the consultation cubicle crouched on my knees yet again, sizing up a woman for compression stockings. The patient sat in her faded cotton underwear, her boiler suit hanging on the back of the chair, and I had the measuring tape wrapped around her thigh. I gripped the tape and tilted my head to the side, checking and double-checking the numbers. Glancing down, my eyes focused on the green varicose veins bulging from her calves. The hairs on her legs were blond and fine, and I realised she must never have shaved them.

I have to spend most of the day lying down, she said. I'd planned on getting the veins removed before we came here. Do you think that's something the doctors could still do?

I shrugged, lowering the measuring tape to the circumference of her knee. You'd have to speak to them, I said.

Sometimes I wish I could just pierce the legs open and pull the veins out, she said. My father used to suffer from varicose veins and his father before him.

I nodded, remembering my own mum and her showing me the wound near her groin. They'd made little incisions along her leg and pulled the veins like thread up towards the opening at the top. Afterwards, I'd imagined what the veins must have looked like in the petri dish, shrivelled and dehydrated.

I let the measuring tape fall slack and got to my feet. I'm measuring you as medium in size. But I'll need to check what we still have in stock. Hopefully there's a pair left in thigh-length.

What colour do they come in?

Does it matter?

No, I suppose it doesn't.

I left her sitting there behind the curtain while I went back into the dispensary to search the shelves. I found a damaged box and was pulling out the sand-coloured stockings when Valentine arrived.

Anything I need to know? he said, as I let him over the threshold of the dispensary.

I don't think so.

He looked around before replying. This place is a pigsty. Have you seen it?

I stepped back, aware of my cheeks reddening. I'm not exactly twiddling my thumbs here, Valentine. But even as I spoke I couldn't seem to muster any sort of confidence into my voice. I might as well have been mute.

He straightened his shoulders and tilted his head forward. Perhaps tidy as you go . . . His teeth were protruding from his mouth and I wondered if they were still his own or a mouthful of dentures. I could report you, he said. Accidents happen when the workplace is neglected.

I placed the box I was holding down on the counter. I'll try to keep that in mind, I said, momentarily closing my eyes, willing him to stop as though his voice was capable of causing me physical pain. I'm not actually feeling the best, I added. Do you think you could fit my patient's stockings for me?

I don't think so, he said with a laugh that came out in

puffs. You'll finish what you've ... But his words began to trail off and his eyes fixed on something behind me.

I turned to see one of the soldiers walking towards the hatch. It was only the rifles and their walkie-talkies that differentiated them from us. If they were to remove those items and walk through the crowd, they'd disappear and become anonymous.

I'd never really understood the attraction of joining the military. Perhaps it was the routine, the discipline of being told what to do. Did they miss the thrill of real combat? I suspected our current existence was something of a let-down in comparison. They slept in separate quarters, absent of family, and worked a shift pattern I could never quite grasp. Generally they appeared indifferent, as if this was just another volatile environment that needed monitoring.

Wolfe, ID number 0377? the soldier said, seeming to already know the answer to his question.

Yes ...

Wolfe is no longer on duty, Valentine interrupted. Is there something I can assist you with? He had his pharmacist's smile on – the caring and listening one – but his hands were clasped together and they were ever so slightly shaking.

I'm not here for my health, the soldier said. I've been requested to collect Wolfe.

Can I ask why? I said.

The soldier didn't reply, only ushered with his hand for me to follow.

I hesitated, reluctantly gathering my blankets and spare suit. I stepped out of the dispensary and the soldier took me by the arm.

Valentine trailed behind us. Where are you going?

That's not your concern, the soldier replied.

But . . .

It's OK, Valentine, I said.

I pressed my folded belongings against my ribcage, my heart already beating fast; I began to think that it was audible. My patient who was waiting for her stockings stared on as I was marched out of the door, and when I looked back Valentine was rooted to the spot.

What exactly is this regarding? I said as we turned a corner, but again there was no response. Please . . . Panic began to choke my voice and I tried to push it down. Was this how it went? Was I the one to be punished because I'd dared to open my mouth and ask for help? I thought about releasing myself from the soldier's grip and running but the barrel of his rifle kept catching my eye. I fantasised about taking hold of it, of feeling some sense of control. I imagined him on his knees and me hovering over him with the gun steady in my hands. But I did nothing. I focused on the squelching noise my laceless gym shoes made on the concrete. Should I have turned the gun on myself? Perhaps that would have been easier.

He directed me down another corridor, our pace quickening until eventually we were in the main compartment of the chamber, coming to an abrupt stop outside an entrance to our leader's lair. A steel door was sealed and the soldier banged his fist against the metal. There was the noise of a handle turning from the other side and when the door opened the soldier pushed me forward, over the threshold, the door closing behind us. We stood in a hatch with another door facing us, and slowly it too opened from the other side. Was this where they brought you to die, so the others didn't see? I hoped for it to be painless. Perhaps the bullet would be in me before I'd even realise. It was the anticipation more than anything. I remembered reading in history books about royal families being gathered in drawing rooms – men, women and children – sitting as though they were waiting to get their portraits taken before the soldiers came in and shot them, all of them. Did I believe in heaven? I liked the idea of life starting all over again, on an earth in another galaxy where people were better to one another.

I was passed to a different soldier and he was ushering me into a room where there was no more concrete. Instead, there was plush carpet and floral wallpaper, and as we walked an electric impulse passed from the soldier to me. It was like the carpets in Las Vegas casinos – they had always seemed to give me a static shock for some reason. It had freaked Daniel out and he'd refused to hold my hand for fear of me shocking him. These memories of Daniel always arrived without warning, often painfully like a winding in the chest, and I begrudged his ability to so effortlessly alter my train of thought.

Chrome fixtures and antique furniture surrounded me. Lilies protruded from a vase and I couldn't help but reach out to them. They were made of silk, but for the briefest of moments I imagined them to be real – that pollen might fall from their stems and stain my boiler suit.

It hadn't occurred to me that our leader would be living a more bearable life. Perhaps I had been foolish to think otherwise, cheated into believing we were all in the same boat. But here I was, gripping the leaf of an artificial lily in what could only be described as his hallway.

The soldier yanked me back. Sit, he said, directing me to a cushioned seat pressed up against the floral wallpaper. It really was like a hotel lobby. Perhaps behind one of the many doors I'd be met with a blackjack table and slot machines.

We seemed to wait for a long time. The soldier stood with his rifle pointed to the ground, his fingers hovering next to the trigger. Please, I said. I haven't done anything . . .

He stared at me. It was you who requested this meeting with our leader. He shifted his stance and the gun shifted with him, bobbing slightly next to his hip.

But I never asked to speak with him . . .

So you no longer wish to see him?

I . . . I'm about to meet him?

I couldn't remember the last time I'd seen our leader in the flesh. We were told that underlying health conditions prevented him from circulating among us, that he was forced to shield and protect his immune system. And I imagined him as a prophet now, busy carving out the pages of his own holy doctorate. If his intention was to create some aura of mystery, then it appeared to be working, because, as I sat there, all thoughts for my own safety disappeared and I was filled with an anxious excitement.

One of the doors opened and a woman in a black tailored skirt and blazer stood over the threshold. We're ready for you now, she said, speaking with a voice that was so familiar.

Are you the voice we hear on the speaker system? I said, marvelling, almost leering at her.

My name's Alison.

It was bizarre hearing someone's first name being spoken. First names were redundant in the main chamber. Surnames were enough to identify family groupings, but names assigned at birth were considered a cast-off from a life that no longer existed.

34

Suddenly I realised how ridiculous I looked in my boiler suit. Her outfit was so striking that I needed to touch it, and as she came to where I was sitting I ran my hand over the seam of the fabric. She stood, letting me feel the material, before clearing her throat. We don't have much time, she said, finally pulling her skirt free from my grip.

The soldier had to force me up on to my feet and I clung to my blankets, the legs of my spare boiler suit dangling in front of me.

You can leave your things here, Alison said.

I glanced at the seat I'd been sitting in and back to her.

Your belongings are safe here. No one will take them.

She held a clipboard and I focused on the metal lever that lodged paper in place. I had this urge to place my finger underneath the springs and feel its pressure; allow its weight to indent my finger. Of all the things that surrounded me, it was the clipboard I found myself lusting for the most.

Behind the open door the lights were bright and it took a moment for my eyes to adjust. There were paintings on the walls – classic portraits and landscapes but also modern and abstract images. Seeing them there nearly brought me to tears.

Are you an art-lover? he said.

I was so taken by the images that I hadn't initially realised our leader was waiting, sitting at a table. I recognised his voice too – smooth and reassuring, capable of casting a spell over the best of us. I hadn't voted for him in the country's election but I could see why people had, and I, a believer in democracy, had accepted the outcome. He had been a military war hero before entering politics, and held a particular affection for the army base where I worked, and I suppose for the people stationed within it.

He inspected me with rimless glasses. The lenses looked as though they were made from real glass, not like the plastic lenses forced upon the other inhabitants who were visually impaired.

Taking in my surroundings, I realised I was standing in a boardroom. The furniture was all wood, maybe mahogany, although I was terrible at deciphering what type of wood things were made from.

I don't know anything about art, I said.

He was wearing a zippered tracksuit with his initials, ND, emblazoned on the chest pocket. Sit down, he said pointing to the chair opposite.

I pulled the swivel chair back and sank into its leather. Alison sat down too, taking the seat next to him.

A bowl of pistachios sat in front of them.

I've heard very good reports about you. You're quite the pharmacist, he said as he reached over and gathered a handful of pistachios. Ralf really had only kind words to say.

One of the pistachios fell from his palm and rolled across the table towards me. Ralf? I said.

Yes, Canavan. He asked to borrow my ear. And he doesn't often ask for a favour.

He cracked open a shell, popped the pistachio into his mouth and chewed down.

So, Ralf tells me you have something of a predicament.

He continued to part pistachio shells, throwing the nuts into his mouth, all in quick repeated succession.

Can I have that? I said, pointing to the stray pistachio.

A little mountain of shells sat in front of him. He leant forward and looked at the pistachio, seeming to ponder it. You're not allergic, are you?

No.

His lips parted and I could see his jaw moving as he ran his tongue over his teeth, dislodging a piece of nut. Forgive me, he said and slid the half-empty bowl towards me before settling back into his seat. Help yourself.

I reached over cautiously, taking one pistachio and prising the shell apart with my thumbs. A tiny green nut rested in the palm of my hand and I stared at it, all other thoughts gone from my head. The only thing that mattered was this nut and its solidity. Alison was talking but I wasn't listening – it was static like a radio, its wavelength moving over my head. I placed the nut on my tongue and let it sit there for a moment before passing it back to my under-used molars and crunching down. I exhaled, rolling my eyes with the pleasure of its texture.

Would this be agreeable to you? our leader said.

I started gathering more nuts in my hand. Agreeable . . .

We've taken the liberty of selecting a suitable candidate, Alison said. We can't have an open call for applicants. A role of this particular status would cause instability and competition among the inhabitants. And we don't have the manpower to facilitate formal interviews.

I had my own small stash of nut shells now resting in front of me. Inhabitants? I said, shaking my head. I want a soldier to help guard the pharmacy.

Alison laughed. Is there something you've misunderstood?

We can't ask the soldiers to utilise their time in this way, our leader said. It's just not appropriate.

But . . .

Our leader chose the candidate himself, Alison interrupted. I hope you appreciate the effort involved.

What do you make of Ralf's latest piece? our leader said, pointing towards a painting of a dog dressed as a jester.

I stared at the large painting hanging to my right. It's interesting, I guess . . .

What do you think it means?

I stared at it. It seems fanciful. Like a joke is being played on us but only the dog understands.

He started laughing. Yes, I think I agree with you.

Ms Wolfe, here is the candidate we've selected for you, Alison said, sliding a paper file across the table.

I think she will make an excellent assistant, our leader said.

If I . . . I hesitated, a nervousness pitted in my stomach. If a soldier can guard the kitchen porters, then surely . . .

Do you care to explain what happened to make you suddenly feel so uncomfortable? he said.

I paused. I'm sorry. It's fine.

The candidate comes from very good stock, he replied.

I opened the folder and inside sat a double-sided A4 piece of paper. It was like looking at a CV from before – when pharmacy students used to ask for summer placements and I'd have to read through their statistics: their grades, why they wanted to work in this particular pharmacy, their previous experience, their strengths and weaknesses and finally their hobbies, desperate to prove to me how interesting a candidate they were. And I wondered then what our leader considered to be my particulars. Was everything worth knowing about me reducible to a two-page document as well? The concept of typing text on a computer seemed farcical now. And printing. I tried to remember the noise of a printer spitting out paper but it was gone.

The candidate on the sheet before me was eighteen and the daughter of the cultural advisor. Surname Levitt. She had been due to start veterinary school before coming here. I breathed in through my nostrils, fearing that perhaps she'd be overly keen to talk science and medicine. And clearly she must have liked animals, so potentially she'd be too caring. I continued reading down the page and noticed that in previous summers she'd packed parcels for an online pharmacy. Instinctively I was nodding my head, acknowledging that perhaps this wasn't such a bad idea after all. Online packers got things done. I knew – I'd once worked in an online pharmacy and we'd had to turn over hundreds of prescriptions for Viagra in quick succession.

Levitt, I said, letting her name circulate in my mouth, recognising this sudden shift in my circumstances. Management had never appealed to me before but there was something attractive about its new possibilities. There would be no appraisals to complete or learning objectives to tick; maybe I could just mould this Levitt into exactly what I needed her to be. And I supposed two women in the pharmacy was better than one.

Yes, thank you, I said. I think she is exactly what I'm looking for.

Fantastic, our leader declared. Miss Levitt will be delighted with her new role, I'm sure. We'll pull her from laundry straight away.

She doesn't know?

You can expect her from tomorrow, Alison said. She resides across the boundary line from you, but this should cause no issue with her signing off on her current role.

She's from the other side of the bunker . . . ?

Is that a problem? he said.

I shrugged. No, I guess not.

Alison began to usher me out of my seat but our leader raised his hand. I would like a moment alone with Ms Wolfe.

Alison paused before lowering her head slightly, and departing while I sank further into my seat. For a brief moment I felt oddly calm, as though I was in my natural habitat. Maybe it was the pistachios.

Our leader waited for the door to close behind Alison before speaking. And it was only then that I permitted myself to look at him properly – the dark hair I was used to seeing was practically all white, and there was a balding patch on top – a comb-over had been attempted but it was patchy and haphazard. His skin was no longer golden but sullen, a shade of white to match his hair. I remembered watching a documentary about an officer who survived the sinking of the *Titanic*. There was an old photograph of him before the ship set sail and he had a thick head of black hair. But there was also a photograph of him a year after the ordeal and his hair was entirely white, as if the shock of what he'd witnessed had scared the pigmentation out of his body. I wondered if it was the same here. Had the pressure of the job eroded our leader's health? I tried to guess what he suffered from – the doctors had always dealt privately with his health concerns. Whatever it was, there was little semblance left of the man who had stormed into power at a volatile and divided time, pledging a better alternative for *everyone*.

Ms Wolfe . . . Sarah. May I call you Sarah? The *Sa* was booming, like singing a song but the *rah* was low and elong-ated, like being called out from a distance. And I didn't like it; didn't want to be spoken to with a name that my loved ones had used so tenderly. I wanted it to stay dead with them.

I would prefer Wolfe, I said.

He laughed. I hate Nathan too, or Mr Douglas. My friends all call me ND. Please feel free to do the same.

OK . . .

He was staring at me. Would you describe yourself as a discreet person?

I suppose.

Looking at you here, I would say that indeed you are. He straightened his shoulders. There are many reasons to stay discreet in this environment. For example, your being given special attention – that will have to be handled discreetly. And the pistachios are another example of a need for discretion. Our other brothers and sisters, they would not be capable of controlling themselves. And there is simply not enough to go around.

My eyebrows furrowed. I won't say anything, I said. If that's what you're worried about.

He nodded. I think you and I could be of continued help to one another. He tilted his head to one side, perhaps trying to gauge me in some way. If someone did something to you, touched you or hurt you . . . you can tell me. Perhaps if you had a name . . . We have ways of managing these things.

I could feel a familiar tightness constricting in my chest, a weight trying to tie me down. I hope your wife is keeping well, I said, blurting the words out. I do miss her exercise classes. We all do.

Thank you, I will certainly pass on your kind regards.

Silence began to fill the room and I stared at my discarded pistachio shells.

What do they say about me? he said. Your patients . . .

I . . . I'm not sure what you mean.

They must have opinions. Everyone does.

I don't tend to get involved with politics, I said.

He smiled, as if my response amused him. Ralf really does seem to think the world of you, he said.

The seam of the zip on his tracksuit bulged from his stomach. It mesmerised me – the notion of the zip bursting, the locking of the metal teeth falling out of kilter. My eyes took in the rest of his tracksuit – the velour texture and the thick thread count of his initials stitched on to the chest pocket. The excessiveness and decadence of him was entrancing.

He rose from his seat then and waited for me to do the same. Let's touch base again soon, over dinner perhaps.

What, real food?

He nodded.

The word *dinner* echoed in my ears. The prospect of eating food that could be pierced with a fork seemed overwhelming. And something to drink – did he also only drink water pumped from a well? I blinked, imagined him guzzling bottles of sparkling spring water.

You will have much to consider with your new assistant, he said guiding me to the door. I trust you are satisfied with the outcome of this meeting?

Yes . . .

He started to laugh. I like you, Sarah. You remind me of someone I used to know. Someone I'd like to see again. He rested his hand on my lower back. I'm giving you an olive branch, he said. I highly encourage you to take it.

I found myself nodding, as if I knew there was no alternative.

Until we meet again, he said, opening the door.

Alison was waiting for me on the other side. One of the soldiers will escort you back, she said, pointing to a different one from before. As I turned to follow his lead she called me back. Aren't you forgetting something? she said, nodding to my things on the seat, and I gathered them, clutching them once again to my chest.

This soldier didn't feel the need to take hold of me and I followed him through one steel door and then another. There was a clear birthmark on his forehead, like a perfectly formed droplet from an oil spill. A pang of jealousy stabbed through me – to have something unique, something that couldn't physically be scrubbed away, was everything.

He glanced around, ensuring we were alone, before removing a business card from the chest pocket of his boiler suit and handing it to me. It was blank except for four surnames and ID numbers written in tiny, neat black handwriting:

*Baxter 0636*
*Clement 1004*
*Floyd 1882*
*Maxwell 2597*

Aside from Baxter the other names meant nothing to me. I waited for him to speak but he remained silent.

What am I meant to do with this? I asked.

Watch them. Monitor their behaviour, how they take their medication, their conversations. And then report directly back to the leader, or myself.

That would be a breach of patient confidentiality, I said, nearly laughing at the absurdity of the request.

When the order comes from him, their confidentiality is waived.

No, I'm sorry, I said, shaking my head. I can't.

Of course you can.

43

He escorted me through the last steel door, the noise of the lock spinning shut behind us. Suddenly I was thrust out into the main chamber with its dull lighting and persistent buzz of generators. The soldier pointed his gun forward, ushering me in the right direction, but I was unsteady on my feet, as though I'd been woken from a confusing and distorting dream.

Afterwards, there was no thought process. I just walked until I was at Stirling's surgery and knocked on the door, not waiting for an answer. Nurse Appleby was occupying the desk in the waiting room.

Can I speak with Dr Stirling?

He's extremely busy, she said, gesturing with her hand to the row of patients already sitting.

It's about a prescription he wrote for some compression stockings.

She stared at me but I didn't move. Fine, she said, you can squeeze in before the next patient.

There was one free seat and I sat down. The waiting room had posters on its walls like the pharmacy but these images were darker – there were no smiling faces or colourful promotions; instead depictions of bacteria and spores, things that would be enough to bring down the steel wall across the boundary line. A standard feature of a community-sized bunker; a precaution to minimise the spread of disease if an outbreak were to occur.

Stirling opened his door and ushered out his patient with a smile. When he saw me he didn't appear surprised. Appleby was already by his side, resting a hand on his arm.

The pharmacist wishes a moment of your time, doctor. It's about a prescription . . .

You keep prescribing support stockings, Dr Stirling, I said. And we're steadily running lower on stock.

I see . . . You'd better come in for a moment and brief me on exact stock levels then, he said, waving me through. His tone was indignant, as though I was nothing but a nuisance to him. It was a tone doctors had perfected for pharmacists.

He closed the door and finally we were alone.

How are you? I said.

He shrugged. How is your hand?

It's fine, thanks, I replied, waving it as if I were trying to swipe a fly. I stared over at the bed where Templeton had lain. I imagined what his skin would look like now. Had maggots eaten away his flesh yet, begun to work through muscle and tendons?

Have other people been on it? I said, nodding towards the bed.

Of course.

Can I lie down on it?

Are you OK?

I cast my eyes to the floor. Please, only for a minute.

Fine, he said. If you think—

I climbed up on to the examination bed, my fingers sinking into the fake leather. I stared up at the ceiling before turning on to my side, trying to process the sequence of events that had brought me to this point.

Will you lie next to me? I said.

I'm not sure that's a good idea.

Please, I said patting the empty space. Only for a moment.

He sat first, his back facing me, before swinging up and resting his legs beside me, his eyes focused on the ceiling while our shoulders touched.

Do you think about Templeton? I asked.

Of course.

I think about him all the time, I said. Him wanting to kill himself . . . Maybe he had the right idea.

Stirling turned to look at me but I continued to stare straight ahead.

I heard this rumour . . . that he raped young girls.

Who told you that?

I shrugged. Do you think it's true?

He didn't reply.

I don't know how I'm meant to feel. Should I be pleased now?

What's done is done, he said slowly pulling himself upright, planting his feet on the floor. I sat up too, my legs dangling over the bed.

I'm getting an assistant, I said.

That's a good thing, isn't it?

I thought so . . .

It'll be company for you, at least, he said.

You sound like a self-help book.

He took my good hand and pulled me down from the bed. You've taken up too much of my time, he said, but he spoke with warmth in his voice. He opened the door and the patients were still waiting. Thank you, Wolfe. Please do let me know if anything further is needed.

I left the surgery and turned down the first corridor, removing the business card from my pocket. It was thick and its edges sharp – clearly of the highest quality. It was the type of object people aspired to own – a brandishing of wealth and status. The business cards that used to get handed to me from unannounced drug reps had always been flimsy and cheap. I pressed my finger into one of the corners and was impressed to find that it held its own weight, no hint of buckling under the pressure. And I wished to have the same integrity. I swallowed, the remnants of pistachio still on my tongue. Whatever was being asked of me now, it didn't feel as if there was room for choice. But it was an opportunity to disrupt the monotony of my existence, and perhaps I craved that most of all.

# 4

I stared up at Canavan's bunk, making out its sunken shape in the blue night-light glow, when the generators cut out, plunging the entire bunker into total darkness. The power cuts usually only lasted minutes but knowing this didn't make it any easier. I gripped my blankets and tried to visualise something that could trick me into distraction. I thought about the huge shopping mall and multi-storey car park that sat directly above us. I'd treated myself to some lovely boyfriend-style jeans and eaten ramen noodles with Officer Holden while his wife was at work. He couldn't operate his chopsticks and I'd revelled in his having to ask for a fork. I so clearly remembered the feel of his hand gripping my thigh under the table.

I shifted position. I could hear people breathing, quick and erratic, while a child cried out in the distance for her mother. I brought my hand up in front of my face but I couldn't make it out. We had been told this particular bunker housed 0.2 per cent of the city's population – the country's best minds huddled together – but in reality it was mostly populated by politicians and bankers, the odd media mogul thrown in for good measure. They had had enough money and influence to protect themselves and their loved ones, but there was nothing particularly special or impressive about any of them. Where were the experts in science or academia?

Could I assume that they were safe in another of the city's bunkers?

We were a poor mix of a gene pool, too. My mum's North African heritage must have been missed on admission – pale enough to slip through the net when combined with the gift of a Western surname. When I was little I used to force my parents to put their arms next to each other. The contrast in their complexions fascinated me – my brother and I a perfect blend of them both.

I closed my eyes for a moment, but when I opened them there was still only darkness. I envied those who had already fallen asleep, oblivious to the situation. In these pockets of darkness it seemed as if anything could happen. What if the lights never came back on? I wondered if the shopping mall above was still intact, empty, with no life to inhabit it. My mum always said you had to live in a place to keep it alive. I imagined living in a house on a hill so I could see out for miles. I thought maybe it would sit on a clifftop by the sea but then I remembered I lived in fear of tsunamis. The house would have a wood-burning stove and solar panels, and there'd be land for growing crops. I wouldn't have to rely on anyone for anything. I shifted again, the frame of my bunk swaying slightly. I assumed there would be soil somewhere, still healthy enough to support life and enough daylight to ensure things could once again prosper. Mum would have loved it.

The yellow day bulbs suddenly flickered on, the hum of the generators restored. I wasn't even sure if I'd slept, but, feeling somewhat reluctant to face Canavan, I jumped down from my bunk, landing painfully on the balls of my bare feet. My spare boiler suit lay crumpled on the floor, which must have fallen off my bunk during the night and I gripped it, relieved and a little astonished to find it had not been stolen.

I decided the suit I had on was still good for a few more days, and slipped on my gym shoes. A shower too could wait another day. They'd never thought to gift us cotton towels, only disposable paper ones – perhaps to deter us from wasting water. And if I was emitting an odour now I was oblivious. I used to be hypersensitive to smell – to my own scent, to the scents of others. But my nostrils had grown immune to the stenches that surrounded me; only new and unfamiliar smells filtered through.

I saw Mrs Foer watching me. Her blanket was up past her nose but her eyes followed my movements, and the creases around her face suggested she was smiling.

I went to collect my food pouches and turned to the clocks. Alison's voice came over the speaker system and there was something particularly satisfying about now being able to put a face to her words. There was a smugness within me, relishing my knowledge of a world behind the scenes. I closed my eyes and let the image of her come to the forefront of my mind as she spoke: Tonight's monthly movie is *Father of the Bride* part two and it will be showing in the recreation rooms from 7 p.m. The rooms will be busy so arrive with plenty of time. The designated agony aunts will have pop-up tables in the doctors' surgeries today from 2 to 4 p.m. I'm sure they will be able to help with any worries or general concerns that you have. And now let's be forever mindful that: *when we are moving forward together, success is guaranteed.* Have a wonderful day, one and all.

I weaved my way down the corridors, a nervousness already anchored in my stomach, but as I rounded the final corner I saw Valentine pacing back and forth across the pharmacy entrance. A strand of grey hair stuck to his forehead, his eyes and mind focused on the floor. I came to a stop in front of him and he looked up with a glimmer of disbelief in his eyes. He planted his hands on my shoulders, gripping them.

Christ, Wolfe, I thought . . . Well, I don't know what I thought. He hugged me then and it was as if he didn't want to let go.

What's wrong?

What's wrong with *me*? What happened to you? he barked. I've been up all night worrying. You were just dragged off . . .

It wasn't that bad.

He released me from his embrace and stepped back, waiting for me to say something, but nothing came. So what happened?

I opened the pharmacy and he followed me in. Wolfe, are you listening to me?

I . . .

Is it something to do with me, or the pharmacy? Have we done something wrong?

I faltered. I made a dispensing error, but it'll be OK.

Shit, he said, following me towards the dispensary. It's a horrible feeling when you make a mistake. But we've all been there, Wolfe. Until we're all robots there will still be human error.

Thanks, I said, attempting a smile.

Have you written the error up?

Not yet.

Well, you really should, while it's still fresh in your mind. We always learn from these things. It's vital we keep a good audit trail.

I placed my belongings on the counter and started unlocking the medicine drawers. I'll do it today.

He nodded. Of course – you don't need to do it right this minute.

Valentine was a classic pharmatron. If I cut him down the middle I'd discover his insides were illuminated in green like a medical cross. His blood probably ran green too, matching the dyed medicinal water often displayed in the conical flasks of shop windows.

OK, I said, willing him to leave.

What was the error, if you don't mind me asking?

My shoulders slumped and I turned away. I . . . I gave a patient miconazole paste for oral thrush but I didn't realise they were on warfarin.

Oh, that is a bad one. How did you discover the error?

Luckily the patient had an appointment with Dr Stirling and he picked up on the INR reading.

Valentine shook his head. But they're still happy to let you practise? Considering the severity of the error . . .

They don't exactly have many options.

When I turned around there was a young woman entering the pharmacy. She lingered on the shop floor for a moment, as if she was deciding to buy something despite nothing being for sale. She was taller than me, with dark blond hair, cut short. But it suited her. From her face it looked as though she would have had her hair exactly in this style regardless of her circumstances.

Eventually she came to the Perspex hatch. Sorry I'm late, she said.

Can I help? I asked, somewhat suspiciously, while Valentine hovered around me.

She bit down on her lip. I'm reporting for work, as I was told to. She paused. Did no one tell you I was coming?

I had pressed my hipbone into the counter as she spoke

and it was only when she stopped that I acknowledged my discomfort and took a step back.

I was expecting you, I said in an almost theatrical tone. Come in. I pointed to the dispensary door, unlocking it and stepping aside. I'm Wolfe, the pharmacist you'll be working with.

Levitt, she said.

What's happening here? Valentine asked.

Oh, this is my new assistant. She's to work with me and help reduce my stress load.

He was staring at me. So I assume I too shall be receiving an assistant . . .

I shrugged. I guess if that's something you want you'll need to take it up with the superiors.

Valentine hesitated before making his way out of the dispensary. Don't forget to fill in that incident form, he said, lingering a moment longer, before heading for the door and having to sidestep to allow my first patient over the threshold.

The man forced a paper prescription through the hatch. Dr Bishop gave me this one to try, he said. He assures me it's a much stronger antidepressant than the one Dr Stirling prescribed.

Right, I said, then turned to Levitt. Just shadow me until I'm ready. OK?

Sure, she replied, and I brought my attention back to the patient. Surname and ID number please.

As he spoke, little flecks of his spittle landed on the Perspex. He was at the beginning of the alphabet and I had his drug chart in my hands almost immediately.

Ah, 60mg of duloxetine. Interesting choice, Dr Bishop, I said, more to myself than to anyone else, but I could feel Levitt's stare on my back. I flicked through the patient's drug chart until I found the write-up for fluoxetine and scored it out with a red marker. There was something gratifying about using the red one in particular – the way the ink seemed to permeate the paper, the sweep of its fibrous point. And the smell; I could have sniffed it all day. I imagined overdosing on its fumes, like Tipp-Ex, but suspected the ink would have dried out long before completing its task.

I could hear Levitt clearing her throat as if she was about to say something but nothing came out. I retrieved a black marker and on a fresh sheet of his drug chart started writing out the new medication.

Do you have to write down everyone's medication by hand? Levitt said.

Her voice startled me and the *t* of the duloxetine blotched out at the flick. Yes, I said.

They couldn't have put all this on a computer for you …

I turned to look at her. I guess they didn't have time, or I don't know …

She shrugged. I doubt you'd even need an assistant if they had computerised everything.

I pulled open one of the medication drawers. They were built into the wall, like a cavity, and when its full length was extended it reached nearly a metre. It seemed to take Levitt by surprise and she ducked out of the way, so as not to collide with its curved metal corner. The duloxetine packet was yellow and silver and I inspected it against the new prescription before popping one capsule out of a blister strip. The capsule, the same colour as the packet, fell into my palm. It was like the colour scheme of my old living room. Everything had been this bold mustard and grey – lampshades, cushions and curtains all tying in together. I placed the capsule into a measuring cup and passed it through the hatch. As the patient poured water and swallowed I realised I hadn't changed the jug over since Valentine's shift the night before. I watched on as he gulped the stagnant water, refilling his paper cone. He opened his mouth for my inspection and I nodded.

There was no one else waiting when he left and I found myself reluctantly turning back to face Levitt. So, any questions so far?

Is this pretty much what you do all day?

There's more to it than that, I said, defensiveness thick in my throat. There's a lot of responsibility.

Like what? She crossed her arms in front of her chest and fanned her fingers over her elbows. The skin between her fingers was red-raw and inflamed. She must have seen me looking, because she curled her hands back in towards herself.

I'm here to provide advice on minor ailments and free up some of the doctors' time so they can deal with more important matters, I said. If a doctor makes a medication error and I don't pick it up, it's me who takes more share of the blame.

She narrowed her eyes, not blinking. But mostly you're here to make sure we don't top ourselves, aren't you?

I paused. Yeah, I suppose that pretty much sums it up.

She let out a silent laugh, her lips creased upwards in pleasure. I could see then that she had a tooth missing. It was a shame, because she was otherwise really rather striking.

I count the stock, I said. So I'll notice if anything goes missing . . .

She held up her hands in defence. Don't worry, that's not really my bag.

Maybe you could start by rinsing the plastic cups, I said,

56

turning to greet another patient who was walking through the door.

She stood straight, rolling up the sleeves of her boiler suit. Sure, no worries. Anything is better than being in laundry.

I pointed to the tap. Let it run for a minute, then it'll turn clear. The hot might even come out as lukewarm if you're lucky.

The waiting patient began to give me her details but I was aware of Levitt humming a tune; it seemed familiar but its name escaped me. There was the memory of Daniel trying to serenade me with the hum of a rap song. I somehow dispensed the medication on autopilot, still holding the box I'd popped the tablets out from, passing them through the hatch. The woman wore a pair of glasses, the approved plastic lenses looking flimsy in their frames. She peered into the cup but it didn't look as if she could see much. Her hand reached for the water jug but she missed the handle on her first attempt.

Do you need some help? I said.

I don't even know why I wear these, she replied, lifting the glasses from her face. There's hardly any difference when I take them off. She threw the tablets into her mouth and then poured water into the now empty measuring cup, spilling a little on the floor. OK, so they don't want us having glass, fine, but honestly, what sort of an existence is this?

I'm sorry, I said, knowing there was nothing I could do.

She shrugged, thrusting her tongue out for me to see. Maybe I'm the lucky one, spared from having to see this place.

I was watching her leave, her steps calculated and cautious, when Levitt asked, What's next?

She'd stacked the plastic measuring cups in a pyramid and drops of soapy water dripped on to the ribbed stainless steel drying rack below. You might as well clean the work surfaces, I said. Just give me a second to check the fridge temperature, I added, so I'm not in your way.

How come you have a fridge? she said. Haven't seen one of those in a while.

Some medicine needs refrigeration. Eye drops, some tablets . . .

And insulin? she said.

I paused. We don't actually have any insulin-dependent diabetics in the bunker.

Why?

I don't think . . . We couldn't guarantee a supply of insulin for the duration.

She cast her eyes to the floor. Oh, OK, I see . . . She started gathering paper towels in her hand. Do you have a surface cleaner?

Soap and water, I'm afraid. I'm not trusted with the disinfectants.

She got to work and I watched her for a moment, before turning back to the drawer where we kept the markers. I couldn't decide which one would be least missed.

Are you going to watch the movie tonight? she asked over her shoulder.

Me . . . ? No, I don't think so.

You don't like films?

I settled on a green marker, having little use for the colour, and, checking to ensure Levitt wasn't watching, I slipped the pen into one of my side pockets. I love films, I said. Just not the ones they show in here.

Levitt paused. Surely it's better than nothing?

Is it . . . ?

Good morning, a woman interrupted, and when I looked up I realised it was the mother and little boy whose hand I'd held in the food queue. The boy was gripping her leg, asking to be picked up.

Baxter, I said, my thoughts immediately shifting to the business card nestled in my breast pocket. Hi, little man.

Hello, his mother said.

How can I help?

I need pads, she whispered, not wishing to meet my eye. It's that time of month already.

What's your ID number?

She rattled the digits off and I pulled out her chart. I see you're not especially regular, I said, reading the last date she had requested them. Five to six weeks, give or take . . .

I've never been regular, she said. Please, I'm already bleeding, and she pointed to her boiler suit but I chose not to look.

Here are three, I said, slipping them through the hatch. That's all I'm allowed to give at the moment. Her face was turning red and little Baxter tugged at her hand, trying to lead her away. Please try to make them last as long as possible, I said, pausing to take a breath before I forced myself to continue, until they're fully saturated.

She gripped the sanitary towels in her hand and made to leave.

Look, I whispered, are you here on your own?

Sorry?

Is it just the two of you in the bunker?

She paused, seeming confused, maybe even taken aback. No . . . My husband is one of our leader's senior defence advisors.

I was aware of Levitt shifting behind me. OK, I said. Well, if you need more, I'll see what I can do.

She nodded, gripping little Baxter's hand. And as she turned to leave I could see a small smudge of red on the fabric of her boiler suit, almost in the shape of a butterfly. I was reminded of those old sanitary towel adverts on television. It was always these on-the-move women not letting a period get in their way. And there was the water dyed blue. I imagined how horrifying it would be if we bled blue. I missed tampons. Toxic shock syndrome would have been a really inventive way to go.

The BEEP BEEP BEEP of the speaker system warned us to return to our respective sides of the bunker for the emergency drill. People were rushing across the boundary line, perhaps returning to their beds. The soldiers preferred us in our bunks but I liked to stand by the dividing line and witness the wall coming down, before watching it rise again. There was something fascinating about the mechanics of it moving to the ground and separating us. With each drill I noticed more and more people coming to stand on either side of the line, as if it was somehow less intimidating with time. I could see Levitt on the other side but I doubted she noticed me. She was talking to an older man who I assumed to be her father – his hair was short, his face clean and distinguished, the way I imagined a senior advisor to be.

The beeping intensified, no longer any interval to identify one beep from another, and the steel wall was now being lowered from the ceiling. I bit one of my fingernails, ragged and too close to the skin, while I fought the urge to crouch, only to hold a glimpse of the others across the line for a moment longer.

No one spoke when the wall locked into place. I looked around and recognised the head teacher. The school on our side had put on a play not so long ago – a retelling of the bible story *Samson and Delilah*. It was bizarre – children aggressively chanting *the Philistines are coming*, while a little girl used her fingers to simulate scissors, chopping off the hair of a boy who pretended to sleep. The girl must have pulled on his hair too violently because the boy began to cry, while the other children stood with wide demented smiles. And I knew I was meant to feel for little Samson – mourn the loss of strength through his hair, be enraged by Delilah's betrayal – but I felt none of those things. In an environment dominated by men, it was refreshing to see this girl relishing in the removal of his power.

At the end of the performance the head teacher had stood up and asked us all to join him in applauding the cast. And only on seeing him again at the dividing wall did I remember he was called Mr Clement. I realised then that the man I was staring at could potentially be the same one on ND's business card. I edged a little closer in his direction then, tried to imagine what I'd say when I arrived at his side.

But the beeping started again and I instinctively took a step back as the wall began to rise. The boundary line was marked out with dashes of industrial yellow paint and despite the footfall it was hardly worn. Some inhabitants waved to one another as though they'd been reunited with long-lost friends. I never waved, but I would sometimes find myself searching for people I used to know, hoping they were on the other side. Maybe that was why I never ventured over – for fear of realising that there really was no one waiting for me.

For a while I kept imagining I'd seen my mum. I couldn't explain why; I knew she was dead. She was dead long before

I came into the bunker. Maybe she could see what was happening in the world before everyone else and that was why she took her sleeping pills. We were to be comforted by the fact that there had been no struggle or pain. And I'd taken note of this, banking the notion for future reference. I had been the one to discover her. She looked so peaceful, as if there was really nothing to fear. We made death into a bigger deal than it was, she had said, while other creatures dealt with it quite gracefully. I wondered if she would have thought I was a coward for wanting to live, for disowning part of myself to fit the bunker's mould. My silence was complicit.

When I looked back, aware of the displacement of people, Clement was gone.

Reluctantly I returned to my bunk. The Foers were absent but Canavan was slumped across his bed just as I'd expected him to be. He saw me and pitched himself up, his palm supporting his chin.

How was your day at the office? he said. I was starting to worry you wouldn't come home.

I placed my hands on the frame of his bunk and whispered, Ralf?

So you were approached by Human Resources, then?

Indeed.

He smiled. And did you get what you wanted?

To a degree, but with strings attached.

Nothing is free in this world, he replied, arching his back before sitting up. Speaking of which, do you perhaps have something for me?

I reached into my pocket and retrieved the marker, before sliding it underneath his blanket, our fingers touching briefly as he took it from me.

Thank you, Wolfe.

I started to climb. You didn't need anything from me, I said. He's given you a blank canvas in his lair.

Canavan tried to laugh but it came out as a puff of air escaping through his nostrils. It doesn't exactly feel like that, he said.

He'd have given you a pen. A whole pack, even, I said, suddenly at risk of crying. Why ask me?

I wanted to see if you'd go through with it.

And now what?

Now we both have something.

I lay flat on my bunk, closing my eyes momentarily before opening them again. *Now we both have something.* His words dangled there in front of me, as if I could reach out and prick them. But what did I have? I felt loose and untethered. I thought of my mum again and of her desire to finally take us to Cairo when we were teenagers – when she thought we were capable of absorbing the culture. But every day of that trip she herself had appeared displaced, struggling to articulate exactly what it meant to be back in her homeland. Instead, we'd embarked on a tour of all the big attractions. At Giza she paid extra for a guide to take us inside the largest of the pyramids. It was a labyrinth of airless, crouching tunnels with rumours of black magic and booby-traps, until we finally arrived at a huge tomb at its centre. I watched tourists climb into stone coffins, their arms crossed over their chests, the flash of their cameras blinding. Panicked, with a genuine fear of forever being stuck in that lifeless place, I'd clambered out, my back hunched over, until I was at the surface, gasping for breath. The pharaohs had given up their organs to rest there, had had their brains removed through their noses. So what was my offering for the privilege of living in this sealed tomb?

# 5

Do you want to play a game? Levitt said. She was perched on one of the plastic chairs in the dispensary with her legs crossed and her hands cupped over a kneecap.

What kind of game?

I'll list symptoms and you have to tell me what my illness is.

I contemplated this for a moment. I hated talking about health when I didn't have to. It bored me to tears. Once, in my previous life, I was getting my hair cut and the hairdresser, knowing I was a pharmacist, wanted to ask me about a cough she'd had for over two weeks. It was raspy rather than phlegmy, and she had infuriated me so much that I hadn't bothered leaving her a tip.

I'll go first, Levitt said.

Fine.

OK, so, she said clutching her chest. I'm breathless, so breathless . . .

Asthma?

She shook her head. Oh, and my vision, she said, rubbing her eyes. Why so blurry?

I squinted, feeling the need to look at her eyes.

I think my eyelids are beginning to droop.

My mind was blank and I continued to stare at her.

Oh, no, my face feels weak . . .

A stroke, I said.

Now the abdominal cramps have started, she declared. I'm going to be sick. I'm going to shit myself.

Templeton's cramping body flashed before me, his grip on my hand. I wanted so much not to see him any more.

I don't know, I finally said.

It's botulism, she replied, thrusting her hands out in exasperation. Honestly, for a pharmacist you are terrible at this.

Who even gets botulism these days?

I could hear the pharmacy door opening and without leaving my seat I tilted my chin upwards, looking out to see who was coming. To my surprise it was Stirling striding across the shop floor. His white lab coat was buttoned and there was an ink stain on one of the side pockets.

Hi, he said, and I could sense Levitt pretending to busy herself behind me. Do you think I could speak with you for a moment? Maybe alone . . .

Sure . . . I said, and turned towards Levitt. Would you mind giving us a minute?

Where am I meant to go? And from her tone I was reminded that she was indeed still a teenager.

Just step outside the pharmacy. We won't be long.

She reluctantly shuffled out, perching herself on the ledge of the false window outside, and for a moment I expected her to remove a phone from her pocket.

Is everything OK? I said.

Yeah . . . He ran a hand through his hair, pulling on a tuft of short curls. I was wondering if you wanted to meet up at some point? I mean, you might be busy and that's fine too. So no worries either way.

What?

I haven't seen you in a while . . .

66

Well, you know where I am, I said.

He paused, seeming a little taken aback. It's just you usually visit the surgery.

I shrugged. I didn't really know that you liked me visiting.

Well, I do. He paused. I'm on night shifts this week but I thought we could meet in the recreation room one evening . . . Maybe after you finish and before I start?

Why?

His cheeks filled with colour. Don't you think it's good to spend time with other people?

I hesitated, contemplating the strangeness of spending time with him outside of his surgery. At least in the surgery I could be honest and frank, as if I were one of his patients and he was bound by his profession to cast no judgement. But in the recreation room, who would I be? And there was the real risk of getting too close – in daring to invest in others when it could all so easily be taken away.

So, what do you think? he pressed.

Tonight? I said.

I . . . I can't tonight. But tomorrow?

OK, I said. Tomorrow.

OK, fine, he replied, in a tone that made it sound as though it wasn't even his idea. Say, fiveish?

Wait – is there anything on in the recreation room tomorrow evening?

He shook his head. I've already checked. And then, awkwardly, as though he couldn't quite bear to be alone with me any longer, he waved Levitt back.

She walked in casually, catching his eye as she passed. All finished? she asked, somewhat flirtatiously.

I think so, he replied.

I was already trying to tally up their age gap. Would she be his type? She was probably everyone's type.

Well, see you later, Stirling said.

See you later, I replied, watching him leave.

I could hear Levitt turning the tap on behind me. He's quite handsome, in a sort of geeky way. Don't you think?

I guess . . .

She started rinsing the used measuring cups, holding them under the running tap. How come you guys are so friendly?

Are we?

I would say so.

We worked together in the hospital on the army base, I said. Some of the doctors could be real dicks but he was always decent. Took on board my recommendations, you know? I guess we've kind of become friends since then.

Is he a good doctor?

He's a great doctor, I said, aware of the defensiveness in my voice.

She began stacking the measuring cups on the drying rack. The skin between her fingers looked as if it had been weeping.

Odd that they're all men, she said. Like, have they forgotten that women were doctors too?

You don't need to do that if it aggravates your skin, I said, nodding towards her hands. I can give you something else to do.

No, it's fine. I like washing things.

You can wash the shelves in the front shop if you're really looking for something to do, then. It's filthy out there, and I couldn't tell you the last time Valentine or I had the chance to clean them. I can give you gloves.

She nodded, filling the basin with lukewarm soapy water. She placed a roll of kitchen paper under her arm and lifted the basin out of the sink with both hands, its weight causing her to take slow and steady steps.

I'll get the door for you, I said, already opening it.

She stopped at the first row of shelves and placed the basin down by her feet. She removed the empty drug boxes, before dampening a piece of kitchen paper and gliding it across the shelf. I busied myself with the drug charts I'd accumulated from my shift. On the top was the chart for Floyd, one of ND's concerns. There had been nothing of particular interest with regard to this patient, although there was little to draw me to any of them for that matter. I flicked through Floyd's drug chart again, for what felt like the tenth time, but still no clues were hidden within. I wasn't exactly sure what I was expecting to find. I suppose I was hopeful that there would be nothing – that I'd be able to settle on some tangible belief that I was in no way breaching my patients' trust. My aim was to approach this as I would any other pharmacy-related task in my previous life: to work quietly and pragmatically and pray for no confrontation or issues to arise. Because there was nothing like the sinking sensation of a patient returning to cause difficulty; of feeling some moral responsibility towards them.

When I glanced up I could see Levitt had placed the boxes back on their shelf in a fashion that displayed them in a semi-circle. As the hours passed she seemed to take pleasure in the task. She designed ailment sections: colds and flu, constipation, allergies and hay fever. She built a display out of the different gastric acid and reflux tablets.

Tell me this, she said holding a nasal spray up towards me. Did we really need all this self-medication?

I shrugged, opening the hatch to hear her better.

You were just a cog, weren't you? she said, smirking. A cog in the old consumer wheel, cranking the gears, telling us what would make everything better. She tapped the side of her nose. But don't you worry, Wolfe, your secret is safe with me.

Perhaps I should find something more rewarding to do? I said. More noble . . . Laundry maybe?

Don't be daft, she replied, spluttering a laugh. Laundry was awful. Awful. This is cushy – a delight in comparison.

And I was laughing because I liked her. I really liked her. It was easy to pretend we were actually working together in a normal pharmacy, leading normal lives, our realities momentarily suspended. In many regards this was the easiest pharmacy job I'd ever had: there were no dosette boxes to check for the elderly, no methadone to pour for the drug addicts, no real clinical knowledge to worry about because most of the patients didn't suffer from anything particularly complex.

Still laughing, I opened the stationery drawer and pulled out the calendar. A picture of a little pug on top of a hill stared back at me. I paused, inspecting the image, imagined the poor thing having to scale its ascent, probably struggling to catch its breath. I'd once been shown a photograph of a pug's skull and the image had stayed with me. It was unnatural, as though its breed was an evolutionary mistake. With one of my permanent markers I scored off another day as if it was something disposable, as if I was counting down to a holiday. When each day felt like the last, it was good to have something quantitative to show for it, and pharmacists liked things being quantitative.

You sleep on the other side of the bunker, don't you? I said, watching as she crossed over the threshold into the dispensary.

Yup.

What's it like?

What do you mean? she said, wiping her forehead with the back of her wrist.

Is it a mirror image of this side?

What? You've never been over there?

No . . .

Why not?

I was aware that, regardless of what I said, it was likely to sound childish. I don't know . . . I just don't like the idea of it.

She stared at me. It's really not a big deal, she said. No different from being over here.

What's the pharmacy like?

It's exactly the same. The posters are maybe different but I'm pretty sure the layout is identical.

And the pharmacists . . .

A male patient walked through the door and my words trailed off. He faced up to me without speaking and I found myself focusing on his forehead. He brought his lips to the Perspex and blew, letting his breath steam up a perfectly formed circle. He pulled back and inspected it, drawing a triangle with his index finger, before wiping it away with his palm.

It's an itch, he finally said. I'm clawing everywhere.

I sighed; I couldn't hide it. Hang on. I'm coming round, I said. I'll need to inspect your hands. I reached under the counter and retrieved fresh disposable latex gloves. I pulled them on and raised my palms up, as though I was about to cut open his body. I stepped out of the dispensary, locking Levitt in behind me, and turned towards him.

I held his right hand up to the light. Is it itchy between your fingers?

It's itchy everywhere.

I, too, was starting to feel itchy. I tapped between the webbing of his fingers. Yes, I think I can see the burrows.

That doesn't sound good . . .

I was already making my way back into the dispensary. Surname and ID number, I said.

I started flicking through the drug charts but there was no file for him. I gathered an empty booklet from under the counter and arched my shoulders over as I carved permethrin 5% cream into the paper. I removed a tube of the cream from a drawer and returned to the shop floor. From the corner of my eye, I saw Levitt wiping a stretch of counter backwards and forwards but I knew she was watching.

Use this, I said, handing him the cream. You'll need to put it on here, behind the curtain. Toes to neck and you must show your face so I can ensure nothing is consumed.

What's it for?

Scabies. Keep it on until tonight, for at least eight hours, before washing it off. I paused. And you'll need to boil-wash your clothes and blankets. I'll give you a temporary paper suit until your clothes are clean.

But it's freezing . . .

I shrugged.

He snatched the tube from my hand and walked behind the curtain. He was staring at me from over the top of it and I could hear the Velcro strips of his boiler suit being pulled apart. Anything else I need to know? he said.

If you've had skin-to-skin contact with anyone you'll need to inform them.

He snorted a laugh but shifted his gaze to the floor. I was aware of his movements from the other side of the curtain – the shadow of his arm stretching upwards across his chest, him bending to his toes. I suspected Levitt was watching too.

He handed me the empty tube of cream and I left him there to go back into the dispensary for a disposable paper suit. I pulled it from its packaging, its touch slightly fluffy, like a dried out wet-wipe. After, he reappeared from behind the cubicle and said, Some say the pharmacists are useless but I'm not sure I agree.

I peeled off my gloves and dropped them into a bucket. You can leave now.

Levitt was leaning against the counter, her hands resting by her sides. Are they always like that? she said. Assholes . . .

Sometimes.

So, what's next on the agenda?

I think you're ready to start date-checking the stock and familiarising yourself with the drugs and their names. I pulled open one of the dispensary drawers. Check each expiry date on the packaging, mark the short-dated boxes with a dot and move them to the front, I said, handing her the blue marker. It's always the blue one, OK?

That's fine, she said, taking it from me. But I don't know what the date is . . . How will I know if something's passed its expiry date?

I stared at her for a moment, forgetting that not everyone had access to a calendar. And I couldn't quite comprehend it – having no real bearing in the year. Only being told what the superiors deemed worthy of reporting over the speaker system. Maybe it was liberating, like the lost week between Christmas and New Year.

Opening the drawer, I pulled out my dog calendar again, offering it to her. You can look at this any time, I said. You don't need to ask me.

She smiled, looking at the page. I thought it was autumn, she said, although I couldn't have told you it was November.

She set about quickly, starting at the bottom, her legs crossed on the floor. I was suddenly envious of the task I'd set for her and wishing I'd kept it for myself. I used to consider it a small victory finding an out-of-date drug; it helped to pass the time.

What happens if I find something *past* its expiry? Levitt said, holding a box of amitriptyline in her hand.

It still gets dispensed, but we just try to use it up first before the longer-dated stuff.

What, really? You still give it to people?

We wouldn't have before, outside, but now it's better than nothing. In fact, I'm sure it's totally fine. My dad carried on taking tablets from his cupboard when they were seven years out of date and he swore they worked perfectly.

And he's OK? she said automatically, naïvely.

He's not here, I replied.

Slowly, she nodded, her focus shifting back to the medicine drawers and their contents.

Can I ask you something else? I said.

Am I doing it wrong? she said, her nose scrunched in concentration.

No. This isn't about the pharmacy.

She glanced up. Sure.

Am I right in thinking that you were planning on going to veterinary school?

Why are you asking?

Sorry, I don't mean to pry ... Another patient was walking in and I busied myself at the hatch. It was a quick transaction of pills. Then a stream of three more patients arrived in rapid succession, as all the while Levitt quietly made her way along a drawer of expiry dates.

Yes, she finally said when we were alone. That was the plan anyway. She lifted her head, pointing her chin to the ceiling. It would have been nice to move away from home, she added with no shift in tone, as if she was indifferent to the topic.

You must like animals, I said, and immediately wished I'd found something more insightful to say.

I guess, she replied. I had the grades for medicine but it really didn't appeal to me. All those sick people, all with opinions . . .

Pet owners have opinions too.

Yeah, but still I don't think it would have been as stressful, plus the pay was meant to be amazing. I could have become one of those supervets that fit bionic cat feet.

I laughed again – a real honest, hearty laugh. But you'd probably have had to stick your hand up a cow's ass. Or lamb a struggling sheep. Have you seen the mucus that comes out of them? I pulled a lamb out of a sheep once and it was disgusting.

She was laughing now too, the noise of her laughter infectious. Really? she said.

I was on a friend's farm around Easter time. And he forced us all into helping him with the lambing.

What did it feel like?

Warm. I was worried I wouldn't be able to do it – get the thing out. You take it by the front legs and pull. And there's so much blood. I hadn't expected there to be so much blood. I paused. I even castrated the little guy – it was like fitting a tight elastic band around his balls. It was weird. We had lamb for dinner that night and it didn't seem to bother any of us.

Do you think they'll still be around? she whispered, so quietly that it seemed like I could have imagined her speaking.

What?

Animals. Do you think we'll see cows and sheep again?

I paused. I don't know. Surely.

My dad – he shot our dog.

I pushed the palm of my hand into my right eye socket and it felt comforting. He did it a favour, I said.

I know, she replied. I know.

The pharmacy door creaked open and a woman walked in. She seemed to be guiding someone else in behind her, keeping the door open with her back pressed against it. The other woman was slow across the threshold and the first woman steadied her. They took deliberate steps towards me before finally arriving at the Perspex. The woman who could barely walk wouldn't look up but she was young, maybe Levitt's age, and I noticed bruising, sneaking out from the collar of her boiler suit and up across her cheeks and face.

The woman who guided her spoke. We have an emergency prescription from the doctor, she said, forcing the piece of paper through the hatch. My eyes were immediately drawn to the doctor's signature. Dr Hays.

I understand, I said, taking it from her.

Can I help? Levitt asked. I could pull the drug chart for you . . .

No, I said. This prescription won't be getting written up.

The emergency contraception box was purple but I wasn't sure what shade you would call it – off-lilac, chalky? I popped it out and passed it through. I turned to retrieve the permethrin cream when I heard the same woman's voice say, One little pill, my darling. You're doing so well. I turned back with the cream in my hand. Do you need to inspect her mouth? she asked.

It's OK. I removed the cream from the box and passed it through the hatch. I'm sorry, but you'll have to apply this here as a precaution. I paused. There's a chair she can sit on behind the curtain.

The silent woman still wouldn't look up and I could see the start of tears running down her cheeks. I'll apply the cream for her, the other woman said. Would that work?

That'll be fine, but I'll give you some gloves.

She guided the silent woman behind the curtain and I tried not to listen. Her breathing was painful and I could feel the hairs on my arms standing straight. Levitt seemed stuck to the spot and no one else came in. It was as though all the inhabitants of the bunker knew. The silent woman's breathing grew even shallower and I began to fear she might be hyperventilating, but after nearly ten minutes the other woman emerged from behind the curtain with the tube of cream rolled up from the end.

I can give her a paper suit, or she can have my spare boiler suit, I said.

It's OK. Laundry have kindly provided her with a fresh one. Thank you, though. She paused. There's bleeding. Down below . . . I know she's not due her supply yet but the doctor seemed to think that under the circumstances you'd be able to provide her with some pads.

Of course, I said, reaching into a drawer. My fingers fumbled through stacks and I grabbed a handful, not even counting them before passing them through the hatch.

Thank you again, she said, letting a sad smile settle. You've been very respectful, she added, before going back behind the curtain and retrieving the silent patient, holding her around the waist and moving her forward until they were out of sight.

And I thought of that *Samson and Delilah* play again: how it had been a fleeting illusion, a momentary transfer of power before Samson's hair grew back and he destroyed everything. There were rumours already circling that a man had been chemically castrated – something of a cure and a warning – an attempt to convince us that these *indiscretions* were the actions of one person, and one person alone. No systemic change was needed because really there was nothing to change. But did anyone believe that? Was the leader naïve to the realities of our existence? Maybe he didn't care. Maybe he was part of the problem. It was easier to romanticise a society once you had extracted yourself from within it.

# 6

The next morning as Levitt and I sat in the dispensary there was a tension in the air. Maybe it was just the ventilation system but I had this overwhelming sensation that it was about to rain, clouds so full and dark, only moments away. I cast my gaze to the artificial windows that offered nothing but a view of concrete or an approaching patient, and tried to pretend that rain was indeed battering against the glass. Perhaps somewhere above us, it was.

It had been a relatively quiet morning in comparison to others. When that happened it was often for no particular reason – sometimes people just didn't have the energy or desire to collect their medication – but I knew on this occasion it was something more. People had grown superstitious, and the rape victim from the previous day was reason enough to take cover. In real pharmacies there would have been a sense of excitement at the blessing of an easier shift: backlogs of work could be tackled, cups of tea could be consumed before going cold, staff speaking to one another with humour, no anxiety or hostility wrapped up in their exchanges. But Levitt and I had little to do and it seemed as though this reprieve from normal order only served to slow the passing of time.

Maxwell, ID number 2597, arrived when I was wiping down the plastic 5ml medicine spoons, dust having gathered on them from sitting in a drawer unused and unneeded for so long. Of all the patients I was tasked with taking a particular interest in, he was the one who intrigued me the most. There was something unpredictable about him, compliance to his medication completely erratic to the point that I didn't even know why he bothered. Often he came with his wife, but behaved as though he was only there to keep her company.

He rattled the digits of his ID number off to me but I knew them by heart, having stared at the carvings of them in ink so many times. I had considered tearing the business card up and forcing the pieces down the plughole, but part of me liked having it, felt it brought a sense of control.

How are you this morning? I said.

He stared at me, shrugged. I'm not a great fan of small talk, he said.

I could feel him watching my every move – the way I flipped his drug chart open, the way I opened the correct medicine drawer – he was taking it all in.

Where's your wife today? I asked, handing his antidepressants through the hatch.

You don't miss anything, do you? he said, throwing the tablets into his mouth. He filled a paper cone with water and gulped the contents. Do you believe in depression? he said.

What do you mean?

Exactly what I've asked. Do you believe depression is a medical condition?

I nodded. Of course.

He raised his eyebrows. I'm not so convinced it's even a thing ... Like what about all those people before us, for thousands of years ... Surely this is a modern invention.

It's a chemical imbalance, I said. It's a thing.

He was smirking now. What about paranoia, do you believe in that?

Yes, I believe I do.

He brought himself closer to the Perspex, tilted his head upwards and thrust his tongue out so far that I could see his tonsils.

I arrived in the recreation room a little after five, and immediately saw Stirling sitting in one of the worn leather armchairs. The sleeves of his boiler suit were rolled up to his elbows and his hands gripped a book. I found myself sidestepping, hiding behind one of the open bookcases, wanting to stare at the profile of his face. Whatever it was he was reading had truly caught his attention and he was smiling. And it was nice to see him this way, in what I imagined would have been his natural disposition.

He looked up then and his eyes fell upon me. He tilted his head to one side as he tried to inspect me between the gaps. I stepped out from behind the books and made my way towards him. I slumped down in the armchair opposite and he nodded.

What are you reading? I asked.

*The Comforters* by Muriel Spark, he replied. It's a strange little book. I think from the cover they probably thought it was chick-lit or something when they brought it in but it's probably the best book you'll find here.

Thanks for the recommendation, I said.

He turned down the corner of the page he was reading from and closed the book over. Have you eaten yet? he said.

No, why?

I brought extra pouches, he said getting to his feet.

Where are we going? I asked, as I forced my blankets and suit under my free arm to keep up with his sudden pace.

He guided me through rows of bookcases until we came to a small opening of carpeted space. He took my blankets from me and, with his too, started spreading them out across the floor. He was very particular in his movements, flattening his hands across the bobbled fabric, stretching the corners out. He nodded before kicking his gym shoes off and stepping on to them. I looked at his toes – the nail beds were healthy, no hint of a fungal infection. I imagined him previously walking around his house or garden barefoot, letting the ground alter his footprints. I remembered reading an article that said shoes were an unnecessary item – that we should be walking around barefoot everywhere, letting the skin become hard and calloused – we would have walked more efficiently and our bodies would have fared better for it.

I realised he was staring at me. Are you not taking your shoes off? he asked.

I reached down and pulled off my gym shoes, lining them up next to the edge of the blankets. I didn't want him looking at my feet – the middle toes were slightly webbed together. I stepped on to the wool and there was an awkward pause before he sat himself down and waited for me to do the same. As I crossed my legs he reached into the pockets of his boiler suit and removed the food pouches. He spread them out in a line between us, an array of all my favourite flavours: strawberry and apple, raspberry and pear, apricot smoothie.

How do you have all these? I said.

He hesitated before saying, I have my ways. Help yourself.

I reached out and took a raspberry and pear one. This OK? I said, holding it up for his inspection.

He nodded, already twisting off the cap of the apricot smoothie with his teeth. He took a few gulps before saying, Is this too weird, us hanging out like this?

I smiled. It kind of feels as if we're about to start doing yoga or something . . .

We could if you wanted to, he said.

A doctor who does yoga . . . Is there anything you can't do? I said, gently mocking.

I'd like to have travelled more.

Where would you have gone?

South America, I suppose. Peru . . .

So why didn't you?

He exhaled. Too busy trying to become a doctor, I guess.

A silence fell between us and I rushed to find my words. Peru's nice, I said. The people are friendly. But I wasn't massively impressed with the food.

So when were you in Peru?

When I was on my honeymoon.

He paused. What was it like, being married?

I tried to shrug but it came off deflated. It was great until it wasn't.

And where is he now?

Not here.

He looked down, started picking at the bobbled wool of the blanket. I've never asked you why you decided to become a pharmacist, he said.

I kind of fell into it, I replied, had been told it was a good profession for women, for family life . . . But if I could go back now I would choose something else.

Why?

The empathy needed . . . I don't think it comes naturally to me.

And I realised then as he stared at me that there had been no strategy or thought when it came to becoming a pharmacist, except that I was good at science and desperate to leave home. Being given a profession – it felt like being institutionalised – I'd spent so long training to do this one particular vocation that I felt like I couldn't just walk away. And it had paid well. That was why I'd taken the locum job at the army base. The plan was to save everything and then leave for a place where nobody needed to know that I was broken. I had been convinced travelling was the only thing that would cure me of my divorce. Maybe that was why I found the bunker's confinement so hard.

Stirling's voice cut through my thoughts. You probably wouldn't be here if you weren't a pharmacist, he said.

I suppose you're right. I paused. Believe it or not, when I was little I really wanted to be an astronaut. I know it sounds stupid but I've always thought there was something mystical about outer space. Maybe it's that feeling of escapism, or not being tied down. I sucked on a mouthful of artificial raspberries and pears. My parents took me to the Space Center in Florida when I was little and it blew me away. There was this astronaut's glove encased in glass and I just stood there staring at it. I couldn't comprehend that this glove had been in outer space.

How old were you? Stirling said.

I don't know, maybe eight, nine. Even the risk of death, the power and fuel needed to catapult a rocket into space didn't bother me. It was the *Challenger*, I think, with its first civilian passenger, that exploded seconds after lift-off, but even still I remember thinking that I wouldn't have minded dying that way.

Did you hear about those people who applied to move to Mars? he said. I couldn't believe the numbers volunteering for the mission. I mean, they would never have breathed fresh air again, or been able to go outside without some sort of artificial breathing device. He snorted a laugh. They vowed to abstain from sex because there would be no means to deal with a growing population in such a hostile environment.

It doesn't sound too different from being in here, I said, somewhat flippantly.

Yeah, I suppose you're right.

We fell into a silence then, the only noise that of us sucking on the contents of our pouches.

Dr Hays mentioned there was another rape victim, he said. I heard she was in a bad way.

And as I tried to think of something to say, something to match the gravity of the conversation we found ourselves discussing, I realised Officer Holden and his wife were metres away. She was facing me, her back pressed into a bookcase, and he seemed to be bearing down on her as they debated something. Her eyes locked on me and I tried to look away but it was impossible. Having slept with her husband, I somehow felt I knew her. Afterwards, when Holden and I would lie together in bed, he'd often place his arm around me, and my head would rest in the crook of his elbow. It was as if our bodies fitted best together this way, in this resting position where we didn't have to look at one another, and sometimes we'd talk about her – her likes and dislikes, her quirks and kindnesses. It bothered him that in a restaurant she'd wrap scraps of food up in a napkin and take them home to feed the birds in their garden. I liked to imagine her birds flocking to a safe pocket of earth, fuelled by the crumbs she'd lovingly offered. Weirdly, I never felt guilty about the affair – I considered myself an outsider observing a scene from a film or documentary, intrigued by his life that was separate from my own. I was passing time and empty space with him. Maybe it was some sort of hangover from childhood when I watched my parents struggle through an unhappy marriage, until finally they separated and I felt nothing but relief.

Wolfe, are you OK? Stirling said, turning his head to see what held my attention.

What is this? I said, stretching my arms out between us.

He paused. Friendship, I think . . .

I got to my feet suddenly and began pulling at my blankets, forcing him to move. I'm sorry, I need to go, I said. I'm not sure this was a good idea . . .

Standing, he watched as I continued to grapple, folding my blankets haphazardly across my chest. Why? he said. Did I do something?

No, I just . . . But I didn't know how to tell him that it was all such a futile exercise, that I wasn't worth his time or kindness. I wasn't deserving of it. And, even if I was: what good would it have done?

My bed swayed with the shift of Canavan's body above and it seemed inevitable that his face would appear. I closed my eyes and lay perfectly still. He flicked my arm and I tried to ignore him, the way I would have done with my brother. He flicked me again and when I opened my eyes he was staring at me.

You've been summoned, he said.

Where?

Don't *where* me, he said. You've left quite the impression on him, haven't you?

I hesitated. It would appear so . . .

He narrowed his eyes. What did you promise him?

What did *you* promise him? I said.

He seemed to think about this before responding. Everything.

But why?

I'm here, aren't I? Isn't that the point? We all wanted to be here . . .

I sat up and tried to cross my legs. Where d'you keep the marker pen? I whispered.

I keep it up my ass, he replied with only a flicker of a smile behind the eyes.

He rolled up a sleeve of his boiler suit and dropped the arm back down. Nearly every inch of skin was covered in little drawings and random words. I could make out a house with smoke rising from its chimney, a tiger, a giraffe and a car, among other things.

I like the giraffe, I said.

Everyone always thinks giraffes are cute, but they're brutal. Have you ever seen them fight? Their necks are formidable.

I'm glad you're here, I said.

He brought his face closer and I thought he was about to whisper words of wisdom but instead he said, Do you think I need something for this? He was pointing to a small boil near his right ear. The skin looked almost transparent, with the pus trying to push its way to the surface.

It looks infected, I said. You'll probably need to get an antibiotic. I'd say if it felt ready you could prick it with a sterilised needle and drain the pus, but . . .

Yeah, yeah, I know. No needle, no alcohol.

Canavan . . . I paused. He wants me to tell him things, confidential things about my patients, and I just don't know if I can.

He looked at me, holding my gaze.

Wolfe, the fact that you're saying this to me means you're already going to do it. You don't need my assurance. You've made up your mind. So just do yourself a favour and tell him what he wants to hear.

Normally, I pleaded with my bowels to move. I'd never been someone to go regularly, but before arriving at ND's lair I rushed to the toilet several times. The lair sat like a metal box at one end of the main chamber, its structure spreading both ways over the boundary line. I was aware of children laughing. It was the loveliest sound in the world and I wanted to bottle it. A man further down my row of bunks often cried himself to sleep at night. You could hear his cries echoing off the walls. Canavan told me the man's estranged wife wouldn't come with him to the bunker, and so his child had stayed behind too. I wondered if he thought about his kid laughing – that chortle only children can make – it perhaps running on a loop in his head.

I faced the soldier standing guard and before I'd even opened my mouth he was talking into his mouthpiece. I could hear the handle of the door turning from the other side and when it opened out towards me I was struck by its thickness. I hadn't noticed it before. It was perhaps three times thicker than any other doors I crossed through. A soldier from inside ushered me forward and the door closed and locked again behind me. He walked without speaking and I followed him until we reached the familiar floral hallway. He pointed to the armchair and I sat down, clutching the armrests. The painting that faced me was of a cherub in white robes, clutching a bow and arrow. The cherub's rear was exposed, and despite the robes it looked like a plump love heart – like a bottom that wouldn't have existed in reality.

I heard a clatter from a room off in the distance and a door flew open. Dr Bishop, head of the medical team, marched past in a fury, oblivious to my presence. And in his wake was the leader's wife, calling after him, asking him to calm down as she followed him towards the first set of doors. It felt strange to be seeing her in the flesh, especially without her exercise clothes on. She was beautiful, curvier than before, and I pondered whether she'd given up on exercise, or if it still dictated her days.

Another door opened and Alison was standing on the threshold, this time wearing an elegant jumper with tapered ankle-length trousers and ballet pumps. I glanced down, once again taking in my boiler suit. I knew it was stupid to pine after clothes.

He's ready for you now, she said, pressing herself against the wall to create as much distance from me as possible, concerned perhaps that I might try to touch her again.

I walked into what appeared to be a home cinema room and was so struck by its sight that a sigh spontaneously escaped from my lips. The lights had been dimmed but were not yet dark enough for the full cinematic experience. ND was sitting in the front row and he waved a hand over for me to join him.

Alison didn't follow. Can I get you anything else, sir?

More tea, please, Alison. He smiled at me. Can I offer you something to drink? Tea, coffee?

Coffee . . . Please.

Better make that decaf, he said to Alison rather than to me.

He gestured for me to sit and I lowered myself into the seat one away from him, shifting my gaze from the blank screen to his outfit. He was wearing an elaborate dressing gown of silk swirls and cord trim, his initials beautifully embroidered on the chest. He turned his body towards me and crossed his legs, the knot around his waist bulging slightly.

Good evening, Sarah.

I winced, my name still sounding caustic and harsh. I focused on my hands, clasped one over the other. Good evening, I said.

He glanced back and waved a hand at Alison. The tea and coffee will be all for now, he said.

I let my fingers glide across the fabric of my cinema seat. Blood-red and again with the initials ND finely embroidered in gold stitch across the arms. The length of planning that had clearly gone into his lair unnerved me. Did all leaders get to style a lair in a bunker when they took up office in the event that a disaster might occur? Or had this been something he'd known was coming? Perhaps he had been preparing these measures while the rest of us were carrying on with daily life. I imagined a big red War button being pushed, something as basic as that, and there being no way to reverse the decision. But maybe I'd watched *Dr Strangelove* too many times.

Suddenly, I was aware we were sitting in silence and wasn't sure how much time had passed.

Thank you for my assistant, I said.

Does she live up to your expectations?

I nodded.

I'm grateful you've come, he said, making it sound as if I'd had a choice. And he smiled again, letting it linger on his lips. So, I wait with such anticipation . . . What do you have for me?

The door opened and Alison walked in, balancing a tray. She placed it down in the seat that divided us. A cafetière of decaffeinated coffee, long-life milk and cubes of sugar if you require them, she said, pointing to each as she spoke. She made a nodding gesture to ND before departing up the aisle and out of sight.

I'm aware I promised you dinner, he said. So I'm sorry to be breaking my promise on this occasion. He paused. But we'll work up to that. We don't want to send your digestive system into shock, do we?

I was staring at the sugar. I wondered what would happen if I ate the full bowl. Would it kill me? It was times like these when I really wished we still had the internet. My hand was shaking but I pushed the coffee plunger down, mesmerised by the way the particles dispersed. I poured the liquid into a china cup and stared at the small waves I'd created. I used to take coffee with milk but I was thinking that maybe I'd rather go without – try to feel the full effect of its powers despite it being decaf. And sugar? Would I put it in my coffee? I wouldn't have before. I used to think sugar was toxic but now I was desperate for its sweetness. I plopped two cubes in and watched the dark liquid seep through the grainy particles as they sank to the bottom of the cup. I didn't stir; I wanted the dregs left at the end.

My hand was still shaking as I brought the cup to my lips. I inhaled its scent before taking a sip and letting the sugary, rich concoction swirl around my mouth. I sucked it between my cheeks and let it fall over my tongue. We used to visit so many artisan coffee shops, spending our weekends on coffee highs. Daniel had been obsessed. What would he say if he were here? He'd probably have moaned that it was far too hot – that the beans had been burnt. And he'd acknowledge that the beans were stale – that there was a bitterness that wouldn't have been present if they'd ground them fresh.

ND was drumming his fingers on his knee and I realised he was still waiting for a response. I've encountered all but one of the family groups in the pharmacy, I said. The only name who doesn't seem to come on my watch is Clement. The teacher.

And are you finding alternative means of obtaining information?

I hesitated. I will . . .

Fine. Go on.

The Baxter family have little to say. I've yet to see the husband but the wife and child are pleasant – nothing particularly suspicious. She takes no regular medication but comes for pads during her menstrual cycle. The little boy barely talks but he's lovely.

Does she speak of her husband?

Very little, but when she does it is with admiration and love. She was happy to tell me that he is one of your senior defence advisors.

I see . . . ND raised his eyebrows for the briefest of moments before settling on a neutral, passive expression. OK, what else?

I took another sip of my coffee and let the mixture touch every part of my mouth. Maxwell . . . A couple with no children. Both are taking antidepressants. She attends the pharmacy daily and rarely misses her doses but he . . . his behaviour and attendance is erratic.

What do you mean, *erratic?*

Well, when he does come to the pharmacy . . . I started

shaking my head, struggling to articulate my impression of this stranger. He seems distracted, like he has the weight of the world on his shoulders. And he's rude. Not that I think he means to be rude, more that internally he's too busy to realise he's being rude. I shrugged. My mum would have called him a *troubled soul*.

But you have no idea what troubles him?

I shook my head, taking another sip.

OK, and what about Floyd?

I really have little to say about the Floyd family. He is the only one who attends the pharmacy for regular medication. He's quiet, reserved, never makes a fuss but always says thank you.

What medication is he taking at the moment?

Nothing significant. A statin for cholesterol.

ND began pouring tea from a china teapot but its colour looked black and stewed.

I have it on good authority that you are an avid film fan, he said. Is this so?

Yes. Absolutely, I said, my relief at the change of conversation perhaps visible. Or I used to be, anyway.

He pressed a button and the projection screen came to life. What are your favourite films?

I like independent films, I said. And Hitchcock, and some of the other old classics like *Whatever Happened to Baby Jane*. I like foreign films too . . .

Well, are you in a rush to get back?

I brought my cup back up to my lips and took a sip before saying, I suppose not.

Pick us something to watch from my collection, he said, offering me the remote control.

Why?

He shrugged. It'll be nice. I can't stand the nonsense my wife watches. For once I'd like to be in the company of someone who takes their film choices seriously.

I took the control from his hand and our fingers briefly touched. I turned to face the projection screen.

I don't know how this works . . .

Press *menu* and scroll through the categories until you find something you like.

I started scrolling, my mind in overdrive as I tried to retrieve knowledge from my previous life. I had this burning desire to please him, to show him I had good taste despite not knowing why it mattered. The cursor landed on *Barney's Version*. Have you seen this? I said.

He squinted forward, inspecting the image. I've always liked Paul Giamatti, he said, settling into his seat. I've never seen this one but I trust your judgment. Press *play*.

The lights dimmed further and the opening credits played out. In the darkness he reached across and touched my arm. Don't let the rest of your coffee go cold, he said, lifting the cafetière in his hand. My cup rested on my lap and I raised it, allowing him to pour me more, and he did so without spilling a drop, returning his attention to the screen.

I'd forgotten how much I loved this film. The first time Daniel and I watched it we had been in Australia. We hadn't especially liked Australia but the memory of having gone to see this film was a happy one. It had been playing in an old movie theatre called the Astor where they still ran double bills. Settled in my plush embroidered cinema seat, and with the china cup still warm against my stomach, I let the film absorb me.

We were more than halfway through the viewing when I had to remind myself where I was and who I was sitting with.

I sank a little further into my seat and imagined Paul Giamatti sitting in his own bunker, perhaps also watching a film. And I really wanted to know what his bunker would have looked like.

When the lights came on I was surprised to see I'd left the dregs of my coffee. It wasn't the longest film I could have chosen. If I'd been more tactical I would have gone with an epic like *Gone With the Wind* or *Schindler's List*, something that would have given me hours of escapism, but I found myself believing that there would perhaps be other opportunities.

That was a fine choice, ND said. I'm not sure I would have come to it on my own without your guidance.

Thank you, I said, placing my cup down on the tray.

Jog my memory, he said somewhat abruptly, have you always worked in army hospitals? There was a change in his tone and it seemed as if something was at stake but I was unsure why.

No, I've worked all over – public hospitals and community pharmacies. I worked for an online private prescription pharmacy too.

And what did that entail, the *private* services?

I laughed. You make it sound more sinister than it actually was. It was mostly filling prescriptions for sensitive and embarrassing issues . . .

Such as?

I brought my eyes up to meet his. Sexually transmitted diseases, erectile dysfunction, male hair loss . . .

And what took you away from that?

I hesitated. My husband.

Ah, he said, raising his eyebrows. The husband . . .

He took a job and I followed.

And then?

We had problems. I shrugged again, turning to focus on the blank screen. We couldn't work past them. He left, and I applied for the pharmacist post on the army base.

He nodded, all thoughts once again disguised behind his calm and assured resting face. Perhaps your conscience was guiding you wisely for the future.

I opened my mouth to speak but he reached out and patted my lips with his hand, like someone comforting their pet. Continue your good work and we will meet again soon, he said. He gestured then with his hand for me to leave.

OK, I replied, pulling myself out of my seat.

And this goes without saying, but we keep our little encounters strictly private.

I nodded. Yes.

Oh, and I nearly forgot to ask: is there anything you don't eat?

I can't remember.

I'll take that as a no, then.

I reached for the handle of the door, turning and pulling, but it wouldn't budge.

Push, he said, but it didn't matter because Alison was on the other side, opening it.

I was hurried along the floral corridor, escorted by the arms of soldiers and thrust out into the darkness of the main chamber. The taste of the coffee was strong in my mouth, the film's credits still rolling fresh in my mind. It had been an easier experience than I had anticipated; small, discreet sacrifices that I believed offered nothing significant. What, really, was I telling ND that I wouldn't have told a doctor caring for his patients? I was acknowledging their wellbeing and shining a light on their mental health. I smiled to myself then, a warm flush spreading across my cheeks as I thought about what I'd watch on my next visit. By nature I had an addictive personality, and the lair was something I knew I could easily grow addicted to.

# 7

I was tapping my fingers on the Formica worktop when Levitt arrived. She was six minutes late and I felt the need to acknowledge this in some way. A snide remark like *good afternoon* was what most pharmacists would have said but I couldn't bring myself to say that. Even in my previous life I'd shrug and say *no worries* when someone strolled in late, offering a weak apology. This time I mustered: Everything all right?

She nodded, not wanting to meet my eye. Her skin looked paler than usual. Sorry, I know I'm late, she said. I've not been well.

Are you fit to work?

Yeah, I'm OK. Feeling better already.

I turned and was greeted by one of my regulars. This time he was complaining of a persistent cold. There's blood when I blow my nose, he said offering me a look at the tissue he held in his hand. It's a constant stream of mucus.

From the lightness of the blood it looks as if you've just burst a small blood vessel from blowing your nose a lot.

He surveyed me before saying, And there's a cough too. I can feel the phlegm sitting on my chest.

Is it discoloured? If it's tinged green then that would be a sign of a chest infection and you'd need to see a doctor.

I don't know, he said, and he coughed into his used tissue, forcing the mucus up and out of his mouth. He lowered the tissue and displayed its contents to me.

No, there's no infection there, I said. It's viral. You'll need to let it run its course.

Levitt began tidying the medicine drawers, her posture tense and disgruntled. What's wrong with you? I asked.

Nothing.

Have I done something to upset you? Is it the pharmacy?

No, Wolfe, I love it here, OK? Can you just leave me be? She exhaled, before thrusting herself down to the ground and crossing her legs. Discontented, she then stretched out across the floor, lying horizontal.

What are you doing? I said.

It helps me think. You should try it.

I hesitated, glancing towards the empty shop floor, before stretching out next to her, and we just lay there, staring up at the fluorescent lights.

Levitt reached out and took my hand, clasping it. I wish we could just lock the door and lie here all day, she said.

I nodded. A robot could do this job. Maybe a robot *should* do this job.

She laughed, but it seemed more like a noise of despair. People made out robots were going to revolutionise everything, she said. That they would have made our lives so much better, given us all more time. But honestly – I think it would have made us miserable. We wouldn't have known what to do with ourselves. Would have realised that we had no real purpose.

You're a wise old soul, aren't you?

I don't feel very wise, she said.

I turned to look at her. What's going on with you?

Look at the ceiling, she said. It's easier to talk when we don't have to look at each other.

I placed the hand that wasn't holding Levitt's across my chest and there was something meditative in the sensation of it rising and falling each time I took a breath.

Are you going to tell me what's going on?

Levitt's eyes lingered on the ceiling and I wondered if she was staring at the discoloured blotch I often stared at. It had always been there and I still couldn't decide what it was or what had caused it. I could almost feel the cogs of her mind turning, words trying to formulate on her tongue.

Wolfe, if I tell you something, can you promise to keep it a secret?

OK. Sure. I promise.

My thoughts were still lingering over the blotch on the ceiling so it took me a moment to process what she had said.

Sorry?

I think I might be pregnant.

No, I said, shaking my head.

She sat up then, crossing her legs again.

How do you know? I said, struggling to sit up too.

I've not had a period in months . . .

That could just be your implant, I said, now rubbing my own, feeling the bump in my arm where it was buried. It's probably just confused your cycle. It'll be nothing . . .

Maybe . . .

Have you done a test?

I can't go to the doctors.

I have some here, I said. Do you feel pregnant? Do you have any symptoms?

For a while I had really tender boobs and I could barely touch my food pouches but I just thought I'd picked up a bug . . .

I suppose it must happen with the implant, I said. Statistically speaking, I mean.

I've heard rumours about it happening to other women in here. Someone from your side of the bunker . . .

Your dad's the culture advisor, right?

Where are you going with this?

I shrugged. I thought I heard somewhere about him being a devoutly religious man. Like, a lot of his cultural policies were based around that, so I guess I thought . . . Well I don't know what I thought.

I don't have his unwavering beliefs, if that's what you're getting at, she said. Maybe it would be better if I did. He certainly wasn't impressed by the health advisor's insistence on the implants. He thinks all we need is stronger faith and willpower. *Why would anyone want to do such a thing in here anyway?* She spoke in a mocking manly tone. He believes we're in Noah's Ark – enough of us to continue on, and a fable for those who didn't listen to the warnings from our leader.

You need to do a test, I said and started rummaging through the dispensary drawers. The doctors always tested their patients after a rape incident but I'd yet to have anyone come in and ask me for one. I found them in a bashed box underneath the aero chamber devices we gave to people who couldn't co-ordinate their inhaler technique. The test was in a white foil wrapper – a rectangular piece of plastic with the swabbing fabric embedded within – a square space in the centre for urine. When I first qualified as a pharmacist, patients used to bring their own urine samples for me to test, the plastic sample bottles often still warm. It was strange to think I knew what their bodies were doing before they did.

I ripped open the foil and handed the test to Levitt.

She stared at me.

You can pee anywhere on it as long as it touches the swabbing.

I can't do it out there, she said. Not in the toilet blocks with everyone else.

There's always the bucket here for washing the floor. I shrugged. I've peed in it loads. Actually, I prefer it to the toilet blocks.

She hesitated before getting to her feet and retrieving the bucket. Just keep an eye out for anyone coming, she said, already undoing the Velcro of her boiler suit. I found myself staring at the off-white of her bra straps before turning away. From the corner of my eye I watched her squat down, balancing herself over the bucket. I heard the hiss of her urine flowing and hitting the plastic.

You can look, she said, and as I turned back she was still fighting with her boiler suit, trying to pull it on, while the sleeves escaped her. I held up the fabric, as if I was helping her put on a coat. What now? she said, clasping the test in her hand.

Three minutes.

She seemed unable to move and I forced the test from her grip. I placed it on the counter and lifted the handle of the bucket, tipping its contents down the circular sink. I was still washing my hands when I realised someone was in the pharmacy.

I'll serve, Levitt said, the Velcro of her suit now intact. Good morning, she said somewhat cheerily, and I couldn't understand how she could detach herself so easily from what was developing behind her. I heard her asking for the surname and ID number, and she was greeted with a monotone, irritable answer. It was Maxwell, number 2597. Levitt moved behind me, opening the dispensary drawers, pulling out a box. I could hear her popping two tablets into a plastic cup, the sound as vivid as her urine hitting the plastic bucket. Can you check this? she said.

She put the cup on the counter for me to look at and I peered inside, acknowledging their oblong shape. I glanced at Maxwell's drug chart, deeming it to be correct before signing the dosage box with my black marker. Levitt collected the cup and slid it through the hatch. Seconds later Maxwell was thrusting his tongue out towards Levitt and she was on her tiptoes, bobbing her head from left to right, thoroughly inspecting his mouth while he grew more irritated.

Is there something wrong? I said to him. You seem particularly anxious today.

He stared at me, his whole body seeming to tense.

We're here to help, I said. If you need someone to talk to in confidence . . .

He left without saying a word and I slid his drug chart to the side.

Do you think that's been three minutes? Levitt said, staring at the test from across the dispensary.

I think so.

She didn't move.

Do you want me to look at it?

No. It should be me.

You're still not moving, I said.

I'm aware.

Everything is going to be OK.

But how can you be so sure?

She took a step forward, and then another, and another until her stomach was pressed against the edge of the worktop and she was looking directly down on the test. She said nothing. And I knew then that it was positive.

Wolfe . . . Her voice shook.

I came to where she was standing and placed my hand on her arm. I was able to grip her bones through the fabric. OK, I said, turning her to face me. Levitt, look at me.

She slid the test along the counter until it was directly in front of me. Two blue lines. There was no denying it; no denying their clarity. I lifted the test to my line of vision, as if it would only be true if I stared at it more closely. One of my many pregnancy tests once had what I'd thought was a hint of a second line – a glimmer, trying to make its way through.

She wrapped her arms around herself. What am I going to do?

I could see a figure walking past the window and sensed the door about to open. Someone's coming, I said, pulling her arms down to her sides.

She walked to the sink and busied herself with the taps, collecting plastic beakers and cups. She left the test sitting out as though it was nothing to do with her and I grabbed it, stuffing it in the breast pocket of my boiler suit.

When I turned around there was an older man standing at the Perspex hatch, waiting with a smile. It's criminal that they make you work on the Sabbath, he said.

I tried to smile back. People still need their medicine on a Sunday, but we'll be finishing soon enough.

As he swallowed his tablets and opened his mouth for inspection I noticed a gold molar glinting back. I'd always found it strange that people liked putting gold in their mouths – a precious metal surrounded by decaying food, gathering in its crevices.

Levitt turned to me after he'd left, a damp beaker still in her hands. Can you help me get rid of it? she said.

My head was shaking *no* without me being fully conscious of it.

I was reading the Drug Formulary yesterday, she said. And was thinking that if I took a massive dose of levonorgestrel then maybe it would do something . . . It must do something for the rape victims.

I shook my head again. It's too late for that, I said. That's a precaution. You're already pregnant.

So that's it . . . Nothing can be done, she said, her voice sounding like it would break. Her breathing grew erratic then and she shook her head violently from side to side. No, there must be something I can do . . .

You're not going to try something stupid, are you?

How would I even go about it? she asked. Do you know? It's not like I can look it up on the internet, or fall down a flight of stairs . . .

I was quiet for a moment. You could speak to Stirling, I said. He might know what to do.

And you trust him?

The familiar beeping suddenly started sounding over the speaker system and we stared at one another. For the first time I found myself being grateful for the interruption, fearing I was at risk of saying something to Levitt I wouldn't be able to retract.

These fucking drills, Levitt shouted. They're so pointless.

Look, calm down, I said. Everything's going to be OK. Let's just go and we can talk about this after.

We shuffled out of the pharmacy, walking side by side, our footsteps falling into the same rhythm – a squelch of rubber then silence before it repeated again until we reached the boundary line.

I guess I'll see you after, Levitt said, before crossing over.

My eyes followed her movements as she weaved around people, stopping a few rows back from the front. She nodded to someone on my side and I glanced around, trying to discover who the nod was directed at, but there were too many bodies and heads bobbing in every direction. The wall began descending and the beeping pierced my ears. With the wall locked into place I turned myself around in a circle, suddenly feeling as if I had to find someone of significance to me. Where was Canavan? And Stirling, too, was nowhere to be seen. Clement the teacher was once again standing in my periphery with his wife. I crept closer, settling in front of him to eavesdrop on his conversation. But it was nothing – him moaning about the lack of toilet paper in the men's washroom, and that one of the urinals was blocked, while his wife replied with a repeated uh-huh. And there's never enough hand sanitiser, he added. How are we meant to maintain any decent level of hygiene if they don't provide us with sufficient supplies? The beeping sounded once again and I shifted my gaze back to the wall, watching it rise.

Back in the pharmacy, Levitt hunched herself over the counter, facing the shop floor. When I asked if she wanted one of my food pouches she ignored me. She ran a hand through her hair and tugged at a knot, letting dirty-blond wisps float to the floor.

How can this be happening to me? she said, with what I considered to be a tone of self-pity. Anger began to rise within me, my jaw tight and uncomfortable. But Levitt was oblivious. I'm so tired, she said. All the time. Her shoulders sagged, her face dipping downwards, and suddenly I realised she was crying. I wasn't sure if I should hug her – it somehow seemed insincere of me, but her body began to shake with the weight of her silent cries. I cautiously wrapped my arms around her and let her chin sink into my collarbone – a space in the body that was made for cupping people. Her body heaved up and down as she breathed and I wondered how long it had been since she'd really cried like this, if ever. She didn't seem like the type to often let go.

Look, you might as well finish up now, I said. I can manage without you, and that way you won't have to face Valentine.

She shook her head into my body and my shoulders swayed backwards and forwards. No, I'd rather be here. It's easier to avoid people when I'm here.

OK, well, just take a seat and keep me company, then.

She sat down and sniffed, wiping her nose with her sleeve. I just can't accept it, you know? Her breathing grew rapid, short bullets through her nostrils. Have you ever really regretted something? Had a moment when you thought: *I really shouldn't have done that*?

Yes, of course, I said, thrusting my hands out as though I needed her to acknowledge the space we occupied. But things are never usually as bad as you imagine them to be.

But this . . . She lowered her voice. Maybe it's a nightmare that can be forgotten? Do you think? Like, I'll remember how it felt but the story will be jumbled and make no sense. She started laughing then, this awkward childish laugh.

Levitt . . . it was consensual, wasn't it?

What? She curled a little further into her chair, bringing her knees up and hugging them.

I need to know that this wasn't something that was forced upon you.

She still had that childish laugh chortling at the back of her throat. Would it make things easier for me if it had been forced? She dropped her chin, like it had been held up by string and was suddenly cut loose. No. It was consensual.

Who is he?

Does it matter?

Well, does he have any idea?

She shook her head.

I ran my hand along my neck, feeling the sprout of one coarse hair. Did you ever think you'd want children? I said. Was it something you had imagined?

I guess I thought when I was older . . . Most people imagine they'll have kids at some point, don't they?

So, you want a child, you just don't want one now?

Another tear trickled down her face, rounding under her nose. You're judging me. I'm *eighteen* . . .

I stared down at my gym shoes. I'm sorry, I don't mean to, I said, but I didn't sound convincing.

So, you'll speak to Stirling for me? she whispered.

If that's what you want.

Yes, she said, nodding. That is what I want.

At my bunk Canavan appeared to be sleeping but there was no sign of the Foers. The blue glow of the night-lights acted like a forensic torch, highlighting the discoloration of my canvas – the cementation of my germs and dead skin cells. I lay for a moment before getting on to my hands and knees, trying to stretch out the blankets underneath me. I tugged and tugged despite my body anchoring the wool.

What are you doing? Canavan whispered, peering down.

I'll be done in a minute, I said, giving the blankets one last tug, my head now poking out from the frame, hanging there in mid-air. I couldn't explain why but it seemed like the most important thing in the world that I get my blankets perfectly straight across the bunk. I thrust my body forward again and before I could stop it something flew out from my boiler suit pocket, tumbling down. Canavan was watching and saw the plastic pregnancy test clatter to the floor. The noise seemed to echo around the entire bunker before everything went quiet.

What is that? he said.

It's nothing, I replied too quickly.

I started to clamber but he was already away. Don't move, he said. You've flapped about enough. His feet were planted on the ground and he picked up the test, turning it over in his hands, seeming confused before acknowledging the two blue lines. He brought his head up slowly and stared at me. What have you got yourself into? he said.

My body was acting against me, my knees pinned to the blankets. Give that to me, I whispered.

Wolfe . . .

Please.

He handed it to me. I can't undo seeing it, he said in a voice I didn't recognise.

I gripped the test, the swollen felt and the absorbed urine pressing against my skin, the blueness of the lines feeling as if they could leave their imprint on my hand. And I realised that I wanted Canavan to think it was mine – that I was capable of such a thing. He was looking at me differently already; I could see it in the way he tilted his chin towards me, in the way his green eyes hovered.

Footsteps came towards us, a man perhaps trying to reach his bed, and Canavan pressed his body into the frame of our bunk, letting him pass. The man continued until he'd reached the end of our closely knit row. Canavan stood back and placed a hand on my head, ever so slightly rubbing strands of my hair. What are you going to do?

I'm going to take care of it.

He climbed on to his bunk and settled above me, the weight of his body seeming to move with each breath, his canvas stretching further, almost eclipsing me.

I brought my foot up and tapped him through the canvas. He didn't move but I knew he was still awake. I nuzzled under my blankets and placed my hand in through the gaps of Velcro. I let my fingers trace over my stomach and belly button. I tried to imagine what it would feel like to be pregnant – flutters that would develop into kicks, arms and limbs contorting underneath, the stretching of skin, the pressure on my bladder. There would be heartburn so bad it burnt my oesophagus; a ball of acid made worse by cravings. Or maybe it would be nothing like that.

# 8

Levitt gripped the sides of Stirling's chair. We've been over this already, she said. I make a point not to look at my body. I've no idea if my nipples are darker.

Do you know when your last period was? Stirling said. There was a mark of something unfamiliar on the collar of his lab coat, black like tar, and his stethoscope wasn't quite sitting evenly around his neck, the metal disc for listening into chests resting flat against his own.

She shook her head. I'm not sure. A while ago now.

Can you be any more specific?

It's difficult to keep track of time.

OK, I understand, but does anything trigger a timeline at all?

She hesitated. My periods have never been regular.

You've not asked me for sanitary pads, I said. So that might indicate . . .

I get pads from the pharmacy on my side of the bunker.

So when did you stop asking for them? Stirling said.

I haven't stopped asking for them. She paused. I thought it would be less suspicious if I just kept going.

What do you do with them? I said.

I trade them.

I'll need to examine you, is that OK? Stirling said, pointing to the examination bed.

Levitt stood. OK.

Stirling was already pulling back the curtain. If you remove your suit and underwear there is a white sheet you can place over your body. Once you're ready, call me and we can get started.

Can Wolfe stay?

Of course. She'll be with you the whole time.

Levitt walked behind the curtain and we could hear the pull of the Velcro as she undressed. Stirling's head was tilted to one side and he seemed to be inspecting me while we waited.

I'm ready, Levitt called out.

Stirling pulled the curtain back slightly, allowing us to enter. I stood at the top of the bed, where Levitt's head was resting on a pillow, and Stirling stood at the bottom. I stared at her bare shoulders, the elastic of her bra straps ever so slightly cutting into her skin. She was nothing but skin and bone.

Stirling started pulling on latex gloves. He seemed relaxed as he did so, as if everything we were doing was perfectly normal.

Levitt focused on the ceiling.

Stirling's sterile hands were now lubricated.

This might be a little uncomfortable. Maybe like having a smear. Have you had one of those before?

Levitt shook her head. She offered me her hand and instinctively my body wanted to deflect, it feeling all too much like Templeton; I wondered how Stirling managed each day with his patients. Reluctantly, as if I had no choice, I reached out and took her hand.

OK, let's take a look, Stirling said.

Wait a minute, Levitt replied. I'm not ready. I don't

think . . . She started to pull up from the bed and I leant forward as though my body was involuntarily trying to press her back down.

It's going to be OK, Stirling said. I promise.

Levitt stared at him. What will you be looking for?

Your cervix. From ten weeks of pregnancy there should be an obvious softening of the cervix.

Have you done this before? she said.

In the bunker? No. But before, yes.

Are you going to get rid of it now?

No. All we're doing is examining. He paused. I'm going to start. OK? Are you still happy for me to proceed?

Levitt nodded, gripping my hand a little tighter. Stirling lowered his head at the other end of the examination bed and Levitt winced. Her legs were bent at the knees and pushed apart, making the sheet that covered her resemble something of a tent.

You still OK? he said.

Did you always want to be a doctor? she asked, her voice directed towards the ceiling.

Stirling didn't answer straight away; perhaps he was giving her question real consideration. It occurred to me that I'd never thought to ask him this question myself.

Being a doctor runs in my family, he said. It was kind of expected.

I was going to be a vet, she said.

Well, maybe one day you still will be, he replied, and it felt strange not to be seeing his face as he spoke. He stood up then and bent forward, pushing the sheet back past her knees towards us. I watched his fingers fan out as he placed his right hand on Levitt's stomach. It looked as if the left hand was still inside her. I'm checking for something the midwives used to call Hegar's sign, he said. It should indicate a swelling of the uterus.

After a moment he stood straight again, taking a step back with both hands raised out in front. That's it, he said. It's all over. He peeled his gloves off and dropped them into a bucket by the examination table. We'll leave you to get dressed, he said, then we can chat things over.

Levitt released my hand from her grip. It was OK, she said. It wasn't too bad.

I nodded before walking back behind the curtain to join Stirling. He was washing his hands in the sink, scrubbing the skin and nail beds raw with antiseptic soap. He seemed deep in thought and I wished to be able to read his mind.

Levitt came out a moment later and sat down in one of Stirling's plastic chairs. There was something childlike in the way she sat – slouching across the seat, her eyes fixed to the floor. Was it seeing her small-shouldered frame lying under the sheet? Was it because I couldn't imagine her body being able to carry a child?

You might as well sit too, Stirling said to me, pointing to the other free chair. Suddenly, I felt like her parent – the type that thinks they're modern and progressive for encouraging their child to access information on contraception and sexual practice.

What do you think? I said.

Well, you're definitely pregnant, Stirling said to Levitt. The cervix is presenting the way we'd expect and I could feel the uterus expanding – something we shouldn't be able to feel until at least twelve weeks of pregnancy.

So, three months, that's how long you think? she said.

No. I think it's further along than that.

Like what? I asked.

Difficult to say ... But from your symptoms and the way your cervix presents I'd say you're comfortably into your second trimester. Sixteen to eighteen, maybe even twenty weeks ...

Halfway? I said, blurting the words out.

No. That can't be right, Levitt said, suddenly on her feet. I mean, look at me. There's nothing there.

Some people just don't show, Stirling said. Were you athletic before you came in here? If you've strong stomach muscles then it will easily disguise the bulge of a baby.

Levitt just kept shaking her head.

Sometimes the baby will emit such a low dose of the pregnancy hormone, he continued, that the body doesn't quite understand what's happening and struggles to adjust accordingly. He paused. You're malnourished, so the baby will most likely be smaller.

If she's malnourished, will the baby be OK? I asked.

Levitt swung her whole body round to face me. Wolfe, why are you even asking that?

Keep your voices down, Stirling said.

Please just tell me how to fix this, she said, her voice laced with panic. I can't have this baby.

Stirling's cheeks puffed up with air before he exhaled. He couldn't seem to find the words that he needed.

We don't have many options ... It's too late for a medical abortion.

Why? Levitt said.

It's like trying to induce a miscarriage and it's only really recommended up to ten weeks of pregnancy.

That's just the tablets, right? Couldn't we just try it anyway? she said.

Stirling shook his head. And if it doesn't remove all of the foetus . . . What do you think happens then?

Levitt fell quiet and looked down at her hands. OK, well, what's left?

Surgical removal. I'll give you something to start dilation and then remove the foetus by forceps. It's the only option we have after about fifteen, sixteen weeks of pregnancy.

Are there risks? I said.

There's risk with everything.

Specifically, what?

Stirling shrugged. Where do I begin? Womb infection, blood loss, damage to the cervix. The earlier an abortion is carried out, the less likely it is for there to be complications. By my estimation we have about four weeks before it would be considered clinically unsafe to carry out a surgical abortion at all.

So it's still doable? Levitt said.

The rule of thumb used to be twenty-four weeks. Some abortions could be carried out after this stage if it was considered life-threatening to the mother. But in here our equipment limits us.

Levitt ran a hand through her hair. Have these surgical abortions been done before in the bunker, rather than the . . . tablet ones?

A few have been carried out, but, as I said, not by me.

Levitt recoiled then. I tried to reach out to her but she backed further into her seat.

Does it look like a baby when it comes out?

You wouldn't see anything, he said.

OK. Her body began to shake, her knees jittering. I think I'm going to be sick, she said before preceding to dry heave, the noise coming from the back of her throat, but there didn't seem to be anything to bring up when she reached the sink.

We need to act soon, Stirling said.

Can't we just do it now? Levitt replied.

Now? No, not now. I've got a clinic this afternoon.

Tonight, then?

Stirling looked up at the whiteboard screwed to his wall, a scrawl of handwriting describing his schedule. The doctor's bag that rested on the desk next to him had his initials embossed on the leather. I owned nothing that was branded. Did that mean nothing was actually mine?

I cleared my throat. You could keep the baby, I said.

Levitt stared at me. I sensed Stirling's eyes on me too.

That's not an option, she said.

Why not? It might be the safest option.

I can't have this baby. Not here, not like this.

I turned to Stirling. The other abortions – were they carried out safely?

He hesitated. They botched one woman, he said, but she was in her late thirties and already a health risk.

What happened to her? Levitt said.

He was slow to respond. She died along with the baby.

Levitt got to her feet. My parents will be looking for me now my shift is over. What time tonight?

If we meet back here after eight, I should be able to make that work. You'll need to excuse yourself for the entire evening, though.

Levitt reached the door before stopping and gripping the handle. I'll see you tonight, then, she said, and then she was gone.

Stirling turned to look at me. Keep the baby . . . really?

I think she should.

He was shaking his head. You know a baby won't survive in here, he said. Look around you.

But I think a baby *could* survive.

It's too dangerous. You're not even thinking about the risk to Levitt's health.

Of course I'm thinking about Levitt, I snapped, swallowing a lump in my throat.

We sat in silence for a moment.

Look, I'm not due another patient for an hour or so. Why don't we go for a walk . . . ?

Where?

We could go to the dining hall, maybe?

I hate the dining hall.

Well, somewhere else, then.

I wish we could take a walk outside, I said. Just inhale fresh air. Sometimes I feel like I can't breathe in here.

He got to his feet. I'd forgotten how tall he was – how imposing his height could be – but he was also so thin. I didn't remember him being this thin when we first met on the army base.

We walked out and along the corridor. It was quiet, as though people had dispersed into crevices despite there being nowhere obvious to go. Our steps fell in line with one another and we walked without conversation, turning left down another corridor. We were headed towards the main chamber of the bunker, to the entrance of the leader's lair and the boundary line, and I was aware of my eyes being drawn to the soldiers and their rifles.

We came to a stop with our toes edged over the yellow-dashed paint.

What do you think? Stirling said. Shall we take a walk across?

I paused. Have you been over before?

He looked at me strangely. Yes . . . Why, have you not?

No.

Why not?

I shrugged. I don't know. It just doesn't feel right . . . Like they're our rivals or something.

It's exactly the same, only on the opposite side.

I know . . .

He pulled my arm, trying to tug me over the line, but I held strong.

What are you afraid of?

Maybe I'm scared we'll get stuck.

We're only going for a walk and then we'll cross right back over. He tugged at my arm again. Wolfe, you're being irrational. Come on, you might even enjoy it. And suddenly we were across the line and continuing to move forward. I glanced back to see new soldiers guarding access to ND's lair from an entrance I'd never passed before.

This isn't so bad, is it? Stirling said.

I still don't like it.

He let out something that resembled a laugh. I think you're being dramatic.

Turning, we came to one of the main sleeping quarters. A woman brushed past us and met my eye before carrying on with purpose. I wanted to follow her before she disappeared from view. I wanted to grip her by the shoulders and shake her. Would she have told me something I wanted to hear?

We turned another corner and passed one of the dining halls. From inside we could hear the hum of human noise but we didn't stop to linger.

You know I'm right, Stirling said. About the baby . . . It's the safest option.

I didn't reply.

Was . . . He hesitated. Was she raped?

I shook my head. She's adamant that she wasn't, but she won't tell me anything about the father. He doesn't know . . .

We found ourselves outside the pharmacy. I peered in through the window and saw a man working in the dispensary – he was young, younger than Stirling. But aside from him everything else appeared identical. He was preparing medication for a patient whose back faced me.

What do you think? Stirling said.

It feels like being in a gallery and thinking that you have to find some sort of emotion, force some sort of expression to the surface. It's not what I expected . . .

What did you expect?

I guess I thought one side would be better or worse than the other. But to be exactly the same . . . it's disappointing.

I'm sorry, he said.

The waiting patient turned so I could see his side profile as he swallowed his medication, and immediately I recognised him as Maxwell. Instinctively, I darted away from the window. Can we go back now? I said. Like, now.

Sure, Stirling said. Is everything OK?

I turned, searching for familiar markings to guide me back across the line. But I was lost in the mirror image of a place I thought I knew.

Do you remember how to get back? I said, trying to contain my anxiousness.

He pointed me in the direction in which we'd come and we started walking, our footsteps seeming loud on the concrete. I'd always liked the idea of having concrete floors in a house – I considered it to be modern and stylish. But concrete sucked the life out of a room. It was cold, so cold that even when the thermostat was up a shiver never left the back of my neck. And I kept glancing over my shoulder, expecting Maxwell to be behind me. Maybe I should have stopped and confronted him, because it felt as though he was laughing at me behind my back, and I couldn't stand that. Couldn't bear the idea of being taken for a fool.

I was aware of Stirling's hand brushing against mine. I glanced down to see his pinkie nudging my own before parting. Our hands brushed together again and I caught Stirling looking at me from the corner of his eye. And as if it was nothing he gently took my hand and linked his fingers in – intertwining them with mine – and I didn't know what to do except move forward, weaving with him down another corridor until the boundary line was once again in view. But anger was embedded like poison within me, tainting the moment. So strange that often I wasn't enraged by terrible injustices, considered them inevitable, but something small could trigger my temper. The audacity of Maxwell was staggering to me. Did he not care that he was taking medication away from other patients? How had he even managed to get a doctor to prescribe him something on this side?

There was the rattle of pipes and I glanced upwards, noticing condensation gathering on the metal. I was suddenly overcome with exhaustion and would have given anything for sleep.

As we crossed over the yellow-dashed line I checked over my shoulder again to see the soldier with the droplet birthmark standing guard in front of ND's lair and I supposed part of me considered it fate. I stopped, pulling my hand free from Stirling's.

Embarrassed someone might see us? he said, trying to laugh as if it was all in jest.

No, I replied, probably more quickly than I had intended to. It's just that I'm heading this way, I said, pointing in the opposite direction from the doctors' surgery.

Ah, right, OK, he said, lingering for a brief moment. I'll see you tonight, then . . .

Yes, I replied. I'll see you at eight.

I watched him walk away before I retreated towards the entrance to ND's lair. The solider with the birthmark looked at me blankly. There was another soldier standing beside him but he was gazing off into the distance.

Hi, I said.

He continued to stare at me, still expressionless. Excuse me?

I'm the pharmacist . . . Do you remember me?

He took a step forward. Perhaps you need escorting back there, then?

I hesitated, trying to pick up a flicker of recognition in his face. OK . . .

Come, he said, taking my upper arm in his hands and turning me forcefully around.

He marched quickly and I struggled to keep up. Have I got this wrong? I said. I thought I was to speak to you or our leader . . .

He stopped. I was told you were discreet, he said through gritted teeth.

Sorry?

We were standing at a junction by the dining hall. He looked both ways, ensuring the vicinity was clear before speaking again. What is it you want to tell me?

Maxwell, ID number 2597, I said.

What about him?

He's collecting medication from the other side of the bunker.

He paused. How do you know?

I saw him, I said. I don't know what he's taking there or even how he's getting it but he resides on this side of the bunker, sees the doctors here for depression. He should have no reason to be going to that pharmacy.

The soldier's face became passive again. OK, is that it?

Is that it? I said, with rising irritation. Should I not have bothered saying anything at all?

Just go about doing what it was you were doing, he said. And don't come back to the lair unless you're invited.

But what if I've something else to tell you? Where am I meant to go?

He paused. Leave that with me, he said, already walking away.

I stood there rooted to the spot for some time, a fury growing inside me that felt both justifiably pure and irrational. Had I wanted him to pat me on the shoulder and tell me I'd done a good job? Suddenly I felt foolish and wished I hadn't said anything at all. I could so easily have pretended to have seen nothing and let Maxwell continue to sporadically collect his medication. How naïve of me to have assumed everyone was playing by the rules; so much of what was expected from us relied on nothing but good faith.

Stirling opened the door to his surgery with his lab coat off, his boiler suit looking worn, and it occurred to me that he might be wearing the one gifted to him by Templeton. He ushered us quickly into the examination room, locking the door behind us. The room smelled of diluted antiseptic like my grandmother's bathroom, but most striking of all was the classical music whispering out from some hidden device.

I didn't know you could listen to music, I said, my eyes closing momentarily to absorb the notes.

Only the classical stuff, he replied. It's meant to relax us.

We congregated around the examination bed, staring at the clean white sheet. How many white sheets did he go through on a daily basis? Were some salvageable, or did the majority have to be destroyed?

Stirling turned to Levitt. Are you ready?

I think so.

This is going to have to take place in two stages. Firstly, I'll quickly examine you again. Then if we're good to go I'll give you a dose of misoprostol to swallow. This will take a few hours to fully dilate your cervix. During this time, I'd keep a low profile. There will likely be cramping and you will bleed so we'll give you some sanitary towels. Are you following me?

I thought we were just going to do the whole thing now, she said.

The misoprostol won't work straight away. We'll meet back here at eleven and I'll finish the procedure. I'll administer a sedative and then it should only take ten to fifteen minutes for me to remove the foetus.

He stopped.

Do you have any questions?

She clasped her hands together and looked down at the floor. No, I don't think so.

If you hop up on to the bed just like before, we'll get started.

While we waited for Levitt to undress behind the curtain, Stirling scrubbed his hands before spending a long time drying them.

I'm ready, Levitt said.

I should stay here, I said quietly. The examination wasn't so bad. Levitt said so herself.

Stirling came to where I was standing and stared at me. I think it would be better for Levitt if you were beside her.

My voice was mute but tears began to fall. All I could do was hide my face in my hands and hope that Levitt couldn't hear me. Stirling placed his arms around me but his clean hands were outstretched. He was whispering, telling me to calm down. Catch your breath, he said.

I tried to compose myself, wiping my face, patting down strands of my hair. Stirling mouthed, OK?

I nodded before slipping in behind the curtain and coming to Levitt's side.

What's wrong? she said, staring at my puffy eyes.

Nothing, I replied.

Stirling came in behind me with a fresh pair of gloves on his hands. If you can position yourself like you did before we can get started . . .

Levitt spread her legs apart and I looked up at the ceiling, focusing on the buzz of the strip-light.

I remembered the injections and the cycles of pills. I remembered taking my temperature and agonising over the tiny window of ovulation. Daniel even gave up cycling, and he loved cycling. But it wasn't Daniel. His sperm count was above average and I had been shamelessly surprised. Weren't we meant to be slowly becoming extinct because the male sperm count was dropping? The doctor's office had been painted a strange shade of blue; I'd read somewhere that people were less likely to eat in a blue room. You won't conceive, the doctor had said. Your womb is hostile. And I'd tried to imagine what that must have looked like from the inside – acidic and aggressive like a spore. Before, I had pitied patients with arthritis – their bodies rebelling against them, fingers swelling and crippling, bones breaking and crumbling, killing goodness within. But hostility had spread and seeped out of me and I had seen the distaste in Daniel's eyes so clearly. We'd said we'd sell everything up and go travelling again when we were old and the kids were grown. We were going to have three and that was all there was to plan.

Was it strange that I still mourned something I'd never had? I tried to reason that perhaps I would have made a terrible mother. I was selfish by nature. Even houseplants had been an inconvenience that tied me down.

The examination seemed to be over in a matter of minutes.

Stirling stood straight. OK, we're all set. We'll meet you on the other side.

When Levitt came out she hesitated before taking a seat. She crossed one leg over the other before shifting and uncrossing them.

Stirling unlocked the medicine cabinet where he kept his emergency supplies. He removed a box from the shelf and popped two tablets out on to a clean paper towel, bringing them to Levitt. Wolfe, can you get her a glass of water, please?

There was a disposable plastic cup sitting on the ledge of the sink and I rinsed it a few times before filling it to the brim.

Levitt held the cup in one hand while the tablets rested on her thigh.

Stirling and I stayed on our feet.

Where do you put it? she said. The foetus.

With everyone and everything else that dies. But it'll be discreet, respectful.

I felt it kick, you know. Little flutters.

Stirling was quiet. The bunker ... it's not designed for a baby. We need to just focus on the present and remember that. Once we're out in the world again, maybe then, if that's what you want . . .

Levitt nodded, picking up the first tablet. She inspected its markings closely before letting it wobble a little in her palm. She placed it on her thigh, lining it up with the other.

Silence filled the room.

The thing is, she finally said, I don't think I can take these.

Stirling shifted his weight from one foot to the other. We can't guarantee a baby's survival in this environment, he said.

Will I be forced to have the abortion?

No one will force you to do anything, he replied.

She seemed to think about this. No, I can't do it, she said. I thought I could but I can't. Maybe if I'd come sooner . . .

Stirling was staring at her. So what you're saying is that you want to carry the baby to term?

She hesitated. Yes, I think so.

As a doctor I have to inform you of all the risks. We are malnourished. What I'm saying is, there's no way to be sure you'll even deliver a healthy child.

I know.

Are you sure about this? Stirling said. Really sure . . .

I've got vitamin D and folic supplements in the pharmacy, I said, a sudden buoyancy rising in my voice.

Levitt shifted in her seat and one of the tablets resting on her thigh tumbled to the floor. I'm sure.

If something happens to the baby from here on in . . . Stirling said. If it stops growing, if you have a bleed or an injury – you will still have to deliver the baby.

I understand.

Stirling ran a hand through his hair, pulling sharply on a tuft of curls. We'd be working with inadequate equipment and medication . . . A lot of what will happen will be off the cuff, can you accept that?

I trust you, she said.

He paused. OK, then. We'll see this through.

What happens after? I said.

I don't know, he said, shrugging. If we can get a healthy baby into this world, into this bunker . . . then I suppose anything's possible.

OK, then, I said, trying to stifle a smile.

But I don't want anyone to know, Levitt said abruptly. Not until it's time for the baby to come.

What? Why? I said.

She paused. It's not that easy to explain . . .

Yes, it is. If people know, they can help us, I argued. And people will notice. It's not easy hiding a pregnancy.

You're only going to get bigger, Stirling said.

But Levitt was still shaking her head.

Levitt, you need to look at this from a positive angle, I said. This is a hopeful, happy thing—

Stop it, she said firmly. Please, just stop.

We stood in silence, like a stand-off, staring at one another.

My father will never forgive me, she finally said. If he finds out, I don't know what he'll do.

I assumed if anything he would be pro-life . . . I said.

She tried to laugh. Yes, when it's not his daughter. When it's not on his doorstep. She paused. He'll take this whole thing out on my mother. Blame her for my decisions. You don't understand what it's like, she added, the words spilling out of her.

Silence filled the room again.

We'll need to think about disguising the bump, then, Stirling said. What size of boiler suit are you wearing?

Levitt started reaching for the tag on the inside of her collar. A small maybe, possibly a medium.

We need to get our hands on larger ones, he said. The baggier the better.

I exhaled. More blankets too . . . I suppose it's good that you work in the pharmacy, I added. Keeps you out of the way.

But sit down as much as possible, Stirling said. Don't overexert yourself.

OK, Levitt said. Thank you.

# 9

I was staring at a new month in the calendar. This time it was a great big Dalmatian poised with one paw raised in the air, its face a smudge of spots. I'd heard somewhere they were a difficult breed of dog, all energy and bounding legs. Levitt slid the contents of a medicine cup towards me for inspection and I nodded. As she handed the medication through the hatch I found myself smiling, elated by the thought of a baby growing inside her, before allowing a seed of doubt to creep in at the sight of her slender silhouette. Even her chest was flat. Were her breasts capable of feeding a baby? What kind of milk would her malnourished body produce? I had no idea.

She was nodding at what the patient was saying and I recognised him, his drug chart sitting on the top of my pile. I silently recited his name – Glass. He always made polite conversation and very rarely missed his medication. I suspected he took the same philosophy I applied to brushing my teeth.

And how are you today? he asked, looking past Levitt to greet me.

I'm fine, thank you, I said.

Good, got to stay positive, he replied before turning away.

He stopped at the door to let someone enter and only then did I realise it was Officer Holden's wife. She came to a stop at the counter but I couldn't find it in me to approach her.

Hi, can I help? Levitt said.

Can I speak with the pharmacist?

Wolfe, this lady would like a word.

I came to the Perspex.

Can we speak out on the shop floor? she said.

I nodded, before reluctantly leaving the dispensary. I followed her to a corner of the shop, where she turned abruptly. I was aware of everything: how I spread my hands across my boiler suit, that my hair was still damp, that there was a cluster of spots on my chin I hadn't bothered to squeeze. I wondered if she questioned why it had been me with Holden. But mostly I was wondering why after all this time, when I'd been very conscious of staying clear of them, did she now want to speak with me.

She cast her eyes down to the floor. I suppose it is something of an embarrassing matter, she said.

There was a long pause. Was now the time to confess? I was under no illusion that she knew exactly who I was. I opened my mouth to speak but wasn't quite sure what I was expected to say.

I have reason to believe . . . She took a gulp. A bug – a louse or something fell from my head, she said. I've discovered a few. I'm trying not to touch my scalp.

So, you think you have head lice?

She nodded, unwilling to look at me. Perhaps I disgusted her.

That's OK, I said. It's really common and easily treated.

She continued to nod. Yes, I know. I went to the doctors' this morning but they were too busy to see me, and the nurse said you would be able to provide treatment. She gave the quickest glance at me and I could see redness travelling across her cheeks. The nurse insisted I come along to reduce the risk of spreading. So here I am.

It's not a problem, I said. I can give you the treatment now. I raced back into the dispensary where it felt somewhat safe, but she was following me, waiting by the hatch.

I'm going to give you a lotion that you can put in your hair straight away and leave in all day, I said. I'll give you a plastic comb too, for later. Can I have your surname and ID number?

You already know my surname, she said. And I don't want any record of this.

I have to, for medical reasons and for stock use.

She ran her fingers across her forehead. I really would prefer otherwise, she said. Please, surely exceptions can be made . . . And suddenly it seemed as though she was pleading with me, and I couldn't bear for her to be pleading with me for anything.

OK, I said. I'll figure something out.

Levitt gave me a look of warning, but I didn't acknowledge her. I pulled open a drawer and removed a large bottle of head lice lotion. She had quite a lot of hair and I'd have to advise that some of it, if not all of it, be cut off to reduce the risk of reinfection.

I returned to the shop floor, gripping the bottle. If you want to go behind the curtain I'll watch over while you apply the lotion, I said, offering it to her. It shouldn't take long. It's really the scalp that you want to concentrate on.

She seemed reluctant to take the bottle and from the way her eyes glazed I began to think she was close to tears.

The thing is, she said, I have this irrational fear of insects. I know it might sound silly to you, but I just don't know how I'll manage to do this. Her breathing was heavy and I realised that her upper body was moving while her legs remained stationary. She was shifting her weight forwards and backwards, in a repetitive rhythmical motion. I can't stand the idea of them being up there, crawling about, she added. I just can't touch them.

I stared at her, beginning to understand what it was she was asking, and the enormity of what that must have taken out of her.

Would you like me to apply it for you? I said.

Please.

I'll just go and get some gloves, OK?

She nodded and sat down on the lone seat behind the curtain. When I returned she'd taken the elastic band out from her hair and was looking straight ahead, the way she would in a hairdresser's. Perhaps she was thinking of me as the worker and herself as the client. I opened the nozzle of the lotion, my hands cased in latex, and she sat perfectly still. I was very aware that I didn't want to hurt her as I parted strands of her hair. It was like applying hair dye. I moved her parting and squeezed out lines of lotion, before rubbing her scalp with my fingers. I could see the eggs clearly, stuck to the root shafts of her hair. I tried not to look for lice – usually they were so small that it was easy to miss them, but my eyes caught a few that were quite large and I knew then that she'd had the lice for some time. How much blood had they already extracted from her scalp?

I worked methodically through her hair and the whole time I thought about Holden. I thought about him coming to find me in the army base and leading me into a windowless room. It was the first contact we'd had since he'd called things off. We'd only stopped because we'd been found out. I had taken hold of his wrist, wanting nothing more than to keep him there with me. He'd been unresponsive and I'd placed my hand on the buckle of his belt. No, he said, swiping my hand away.

Please . . . I said, practically begging.

I need you to sit down, he replied. I've got something important to say.

I had watched his mouth move, a beautiful oval shape, the image of white teeth behind moving lips as he told me about the bunker and what was imminently planned. I'd known the world was in a bad way but I hadn't anticipated his words – hadn't expected those sentences to ever tumble from his mouth. I'd focused again on the belt I had tried to remove moments before. The irrelevance of the item. How could he worry about the looseness of his trousers when he knew the world was going to end?

You can't take anything with you, he said. No photograph, no piece of jewellery. Nothing. Everything you need will be provided.

Not a soul was to know. If word got out, there'd be no place for me in the bunker. I had the weekend to spend with whomever I pleased and then I was to report for work as normal on Monday. He was so calm as he spoke, as though he was reading lines from a rehearsed script. I half-expected someone to shout *cut*, allowing his words to lose all meaning and effect.

It felt as though I'd touched every inch of Holden's wife's scalp by the time I was finished. I gathered her hair and tied it in a neat bun before stripping off my gloves. She stood and we stared at each other. I fought to keep my eyes up, to avoid shifting my gaze. We were of similar height; she was perhaps an inch or so taller. And suddenly I wished to take in each and every detail of her – the smudge of freckles across her nose, the crinkle of cartilage on the tops of her earlobes. Perhaps the reality of what I had done with her husband was finally hitting home because I found myself wanting to apologise. There were so many things I needed to apologise for.

I'm sorry, I whispered. I'm so sorry.

Does it make you feel better to say that?

No, not really.

Her mouth made this strange squeaking noise. She tilted her head back and I thought she was about to speak when her spit hurtled towards my face, landing on my cheek. And for a brief moment I wasn't sure what had happened, because she looked exactly the same as she had seconds before. Slowly, I brought my fingers up to my cheek and touched her saliva. I let my hand fall away so I could see its residue on my fingers – transparent and bubbled. She bobbed her head to one side but she looked sad, sadder than she'd been this whole time in the pharmacy.

That didn't make me feel better either, she said.

I shook my head but it was more like a tick, as if I'd tried to reset something. I brought the sleeve of my boiler suit up and wiped the rest of her spit away, leaving a damp patch on my sleeve.

You're not a bad person, she said. I think in my head I wanted you to be, but really you're not.

I watched her leave before making my way back into the dispensary.

Who was that? Levitt said.

No one, I replied.

You don't make special allowances for *no one* . . .

Would you just leave it? Please.

I came to the hatch to greet the next patient. There's still fluid in my ankles, he said, sliding a prescription through the hatch. Dr Bishop is suggesting I up the dose of my water tablets.

I nodded. I think that's a great idea, I said. Wonderful.

I watched him fumble with the cup, slowly throwing the extra tablet into his mouth. Even just watching the delicate way he placed the measuring cup back on the counter irritated me.

I was returning the furosemide water tablets to their slot in the drawer when another woman ran in, thrusting the door back on its hinges, forcing it to clatter against the wall.

Help, she shouted. Please, help me.

Levitt and I both stood to attention, my senses on high alert. I was already searching for the bruises or marks of abuse on her body, a pool of blood gathering in the crotch of her boiler suit, but there was nothing. She was hysterical though, hardly able to catch her breath.

What's wrong? I asked. Are you OK?

No one will help me, she said. Please . . . She was gripping the counter now, and from the way she moved her body I thought she might crack her head against the Perspex.

It took me a moment but finally I recognised her. I can only help you if I know what's wrong, I said.

He's missing, she shouted. And no one seems to care. I've been to the soldiers, I've talked to everyone who knows us . . . He's nowhere. Her nose was running and she wiped it away with the back of her hand. You can't just disappear . . . Not in here.

OK, please try to calm down. Who is missing? I asked, already knowing the answer.

My husband. Maxwell, she said, her voice merely a whisper now. ID number 2597. Please . . . All I want to know is if he came in for his medicine today. At least then I'll know he's OK.

I parted my hands, rubbed my fingers against the soft skin of my palms. I'm sorry, I said. I can't give out that information. It would be breaking patient confidentiality . . .

What? Are you joking? she shouted.

I shook my head, attempting my most solemn expression.

My husband is missing and you won't tell me if you've—

Wolfe, Levitt interrupted. Can I check? What if I do it and then you don't—

No, I said firmly, aware of my heart racing, perspiration gathering on my forehead. I focused on Maxwell, not daring to look at Levitt. You've done the right thing, reporting your concern to the soldiers. I suggest you speak to your friends again. I'm sure he'll turn up. As you said, you can't just disappear in a bunker.

Maxwell exhaled, her eyes full of disbelief. Aren't we all meant to be helping one another? she said.

I'm really sorry, I replied. I'm only doing my job.

She stood there a moment longer, shaking her head in anger, her mouth open as she took pained, deliberate breaths.

There's nothing I can do . . . I said, my words hanging there with the fear of her never actually leaving. I busied myself, shuffling drug charts across the counter, opening and closing drawers as though I was looking for something in particular, until finally she walked away.

What's going on, Wolfe? Levitt said, staring at me.

Don't ever put me in that position again, I snapped. You had no right to interfere.

Levitt took a step back, cautious, her trust wavering before my eyes. That woman was terrified, she said. That was real. And you couldn't make an allowance for her when you could for someone else . . .

It's a breach of patient confidentiality, I said, a lump rising in my throat. And what exactly was your plan: to break rules and end up in the firing line when you're already trying to keep a low profile?

She faltered. I'm sorry, she said. It won't happen again.

I gripped the handle of a medicine drawer, saliva gathering in my mouth as if I could be sick at any moment. An instant sense of guilt lodged itself into my stomach; the horrendous fear of knowing that Maxwell's disappearance was no coincidence. I could try to fool myself into thinking otherwise, reason with verbal logic, but it would do nothing to take that sensation away from my churning insides. I needed the toilet suddenly, could barely contain myself, but I knew I'd feel no better afterwards.

I stared at the floral wallpaper in ND's hall and convinced myself that monkeys were hiding within the pattern – the tails circling their bodies, distorted among the flowers but definitely there – the eyes, the pouting lips, jutting chin, and arms instead of branches. I blinked. Was the wiring in my brain wrong? Turning away, I focused on the fibres of the carpet, tapping my foot to a count of ten before bringing my attention back to the wallpaper. Monkeys – definitely camouflaged throughout. I rose to my feet, pacing to the opposite wall to see if monkeys were hiding there too. It reminded me of an expensive textile shop in the city – they had this wallpaper that appeared to be a classic floral design, the colours antique blue and pink, but on closer inspection it was a continual repeat of two delinquents pissing in a fountain. They had managed to take something unfortunate and make it beautiful by deceiving the eye.

I took my seat again and clasped my hands over my knees. I wished I could remember the name of that textile company. These lapses in memory seemed to be happening all the time – things on the tip of my tongue, something feeling so close yet completely out of reach. The designers would most likely be dead now. I made a mental note to scavenge their offices once I was out – one day my home would have their designs if nothing else.

A door I'd never been through before opened and instinctively I rose from my seat. But it wasn't Alison who greeted me – it was a balding man who wore towelled slippers on his feet as though he was in a hotel. He'd tucked his shirt into burgundy chinos that were too short in length and I could see the word *Wednesday* embroidered into the fabric of his socks. I couldn't remember what day it was and this panicked me; it seemed essential that I should know. Was it indeed a Wednesday?

Follow me, he said, standing over the threshold.

He led me into a large kitchen with gloss cupboards and wooden surfaces. At a breakfast bar two place mats were sitting next to each other, minus cutlery. He nodded to a stool and I hesitated before perching myself up on top. He'll be with you shortly, the man said, busying himself on the opposite side of the counter. Next to him a microwave buzzed with life, a glow of light coming from inside. It pinged, a piercing noise that startled me. The man put on oven gloves and removed a plate, placing it on the counter. Two meat patties sweated on the plate, fat oozing out.

Do you want a cheese slice? he said.

Cheese?

Well, it's the closest you'll get to cheese in here.

I nodded.

He opened up two artificial-looking burger buns and squirted ketchup inside. I was watching him smooth the ketchup out with a knife when ND appeared behind me wearing a tracksuit. I got to my feet as if I was standing to attention but he smiled and ushered for me to sit. I gripped the counter and pulled myself forward in my stool until my torso was pressed up against the edge, my feet planted on the foot bar.

Hello, Sarah, he said. Lovely to see you, as always.

I watched his cheeks wobble slightly as he swallowed saliva. He rested his hands on the back of his stool.

The man behind the counter placed two plates on the mats.

Can I? I said, pointing to my plate, needing reassurance that it wasn't an illusion.

Well, I did promise you dinner, ND said. I've always thought sitting down over a meal was the best way to truly understand a person, he added. You pick up so much even from a person's likes and dislikes. He pulled his stool back and settled himself down with a thud. Alistair, do we have something nice to offer our guest to drink?

Alcohol?

No, not alcohol, he said. She wouldn't be ready for that.

Alistair opened a cupboard door, which turned out to be a fridge. He removed a bottle of Coke and broke the seal of the cap. He poured the Coke into glass tumblers, the rims looking thin and fragile. When he placed my tumbler down for me I couldn't help but bring it to my lips, my front teeth clinking against the glass. The bubbles fizzed in my mouth and I swallowed, resisting the urge to burp.

Don't let your cheeseburger get cold, ND said, his own burger untouched.

I took the bun in my hands, biting down, letting the taste of meat circulate around my mouth, almost metallic.

ND slid his hand along the counter, letting his fingers tickle my arm. Are you enjoying that?

Like a reflex, I pulled away. It's delicious, I said.

Well, there's no reason why you can't continue to eat like this in my company.

He smiled and there was a white, mucus-like substance resting around the edges of his mouth. Alistair, you can leave us now, he said.

Alone, he began chewing on his burger when I was nearly finished. I'd practically inhaled it, chunks of artificial meat swallowed with barely a chew. The cheese was the best part. It tasted of barbecues and made me think of all those times I'd sat outside, waiting for food that took too long. I used to remind Daniel to eat before going to a barbecue because the food was rarely ready on time.

ND took a sip of his drink and cleared his throat. So, what nuggets of knowledge do you have for me today?

There was a small dollop of ketchup on my plate and I scraped it off with my pinkie, bringing it to my lips. Maxwell has gone missing, I said. Did you know?

He paused, mid-chew. How do you know he's missing?

His wife came into the pharmacy, hysterical, wanting to know if we'd seen him. If he'd collected his medicine . . .

And what did you say?

That I couldn't tell her anything.

Well, as you said, he was never regular in taking his tablets. ND took another bite of his burger, chewed and swallowed in a very calm and measured way. Not that I condone that sort of behaviour but I suspect he has just found himself a new partner on the other side of the bunker. These are certainly trying times for anyone's relationship. Perhaps a little time and space will do them the world of good.

That familiar tension was back in my stomach, saliva once again gathering behind my molars. Do you think so?

Life goes on, he said, forcing the last of his burger into his mouth, his jugular bulging as he swallowed. And I wanted to laugh then – laugh at how ridiculous he sounded.

The thing is, I said, I don't think he has shacked up with someone else on the other side of the bunker. I think that maybe something has happened to him . . .

Are you a detective now?

I didn't answer. I focused my energy on trying to remain composed, the reality of the situation slowly dawning. So easily manipulated by the smallest of pleasures; not a scrap was left on my plate. Would other inhabitants have been better principled? Or would everyone have eaten the cheese-burger if it had been placed in front of them?

Stop looking so glum, ND said. You don't need to worry. There's ice cream . . .

I don't want any ice cream.

He grabbed my plate and threw it down on the counter in front of me; it smashed into pieces, little shards brushing against the sleeves of my boiler suit. And I was so taken aback by the outburst, astonished even, that I sat there unable to move.

You are lucky to be here, he said. Don't forget that.

Yes, I whispered. I'm sorry.

Perhaps you could appear more grateful, then, he replied.

I began to nod; I couldn't help it.

Now, one scoop or two?

# IO

There was no sleep the night before Daniel left. Perhaps I had never really slept properly since. This is over, isn't it? he'd said, and I couldn't reply. We sat next to each other on the sofa, the light starting to shine in through the slats of the blinds. I kept staring at them, wishing I'd turned them the other way – maybe the room would be darker still if I'd swivelled the cord the other way. And then we would have been able to sit longer, pretending that there didn't have to be any outcome in daybreak. He lifted his feet and placed them on the coffee table, crossing them at the ankles. The socks didn't match. I kept running my hand across my neck. The clock in our living room ticked loudly. Sometimes I wouldn't notice it, and other times I'd want to take it off the wall and place it in another room.

I thought we'd make it, he said. I never thought it would be us.

I tried to think of words that might reverse us in some way but nothing came. I'd always been a defeatist by nature.

Sarah?

We had a good run, I said.

What do we do about the dog?

Did you even want to be a father? I said.

He hung his head over the back of the sofa and stared up at the ceiling. It shouldn't have hinged on this, he said. This shouldn't be the only way to be happy.

I turned to look at him before shifting my gaze. We'd made a beautiful home. Had spent so long trying to get the right shade of grey for the room. I could feel a tear running down my cheek and I didn't bother wiping it. I let it slide to the bottom of my chin before swallowing the other tears away. Daniel . . . Don't leave me. Please.

We can't bring happiness to one another any more. Once it's gone you can't get it back, he said.

And I nodded because I believed it too. We'll have to make a clean break, then, I said. I can't watch you make a life without me.

Yes, clean break.

You take the dog, I said.

OK.

I rolled on to my back and pulled the blankets down from my face. There was the white canvas and Canavan's body bulging from the seams, but it didn't look as though it was about to give way any time soon. Below, I could hear the Foers whispering to one another. Merry Christmas. Love you, she said.

There was a pause before I heard him say, Merry Christmas. Try and enjoy it.

Canavan turned above me and suddenly his green eyes were staring down. Is today the day? he said.

By that do you mean the day our Christ was born?

I have no intention of getting up today, he said.

Apparently the food pouches are Christmas-themed.

He dragged his body forward so his head was dangling uncomfortably close to mine. I filled my boots at ND's yesterday, he whispered.

What did you have? I asked, already visualising Alistair pulling a steaming dish from the oven.

Tinned beef with all the trimmings, he said. I think they're having goose today. He's not a fan of turkey. Did you know that?

No.

He smiled, showcasing a mouthful of yellow teeth. He shifted his weight back on to his bunk and although I couldn't see his face any more I knew he was staring at the ceiling, perhaps counting some of the rivets that sat in his line of vision. He cleared his throat.

I'm sorry I introduced you to him, Wolfe. All I wanted to do was help you feel safe. He shrugged through the fabric, seeming to hesitate before speaking again. I didn't mean for him to take a shine to you. He reached out with his hand and waited for me to take it.

What should I do, Canavan?

He squeezed my hand. Have you sorted out your little stomach condition yet?

I paused. Yes, it's sorted.

Good, at least that's something.

Two bare artificial trees had been set up on each side of the bunker, close to the boundary line, another perfect mirror image. I was wondering whose job it had been to remember these on the inventory when Alison's voice came over the speaker system.

Attention all inhabitants. We are holding our first ever Christmas-tree-decorating competition. North versus South and our leader will be the judge. Conversation broke out then through the bunker, distorting her voice above, and there were collective calls for quiet. She continued. The recreation rooms will be converted into craft centres for the day so the children can make decorations. Supervised. It is up to you all to work as a team. You will collectively decorate the trees. Judging will commence this evening and the trees will remain in place until the New Year.

Her voice cut out, leaving a deafening static before the chamber erupted in noise.

Did she say the leader was judging? one man asked.

That's what she said, someone replied.

So we'll see him . . . a woman said.

I backed away from the main compartment, thinking it was perhaps a good opportunity to collect my food pouches. I'd never especially liked Christmas; in a way I was almost disappointed that the leader and his advisors were even trying. Was it meant to boost morale, or remind us of the faith and traditions we considered superior?

I thought the 5mg diazepam tablets were the perfect shade of blue. Like a summer's sky, with little flecks of white lactose interspersed for clouds. Everyone seemed to be on diazepam. The supply would not last our duration and I contemplated what would happen when everyone was defrosted back to reality. The female patient who was waiting tipped two of them into her mouth and sipped water, already looking calmer as she returned the cup to me. Thank you, she said, opening her mouth wide. As she made to leave she looked past me, smiling oddly at Levitt, and I began to wonder if she suspected something in her appearance.

I turned to Levitt, my eyes searching for a bump, but the boiler suit swamped her.

Which sweet pouch did you get today? I asked.

Crumble, I think.

Do you want to swap? I've been given mince pie flavour but I hate mince pies. Too many spices.

No, you're OK, she said. I don't like them either. I used to think they were made of actual minced beef as a kid and I've never really been able to shake that off.

I stole another glance in her direction. She was careful not to behave in the way I imagined a pregnant woman would. They usually placed their hands on their backs and forced their stomachs to protrude, or they were forever running fingers across bumps, following the movements of their unborn child. I wondered if there were stretch marks – a reason for me to finally use the oil we kept in stock. A friend had suffered from anorexia and the stretch marks from her weight gain had startled me. To see someone who was still unbearably thin have stretch marks seemed more unnatural than the weight loss itself. But then my sister-in-law had had a tiger's coat stretched across her stomach after childbirth and I used to worry that would happen to me. Would I wear bikinis again? Would I still fit into my old clothes? It had all seemed to matter so much at the time.

Wolfe . . . Levitt said. There's a soldier outside staring in at us.

I came to where she stood. It was my soldier with the birthmark, hunching to see through the artificial windows. His hand rested on the barrel of his rifle.

You haven't told anyone else about me, have you? Levitt said.

I stared at him. No, I said. No one.

What about Stirling? Her voice was low, as though she could barely get the words out.

I could feel another coarse hair poking out from my neck. It wasn't long enough yet to pull on. He wouldn't, I said.

But how can you be so sure?

I'm sure.

She raised her hand and offered him an awkward wave. Maybe he thinks we're closed . . . she said.

But he pretended he hadn't seen her and lingered there a moment longer before walking off.

Those soldiers really give me the creeps, she said. There's no need for them to carry guns. They could so easily murder us all in our sleep. She paused, as if she was expecting me to say something. What do you think he wanted?

I don't know, I said, trying to sound relaxed, unfazed.

Well, he was definitely watching us, she said.

I made my way to the recreation room and lingered outside, listening to the thrum of adult conversation, not at all the noise of children I'd expected. Inside, it seemed as if the entire population of our side of the bunker was in attendance. Two soldiers guarded the door and as I walked through they were patting down a man, removing something that resembled a crayon from behind his collar.

On the floor were colourful foam mats patchworked together for the children to sit on, and like an island in the middle the disused ping-pong table masqueraded as a supply station. I recognised Alison straight away, handing out supplies, with two more soldiers standing guard on either side of her. She looked terrible in her boiler suit, but perhaps that was just because I was used to seeing her in beautiful clothes. People thronged around her and she appeared stunned, as though we were vultures ready to attack. I had to push my way through to see what was on offer: there were stacks of coloured paper sheets, squares of felt, blunt scissors, thread, glue, and a hole punch chained to the frame of the table.

Alison was holding a felt snowman in her hand with black felt circles for coal. As you can see, there are examples to give you inspiration, she said to no one in particular.

Can anyone make one, or is it only for the children? I said.

She stared at me, with perhaps a flicker of recognition, before handing me some scissors and felt. Knock yourself out, she said.

I spotted Baxter and his mother, tapping her shoulder before offering a polite hello.

This is carnage, she said, holding the remains of a star with only four points. I don't think he's actually that fussed but I didn't want him to feel left out.

Can I join you? I said.

Please.

I crouched down and smiled at Baxter but he cuddled into his mother. Perhaps children were indeed better judges of character than adults.

I'm not sure what I should make with this, I said, holding the felt in my hands. I ran my fingers over its texture, my ragged nails tugging across it. I realised that for some of the younger children this would be the first Christmas they'd fully remember, and I found myself being envious of this, of knowing nothing better and simply enjoying the small pleasures being gifted.

Everyone, please remember we've agreed to cut the decorations in Christmas-themed shapes, Alison said, now circling us, a soldier following. Things like Christmas trees, stockings, baubles, holly . . . She stopped next to a boy who was sharing the mat with Baxter, squinting at the shape of what he'd cut. I wouldn't say a pineapple is particularly festive, she said.

Does it matter? the man sitting next to him snapped. He used to like pineapples. I don't have a problem with him hanging a pineapple on a Christmas tree.

But it doesn't fit the theme for the competition.

And are you going to stop him from putting it on? he said, swivelling round to stare at her.

She stood straight and carried on walking. Once you've got your shapes you can glue them on to the cards. I'll punch a hole in the top for stringing them up, she added, her words floating above me.

A woman crouched down beside us, her hand on Baxter's mother's shoulder. We could use more thread, she said. If we all get our hands on a decent length we can make it work.

How? She's keeping count of the spools.

But while she's doing the rounds she won't know what lengths are taken off, the woman replied.

I tried not to look at either of them as they spoke but could feel my eyes instinctively being drawn towards them, my ears pricking up at the hushed words and their cryptic meaning. Thread had been easy to steal from laundry but then people had started tying tight knots around their body parts, man-made tourniquets, until the soldiers had put an end to the self-mutilation. In my previous life I used to worry about babies getting strands of their mother's hair knotted around their little fingers and toes. The thought of their extremities losing full circulation made me feel sick.

I've always threaded my eyebrows, the woman said. They keep a much better shape than wax. She tilted her head to see me staring. I'll thread your eyebrows too if you help me get more, she said.

I lifted the PVA glue and squeezed the nozzle, spreading the liquid thinly across my fingertips. I let the glue dry, which didn't take very long at all, before peeling it off. Transparent strands flaked on to my free palm. The lines from my fingerprints were embedded in them and I stared on, feeling as if I finally had something that was my own.

Barely an inch of artificial branch could be seen for the number of decorations hanging from the trees. As I brushed my hand across the bristles, I imagined some of the decorations to be chocolates wrapped in foil. I could almost taste them.

The children all tried to point out to each other which decorations were theirs. But, to me, both trees looked the same. There were no fairy lights and I accepted this like a personal failing, like when I'd bought multicoloured lights for our tree at home but Daniel had thought they were tacky. There was no tinsel for the bunker trees either, but that was OK. Tinsel was a terrible invention.

Alison's voice boomed out from the speaker system. Please make a safe space for our leader. Back away from the trees so he has plenty of room to commence judging. Thank you.

And suddenly there was a procession of guards marching the leader out of his lair from our side of the bunker. Silence fell as ND emerged from his circle of soldiers and waved to us. He wore a red boiler suit, pristine white gym shoes and a Santa hat, hiding his white and thinning hair. He stopped at our tree first and inspected it, staring up to the top before circling it, his hand settling on a felt penguin. I expected him to search the crowd, looking for the faces he knew. Did I want him to seek me out? Perhaps. But he nodded to a soldier and was ushered forward across the boundary line to the other tree. Like a wave rolling across the shore, there was a collective movement of bodies from our side, passing our tree to stand closer to the boundary line.

ND did the same again, inspecting and circling, gripping a different decoration in his hand before stepping back, his soldiers once again surrounding him. He leant forward and whispered something into the ear of one. They marched him back to the entrance of his lair on the other side of the bunker and within seconds he was away. The soldier he'd whispered to stood forward from the group and raised his hand in the air, and it stayed poised like that for a moment, before he pointed it in the direction of the other side's tree. Shrieks of applause seemed to erupt from across the line but not a sound came from our direction, before someone in the distance started crying.

The soldier who had declared the winner approached a young girl of maybe nine or ten and handed her a feathered angel figurine. With the help of two men she was hoisted high into the air, where she placed the angel on top of the tree. Festive music started playing out through the speaker system then and children from across the line were dancing, bopping up and down.

Suddenly, people pulsed across the line, marching towards the opposite side's tree and celebrations. A girl of a similar age to the one who had positioned the angel only moments ago was now gripping the branches of the winning tree, trying to scale it, but people were pulling her back, holding her ankles and tugging at her boiler suit. And then a fight broke out around the girl. Grown men and women were pushing one another, shouting and pulling tufts of each other's hair. My eyes narrowed on one man biting another's earlobe before the other man retaliated with a head-butt. There was the splatter of blood from a nose, fresh and rich and mesmerising.

Had we always been this competitive? I watched on with a sense of inevitability, as if we were being baited this whole time, while my ears rang with the noise of collective violence. Was it the noise of a man's head being thrust against the concrete floor? Or was it the noise of fists settling into flesh? I thought about airbags in cars and how it was nothing like landing in a giant pillow. The soldiers stood back, staring at the scene with their rifles close to their bodies, pointing upwards. If a bullet were to be shot, would it ricochet off the metal until it found a home? It occurred to me that I'd never actually seen them fire a bullet. The butt of their rifle and its brutal force was enough to keep inhabitants in order. There probably weren't even any bullets in their guns, and, the more I thought about it, the more I believed it to be true.

Eventually the soldiers came forward and started pulling bodies apart. One man lay lifeless on the floor and another man was hunched over him, covered in blood. The man began to weep, planting his bloodied hands on the floor, leaving distorted handprints. Two soldiers dragged him off and another bundled the lifeless body into his arms, carrying him the way a groom might carry a bride across the threshold. And I wondered if they would even attempt to bring him back to life or just dispose of him. The airlock chamber on our side had a circular porthole window in the door, but the soldiers had covered it in parcel paper to stop us from peering inside. I thought about the realities of trying to leave the bunker and having to clamber over all the body bags. And, the more I tried to visualise leaving, the more it overwhelmed me.

# II

I was thinking about a pharmacy I used to work in when Stirling walked through the door. The pharmacy had been positioned in the basement of a building and I imagined my old colleagues camping down there with sleeping bags and supplies, deep enough to avoid the touch of radiation. I'd always liked those people.

I saw Levitt's eyes catch him. Hi, Dr Stirling, she said.

Wolfe, I have a prescription for you, he replied, with an unfamiliar sternness to his voice.

OK, I said. Do you need it now? I'm just finishing my shift.

He slid the paper through the hatch and I let my fingers settle on the prescription, already sensing ND's influence before seeing his name. Stirling watched me; waited for my expression to change. What? I said, stunned to see oxycodone scrawled in Stirling's handwriting. I'd yet to see oxycodone, or any schedule two controlled drug, being prescribed since entering the bunker. Opiate derivatives were being kept for emergencies only, the bunker's inhabitants having no daily use for them.

It's urgent, Stirling said, nodding his head in acknowledgement to Valentine, who had arrived to relieve me of my duties.

Good afternoon, Dr Stirling, he said, standing to attention. What brings you here? He still seemed to regard doctors as gods.

Wolfe is dispensing a prescription for me, Stirling replied.

Hi, Valentine, I said, already crouched on my knees, unlocking the controlled drug cabinet, something that didn't go unnoticed by him.

Why are you—?

If you could bring the medication straight to my surgery, Stirling said, directing his words towards me. That would be preferable.

I got to my feet, two different strengths of oxycodone in my hands, 10mg and 40mg. Full boxes of fifty-six tablets in each.

What's going on? Valentine said, watching as Stirling strode out of the pharmacy.

I pointed to the prescription sitting on the counter.

He glanced at it, his eyebrows furrowed in confusion. Since when are we getting prescriptions for the leader? he asked, turning to confront me. Let alone for controlled drugs . . .

Since now, I guess . . .

Well, what's wrong with him?

I don't know, Valentine. I'm only following orders.

He took the prescription in his hands, raising it towards the light to inspect Stirling's penmanship.

It's a valid prescription, I said.

I just don't understand . . .

Levitt was staring at us, leaning against one of the counters and Valentine clocked her.

Busy as ever, I see, he said, trying to contain something of a snort. You've certainly settled in well, Levitt.

Levitt didn't respond, only collected her things.

I too started collecting my blankets, dropping the boxes of oxycodone into the pockets of my boiler suit. I held the door

open for Levitt and before leaving said to Valentine, Try not
to worry about this. I'll complete the schedule two paperwork in the morning.

He hesitated before nodding, busying himself with the
contents of a medicine drawer.

Out in the corridor, Levitt and I walked in silence except
for the sound of our gym shoes pad-pad-padding across the
concrete. We came to a stop just before the doctors' surgery.
I shifted from one foot to the other, unable to settle, agitation
seeping through me.

Is everything OK? Levitt said.

Why wouldn't it be? I replied defensively.

Is the leader ill? she said. Is there something wrong?

I paused. Look, it's not something you need to worry
about. I'm sure everything's fine. I reached out to touch
her but then for some reason decided against it. You just
focus on looking after yourself. That's all that really
matters.

She looked at me, her eyes narrowing slightly. OK, well,
I'll see you tomorrow, then. But as I entered the surgery she
was still lingering out there in the corridor.

Inside, several patients were sitting in seats and Nurse
Appleby was marking something up on the whiteboard. She
nodded as though she was expecting me and gestured for
me to sit. My knees jittered slightly and I clamped their
movements down with my hands. The patient to my left was
gripping his wrist, his hand upright, and I could see scald
marks embedded across his skin. He shook from the pain
and I wondered how he'd come to acquire his burn; we were
like cavemen, with no means of fire. I winced just looking at
his skin – red, raw and already blistering. I'd burned myself
once on a frying pan handle that had accidently been resting

over a gas flame. The pan handle had momentarily stuck to my skin and I hadn't been able to shake it off. The blisters had risen in little rows of bubbles and the pain had throbbed, like pins pricking continuously.

Suddenly the memory seemed so vivid that I wanted to feel that pain again. We had only evolved as humans because we'd discovered how to cook food. I hated that feeling of going backwards.

On the wall, directly in my line of vision, was a poster with a drawing of a brain. Speech bubbles floated out in different directions. *Don't feel sad on your own,* one said. *Let's talk mental health,* said another. The surgery door opened and Holden's wife walked in. She confirmed her appointment with Nurse Appleby before turning and clocking me. There was an awkward pause where we weren't sure if we were to acknowledge one another before she somewhat reluctantly took the empty seat next to me.

Hi, I said.

Hello.

I placed my hands inside my pockets, instinctively checking on the boxes of oxycodone while my foot tapped frantically off the floor.

It's disappointing what happened with the Christmas trees, she said. At this rate there will hardly be any of us left.

I guess we weren't quite ready for rivalry, I said, immediately wishing I could scoop the words back into my mouth.

I never really thanked you for helping me with my hair, she said.

Have you had any trouble since?

She shook her head. I'm sorry I spat on you.

I shrugged. I deserved it.

Still, it wasn't right. My husband was just as responsible and I never spat on him. She opened her mouth to say something else but Dr Hays called her into his consultation room and she rose from her seat without another word.

The waiting room began to empty before Stirling called me in. He appeared erratic, closing the door behind us, hesitating before sitting down at his desk and playing with the rubber tubing of his stethoscope. Eventually he said, Dr Bishop has always dealt privately with our leader's medication. Always. So you can imagine my surprise when he asked *me* to start prescribing oxycodone for him.

Why? I said.

I don't know ... I asked if I could at least see our leader, assess his pain, but I was told that would be impossible.

So why's Bishop asking you?

He shook his head. I'm getting set up or something ... A defeated expression settled across his face. Clearly I'm more disposable than the other doctors. Accountable, if and when it all goes wrong.

And you agreed to prescribe it ...

What choice do I have? he said. What Bishop says goes. He's the leader's brother in-law ...

My eyes widened in disbelief. Sorry? What?

You didn't know? You assumed he'd been positioned as head of medical through experience and reputation? He tried to laugh. No. I don't think that's how it works in here. My father's the health advisor and he didn't want Bishop anywhere near us. There were rumours of malpractice in his previous life.

There must be something we can do, I said.

Do you think the leader's abusing oxycodone? he said, the words spluttering out. That's the only thing I can think of that makes any sense. With the high doses requested ... I suspect Bishop's been prescribing them from his own supply. He'll have run out now and won't want to put his signature on that type of paper trail.

Who's going to check? I said.

We get audited, Wolfe. It's my father who checks our practice and prescribing, ensures we're not causing the inhabitants any harm. He paused, rubbing his forehead.

Well, maybe that's why Bishop wants it to be you, I said. What's a father going to do to his son?

The weirdest part, Stirling said – the weirdest part is that it is to be you *specifically* who delivers the medication.

Me?

He flattened his hands, palms pressed into the wood of his desk. So, Wolfe, I've got to ask. Why are you taking medication to our leader?

From the pained expression on his face I realised he was bracing himself for something he didn't want to hear. And what answer could I possibly give? Was this a reward, or an infliction? Maybe it was simply a legitimate way of having me in the lair – Canavan the artist, me the drug mule.

I stood with my back to the examination bed. I don't know . . .

He rose suddenly from his chair and reached out towards me. Have you promised him something?

A tear escaped and dribbled down my face. All I wanted was to feel safe, I said. I wiped the tear away before lowering my chin and Stirling placed his arms around me. He was gripping me and I wanted him to squeeze the life out of me.

My nose rubbed gently against Stirling's lab coat. His hand curled around my neck and I could see a plaster on his thumb. What happened to your thumb? I said.

Nothing.

I kissed the tip of the thumb, and then I reached up and found his mouth. My lips were dry and chapped but his were soft, and the warmth radiating from them was soothing, like a blanket.

He pulled away. I'm not sure this is a good idea, he said.

His hair seemed longer and there was unfamiliar stubble on his face, but it suited him. Perhaps the other doctors were meant to take him more seriously now he'd disguised his youthfulness. I tried to kiss him again but he jerked his head back further.

Wolfe, you'd better take that oxycodone to him. His face was stern: a doctor giving advice to his patient. Whatever this is, he said, gesturing with his hand between us, I don't think it's something we should pursue.

And what exactly was *this*? I still didn't know. It was like that Game of Life board game – little binary cars, and a colourful spinning dial that dictated your successes in a theoretical life. I was just a piece in play now, at the will of a supposed drug abuser. How my methadone patients would have laughed if they could have seen me.

Right, I said, at risk once again of crying. Whatever you think, then . . .

A woman almost identical to Alison was escorting me into the boardroom. She too wore a tailored suit, but her hair was lighter and she was a few inches shorter.

You can sit down, she said. He won't be long.

Where is Alison? I asked, realising I hadn't seen or heard her voice since the Christmas craft workshop. I spoke as though we were friends; hoped that my asking for her would provide authority and disguise the nervousness in my voice.

But the nerves were already creeping up into my throat, tying themselves into a knot. I licked my lips and struggled to swallow.

She didn't answer me.

I ran my hand along the top of the table, enjoying its smoothness and solidity. I'd bought a Scandinavian TV unit made of ash once. It had dented easily but there had been something about its colour that I adored. Daniel would place his index finger on its sharp corners. We'll need to cover these up when we have kids, he'd said. It would take their eye out.

As I sat down in a swivel chair, one of the boxes of oxycodone tablets buckled a little in my pocket. I reached in and removed it, staring at the creases on the box. So much of this medication had been prescribed to patients in my previous life. Once a patient was on it, it was difficult to get them off. What must it have felt like to take something like opium? Was it as wonderful as people described? I could have opened the box then and popped one tablet out. There was even a jug of water on the table, willing me on. But, despite the temptation, I didn't. The strength of the tablet would have destroyed me, my respiratory system shutting down in shock.

ND entered, and settled himself slowly into the chair opposite. I see you have come bearing gifts.

I nodded, sliding the box I held in my hand reluctantly across the desk.

And the rest?

I reached in and retrieved the other box.

He inspected them, breaking the seals before peering inside, checking their contents. Eventually he said, Thank you.

My fingers gripped the edge of the table. I focused on the thin hairs that sprouted between knuckles and joints. When I looked up ND was staring at me.

This works quite well, don't you think? he said.

My chest seemed to constrict and I decided this was what people meant when they talked about angina. What works? I said.

He popped one 40mg tablet out from its blister strip. As you have probably surmised, I've decided it will be better for everyone if you deliver my medication from now on. It gives us further opportunity to touch base.

I was under the impression that Dr Bishop preferred to deal with your medication directly.

You'll be ridding him of the burden, he said. Help him dedicate more time to keeping our brothers and sisters healthy.

I doubt Dr Bishop would trust me with the responsibility, I said.

It is not for him to decide, though, is it? It is you I would prefer to see.

I'm not a doctor. I can't possibly . . .

He took a sharp intake of breath and exhaled. You're not listening. I don't want a doctor. I don't need a doctor.

I could hear the bark of dogs in another room.

Do you have anything of interest to share with me this evening? he said.

No, not really . . . All quiet on the home front.

You're going to have to try a little harder, he said. I don't believe life can be as quiet as you perceive it to be.

I can't just make things up.

He laughed.

May I leave now? I asked, already trying to get to my feet.

What's the rush? I'm under the impression that a certain young physician is on back-shift tonight. He's a fine doctor, don't you think, Dr Stirling? I suspect he has a bright future ahead of him.

I stared at ND and tried once again to recognise the man I'd seen so many times on television. But that man was gone. Perhaps he'd never really been there. Nothing but a façade: a voice telling others what they wanted to hear.

What's the oxycodone for? I asked.

There was a pause. It's not something you need to concern yourself with.

Well, if I'm dispensing it and bringing it to you, ought I not to know?

He smiled at me, another laugh being released through his nostrils. You really do amuse me, he said. You're not like the others. He swallowed. Let's say chronic back pain. OK? That should put your mind at ease.

I ran my hands along the rails of my bunk. For a brief moment I considered rolling off the side, just thrusting myself over and embracing the fall. The concrete would be hard – I really tried to imagine it. Canavan's body was heavy with sleep above and I peered over the edge, looking down. I didn't know what I was expecting but Mrs Foer's eyes were staring back at me. I pulled my head in quickly and lay motionless, as if I'd imagined her, before slowly bringing my head back out.

This time, there was the flicker of a smile. She pulled her blanket off and hopped down to the floor, careful not to wake her husband as she passed. I watched as she silently slipped on her gym shoes and stood up straight. She looked up and used her index finger to summon me, like a school teacher ushering me to the front of the class.

I hesitated before climbing down, still unsure whether she was actually addressing me.

He's always been able to sleep better than me, she whispered, her eyes landing affectionately on her husband. I was taking sleeping pills but I don't like that man Valentine. Terrible manner with his patients. So instead I take trips now.

Where do you go? I whispered.

She placed her hands on her hips, drawing in the fabric of her boiler suit. Tonight I'm going to Paris. Would you like to join me?

I nodded.

Foer walked with purpose, never really stopping to think about her direction, and I found myself almost skipping to keep up.

Have you been to Paris before? she said.

I have. But it was a long time ago.

Let me guess: with a lover? It always seems to be a place lovers go.

I went once with my husband. Before he was my husband.

What always strikes me as odd each time I visit, she said, is that I don't see what's particularly romantic about the place. Do you agree?

We got robbed, I said. Outside the Moulin Rouge.

Exactly.

Some weirdo chased us with his bike, cornered us in the entrance to the park and took everything we had.

She gripped my arm. Don't worry. Tonight you won't get mugged. Tonight, we will dine in beautiful restaurants and drink red wine and dance.

I stared at her profile as we continued to walk. Was this woman mad? Was I indulging her? I supposed some part of me wanted to know if she could in fact take me to Paris.

We passed the locked kitchens and rounded the corner towards the doctors' surgery. In a moment we would be passing the pharmacy.

Do you always go to Paris? I said.

No, I've not been there in a while. I often stay in Europe but sometimes if I'm feeling adventurous I'll cross the boundary line and head across the Atlantic.

As we walked we passed the same points and it dawned on me that she was directing me with no real purpose – she just wanted to walk, and perhaps it was a novelty to have someone with her.

We came to a stop by the washrooms. Would you mind waiting outside while I freshen up?

No, go ahead.

It feels safer knowing there's someone waiting for me.

It's fine. I'll stay right here.

She was gone and back in what felt like less than a minute. Her sleeves were rolled up to the elbows, her hands still wet, and little droplets fell to the floor as she continued walking. On the inside of her arm, near the elbow joint, was something like a bruise, but as I drew closer I realised it was a tattoo – like a faded bird, the brushed-away red maybe suggesting a robin. She hadn't struck me as the tattoo type and I wondered what it symbolised. I was suddenly jealous that so much more of her life had already passed. I saw myself as the victim. Mrs Foer would have a deeper well of memories to dip from, and someone like little Baxter would perhaps be able to eventually block this period of his life out. But, for me, it felt like peak time.

Foer and I seemed to crash into one another as she veered towards the recreation room. This way to Paris, she said. Sorry, I'm no good at reading maps. I have to turn the map in the direction we're travelling but I always get us there in the end.

Inside, there were a few people spread out across the large expanse of room. By one bookshelf a woman was curled up with a blanket, a book resting by her side and her eyes closed. It hadn't occurred to me to sleep anywhere other than my bunk, and there was something warming about the concept of sleeping in the recreation room. I believed nothing bad was likely to happen to people when congregated around books. But then I remembered Templeton, and begrudged him yet again for tainting even this space.

Foer stepped around another sleeping body and guided me along a short aisle until we reached the travel section. There was a man already sitting down, his back pressed against the books, his knees drawn up beside him. He looked up, smiling as though he was expecting us, and shuffled further up against the bookcase to make room.

Foer settled in beside him, their shoulders touching, and I sat down opposite, crossing my legs.

I brought another traveller with me tonight, she said.

I see that. He reached over and extended his hand for me to shake. The fingernails were unnaturally long and I could see the deposits of dirt underneath them. I'm Webb, he said; it's a pleasure to meet you.

Hi, I'm Wolfe.

I know, he said, placing a travel guide to Paris on the floor. So, where shall we go first?

I'd rather visit the Eiffel Tower later when it's dark, Foer said. It's beautiful with its lights on.

And yourself, Wolfe, where would you like to go?

I was quiet for a moment. I'd like to take a trip down the Seine.

Excellent idea. We can do that after we've had breakfast, he said, flipping open the pages of the guidebook. Is everyone happy to just go with one of the brunch spots recommended in here?

And I found myself nodding, settling into the wall behind me. There was a strange feeling inside, one of genuine excitement – of previous travel, for waking up in an unknown place and flicking through the guidebook wondering what we'd do – hoping it would pan into one of those perfect days.

This place, Webb said, pointing to a description in the *Let's Eat* section of the guidebook. It's famous for its pastries.

Sounds wonderful, Foer said. Let's go. And she instantly got to her feet, more agile than either of us. We followed her and walked in what appeared to be a circle around the bookshelves until we were back in the same spot. Foer delicately wiped the corner of her mouth with her pinkie finger as though there was icing sugar on it. She licked her lips and I found myself copying her. Webb gathered an imaginary cup and brought it to his lips. Look, he said, pointing to the opposite bookcase. Do you see the roller-skaters coming down the street? There must be hundreds of them. And Foer and I looked in the direction he pointed, nodding, bringing our own imaginary cups to our lips.

I do so love sitting in these little cafés, Foer said. You really get to see the world carry on around you.

I wasn't sure how long we stayed like this before we walked along the river and marvelled at the bookshops and cafés of the Latin Quarter. Our night in Paris ended with a trip up the Eiffel Tower and a drink in the bar, looking out across the city's skyline. We took the steps up to the balcony and let the wind flap around our faces. There was the noise of traffic off in the distance and it was wonderful. It was a release I didn't think I was capable of finding – a temporary pause from my existence – an opportunity to be in control of my own decisions.

When we parted from Webb he placed a kiss on Foer's cheek. He shook my hand again. It was a pleasure to have you here with us, he said, before letting go. We're going to Boston next time and you're more than welcome to join us.

When are you going? I said.

Foer will let you know.

She linked her arm through mine and we started walking again. She seemed to be in some sort of trance, humming to herself. But as we stepped out of the recreation room her body changed and it felt as if she was using me for leverage to keep herself steady. I sensed my free hand coming round and gripping her arm, the arm that was linked through mine. I was sure she would collapse otherwise.

Her head hung low. Do you think it's stupid? she said.

What's stupid? I asked, already knowing what she was referring to.

My husband doesn't understand. He thinks I'm a fool.

I paused. We all need means of escaping.

My daughter wouldn't come here, she said quietly.

Her body weighed on me like an anchor, and I was at risk of her dragging me down to the floor. I'm sorry, I said.

How long were you married for? she asked.

Four years.

Isn't it funny how quickly the shape of a wedding ring grooves the skin of your finger, she said, inspecting my hand. And she was right – the ring had imprinted its way into the skin of my bare hand without me even noticing.

It won't go away, will it? I said.

Where is your husband now?

I assume he's dead.

Yes. I assume the same about my daughter. She was barely twenty but so headstrong. She nodded, as if we'd made some sort of discovery together.

What brought you to the bunker? I asked.

My husband is in banking, she said, and as she spoke a touch of pride momentarily crept into her voice. I imagined the many times she had boasted about this to people in the past. He is a strong supporter of our leader, she added – a benefactor, you could say. But then she began tapping her mouth repeatedly, as if she was chastising herself for speaking at all.

Are you OK?

She shook her head. Boston will be good fun, she said. You should come.

We'll see.

She smiled. It's much easier when everyone going has been before.

I guided her back to our bunks and helped her climb up past her sleeping husband. As she curled under her blankets she said, Berlin is actually one of my favourite places to go. I'll take you there one day.

# 12

I stepped behind the mouldy plastic shower curtain and let the lukewarm water spray over my head. I craved the lazy process of undressing and padding across tiles, of water being almost unbearably hot, of condensation gathering on glass. I raised my hand and pressed the soap dispenser encased in metal. It made a churning noise and released pink-tinged soap. Could you overdose on soap? I rubbed my hands together and started with my hair, working my way down to in between my legs. There was no point wasting soap on thighs and knees, or ankles and toes.

I ran my mind over the memories of arriving, of having to strip naked in front of the soldiers and being sprayed with some sort of disinfectant, as though I was already contaminated. I had discarded my clothes on a growing heap – a denim dress with pockets and thick high-denier tights. It was an outfit I had spent time considering, believing it expressed who I was. Except no one really saw it, only the shop assistant when I stopped for fuel. I had filled the tank, more out of habit than logic, before slipping my bank card into a pocket of that dress. My entire outfit was still lying in the airlock chamber, resting next to the now dead. Was I to reclaim the outfit if we made it out alive? Zip it back on and walk into the sunshine as if nothing had ever happened?

After dressing and collecting my food pouches, I did something I wouldn't normally do – I entered the dining hall. I wasn't sure why I didn't like this space. Maybe it was the congregation of people, the faces I might recognise, or maybe it was because I didn't especially like watching others eat their food pouches. There were long rows of tables and benches, with inhabitants trying to find a space where they could. On the floor between the rows were buckets for waste, and for gathering the vomit that came with the pouches. Despite my weakened sense of smell I still shuddered at the thought. I imagined the doors to the bunker finally being opened and our collective stench being released into the world, polluting it further. Perhaps history books would later document us and ponder how we ever existed in these conditions. How had we managed thus far to avoid an epidemic?

I walked the length of the hall and, against my instincts, took in the faces of those sitting down. But I couldn't see Stirling. I'd lost count of the days I'd been searching, having not seen him since delivering medication to the lair. It was as if he'd swapped his shifts to avoid me, and I realised I had no other real means of contacting him. At the end of the table I turned and walked the length of the room again. The noise was strange – no clanking of cutlery, only whispered conversations mixed in with sucking and the seals of caps being broken. If something were to happen to Stirling, as it had to Maxwell, would I ever know?

Someone reached out then and gripped my arm. When I looked down it was Baxter and his mother sitting, squeezed on to a bench.

Are you OK? You look lost . . .

I stared at her for a moment, letting my confusion settle. I . . . I was looking for someone, but they're not here.

Why don't you sit down?

She was already lifting little Baxter on to her knee to make room for me. And without really thinking about it I was lifting my leg over the bench, straddling it, and smiling at Baxter. I can't find him . . .

Who? she said.

I didn't answer. I just kept staring out around me.

Maybe you should eat something, she said, pointing to my pouches. I can swap with you if there are ones you don't like? After having him, she said, rubbing her chin affectionately off Baxter's head, I'm used to eating leftovers.

Little Baxter reached out then and I gripped his cold fingers.

You're shaking, she said. Are you sure you're OK?

He's beautiful, I said, my voice fragile like glass. You're so lucky to have him.

She gripped him tighter. I know.

I mean, if he were even a little younger . . . he wouldn't be here, would he?

Her face changed then, a sharpness behind the eyes. She bit her lip, opening up a crack and letting red surface. I had an abortion, she said, not bothering to whisper. That's what I was willing to do to give him this chance.

Here? I said.

No, just before we arrived. I was about eight weeks. My husband said it was the only way. The baby wouldn't have survived in here. Better to lose a child before you've held them in your arms, he said. But I think about that baby every day. I imagine it would have been a girl.

Little Baxter brought his pouch up to his mouth and I watched him take a long suck on what I could see was banana flavour. With my eyes still on him I said, I never see your husband.

I don't see much of him either, she said. He's so busy with his work. I worry it's not good for his health. She smiled. Perhaps I'm still clinging to the idea of a work-life balance. She reached out and touched my hand. You're not married, are you?

Not any more.

But there are people here who look out for you?

I believe so.

She seemed to ponder this. My husband makes me go on the top bunk, this one below me, she said pointing to Baxter, and then him underneath us. She stared at me as if she'd asked a question, as if she needed my reassurance about something.

I nodded.

She tucked a strand of hair behind her son's ear. You have a kind face, she said. I always think that when I see you.

Selfish mind, perhaps.

I think you'll be paired up well once we're out of here.

Excuse me?

For marriage and babies, of course, she replied somewhat flippantly. We can't dwindle in number any more than we already have. That's what my husband says, anyway. She began whispering a faint tune into little Baxter's ear. I had no idea what it was, maybe a lullaby or nursery rhyme, but it was soothing and I closed my eyes.

Don't stick your finger up your nose, darling, she whispered. It's dirty up there.

They're my tunnels, Mummy, he replied.

I gripped her arm. Listen to me, I said. I'm meant to be monitoring him, and you, and reporting back to our leader.

Sorry?

Our leader – he doesn't trust your husband . . . I doubt he trusts anyone. I just . . . I just need you to be careful. Because

I couldn't bear if something . . . I grew breathless, empty, and swallowed a gulp of stale air.

Why are you telling me this? she said.

I don't know . . . Maybe I need to feel some form of moral redemption. I paused. It's just so claustrophobic in here, isn't it?

She blinked a few times. I think you should leave us alone now.

Desperate, I reached out for little Baxter's hand. You don't understand, I pleaded. I'm not going to tell him anything . . .

She pulled little Baxter's hand away from me. Please, leave us alone.

I worked on autopilot, pulling open drawers and retrieving medication: 75mg of venlafaxine for depression and 2mg of diazepam. My eyes glazed over as I double-checked them with the patient's drug chart. I passed the tablets through but my patient was theatrical in her swallowing, and when she opened her mouth for inspection I could see a tinge of white poking out from under her tongue.

Look, either swallow the diazepam or spit it out, I said. Stop wasting my time.

She swallowed again and this time I saw nothing so nodded, already turning away and disowning her. I'd hated supervising drug addicts in my previous life – with methadone it was usually a quick transaction but sometimes it would be these buprenorphine tablets that stank of lemon and had to be dissolved under the tongue. It took five to ten minutes for them to fully dissolve and there was something unnatural about having to spend that intimate amount of time with a stranger, cramped in a consultation room, nothing but silence or awkward conversation to carry us through. Once, one of them told me he was planning to get clean for his son's third birthday. I'd nodded, a vacant smile settling on my lips, before turning to look at the patient information leaflets stacked in plastic holders – one explained how naloxone injections saved lives by reversing a potential overdose – an opioid user's best friend. A few days later this same patient was back to get sterile needles, water ampoules and sachets of citric acid. After a while it didn't matter to me if he let his tablets dissolve. I wasn't his mother. But I did wonder how old his son would have been now, if he had lived.

Levitt was watching me, resting her elbows on the counter and cupping her face in her hands. What are they trying to do with the tablets if they don't swallow them?

Pass it on to someone else, trade it . . . Maybe they want to save their tablets up for an overdose.

So those tablets you were dispensing for the leader, they're, like, serious, then . . . ?

Why are you asking?

She shrugged. I don't know, I'm just curious. I mean, I don't know about your side of the bunker but I get the impression his popularity is dwindling . . .

I stopped. What makes you say that?

She crossed her arms under her chest and I thought I could see the small bulge of the baby. It was probably nothing; my imagination getting the better of me.

My dad . . . She shrugged. I've heard him say a few things.

Like what? Asking her was like a reflex, instinctual. But I realised that I didn't want to know; didn't want to hear words that could be used against me.

People are disgruntled. Can't you feel it?

But I couldn't feel it. At times it seemed as if I lived in a different bunker from everyone else. What do *you* feel? I asked.

She hesitated. Listen, it's nothing. We all like to moan and pass judgement, don't we? Being a leader in these circumstances can't be an easy job for anyone, especially if you're ill.

Still, I said. Leadership only works if there's trust . . .

Levitt stared at me, her eyes narrowed. It was as though she was sizing me up, gauging where my loyalties lay through clipped comments and cryptic expressions. And it saddened me to see her looking at me in this way, and that I couldn't be honest with her.

Another patient came towards us. Levitt dealt with her request, retrieving the drug chart, popping tablets and showing them to me, but I couldn't concentrate. Who was this man we had chosen to be our country's ruler? I thought about his varied slogans and soundbites before he won his election – it was so easy to attach yourself to the vagueness of words, constantly rearranged to portray a different meaning.

I watched Levitt plonk herself down in her seat, while the patient left.

Have you taken the vitamins and folic acid tablets I left out for you?

Yes.

And you feel OK?

Stop making a fuss. Stop trying to be a good pharmacist.

Levitt pulled off her gym shoes and laid them on the dispensary floor, inspecting her feet. Do they look swollen to you? she asked.

I stared at them, comparing them to my own. No, not especially.

She bent to slip her shoes back on, and when she sat up she squirmed a little as though she'd been stung.

Are you sure you're OK?

It's kicking, she said. The kicks are strong now.

Can I feel?

She hesitated, looking out across the shop floor. Fine, but put a blanket over your hand in case anyone comes in.

I pulled my blanket off the counter and she draped it over her torso and legs. I slipped my hand underneath the fabric and she clasped it, guiding it across her boiler suit. She tapped her fingers into her stomach and quietly, almost inaudibly, said, Baby. Come on, baby. And then there was this jolt – a foot or an arm or something – but it kicked out and caught my breath. The little body kicked out again, stretching in such tight confinement, and it was the loveliest feeling in the world.

Do you think it's a boy or girl? I whispered, still tapping a rhythm off her stomach.

She paused. A girl, but I guess that's only because that's what I know. She shrugged. I try not to think about it, to be honest . . . Focus on getting it out of my body. She tilted her head to one side. People have been doing this for thousands of years. So it can't be that bad, right?

A lack of medical intervention could be a good thing, I said. We're letting things take their natural course.

But what if it never wants to come out? Do you think they can overcook?

Nah, I said. Although I did once read somewhere that there was a tribal woman in Africa who had a pregnancy documented as lasting over four hundred days.

She started to laugh before suddenly falling quiet. Women *do* die during childbirth. I think about that a lot. She paused. Is it OK to say that I'm scared?

You're young. You're probably at the optimal age for doing this.

How will it all work? she said. Even if by some miracle it arrives safely, how will it survive in here?

We'll figure it out.

Babies need nappies and clothes . . . she whispered.

Jesus was born in a stable. I doubt they had nappies or clothes then.

Do you want kids at some point? she asked.

I paused. I would love to have kids.

I think you'll make a great mum, she said. Better than me.

And I had no idea what I was meant to say. I supposed part of me believed it. What I would have given, then, to be able to feel the growth of a baby inside my own stomach. Suddenly the loud beeping from the speaker system began to ring out, forcing me from my thoughts and towards the boundary line.

Canavan's legs were dangling off the side of his bunk. He was sucking on a pouch and staring at me the same way I imagined a baby would stare when drinking a bottle of milk – dedicated to the job, but interested in the surrounding environment. He pulled the pouch away from his lips and there was a puckering sound, as though something had popped.

Where have you been? he said.

Is that any way to greet me after a long day at the office?

He climbed down, landing straight and overshadowing me. He looked around before speaking. I'm hearing rumours about you harassing advisors' wives in the dining hall. Tell me that's not true.

I focused on the bushy chest hair poking up around his neckline. I was trying to help her, I said. Warn her.

Warn her of what? He gripped my shoulder and brought his mouth close to my ear. You look after yourself, Wolfe – that's it. You're not going to get a medal from anyone for being brave and speaking up.

But . . . he doesn't care about us. Any of us.

No shit.

Someone he told me to monitor went missing . . . I caused that. I made that happen. So I can't have that happen again, not to little Baxter. He needs his parents.

He was quiet for a moment. Maxwell, he said. Is that who you're talking about?

My chest tightened. How do you know his name?

Maybe we should go for a walk, he said, trying to take hold of my arm.

No, I said loudly, pulling away from him. I'm tired. I'm not going anywhere.

Please, Wolfe, he said, a pleading, woeful expression settling on his face. I just want you to understand . . .

Understand what? I demanded.

It was me, OK? he spat. I was the one who took care of him.

I stared at him, my eyes wide. He's dead . . . Is that what you're telling me?

He brought his huge arms up and slowly wrapped them around my shoulders and I didn't protest. Please don't be upset with me, he whispered. I don't think I could bear that. I had no choice . . . And honestly, he was marked regardless, so I don't think you should feel responsible . . .

Why? I whispered. He has all the soldiers he needs; why not get them to carry out his dirty work?

Don't you see? The soldiers keep an eye on him as much as they do on us. It's a fine balance, an ecosystem. We're all doing a little dance.

I closed my eyes, focused on his embrace, wishing for it to be tighter. It's too much, I said. Now I know he's dead, there's no hiding from this any more.

I'm so sorry, Wolfe, he whispered, his voice like a rush of wind in my ear. I'll figure something out. I'll find a way to make things better.

In the blue tinge of the night-lights I tiptoed along to the end of my row and turned left. I counted the next seven rows until I thought I'd found the right one. Stirling had mentioned once in passing that he and his parents bunked in Row M, a column number in the fifties. So many times I'd imagined making my way to him in the night, hoping he'd be able to cure me of this strange pressure I felt in my chest. But, as I weaved past bunks, this particular row feeling narrower and more claustrophobic than my own, I began to doubt myself.

Most of the faces I passed were covered with blankets but a few faces slept exposed. There was the sound of deep and heavy sleep, of snoring and turning, and I continued until I was confident I'd identified the right bunk. It was a bottom bunk and the entire body was covered over with blankets, but from the side profile I was convinced it was Stirling. I hadn't quite considered what would happen if I mistakenly picked the wrong person, but my urgency to find him seemed to eclipse all other worries.

I rested my hand on a shoulder. I patted it lightly but the body didn't move. I tapped it again, this time harder, and someone in the bunk above stirred. I held my breath but it came to nothing. I peeled the blanket away from the hidden face to see the hairline and tip of Stirling's ear. My body released whatever breath was still left in it.

I brought my mouth to his ear and whispered his name. His eyelashes fluttered and he tried to roll away from me but I whispered again, this time planting a kiss on his lobe. I couldn't help myself. He opened his eyes slowly and I held my index finger to his lips. He blinked a few more times, appearing confused before he tried to sit up.

Can you come with me? I mouthed.

He slowly pulled back the blankets and placed his feet on the floor, still dazed. What are you doing here? he whispered.

I gestured with my hand for him to follow. Once we'd reached the safety of open space he gripped me by my wrist. Do you know how dangerous it is to be wandering around bunks in the middle of the night? he said. Something could have happened to you. And I wouldn't have been able to do anything . . . He was running a hand through his dishevelled hair. Seriously, what the fuck were you trying to do?

I pulled my wrist away from his grip and took a step back. I didn't know how else to reach you. You're never in your surgery. Did you swap your shifts?

Yes, he whispered.

Why?

He looked up at the ceiling before responding. I . . . I just thought we needed to give each other some distance. He brought his chin down and stared at me. He looked defeated in a way I hadn't seen before. I'll prescribe his drugs, I'll do that if I have to, but I just don't think I can handle the idea of him having you too.

Stirling, I've not been with our leader . . .

He shook his head, breathing heavily. Suddenly he was brushing tears away with his hand. He tried to turn away but I grabbed him, finding his neck and planting a kiss on a soft piece of skin.

I'm fine, he said. It's stupid. It's nothing.

I'm not worth getting upset over, I said trying to laugh.

He stared at me. Stop doing that.

Doing what?

Making out you're not good enough.

I shrugged. But maybe I'm not.

We'd come to a stop outside the doors to the female washroom. Stirling looked both ways before entering and I stood perplexed for a moment before following him in. He was walking past the cubicles, checking to see if they were empty.

What are you doing? I said. Don't you know what would happen if you were caught in here? I turned myself around in a circle before saying aloud, Is there anyone in here? Dr Stirling has just entered by mistake.

There's no one here, he said, walking back past the cubicles to meet me. We're alone.

I turned and stared at my wobbled reflection in the metallic mirrors. I saw nothing attractive about the woman who looked back. The grey in my hair had run wild. Stirling was going grey too but it was distinguished, a colouring that made him look as if he had life experience. The stubble that rooted through his cheeks and chin was short and attractive. I could imagine him in years to come being the handsome and successful father who waited to collect his kids from the school gates. It was as though I could only measure the success of a person by the way they would be perceived with children.

He came and stood next to me. Do you think much about being outside?

Yes, all the time.

What do you want when you leave?

A cottage with a wood-burning stove in the middle of nowhere.

That sounds lonely, he said.

Do you actually think we'll get out of here?

Yeah, I do, he said.

I ran my hand along my upper arm, my fingers landing on the tiny bulge in my skin where the contraceptive implant was buried. I squeezed it a little.

I can't have children, I said. The words seemed to linger in the air. So . . . really, I'm no use to anyone when we do get out of this place.

What are you talking about?

Once we're outside we'll be expected to breed like dogs. That's what Baxter's wife told me, anyway – we'll be paired up if we're not already married and used to populate once we're out of this hellhole . . .

Wolfe, he said, I already knew you couldn't have kids. I don't care about that.

His words stunned me and I stared at him, mouth open. How did you know?

He cleared his throat. Come and stand in the shower cubicle with me. I don't want to risk anyone coming in. He took my hand and we walked to the furthest cubicle from the door. I stepped in first and he closed the curtain behind us. He looked at me, hesitating before opening his mouth.

When we were still working in the military base, an officer called Holden came to my clinic and asked me to alter a staff member's medical history.

Holden came to you? About me?

He knew my father, so maybe that's why he came to me. Stirling looked down at the shower tray. He threw your file down on to my desk and asked me to remove any mention of infertility.

I let out a shriek of almost hysterical laughter and then tried to claw it back into my mouth. After a moment I said, Did he tell you about us, Holden and me?

No, but . . . he wasn't asking favours for anyone else.

I'm not proud of what happened. There's nothing between us now—

Stirling held up his hand. I did it. I altered the information and signed it off. He paused. I knew if I didn't they'd pick someone else to take your place. He met my eye. You wouldn't be here if it weren't for Holden.

I tapped my fingers on one of the cold white tiles, its grouting black with mould. The irony being that I can hardly bear it here, I said.

Yet you stay, he replied.

What did Holden offer you in return?

I took nothing from him. He shrugged. You and I, we were friends. I didn't want to see you left behind either.

I wrapped my arms around him. I don't want Holden, I said. I need you to know that.

He was nodding, but he'd shifted his gaze back to the shower tray.

Will you sleep with me? I said.

He said nothing.

I can't have children and you don't care and I want to be with you.

He still didn't move.

Did you hear me? I said.

Yes, he replied. I heard you.

Do you want to be with me?

He paused. Yes, I want to be with you.

I kissed him and he hesitated before kissing me back. My hands gripped his neck and I realised just how terrified I was of losing him. I couldn't imagine not being able to see him. I grew frantic, gripping his boiler suit, pulling at the Velcro, running my hand in through a gap and across his chest.

Take off your suit, he said.

We'll be cold.

Turn on the shower.

We threw our suits over the bar holding the shower curtain up, our skin already goosebumping from the cold. I turned the water on and it was surprisingly hot, almost scalding. Stirling centred me right under the showerhead and kissed me everywhere. I was crying but the water washed the tears away. When we were ready he pressed me up against the wall and my legs wrapped around his torso. He was gentle but not too gentle, and everything about him was instinctive. He seemed to understand that I didn't want eye contact then and I must have been panting because he whispered for me to be quiet. We rocked backwards and forwards, our bodies locked together, and I could have stayed like that forever with the warm water falling.

When it was over he tried to pull away but I held on to him and he let out a small laugh, right into my ear. He kissed me and we parted, curling up naked together on the shower tray. His arms stayed wrapped around me and periodically he'd plant a kiss on my cheek or forehead.

Do you think there will still be hair dye outside? I said.

Stirling touched one of the white streaks in my hair. I like it. Bride of Frankenstein, he said, and I playfully swiped his hand away.

We'll have to go soon, I said. It's nearly a new day.

I know.

I glanced down and noticed these strange little hairs gathered around my nipples.

I felt Levitt's baby kick, I said. A little foot or an arm. It kicked right under my hand.

He half-smiled. That's nice, he said. Really nice.

What do you think it'll be like?

He hesitated before speaking. Wolfe, this isn't your baby, he said gently. You understand that, right?

Yes, I whispered. I understand that.

OK, good. He got to his feet and, shivering, pulled our boiler suits down, his mind clearly already somewhere else. And I knew I'd lost him then; this thing that was only ours, that couldn't last forever, was now over.

He handed me my suit, already stepping into the legs of his. He dressed quickly and as I struggled with my damp body to get into my own suit I felt vulnerable, with him now clearly seeing what this place had done to me – the thick growth of my body hair, the unhealthy pigmentation of my skin deprived of sunlight. I was too pale; sickly-looking.

We turned towards the door and I reached for the handle.

Take a look outside and see if anyone's coming, Stirling said.

I peered out but the coast was clear, hardly a soul up yet. It's safe, I said.

He kissed me quickly and made to turn the handle.

You won't leave me, will you? I said.

I won't leave you, he replied. I promise.

And then he was gone.

# 13

Floyd, ID number 1882, was waiting patiently for me to dispense his cholesterol medication. There was something rewarding about removing the 40mg simvastatin tablets from their blister strips – maybe it was the way they popped open without any resistance, me not having to pierce the foil with my fingernails. Looking down, my nails were not in great shape: short stumps from an acquired biting habit and milk spots like little dents calling out for zinc and calcium.

Before coming into the bunker I'd had my nails manicured and painted red. I wasn't in the habit of getting my nails done but I'd passed a salon that sat empty, the beauticians looking bored behind their counters, and on a whim decided to go inside. They had assured me that the gel polish they'd used would last at least three weeks. And I remembered then those first few days of uncertainty in my new contained home, my boiler suit still creased from its packaging, the severity of the situation like radioactive ash, slowly beginning to settle. I'd looked down at those perfectly manicured nails and begun biting at the polish, peeling it off in flakes, layers of nail coming away with it.

Am I getting my medication some time today? Floyd said, with a cheerful, friendly laugh.

I smiled, trying to laugh too before passing the medicine cup through the hatch. How are you today anyway? I asked.

There was no hidden agenda to my question, only that I wanted to offer genuine kindness, make amends in some small way for my previous betrayal.

Floyd opened his mouth and I half-heartedly peered inside. *Comme ci, comme ça.* So-so, he replied.

I nodded.

You look tired, he said with a quizzical expression. Perhaps when we overthrow our current dictatorship you'll be able to negotiate better working terms. Join a union maybe . . . He smirked then, trying to contain a laugh as he walked away.

And I stood there, staring out after him, completely unsure as to whether he was joking or not.

Wolfe . . . Levitt said, coming to my side. I don't want to bother you and it's probably nothing . . . But I keep leaking.

I turned to look at her. What do you mean, *leaking*? Leaking milk?

No, she whispered. It's like I keep peeing myself except I don't think it's urine. And I swear there are tinges of blood. I'm having to wear pads because my pants are getting soaked right through.

I straightened. How long have you had this?

She hesitated. Since yesterday.

Have you experienced this before?

I don't think so . . . It just doesn't feel the same as anything else.

Levitt, this could be serious, I said. You need to see Stirling.

He said something about a mucus plug . . . Could it be that? This strange sickly fluid, like a tinged saline solution.

Why would you leave it this long to say something? I snapped.

I don't know . . .

But the baby . . . I said, with my voice raised.

Stop shouting at me. She smacked her fist off the counter and then recoiled, curling her hand into her body, hiding it under her armpit. I should have aborted the thing, she whispered, so quietly that I could easily have missed it.

What did you say?

Nothing.

I grabbed her throbbing hand and clamped down on it. I knew I was hurting her. You are going to have this baby and everything will be fine. I pulled her towards the door of the dispensary. Leave your things here, I said. Hopefully we won't be long.

We can't just leave.

But I was already marching to the front door, turning the little sign over to say *We Are Closed*. Hurry up, I shouted, my finger hovering over the scanner to lock the doors.

I bustled her by the elbow down a corridor, taking a sharp left towards the doctors' surgery. You're hurting me, she said.

Come on, I replied, gripping her tighter.

Inside the surgery we had to queue to speak to Appleby.

Good afternoon, Ms Wolfe. To what do I owe this pleasure?

My assistant needs some medical attention. Can we briefly see Dr Stirling? We won't take up much of his time.

She began shaking her head. No, I'm afraid Dr Stirling is fully booked this afternoon. You'll not see him at all today. She looked at Levitt. Are you one of his patients?

Levitt went to speak but I interrupted her. She resides across the boundary line but she works in the pharmacy with me so her medical appointments have been moved here for convenience. Please, it's a matter of urgency. If we could just speak to Stirling . . .

A patient from across the line should be seen by one of their doctors. It's standard procedure.

I swallowed, tried to calm myself.

Levitt, will you take a seat, please, I said. I need to speak with Nurse Appleby.

Levitt hesitated, staring at me before retreating to an empty chair.

There's something about her I feel you ought to know, I whispered.

What?

She has somewhat of a reputation on the other side of the bunker . . . Our leader thought she would benefit from structure and distance.

Appleby stared at me blankly.

Let's say she was rather . . . promiscuous . . .

Excuse me?

When I was provided with her assistance it was under the assurance that she stay under my supervision at all times, I said. She's the cultural advisor's daughter. Allowances have been made for her to attend the doctors' surgery here. Stirling is fully aware of this.

Appleby's eyes seemed to burn through me. I'd never been a good liar. She tilted her head, looking past me at Levitt, who sat slumped in a chair.

Since she is part of the healthcare team, I could squeeze her in with Dr Shaffer, who will be returning from a bunk visit shortly. He's always happy to accommodate staff.

OK, fine, I said, somewhat defeated, before retreating to where Levitt sat.

What now? she whispered as I stood facing her.

I don't know . . .

Wooden toys were scattered across the floor but there were no children present to play with them. Levitt gripped my sleeve and tugged me to her level.

I can't have him examine me, Wolfe. Please, you have to help me.

Look, you need to calm down. It's not the end of the world . . .

It is for me, she said, with desperation seeping into her voice. You don't understand . . .

I stared at her. I know you're scared of your dad, Levitt, but this isn't normal. The baby's health comes first.

Her breathing was weak and shallow. Please . . .

Calm down, I said. It's not good for you.

Please . . .

The door opened and Dr Shaffer walked in with his medical bag swinging from his side. He nodded in our direction before turning to Appleby. How are we looking? he said.

Another full session. Dr Stirling is struggling with the numbers in his clinic so I may need to transfer more over to you.

He placed his bag on her desk and picked up the clipboard with names written down in red marker. Are these in order? he said.

Appleby nodded.

I crouched down and placed my hands on Levitt's knees. You need to make a scene, I whispered.

What?

You need to take a strong stance, publicly, and express that you do not wish to be examined by this *particular* doctor.

Levitt stared at me, her eyes bulging from their sockets.

And you need to do it now, while there are enough people to witness it.

What do I say?

I closed my eyes. I think you need to make some sexual reference – something to suggest he perhaps . . . might not be . . . Shit. I don't know.

Levitt took a few deep breaths and got to her feet. I should have grabbed her then and held her back. I knew I was taking something away from the victims who had actually been abused, but I could see no alternative.

Excuse me, Levitt said.

Is there something I can help you with? Dr Shaffer replied.

Levitt kept her focus on Appleby. Is this the doctor who is scheduled to carry out my medical?

My eyes shifted. Everyone sitting in the waiting room was listening – I could tell from the stillness.

It is, said Appleby.

Levitt started to frantically shake her head. No, it needs to be someone else. I can't have this man touching me again.

Excuse me? Dr Shaffer said.

Please, I can't, Levitt said with real conviction in her voice. Not this man.

Dr Shaffer turned to Appleby with his palms resting upwards. I don't know this girl, he said. What is she talking about?

I remember you from the other side. You've been over to give us medicals before . . .

Dr Shaffer was turning around now to look at the patients sitting in a line. It was as if we were his jury. I've never done that, he said, almost shouting.

The door to Stirling's surgery opened and he stepped out, bidding his patient farewell. What's going on? he said, looking from Dr Shaffer to Levitt.

I won't have this man examine me. He makes me uncomfortable. And as she spoke I suspected she wasn't too far from tears.

Stirling came to where Appleby and Dr Shaffer were standing. Whispers were exchanged and my shoulders relaxed because I knew already that it had worked.

Stirling turned to Levitt. Do you have a chaperone?

She nodded, pointing to me.

Would it be agreeable if I examined you with your chaperone present? He spoke calmly, the way he would perhaps speak to a child.

Levitt fell quiet. Yes, I suppose that would be OK.

Dr Shaffer cupped his hand over his mouth and I rushed past, entering the surgery with Levitt in tow.

Stirling remained calm, gently closing the door over.

What have you done? he whispered, turning to face us. I tried to rest my hand on his arm but he pulled away. No, this isn't how it goes . . . He was breathing through his mouth, his body tensing with anger.

I'm sorry, I pleaded, the fear of losing him strong. We didn't know what else to do.

Have you any idea? We can't carry on like this . . . I mean, fuck.

I can fix it, I said. It'll be OK.

He slumped into his chair. I get that you're scared, but accusing one of the doctors . . .

That nurse wouldn't let up, Levitt whispered.

Look, this is important, I said. She's leaking fluid. She has to wear pads but they're being saturated.

Stirling rubbed at the fresh stubble on his cheeks. I'll need to check the pad, then, he said not looking at either of us.

Levitt unzipped her suit. The pull of the pad's adhesive as she separated it from her underwear made a strange ripping noise. For some reason she handed the pad to me rather than Stirling. I turned to him but he only glanced at it, not wanting to take it from me. Are you experiencing any other symptoms? he said to Levitt.

No. I don't think so.

And you're still getting movement?

She nodded.

Well, you're not in labour, he said. But I think you might be leaking amniotic fluid.

What?

Do you mind if I feel your stomach? he said, pointing to the examination bed.

I placed the pad on the floor beside my feet, having no desire to touch it any longer.

Stirling planted his hands on her stomach and moved them around, pressing his fingers into her skin. I suspect your stomach is smaller . . . Which makes sense.

Is the baby OK? I whispered but they both ignored me.

Levitt, listen to me. This is really important. I can't be sure, but I think that you have a small tear in your amniotic sac, and the fluid that surrounds your baby is gradually leaking out. It can happen but it's not ideal. Wolfe is going to give you antibiotics every day that will reduce your and the baby's risk of infection. Drink lots of water. You need to try to replenish the fluid you're losing. And don't move much – take it really, really easy.

What about the baby? I demanded. How can we be sure it'll be OK?

Stirling looked at me. We can't be sure. We need to just hope, and assume that the baby is nearing its full term . . .

The baby has to be OK, I said.

Levitt sat up, quickly sticking the Velcro of her suit back together. We should go, before we cause any more trouble. She stopped then, her hand gripping the handle of the door. Stirling, I'm really sorry . . .

He shook his head and I made to follow her out. Wolfe, can you stay behind a moment?

I watched Levitt leave while relief washed through my body. I'm sorry we put you in this position, I said. I'll make it right, I'll fix whatever damage this has caused.

And how are you going to do that?

I don't know yet . . .

He exhaled, opening the top drawer of his desk. I've got a repeat prescription request for you.

I grew nauseous. Already?

He handed me the prescription. His handwriting was lovely for a doctor, my own handwriting childish and unsophisticated in comparison. Oxycodone was at the top in an increased strength of 60mg, and a stomach capsule was thrown in for good measure.

Alone in the boardroom, I stared at what must have been Canavan's new artwork hanging on the walls. In a large frame a nurse wore a traditional white pinafore and tricorn hat. She had this half-smile and was holding a syringe that squirted purple liquid into the air.

The table was empty with only a couple of folded paper napkins sitting in the centre. I pulled back one of the heavy chairs and settled into it. My feet dangled a few inches off the ground, bobbing slightly with the movement of the chair. I placed the new boxes of medication on the table, running my hands along the Braille. We'd been taught never to cover the Braille with our dispensing labels, drummed into us the same way that we were never to put a label on a box of cream, always the tube. It seemed so redundant now: the disabled access, the elderly scribbling their signatures on the backs of their prescriptions, administering the flu vaccines for winter, persuading people to stop smoking and offering them nicotine-replacement therapy.

I wasn't sure how long I'd been left alone. Eventually a side door opened and ND strolled through wearing a tailored suit, looking thinner than usual. He'd buttoned the blazer, a gold button glinting where his belly button probably sat, and in his hand he balanced a china cup and saucer. He pulled a chair back beside me and plonked himself down, the chair sagging slightly.

He gathered the medication without comment and opened the oxycodone as if he wanted to be sure I wasn't trying to short-change him. Anything new to report, Ms Wolfe? He spoke with agitation, me a thorn in his side.

Nothing of any significance, I replied stiffly, not meeting his eye. They come for their medication, they go. There's really nothing suspicious to note. I wouldn't worry if I were you.

He brought the china cup to his lips, placing the saucer down on the table. A biscotti biscuit still in its wrapper tumbled off the side. You're not me, though, are you?

I reached over, my fingers attempting to touch the biscuit, but he slapped them away. Do you think you deserve that?

I haven't done anything.

Precisely. He rolled his head back and let it hang over the

back of his chair. You and I had an understanding, he said. Who do you think you're protecting exactly?

I exhaled. Baxter's wife aborted her unborn child to be here . . . You don't do that if you don't believe in the cause.

So you're using your own judgement now? How about you just tell me what you see and hear and I'll decide who's still a believer in this leadership.

I see your oxycodone dose has gone up, I said. That back pain must be really troubling . . .

What are you implying?

I shrugged. What are you going to do when it all runs out? At the rate you're churning through them we won't have much left.

He tilted his head, inspecting me closely. What do you think it's like for the few who enter the airlock chambers still alive? he said. How long do you think it takes before they join the dead? They can't open the external doors even if they want to, so do they just wait for starvation, or do they actively try to hasten the process?

I pushed my chair back and rose to my feet, making it to the end of the table before he smacked his fist off the surface. I did not say you could leave, he shouted. You leave only when I say you can leave.

I stopped, taking in short, sharp breaths.

Sit down.

No.

Sit down, he said. I won't tell you again.

Slowly, I returned to my seat. I clasped my hands together to stop the shaking and hid them under the table.

The worst thing you can do in here is care about others, he replied. Suddenly you're invested. He paused. That might be the best piece of advice I ever give you.

I have no family here.

He took the biscotti and threw it to me, it landing in front of me. Don't be so naïve. You think I don't know what sort of trouble you get up to?

I focused on the biscuit, which felt like the safest place to cast my gaze.

Oh, for God's sake, will you just take it? I doubt I'll get your concentration otherwise.

I was pathetic enough to already be pulling open the wrapper. I bit off a corner of the hard little biscuit. It was the same biscuits they used to give me in the hairdresser's. I let the small bite sit on my tongue, my saliva beginning to tingle with the sugar. It was laced with almond and, before I was even aware of it, the entire biscuit was in my mouth, its oval shape touching the back of my throat, and I was aware of the noise my teeth made as they crunched down, the crevices in my molars collecting the crumbs.

I'm going to ask that you prove your loyalty to me, he said. It's the only way I see us going forward.

I hated that phrase: *going forward*. I tried to chew away the biscotti. My mouth was dry and I struggled to clear the roof of my palate.

Going forward ... I said. I don't think there's anywhere else for me to go.

Ignoring me, he said, There is a patient in your care. I need you to administer something to him.

His words were slow to seep in, my mind running over them like a tongue running over teeth. I found myself laughing, this hysterical maddening laughter.

Obviously I can't do that, I said.

He smiled. Let's say there's human error – that exists, doesn't it?

Well, yes, I said. There will always be an element of human error.

So it wouldn't be impossible for, say, this man to accidentally receive the wrong type of medication, would it?

Another wave of nausea pushed up into my throat and I swallowed it down. No, I whispered. I suppose it could happen.

There, that wasn't so hard, was it? He stretched his shoulders back and relaxed into the leather of his seat, the fabric squelching. He reached into the chest pocket of his blazer and removed a single passport photograph, before using his finger to slide it along the table towards me. I stared at it. Go ahead, he said. Pick it up.

I pinched the edge of the photo with my thumb and index finger. Somewhere I still held the knowledge that it was the only correct way to hold a photograph, always by the edges. At first I didn't recognise the man staring back – a photo from his previous life: a military uniform with medals, clean-shaven face, the mouth showing no expression but the eyes wanting to smile. Slowly recognition seeped in – one of the first to arrive for his medicine, hardly missing a dose, always polite, leaving with a sad smile as though he was personally apologising for something outside his control. Glass, I said. His name is Glass. ND was nodding and my mind was already running over his medication. I could see the colours of the tablets in the plastic cup I'd pass through to him.

I turned the passport photo over to see the name *Glass* confirmed in ink along with his ID number. The ballpoint of the pen had ebbed its way into the composition of the photographic paper.

Why him? I said.

Why not him?

Is he important?

ND seemed to contemplate my question before speaking. When we suffer from cancer we always try our best to remove it, don't we? He paused, placing a hand on the knot of his tie. Cancer always starts from the inside, defying its host.

I dropped the photograph on to the desk and it landed face-up but upside-down. Glass's eyes stared back at me – the eyes of a kind man – eyes you'd expect a grandfather to have.

I rubbed my mouth and then my cheeks. There was that familiar sensation of feeling like it was all inevitable, that fighting would be futile.

How do you want me to do it? I said.

I'm leaving that in your capable hands, he replied. You're the pharmacist, after all.

But do it to what end?

To *the* end.

Does he have a family?

If I say no, will that make it easier?

He got out of his seat and hovered over me. He carried an odour of bleach. Maybe I should have been reassured by the knowledge that he was clean, but I found more comfort in my own stench.

He placed his hands on my shoulders and started rubbing them, rolling his fingers over the fabric of my boiler suit. You know, you could have a lovely life. His lips were close to my ear and the fine hairs on my skin stood to attention. I did everything I could to stop myself from shuddering. There's plenty of space in my quarters, he said, rubbing his nose in my hair before planting a kiss on the crown of my head.

He stood straight and I could feel him smiling behind me; could visualise the curl of his mouth and the creases around his eyes. Don't let us down, he said before spinning me around in my chair. We're relying on you.

# 14

I arranged to meet Stirling in the recreation room. The sofa he'd chosen had space for two and faced a coffee table that was de-laminating at the corners. Old lifestyle magazines were spread across it and someone must have spilled water because the horoscope page was now stuck to its surface. Before sitting down I glanced at it, inspecting my own horoscope. I held no belief in astrology but couldn't help but be curious. It said I was likely to experience some surprising but pleasant news, and that I might even meet a potential significant other and not to immediately dismiss their arrival. The magazine could have been ten years old.

I sank into the sofa cushions and our legs touched. He nudged me but his gaze was focused straight ahead. We hadn't discussed the six-year age gap and I wondered if it was something he considered. It seemed like a significant amount of time. I had dated a younger man once before – him nineteen and me twenty-four – but from its inception I'd known it was a wasted exercise. We lived in different cities and he usually came to stay with me, but one weekend I agreed to travel to his university halls. Everything smelled damp and his roommates shared a jug of water rather than pouring themselves a glass. I couldn't shake off this feeling, as though he was role-playing someone he thought he'd be when he was older.

I turned to stare at Stirling for longer than was probably natural.

I never see you with your family, I said. Why is that?

He shrugged. I have no one but my parents here. And we're not exactly close.

I sank a little further into the sofa. Do you think if we were in the real world you'd tell them about me?

What?

Would you bring me home to meet the family?

Why are you asking that?

Because a divorced infertile pharmacist six years your senior can't exactly have been your particular dating preference.

I didn't come here to fight with you, he said, with a wounded tone to his voice that made me hate myself.

I'm sorry. I don't know what's wrong with me, I whispered.

Has something happened, Wolfe? Has *he* done or said something to upset you?

I sat perfectly still just looking out ahead of me.

You would tell me, wouldn't you?

I said nothing; couldn't find the words to explain any of it.

I hate this, he said. I hate that he can essentially do whatever he wants and we've no choice in the matter.

Can we talk about something else, please?

He grew quiet before asking: How's Levitt?

I think she's OK.

The leaking hasn't got any worse, has it?

I shook my head.

A group of people were standing with their backs to us and as they parted I saw Glass sitting in an armchair not too far away. He glanced up and met my eye. He looked like someone I could trust; if I were lost I would have asked him for directions.

The people who surrounded him were laughing and I sat up, desperate to see what held their attention. The laughing intensified and I realised the Twister mat had been pulled out. A girl of maybe seven or eight placed her right foot on a red spot and the other foot was stretched out across the mat to a green one. A man, maybe her father, was hunkered down beside her, wobbling with one foot dangling in the air. A woman was smiling, inspecting them from a standing position, while Glass held the spinning board. His index finger flicked the pointer and it spun into action, commanding them to make their next move. Their laughs continued but there was no laughter from him; he seemed to take his role somewhat seriously. But as I stared on I saw his eyes were giving him away, showcasing his enjoyment. It dawned on me that he was in the company of his family. And I started thinking about my own family: my niece and her painting easel, and my brother with his generous smile, the grey eyes and long eyelashes.

Wolfe, what's wrong? Stirling said. Please tell me what's wrong.

I was crying. I had no control over it.

I don't think I'm well, I said.

He turned in his seat towards me, hesitating for a moment before reaching over and gently wiping my tears away. His touch was so tender, so genuine that it only encouraged the tears. Cupping my face with his hands, he kissed me on the cheek. It's going to be OK, he whispered. Everything's going to be OK. He faced forward then, clasping my palm, practically forcing our hands down between the cushions of the sofa and out of sight.

People stopped to watch the game of Twister happening beside us. I brought my feet up on to the sofa and hugged my shins. I could sense their bodies getting closer, suffocating me. Maybe at any moment a bomb would go off and turn us into fragments of our former selves.

Stirling was now focused on the game too but I'd lost all interest, feeling the need to rebel against the crowd. Why should these people be given a moment of collective enjoyment? I started flicking through one of the magazines, turning the pages with real aggression. There had always been so many magazines in pharmacy staff rooms. A twenty-minute lunch break in a nine-hour shift and I'd try to switch off with trivial stories – *my stepfather killed my mother*, or *my former pupil and our love child*. I stopped at an article in the magazine and stared down, bringing the picture close to my face. It was about hoarding and ways to encourage hoarders to break their habits. It seemed like such a strange concept – that people used to own more than a handful of things, filling houses and garages – paying to store possessions in industrial units because there was no room left in their own homes. I turned the page and there was a promotion for a cross-stich magazine. Buy the first issue and you'd get a free sample and pattern. I turned to the front cover and inspected the date of publication. I couldn't quite believe that people paid money for cross-stitch magazines. It might have been something my grandmother would have done, but even then I wasn't sure. The needle would have been nice to hold, though. I tapped my index finger against my thumb, really trying to imagine the prick.

There was a surge of noise and then a cloud of sighing. I looked up to see the people previously balanced on the Twister mat huddled on the floor. Some of the waiting crowd moved forward, claiming spots on the mat for their turn, the mood suddenly a little sour. I began to relax, as though everything was now as it should be, and brought my attention back to the magazine, flicking towards the back in search of another horoscope. And as I flicked through, I was thinking about the old *Pharmaceutical Journal* I used to receive in the post. It was full of articles about the future of pharmacy, with people showcasing too many teeth in their smiles. But I was only ever interested in the back pages – the section where it described in detail who had most recently been struck off the practising register. They always named the pharmacist and described their conviction. There was the man who was selling Viagra to his friends on the golf course, or the woman caught dispensing antibiotics freely to patients. Then there were the serious ones – where human error played a part and a death had occurred. A shiver would crawl up my spine – those were the ones that made it into the national newspapers, where court cases could be followed. And the pharmacist had to live with the fact that someone had died because of them.

I looked up to see Glass turning the spinner of the Twister board once again. Perhaps it was possible to trick yourself into thinking a mistake had been made. An accident. I turned over another page of the magazine. What were the most common errors? Was it giving beta-blockers like propranolol instead of steroids like prednisolone because they sat close together on the shelves? I turned another page. My thoughts moved quickly. I vaguely remembered there being an incident where an oral diabetic drug was dispensed to a patient who wasn't diabetic, and it took its effect gradually, until the patient fell into a hypoglycaemic coma before eventual death. And I was sorry for the pharmacist, only because I knew it could have happened to any of us – it could have happened to me. Because sometimes the environment you were thrown into was so questionable you felt as if anything could happen. Like when you did a locum shift in a large chain supermarket and the staff shortages were so bad that there was no one there to open the pharmacy department, apart from yourself. But you didn't know how to even get the keys so you'd circle the shop floor looking for a store manager, and tell him that there were no staff in the pharmacy. And he'd act oblivious before pulling someone from the fish counter to man the entire pharmacy with you. And you didn't know how things worked or where things were kept and the lady from the fish counter only shrugged. And you knew deep in your bones that when anyone was pushed to their limit anything was possible.

I came to and Stirling was staring at me. I'm worried about you, he said.

I'll be OK.

But the seed was planted. Glass's medication was churning through my mind again. It would be easy to swap a white diuretic water tablet for a white diabetic tablet of exactly the same size. But was it something I was capable of?

The Foers were sitting together on the bottom bunk. He offered me a polite nod but she smiled, and as I climbed I could feel her eyes following me, trying to signal some sort of secret message. Canavan's arm dangled over the side of his bunk but he didn't raise his head and I let him be. I lay flat and closed my eyes but the bunks were swaying with movement. When I opened my eyes I was expecting to see Canavan's face staring back but instead it was Mrs Foer.

Her head bobbed up and down as she struggled to keep her balance. Wolfe, she whispered. How are you this evening?

I'm OK.

You look a little grey.

I never got a chance to get my food pouches today, I said.

Oh, no, that won't do. That won't do at all, she replied before scurrying away. I heard her returning and when she reached me she planted a sealed pouch of puréed blueberries on to my blanket. You are not moving until you've consumed that entire pouch.

No, Mrs Foer, I can't take that. It's yours.

It doesn't matter – with your type of job you need to keep your strength and concentration up.

Honestly, I can't take it.

She picked up the pouch and waited for me to take it from her. Just suck it, she said. I'm not leaving you alone until I know you've eaten at least some of it.

I reached out and took it from her. Why do you care? I said, my voice thin and fragile.

This strange, perhaps injured look crossed her face. We are all we have now. There's no one else left.

I broke the seal and the lid fell, rolling across my blanket. She continued to watch and as I brought the pouch to my mouth I wondered if this was what it was like to have an eating disorder – to have someone document what passed between your lips – to have that look of fear and sadness flicker across their eyes, telepathically begging you to make yourself better. The sugar of the pouch hit me first, then the tang of the berries at the back of my throat. I hadn't realised how hungry I was. I devoured the pouch, sucking every morsel from its packaging until it lay flat on my bunk, thin like a wafer.

We're going travelling again tonight, Foer whispered. Are you coming?

I don't think so, I replied with the taste of artificial berries still in my mouth. I'm so tired. I feel sick with tiredness.

You're not looking after yourself.

I'm trying.

Come with us. It'll make you feel better, I promise. You missed the trip to Boston.

Where are you going? I said.

Tonight we can go anywhere you wish. We can go to your favourite place in the whole world and have a wonderful time.

Can we go to Rio? I said.

Brazil?

I nodded.

Well, I've never been . . . But I'd love for you to take me.

I have happy memories of being in Rio, I said.

She placed her hand over mine. We can go to Brazil, but don't fixate too much on old memories. I won't go anywhere I used to visit with my daughter.

When are we going? I said.

Later, when it's quiet. Get some sleep and I'll wake you.

And as if her words were capable of casting some sort of spell over me I began to fall asleep, my heavy eyelids not fighting any more. I dreamt, but of nothing tangible or significant, and when my body was prodded awake I came to asking about a cactus.

How long was I asleep?

About four hours or so, she said. I dithered about waking you actually, but then I thought you might not sleep later if you have too much of it now.

I stretched my arms up past my head and nudged Canavan's bunk but he did not move. I was damp and clammy under my blankets and a shiver travelled down my neck. I thought about just turning over, tucking the blankets in nicely behind my back to stop the heat from escaping, but eventually I sat up. An ulcer tipped my tongue; it had been threatening me for days, finally catching me in my sleep. I ran it against my teeth, biting down on the little piece of flesh that protruded from the rest of my tongue. The taste of blueberries lingered on my chapped lips, having seeped through the cracks. I wanted the blueberries to leave a permanent residue, something I could recall later.

I need to clean my teeth, I said.

You can freshen up with me.

I pulled back my blankets and gathered them in a heap, before making my descent. Watch out for Sleeping Beauty, Foer whispered, smiling over at her husband.

We weaved through our row but I kept glancing back to see Canavan – there were tufts of his shaggy dark hair, his face turned away from the world. But then I thought I saw him sitting up, scratching his head, staring at us.

Hurry, Foer said.

Is Webb coming tonight?

Yes, she said, her face lighting up as she turned to reply.

We stopped at the washroom and entered. Other women stood grooming and cleaning themselves, and there was the sound of showers running behind curtains. I brushed my teeth while Foer went to the toilet. In the mirror I inspected myself, pinching my waist with my hands. I'd been forcing some of my food pouches on to Levitt and I hadn't taken the time until now to really inspect my thinning body. The mass of grey fabric swamped me; I could have done with a belt.

One woman was trying to separate entwined clumps of her hair in the mirror. It looked like dreadlocks and she growled as she pulled, strands of her hair falling into the sink. She stared at them gathering in the basin before turning to me. What was that shampoo – the one that smelled so strongly of apples?

I don't know . . .

Do you think it will still be there when we get out?

I was aware of her stepping closer towards me. She looked me up and down before touching a strand of my hair.

You've got access to shampoo, haven't you?

Sorry?

Your hair is so shiny.

Dark hair seems to look shinier, I said.

Who are you fucking?

What?

Is it him? Is it our leader, or one of his foot soldiers? Are they giving you shampoo? I could feel her breath on my face. I used to fuck him too, but look where that got me once his wife cottoned on. I was a model. Now I clean the fucking toilets.

Foer emerged from her cubicle and rushed to where we were standing, inserting herself between us. Wolfe is our pharmacist and she deserves your respect, she said. Never speak to her like that.

The woman eased off but was still sizing me up, her stare working its way down my body. They used to sell shampoo in pharmacies, she said.

What's your ID number? Foer demanded.

This has nothing to do with you, the woman replied.

What. Is. Your. Number?

Look, it's OK, I said, trying to take Foer by the arm.

No, it's not OK. We're going to sort this out right now.

The woman backed away from us.

Please, Foer, I said, gripping her. Let's just go and forget about it.

Foer paused before opening the door. I followed her out into the corridor, where her shoulders fell into something of a more relaxed state and she smiled at me. I'm sorry about that, I just can't abide disrespect.

It's fine, honestly. But thanks for defending me.

She was still shaking her head.

I didn't . . . you know.

You didn't what?

Sleep with our leader.

OK, dear.

Honestly, I haven't . . .

She smiled a knowing smile, leaving me there to linger for a moment. When she turned back and realised I wasn't behind her, she called out, Come on, dear, we've got an adventure to go on.

Webb was already waiting for us by the travel books and we settled down beside him, the wiry wool of the carpet brushing against the bare skin of my ankles.

What do we think? he said, showcasing the spine of a guidebook to Argentina. I had so much fun that time we went to Chile that I thought we could dip our toes back into South America.

Foer stopped him with a raised hand. Wolfe had the same idea but she was thinking Rio, Brazil.

Rio? He brought his lips together, the bottom lip jutting forward and fleshy. It's a tad glitzy, don't you think?

We don't have to go to Rio, I said.

No, we're going, Foer said. We can go to Argentina another night. She stood up to survey the shelves and collected a Brazilian guidebook. It looked almost identical to the one

Daniel and I had lugged around on our backpacking adventures.

She started flicking through the pages, the paper so thin it was like the Bible. Where would you like to go in Rio?

We should rise early and visit Christ the Redeemer first, then head to Santa Teresa for brunch, I said. Perhaps afterwards, walk the zigzagging pathway from Copacabana beach to Ipanema. Laze on the beach and then catch a cable car up to Sugar Loaf Mountain for sunset. Finally, back to Ipanema for sushi. The details just rolled off my tongue, as though I'd been thinking about them for days. And caipirinhas, I said. We must stop and drink lots of caipirinhas.

Webb was on his feet, looking somewhat energised by my description. Foer passed me the guidebook and I turned the pages of the tracing paper until I found the description of Christ the Redeemer. They stared back at me, beaming with what seemed like real excitement. Suddenly I wanted this day so badly. I had this fear of being stuck otherwise – of circling the bunker and crossing the boundary line again and again but not actually ever getting out. I looked at Webb before shifting my gaze to Foer. Were they already stuck? There would be no guidebooks for outside. What if they'd forgotten how to live outside a bunker? Institutionalised, like prisoners not knowing what to do with themselves once they'd been set free.

We'd better start by crossing the ocean, Webb said, and was already leading us out of the recreation room. Foer followed in his footsteps but I lagged behind. The way they were walking they might as well have been intrepid explorers visiting a continent for the first time. I'd read somewhere that people became truly fearless when they lost their minds. It must be nice, I thought, to feel completely invincible.

We turned corners and strode along the corridors, passing the sleeping quarters, the washrooms, and everything else that felt familiar. As we stepped over the boundary line I took a moment to stop and stare at the yellow industrial paint. It reminded me of the paint my dad had used on the floor of his factory. I think it had been blue paint but still it had that robust, plasticky texture, as if it could endure anything. The paint had cost a fortune and he'd had to persuade his business partner that it was worthwhile – that it would really make the place feel like a proper factory where people would congregate to create something. I rubbed my toe over the yellow paint and not a flake budged. I was smiling, as if I knew something others didn't.

Are you coming? Foer called out. Christ the Redeemer waits for no one.

I nodded, following them. We stood among hundreds of other tourists and raised our hands out to mimic the statue's stance. Webb took our photo and then showed us the image. We ate barbecue at a *pay what it weighs* buffet up in the hills of Santa Teresa and climbed colourful terracotta steps, all the while vigilant for robbers on motorbikes who might hold us up at gunpoint. We waded through the warm waters of Copacabana and then Ipanema beach, stopping to towel off and drink sugary lime- and cachaça-fuelled caipirinhas. And I shielded my eyes from the glinting sun over Sugar Loaf Mountain. The three of us sat in a row with our arms around one another, our legs resting flat, our toes pointing upwards. We stared at the helicopter that was about to land by our feet and we couldn't have been happier.

I let my mind drift towards Daniel, memories that made me smile: of him trying to surf in the crystal waters, hopelessly falling back into the sea. I'd worried about sharks eating him and he'd mimicked a shark and pretended to bite my face. And there was his laugh – that deep chuckle that sourced from somewhere down in his gut. The way he was forever fretting over whether his wedding ring was too loose for his finger; the way he'd pretend to drag me to bed by my foot when I'd ask him to carry me. That he had been incredible with kids and would have made a wonderful father. Maybe he got the chance to make a baby with someone else; or maybe it was something he didn't even want. I wanted to tell him I was sorry, and that I hoped he hadn't been alone at the end.

# 15

I was on all fours, my arms outstretched, trying to remove a box of bisoprolol that had got wedged behind one of the medicine drawers, causing it to jam on its runners.

Levitt, can you pass me something long? I said. My fingers brushed against the box but I couldn't grip it. Levitt, are you listening to me? Try the ruler in my stationery drawer.

I turned awkwardly to look at her and she was standing hunched over, her hands pressing into her back. I'm cramping, she said.

Cramping?

Yeah, like period pain.

I brought my arm out from between the drawers and stood straight. Do you think it's the start of something?

It's not so bad, Levitt whispered. Maybe it's nothing.

When I looked up, Glass was walking through the door towards me.

Hello, I said.

Hello indeed. He tilted his head and said, How are you this morning?

I'm fine, thank you. How about yourself? Already he seemed vulnerable to me despite me having done nothing.

Oh, you know, I suppose I shouldn't complain too much.

I've seen you . . . I said. In the recreation room.

I've seen you too.

223

Is that your family you're with?

Some old, some new.

What does that mean?

We are sociable creatures. We make family when we have none.

How do you do it? I said.

What? Make a family?

No, be happy?

He seemed to think about this before speaking. I'm not. But I appear so for the children, he said. They can't know that the worst of the world is happening. We had our innocence, so let them have theirs.

I let his words filter through me. Who are you? I said. I mean, who were you before here?

Does it matter?

No, I guess not.

I pulled open one of the drawers and popped his orange atenolol beta-blocker into a cup. I moved along to the F–H drawer and stopped. I placed my hand over the box I should have been dispensing from, his furosemide 40mg water tablets, and then glanced at the diabetic 80mg gliclazide tablets. But I couldn't do it. I collected the rectangular furosemide box and popped two tablets out into the same cup along with his atenolol. I passed the cup through to him and he swallowed without even looking at its contents. He showed me the inside of his mouth and I nodded.

He lingered for a moment and I asked, Do you need something else?

It's my tongue. And he poked it out. I've got little ulcers all over the tip, do you see? It feels like I've had them forever.

I've got them too, I said. Would you like something for them? I've got a gel that might help.

He hesitated before shaking his head. What's the point? I suppose they give me something to focus on.

I watched him leave. It wasn't until he was fully out of view that I released the breath I hadn't realised I was holding, my chest tight and uncomfortable. How would I have fared if I'd given him the wrong medication?

Levitt began to pace the floor. Can I have some paracetamol? The cramping's getting worse, she said, placing her hand in between the gaps of her boiler suit.

This could be it, I said, flicking through my calendar, desperately trying to tally up the days and months. A picture of an Airedale terrier stared back at me, his name, *Bob*, in the description below.

Levitt stood there, looking helpless.

Do you want me to go and get anyone from your side of the bunker? I asked.

She shook her head.

I popped two dihydrocodeine tablets out of their packaging instead of paracetamol and handed them to her, pouring her some fresh water into a paper cone.

Thank you, she said. And as she spoke I popped a few more tablets, placing them into the breast pocket of her boiler suit for later, believing that would be enough.

But as the hours passed the pain intensified. Any time Levitt sat down she'd quickly shift again, wanting to be back on her feet. A patient walked in and she turned to face the sink, gripping the counter. It was a woman with a collection of cold sores on her bottom lip. I offered her a pea-sized amount of cream to apply in front of me. You should be applying this five times a day, so return in a few hours, I said before she left.

When I turned back, Levitt looked pale. I've no idea what I'm doing, she said, wincing in pain.

You don't need to know everything, I said. We'll figure it out. My sister-in-law didn't know that you bled afterwards, like you're catching up on all those missed periods.

I didn't know that . . . For how long?

I shrugged. I think she said like six weeks.

What? I'll never be able to get enough sanitary pads for that length of time.

It's OK, calm down . . .

Another patient was walking into the pharmacy and Levitt crouched down on to the ground, out of view. The man gave me his surname, Swan, and ID number. He was asking me something about his stomach capsules but I was struggling to concentrate. I gripped a strip of the omeprazole capsules but there was a foil seal on the back that had to be peeled rather than popped. My hands were shaking a little, and as I pulled the seal my finger slid across the foil's edge, cutting open. It was nothing; a paper cut. But it seemed as though I'd discovered a weapon, and I stared down at the prickle of blood, transfixed.

Is your finger OK? he asked.

Did you see that? I said, looking up at him. I mean, I could have tried that a hundred times over and it would never have cut me . . .

These things happen.

I reached under the counter for a box of plasters. He waited for me to position the plaster on my finger before I attempted again to dispense his stomach capsule.

I passed it through to him and he popped the capsule into his mouth, seeming to chew on it before it made its way down his throat. If there's anything I can do to help, he said, pointing towards Levitt's crouched body, please let me know.

Thanks . . .

I remember my wife . . . It's not easy.

Levitt wouldn't leave my side. She stayed for handover with Valentine and pretended to be inspecting the shop's shelves while we exchanged false pharmacy pleasantries. I ushered her to my bunk and was surprised to find my entire column empty. She couldn't climb, so I had no choice but to settle her on Mr Foer's bed. Her breathing grew shallow, her shoulders tight. She swallowed two more dihydrocodeine tablets without any water. Is there something stronger I can take? she whispered.

Stirling has access to the injections.

She gripped my arm and her nails dug in through the fabric of my suit, burrowing their way into my skin. I'm really scared, she said.

Are you sure you don't want me to find your parents?

She shook her head again.

I would have done anything for her then. I would have taken the pain and harboured it myself if I could. And I wondered if that was what it felt like to be a mother. Even with Daniel I'd put myself first. I doubted I would have died for him. But would I have died for Levitt and her baby? Yes, perhaps I would have. Mum had always said she'd die for me and my brother, but I'd never been able to fully comprehend that.

Maybe it's time to get Stirling, I said.

Don't leave me, she said. I'm on a stranger's bed.

I'll be quick, I promise.

I ran to the main chamber and stared at the clocks. Stirling would have finished his shift, so where would he be? I ran back to the sleeping quarters and weaved down his row but his bunk was empty.

Panicked, I ran back to Levitt. She was lying on her side now, her knees pulled up towards her chest. Where is he?

I can't find him.

You can't find him?

He'll turn up.

I think it's coming, she said. I feel like there's a baby's head between my legs.

Do you want me to have a look?

No, she spat. Do you even know what you're looking for? I want Stirling.

I'll look for him again.

You're not leaving me here, she said, already struggling to her feet. I'll come with you.

Is everything OK, dear? Mrs Foer asked, startling us from behind. She took in Levitt struggling to get off her husband's bed. My goodness, she said. It can't be?

I placed my arm around Levitt. Can you help me get her on to her feet?

Mrs Foer took her other arm and we began to shuffle forward.

Where would you go if you were Stirling? Levitt said.

He likes to read.

It's not far to the recreation room, Foer said, but it seemed to be more to herself than me.

Levitt winced then, bending with the pain. Do they know? she said. Is everyone looking at me?

No one is looking at you, I lied.

I pushed open the door to the recreation room. Inside, there were a handful of people – some were sitting in armchairs, flicking through magazines; a few kids sat on the floor with their legs crossed, playing cards. One man was lying out flat with a book placed over his face. On impulse we directed Levitt through the bookcases towards the travel section.

Webb was already huddled there, a book on Dublin resting over his knees. Are you all coming? he said, not seeming especially surprised to see us there.

No, not this evening, I said, easing Levitt down on to the floor beside him. Have you by any chance seen Dr Stirling?

He shook his head.

I turned to Foer. Can you look after her while I try to find him?

Of course, go.

Levitt had curled back on to her side, her eyes closed in pain. Whatever fluid was left suddenly seeped out on to the carpet and relief momentarily washed over her, but it lasted only seconds before the pain intensified.

I'll be back soon, I said. I promise.

I circled the recreation room but still couldn't find him. I ran back out into the corridors and darted aimlessly. Despite it being hours since he finished his shift it dawned on me that he might have nowhere else to go. I turned and headed for his surgery. One of the back-shift nurses was on and I couldn't remember her name.

I'm looking for Dr Stirling . . .

He's clearing his room for a drop-in clinic tomorrow. Do you need something?

I was already striding towards the door. No, just a moment of his time, I said. A small pharmacy matter. I opened the door gently and smiled at her before closing it behind me.

What's wrong? Stirling asked, standing from his chair with real concern.

It's Levitt. She's having the baby.

Shit. Are you sure?

What do we do?

He gathered his doctor's bag and started throwing things into it erratically – latex gloves, a scalpel, hand soap, a sheet that had perhaps once been white but was now a strange shade of grey. His hands shook as he forced the sheet in, fighting with the fabric, pushing it down. Where is she? he said.

The recreation room.

He started nodding. The recreation room is warm and has softer flooring . . .

He forced his bag shut and made to leave.

She's in a lot of pain. Is there something we can give her?

He fumbled, his fingers hitting numbers and unlocking the safe above the sink. Inside, he grabbed a vial of morphine and a couple of syringes and needles. OK, he said, we need to go before someone discovers what I've taken.

I led him in between the bookshelves. On seeing Levitt, he crouched down, his face level with hers. How long between contractions? he asked.

Maybe every four minutes or so, I replied. But I can't be sure.

I'll need to examine you, he said, pulling the greyish sheet out from the depths of his bag. Can you lie on your back?

Levitt moved on to her knees and was tugging at the Velcro of her boiler suit. Help her, he urged, and I took the seam from her grip, pulling the strips apart and easing her arms and shoulders out.

Cover yourself with this sheet. His eyes darted across the floor. We need to find something she can lie on . . .

Foer got to her feet. I can get something, she said, running off.

I continued pulling the suit down until it was past her waist; all the while, Stirling stood with the sheet taut between his outstretched arms, shielding us.

Foer returned with her arms full of green paper towels from the washroom, the texture of coarse recycled waste. Will these do? she said.

I was thinking more like blankets but fine. Get them down. And Foer massed them into a circle, their corners flapping as they overlapped. Levitt shuffled over on her knees and then I pulled the rest of her boiler suit off. I took the sheet from Stirling and placed it gently down over her exposed skin.

Wolfe, can you remove her underwear?

I reached under the sheet and came to her waist, hesitating with the elastic. I pulled her underwear down and off, scrunching the fabric in my hand.

Are you OK, Levitt? Stirling said.

Levitt's body tensed. I can't do this, she said.

Keep breathing, you're doing a great job, he said, sounding genuine.

I stood back, confused by what role I was meant to play, watching Stirling place his hands under the sheet.

OK, Stirling said after a moment, getting back on to his feet. I'd say we're at about six centimetres. The baby's head is down but I think it's back-to-back . . .

What does that mean? Levitt said, breathing out a contraction.

It's not the most comfortable way to deliver a baby. But it's not breech, which is good.

Levitt started shuddering in pain. Can you give me something?

Stirling tore open a needle, screwing it on to a syringe. He drew up the liquid from the morphine vial, tapping the chamber with his index finger to remove any air bubbles. Can you turn on to your side? he said, and Levitt struggled but shifted. He pierced her bum with the needle and pressed down on the syringe, the liquid instantly disappearing into her fatty tissue.

The contractions aren't close enough yet and chances are they might slow down again, he said. Please try and rest, even get some sleep. It could still be a while before this baby comes. But you're doing really well. He nodded, but it was as if he was trying to convince himself. Close your eyes. We're right here. We're not going anywhere.

Sleep would be nice, she said, and her words had a calming edge to them, a slowing of the *ice* in nice.

I'd never experienced real physical pain like this and wished to feel it too. I crouched down and enveloped her in a hug. Her arms dangled by her sides but slowly she brought them up and gripped my shoulders. I kissed her cheek and it was salty with sweat.

Wolfe, she whispered.

It's OK, I said.

If something happens to me . . . You'll take it, won't you? Please tell me you'll take the baby. I can't have . . .

Nothing's going to happen to you, I said.

We moved around her, positioning ourselves in a semi-circle, trying to block off entry into the deeper depths of our aisle, and obstruct any view from the open floor. We had no means of keeping time and could only try to silently count the seconds as a way of measuring her contractions. Her eyes remained closed but every so often I'd see her body tense and convulse in pain. It was as though she'd lost all ability to speak – there was no strength for words. And a silence fell on us all then as we sat huddled, waiting for time to pass.

I reached out and touched Stirling's arm. Lots of babies get stuck back-to-back, I whispered.

He looked at me as if I hadn't made my point yet.

What happens if it gets stuck?

It's not going to get stuck.

How can you be sure?

It's not going to get stuck.

Foer pulled a food pouch from her pocket. She might get hungry . . . But then she probably won't eat until after, will she? It's tea and toast they normally have, isn't it?

I went to read the clocks in the main chamber. The time was 9.54 p.m. It seemed like a good time for a child to be born. For some reason the idea of the baby trying to arrive in the middle of the night unnerved me. I walked back, oblivious to the people and noise around me. Stirling was examining Levitt again, with Foer standing beside him like an assistant, while Webb focused on his travel guide.

How's it looking? I whispered.

She's pretty much at ten centimetres now, Stirling replied. But the baby is still back-to-back.

We can do this, can't we?

We wait for her to feel like she wants to push and then we'll see . . . He turned to look at me. You're going to have to help me.

I nodded.

Levitt started grunting. She seemed desperate to get up from her back and Stirling was immediately by her side. The grunting grew deeper. She was clambering now, desperately trying to roll on to her side.

Do you need to push? Stirling said. Can you feel it?

Levitt was thrusting her head backwards and forwards. I want to squat. I can't lie down. Her breathing was erratic and flustered and I found myself standing there, my fingers moving frantically across her back.

Help me get her on to her knees, Stirling said. Now.

We moved her into a squatting position and Foer started dabbing her forehead with a paper towel. Go with the contractions, Stirling said, when you feel one, push with it. He turned to Webb, who was still gripping his travel book. Go and check the time.

Webb looked confused, as if we should have known he wasn't a part of this, but Stirling shouted at him and he slowly got to his feet.

It's 10.20 p.m., Webb said on his return. As he spoke, he began to retreat from where he stood between the bookcases. He started shaking his head, seeming to finally understand what was taking place. He brought his hands up to his over-grown ears and cupped them. No, no, no, he kept saying.

A groan escaped from Levitt's lips as she attempted the first push and I crouched beside her.

You're doing so well, I whispered.

The contractions continued to come and she pushed and pushed but nothing seemed to be happening. Stirling's lips were moving but there was only static in my ears. Foer shook my arm.

Go and check the time on the clock, Stirling shouted, star-ing at me. I need to know how long she's been pushing for.

I ran off, tripping over my feet and landing on my elbows. Pain started to spread across my side but I clambered up and on, oblivious now to the number of people present in the recreation room. I ran along the corridor but when I arrived in the main chamber I was drowned with disorientation and turned myself around in a circle. I could feel my movements slowing and I had this fear that I'd never be able to find the clock or understand time again. I closed my eyes. When I opened them the clocks were directly above me and I stared at the time before running back to the recreation room.

I forced my way through the growing crowd and up the aisles. It's 12.24 a.m.

Stirling's hands were covered in blood and Levitt seemed to crumble, letting the crown of her head press into the floor as she rocked her body backwards and forwards. I placed my hand on her head. The strands of her hair were wet and I felt her sweat penetrate my skin.

Over two hours of pushing and nothing's happening, Stirling said. Wolfe, help me get her on to her back. I can't examine her properly in this position. We took an arm each, pulling her on to her feet before lowering her backwards on to the floor.

Levitt thrust her head to the side and reached out towards me, desperate for my grip. Once I was in her embrace she pulled me close, her lips touching my face. She kept trying to take gulps of air but couldn't seem to catch her breath.

I'm going to die, she said. I can't do this any more.

No, you're not, I said, staring at Stirling, a fear burning through my body. He wiped his forehead with his wrist, speckles of blood settling on his skin. We need to do some-thing, I said.

Levitt, he said calmly, already removing the scalpel from his bag. The baby is stuck. I'm going to have to make a small cut. You shouldn't feel anything.

I looked away.

No, Levitt said. Please don't.

It's our only chance of getting the baby out, he said.

Levitt was crying and I gripped her head and curled myself around her, my cheek pressing against hers. Her skin was hot, like a fever and I imagined her scorching me. And I began to fear that if I pulled away I'd discover a still body, her eyes empty and lifeless. I tightened my hold; I could have suffocated her. I never thought to check if I'd given her enough room to breathe.

Stirling was shouting now. Push, he said. Again, again, nearly there.

I looked up, firstly to see Levitt blinking and then to see Stirling holding a baby in his hands. It was covered in thick, creamy mucus, more mucus than blood, and I hadn't expected any of it. Stirling cupped the baby's head in one hand, its back and bottom in his other.

But the baby was silent. It's a girl, he said, and as he spoke I could hear the desperation in his voice. Come on, little one, he pleaded. Take a breath. Please take a breath. But still there was nothing but silence. Stirling crouched on his knees and placed the baby on the sheet, the umbilical cord – this huge pulsing lifeline – trailing from mother to child. He started wiping the baby's nose and mouth, blowing on her face. The baby's fingernails and toenails were intact and long. The mucus covered Stirling's hands and he was muttering something to the baby, perhaps pleading with her to breathe. And I was praying – I was asking for this child to be saved because I couldn't see the point in any of this if she wasn't going to be spared. There had to be something worth surviving for; there had to be a reason to try. My breathing was laboured and I realised I was hyperventilating. I clung to Levitt's hand. Her eyes were closed and she too was chanting under her breath.

And then, when the silence had gone on too long and I was sure there was no life in this baby, a cry broke through. It was a cry only a newborn could make, and I thrust my head back and stared at the fluorescent lights above. The baby began to howl for her mother. Foer shook her head, her hands running through her hair, tugging on clumps.

Stirling placed the baby gently on Levitt's chest, pulling the sheet up around them. And as he took a step back he fell to the ground and hid his face in his hands.

I came to where he was crouched and ran my fingers across his shoulders, letting them settle there for a moment before I continued on, walking aimlessly through the aisles of books until I was in the open space of the recreation room. When I looked up there was a sea of people – the soldiers included – and they stared out at me. No one moved. And the baby cried and cried, the noise of her cries echoing up through the pipes and through the walls of the chamber, and perhaps even up to the ground above us.

# 16

Stirling and I stayed locked in his surgery for some time, the rest of the doctors and nurses having finished their shifts. Knowing no one was looking for us offered a small measure of relief. We lay on the examination bed, naked under a clean white sheet, pretending we were somewhere other than the bunker. Difficult memories of the past were banished, worries for the future paused; we focused only on the present, high on the euphoria of bringing Levitt's baby safely into the world. To everyone her name was simply an extension of her mother's surname, but when alone, with her fingers wrapped around my pinkie I'd whisper her first name: Eleanor – after Levitt's grandmother.

Stirling wrapped his arms around me and nervously laughed as I told him about the time I hadn't properly pulled on the handbrake of my battered old car and watched as it rolled down the street, hitting the front of a sports car.

Who's liable if no one's driving? he asked, a smile settling on his face.

I shrugged, smiling too, pressing closer towards him.

He kissed my forehead, a quietness falling over us. I still can't believe it, he said. The notion of this tiny little baby being here. It's incredible, isn't it?

She's the most beautiful thing I've ever seen, I said, rubbing my nose against his shoulder.

You were right, he said. She's good. She's good for all of us.

She's certainly boosted morale, I said, even the women from laundry are falling over themselves to help make cloth nappies.

And it was true – people from both sides of the bunker were coming together, desperate to help in any way they could. Eleanor's presence was nudging us towards the caring and somewhat thoughtful community we should always have been. Even in the pharmacy I noticed it – patients were complying with their medication in numbers I'd never seen before. Some of the soldiers too came to visit for nothing more than to get a glimpse of her, their manner friendly, often jovial. It felt as though something special was happening; that I was someone special merely by association. And I liked it; enjoyed the public display of envy.

Just keep an eye on Levitt, though, Stirling said. Childbirth is overwhelming for anyone under normal circumstances, never mind in here. I worry that it will become a bit obsessive. The attention from other people, I mean.

I think her family are actually being very supportive, which has probably taken her by surprise.

But no word of a father coming forward?

I shook my head.

Teenagers are so fertile, aren't they? It's madness. He paused then, his body tensing. Sorry, I didn't mean . . .

It's fine, I said tracing my hand along his stubble. I suspected he had been a quiet child, a worrier from a young age.

I tried to pull away but he held me close, bringing his lips back to meet mine. Wolfe, you don't need to be defined by your ability to make a baby or not. That's not everything there is to you.

I know, I said. I know that. I'm not going to punish myself any more for something I can't control.

He stared at me, his pupils seeming to dilate. I hate to break this party up, he said, but I've had another request for a prescription.

My head dropped, my nose resting against his chest. I don't want to talk about him when we're together.

His chest puffed out as he inhaled a breath. I just thought I should mention it, he said.

His request will be dealt with tomorrow, so can we please just go back to talking about something nice? I want to talk about anything other than him and being in here.

OK, he said, nodding, and I could feel the nudge of his chin against my head as he did so.

It was late when I got back to my bunk. Mr and Mrs Foer were deep in sleep, both of them snoring lightly, and I looked at them affectionately, admiring their relaxed state. Canavan was curled on his bed, his face to the wall, and I assumed he too was sleeping, but as I began to climb I could hear him turning over.

Could you make any more noise? he whispered, except he was terrible at whispering. Honest to God, what chance have any of us got of getting to sleep with your fucking about . . . ? His face hovered close to my own, and I tried to search for the lines of humour under his eyes, the smirk of a smile, but there was nothing.

I'm sorry, I whispered.

He humphed himself back up and rolled over again.

Canavan . . . I whispered.

There was silence before he said, What?

I wish I'd told you that it was Levitt's pregnancy test. That it was never mine . . .

241

It's none of my business, he said.

Unlike the rest of the bunker, he had taken little to no interest in Eleanor's arrival, practically denying her existence. And I couldn't shake off this sense of guilt, a niggling feeling of betrayal on my part, as though I'd abandoned him or neglected him in some way. Was he jealous of the effect she had on me? Infuriated by my breach of his trust?

What's wrong? I said. You're not your usual self . . . And I miss that guy.

His body moved through the canvas, like a shrug trying to turn into laughter. I suppose you could say I'm having some project management issues.

Do you still do whatever is asked of you?

Again there was a pause. I try to . . . But it can be difficult to justify at times. He dropped his hand beside me and tapped his fingers in anticipation. I reached out and clasped his palm. I used to be able to suspend reality and pretend, you know? But I can't seem to do that any more. I feel like I'm losing all of my memories . . .

I stroked his palm with my fingers, his skin bulky and coarse.

Where do you go when you leave with Foer? he asked in a voice I didn't really recognise, a childlike quality to it.

We go on little make-believe travelling adventures. Like imaginary play but for adults.

And does it help?

Yes, sometimes. I think so.

He brought his hand back up and tucked it into his blankets. Maybe I should try it some time.

Levitt sat on one of the dispensary chairs breastfeeding Eleanor while I removed the boxes of oxycodone from the controlled drug cabinet. The noise of her feeding was audible, a puckering of lips against Levitt's flesh, and I so desperately wanted to know what that felt like.

I placed the boxes of 60mg oxycodone in my side pockets and locked the cabinet, all the while aware of Levitt watching me.

What do you do when you're in the lair? she said, rubbing Eleanor's back in a circular motion.

I shrugged. Nothing really.

A man and a young girl walked into the pharmacy and I came to greet them at the Perspex. Hi, he said. I'm just wondering if you can help. My daughter has sore eyes. He stared at her then, waiting for her to say something, but she remained silent, staring down at the floor. She must have been about thirteen, fourteen. I suspect she's got an infection or something, he said. Both eyes are red and leaking gunk. In the morning they're crusted over and her mother has to wash them to prise them apart.

Can I have a look at them? I asked the girl. You can show me here or I can take you into the consultation cubicle.

She brought her face up, her cheeks turning red.

Yes, there's definitely an infection there, I said. Conjunctivitis. It's quite common and spreads easily. I can give you an eye drop to apply here but you'll need to return every two hours while the pharmacy is open for the next forty-eight hours. I turned to her father then. Make sure no one is sharing boiler suits or blankets with her. And obviously continue to practise good hand hygiene.

Will my eyes be OK? the girl asked, her face twitching nervously. I don't want to lose my sight.

Your eyes will be just fine, I said. The drops are going to sort everything out.

She was nodding, and suddenly she seemed familiar but I couldn't quite place her. And it wasn't until after I'd written up her drug chart and administered the first dose of drops that I remembered she was one of the teenagers who had witnessed Templeton eating the plastic houses from the Monopoly board. It occurred to me then that I'd given very little thought to her and her friends in the many months since it had happened. How long had it been? The length of time it takes to make a baby? I wondered if this girl and her friends still thought about him, lay in their bunks with their eyes closed, replaying the scene. Was the twitch to her face something she had always suffered from or was it a new affliction, a symptom of her environment? She would have been the right age for Templeton.

Glass arrived next. He let a smile flutter across his lips and it looked warming, so at ease that I smiled back. Again, I tried. I stared at the wrong boxes of drugs in the drawer but it was impossible; it was as if I couldn't physically touch them.

How are you today? he asked as I passed his cup of tablets through the hatch.

I'm fine, thank you. And you?

He opened his mouth for my inspection. Things can only get better, he said. I mean, look at that little miracle behind us. Total perfection.

I know, I said, turning affectionately to gaze upon Levitt and her baby.

Levitt smiled at us both, the baby sleeping, her little head resting against Levitt's collarbone.

As I watched Glass depart I was aware again of a figure lingering outside the pharmacy, wide shoulders and the mass of grey fabric from a boiler suit. The body turned and I could see a soldier's rifle pointing upwards, a hand wrapped around the barrel. The soldier bent slightly to peer in through the window and again it was my soldier with the droplet birthmark. He always had the same expression – as though he was on the cusp of saying something profound. What knowledge did he carry within him? It seemed obvious to me then that he'd be there; that it was only a matter of time until I was to be judged on my progress with Glass, or lack of it rather. Perhaps I had been foolish to think that Eleanor's arrival had reset something within the moral parameters of the bunker – that with new life came fresh starts. Clearly I had watched too many '80s films about babies in the past: *Look Who's Talking, Baby Boom* . . .

Levitt was speaking to me but I wasn't listening, and she rose to see what held my attention. He never comes in to see the baby like the others, she said. He gives me the creeps, with his staring eyes. She turned to look at me. Do you think we should say something? Complain to someone?

I shrugged, still holding the soldier's eye. I doubt it would make any difference, I said.

He turned and left, and after a minute or so I tried to convince myself he'd never been there at all.

It feels like everyone is watching me now, Levitt said. It was nice being invisible before. How did celebrities deal with this?

It will take people time to get used to there being a baby here, I said.

Levitt nodded.

I'm sorry if I was harsh with you sometimes, I said. I know I could be forceful, with your pregnancy . . .

She shrugged. Do you think she'll begrudge me for not wanting her? Even for a little while . . .

I shook my head, wanting to think only of tiny fingers and toes, of milky, dreamlike smiles.

Do you still see yourself having kids when we get out of here? she said.

I paused. I can't actually have kids. I'm infertile.

Oh, Wolfe, I'm sorry . . .

It's OK, I said. Really it is. Some bodies just don't work the way you'd expect them to.

And I was still thinking about this when Valentine arrived for handover.

He barely acknowledged me, coming close to Levitt and peering down at Eleanor, his face creasing into a smile. And I stood watching him, inspecting this newly discovered affection. I'd heard him bragging about her to a patient the day before as I was leaving, talking about her presence and how it filled the dispensary with joy, even when she wasn't there.

How is she today? he asked, his voice a low hush.

She's fine, Levitt said.

He paused, his hand extended in mid-air, desperate to touch her. Can I . . . Can I hold her? he said. Only for a moment.

Levitt hesitated, gripping Eleanor. I'm not . . .

The baby's settled, I said, interrupting. Probably not wise to disturb her. Anyway, we'd better go.

The soldiers were expecting me, allowing me to enter the lair and make my way to ND's floral-patterned hallway unsupervised. I didn't bother sitting down; instead I stood for some time inspecting myself in the glass mirror hanging on the wall.

The door to the kitchen opened and it was Alistair who stood on the threshold. He ushered me in without a word and pointed to the table, which had been covered with a white linen tablecloth. Two place mats had been set with crystal wine glasses and silver cutlery. He pulled out a seat and waited for me to sit down. He then busied himself at one of the counters, rolling up his sleeves, clasping a tin opener in his right hand. And like an afterthought he said, Our leader will be with you shortly.

I pressed the prongs of my fork into my fingers. It was sharp, but not sharp enough to cause any real damage, and when I looked up ND was walking towards me.

Why don't you go ahead and pour us some wine, Alistair, he said, lowering himself into his seat. The hefty weight he had once carried was disappearing, but not in a particularly healthy way. He held his hand out towards me, a slight tremor in his fingers. My tablets, please. And I placed them on the counter.

Red or white? Alistair asked behind us.

Any, ND replied, already opening the first box of oxycodone.

I watched Alistair uncork a bottle of red and bring it to the table. ND inspected the label. He nodded and Alistair began pouring, filling ND's glass to the brim, but when he came to my glass ND pinched his index finger with his thumb. Ease her in gently, he said, popping a tablet into his mouth. It'll take her a little time to adjust, with her puréed diet. Let's get some solid food in her before we get too generous.

Alistair proceeded to pour a two-finger measure of wine into my crystal glass.

Go ahead, ND said, leaning forward, already looking calmer.

I brought the glass to my lips and let my nose hang over the rim. Daniel and I had done wine-tasting before but it meant nothing to me now. I took a mouthful and swirled it around, all the while aware of ND watching me. It was rich and overpowering but I let the first sip pass down before taking another. What was wine meant to taste of? Berries? Fermentation? I took a bigger mouthful and swallowed it without trying to ponder its flavours any further.

Take your time, ND said. Savour it.

Alistair was placing plates in front of us. Tempura prawns, he said, taking a step back.

The tails of the prawns poked out from the batter and I ran a finger over them, feeling their almost plastic touch. ND had already squeezed the tail off one and was dipping it into a sweet and gloopy-looking sauce. What's wrong? he said. Don't you like seafood?

I . . . I do, it's just I wasn't expecting to see prawns.

Yes, he said, his mouth already full with another prawn. Alistair is a wonder in the kitchen. He can bring anything to life from the freezers and store cupboards.

Have you always been a chef? I said, trying to address Alistair.

I poached him, ND said between chews. The world will again need beautiful food in the future.

Once I started eating my prawns I couldn't stop. I barely took a breath as I went from one to the next, until all six prawn tails lay limp on my plate. I had the excitement of a child as I held my cutlery, all wariness and suspicion of my company temporarily gone while I wondered if this was what it was like to truly feel normal again. ND topped up my wine glass and as I gripped its stem I was aware of its fullness, sloshing backwards and forwards. I liked the weight of the crystal in my hand and gripped it tighter, thinking it suited me.

Alistair removed the prawn tails and placed another dish down – fillet of steak, he said, medium rare, with walnut mashed potatoes and garlic root vegetables. Enjoy, he added, placing clean cutlery before retreating from the kitchen, closing the door gently behind himself.

ND nodded towards my food. Please, he said. Don't let it get cold. And he reached forward again to top up my glass. And suddenly I was aware of there being a steak knife in my hand and I was carving through the fibres of bloodied meat. In my mouth the meat seemed to dissolve and I swallowed it, desperate to get another piece on my fork. I scooped up some of the walnut and potato mash and smeared it across the cut of steak before loading it all into my mouth. My meat was gone in minutes but ND had barely touched his.

Are you not going to have that? I said, pointing with my steak knife. It occurred to me then that I finally held a real weapon in my hand. What would it be like to pierce his flesh? Would it pass through like butter? I had a burning desire to discover the answer, like a scientific experiment. That moment when you stand on a balcony or bridge and fleetingly contemplate jumping, just to experience its force.

My head was beginning to feel fuzzy and I closed my eyes for a moment. When I opened them he was pouring the dregs of the wine bottle into both our glasses. I took a gulp of warm wine and let it circulate around my mouth before swallowing.

A toast, he said, raising his glass and waiting for me to do the same. To new life, he said.

I smiled, taking a large sip of wine.

How is the baby?

Unsteadily, I placed my wine glass on the table. Levitt's child?

There are no other newborns in the bunker, that I'm aware of . . .

Good, I said. She's good. Defying the odds.

Healthy?

I nodded. My head was heavy and I really couldn't stand the heat. I was aware of ND continuing to ask questions: the weight of the child, hair colour. And I slurred one-word responses, suddenly desperate for him to stop talking.

Are you OK? he said.

I'm just warm.

He cleared his throat. We are doubly blessed in this bunker, he said. My wife, too, is expecting.

I could feel the sweat on my forehead and it took everything in me not to wipe it away. That's wonderful news. How is your wife keeping?

He nodded. Fine, all things considered. A little morning sickness . . .

And a wave of nausea washed over me then.

He took a bite of his steak and chewed, the juice from the meat gathering in the corners of his mouth, pink and repulsive. If I'd known about Levitt's baby, he said, I could have arranged for the poor girl to give birth here, where it would have been more comfortable. Sanitary.

I shrugged, swallowing another gathering of saliva.

My wife and I . . . It pains us to think of that poor child being born in those circumstances, he said, piercing another chunk of steak with his fork. And Levitt too, a good girl like that . . . He wiped his mouth, leaving a stain on his linen napkin. Now, how are we getting on with Glass?

I . . . Well, I'm still working on it.

He raised his eyebrows. Good thing you're finding me in a celebratory mood.

It's taken me a while to work out the finer details, I replied. It'll be subtle but authentic. It has to look like an accident.

So do you have a plan?

Yes, I think so.

And will it work?

I've read about it working.

He ran his tongue over his teeth but said nothing.

Do you want to know what it is? I asked.

No.

It's just, Glass . . . And from the tone of my voice I knew I had no control over what I was about to say. He seems like a decent man. I don't want to do something we'll regret.

We? he said, before taking a bite of his steak.

Another wave of nausea rose up and I struggled to push it down. I . . . I don't know if I've got it in me.

Of course you do. We all do. He pushed his plate away, a chunk of bloodied steak fat resting on the side. How is Stirling? I'm sure he is considered quite the hero after delivering the baby.

I didn't answer.

We certainly don't want the soldiers to discover he's been misprescribing opiates, do we? It would be tragic to lose such a good doctor.

My body buckled over the side of my chair then and I retched uncontrollably. I was aware of my undigested food landing on the floor and I so desperately wanted to keep it in, for it to nourish me in some way.

As I stared at my wine-stained vomit, I could feel ND's hand on my back, patting it gently as if I were his dog. It's for the best, he said, his voice warmer, more fatherly.

I just don't think I can, I whispered.

He gripped my hair sharply from the scalp, causing my face to jut upwards. The pain of it was intense but somehow gratifying. You'll see I'm right, he said. It's best for everyone involved. He released me then, throwing his napkin to the floor. Clean your face, he said, collecting his wine glass. It's disgusting.

I wiped my face before crouching to clean up the chunks of vomit I'd left by my chair.

Leave that, he said, swiping his hand in the air. The dogs will get it.

Rising to my feet I thought about the nuclear accident in the Fukushima power plant years before – it was all over the news: scientists sacrificing themselves to go back in and secure the facility for everyone else. The image of the men in their biohazard suits venturing in was ingrained in my mind. It was selfless, and I'd always wished to be more of a selfless person. But I wasn't; I was selfish, having gone to such extreme lengths to live. What if I'd taken the place of someone who had truly contributed to mankind? All those podcasts I'd listened to with physicists and biologists trying to explain the wonders of the world in the simplest of terms – people dedicating their lives to studying things as intricate as snails and their relationship to the sun because it all mattered – it all meant something.

The wine was too much, ND said. It's my fault really. Your body wasn't ready for it.

# 17

When I woke in my bunk the next morning, Canavan was gone. It felt as though my head was going to explode and I lay there, staring up at the empty canvas, sharp stabs pulsing against my right temple. It took me a while but slowly I climbed on to his bed, and sat trying to be logical, needing to bury the anxiety in my stomach. I couldn't decide if my worry was genuine, or from the hungover fear of what I might have said and done the previous night. Despite Canavan's distancing, and dwindling desire to confide in me, he was always in his bed each morning, never known to be an early riser. I sat on his bunk a moment longer, the canvas smelling only of damp and stale perspiration, while a wave of nausea churned my insides. Perhaps I was hoping to find some fragment of him, maybe a clue to his whereabouts. But there was nothing.

In the kitchen quarters I was handed my ration of pouches before heading to the pharmacy, not bothering to inspect what had been gifted to me. The new Alison's voice spoke over the speaker system but I paid little attention to her, as if somehow I was honouring the real Alison's memory by doing so.

Levitt was waiting for me outside the pharmacy and I stepped aside to allow her over the threshold. She was carrying Eleanor in a wrap made from one long piece of cotton, which an experienced mother had shown her how to wear.

You look ill, she said. Are you OK?

I'm not really sleeping, I replied, rubbing my forehead.

Yeah, I know how that feels, she said, stifling a laugh. I think my surrounding bunkmates are going to start turning on me soon. I swear people must be able to hear us on this side of the bunker.

Well, I've never heard her, I said, turning to greet my first patient of the day.

I'm here for my mother, the boy said. He might have been sixteen or seventeen – a sparse growth of hair over the top lip.

What's wrong with her?

She's had hiccups for over an hour and needs something to make them stop.

Hiccups?

Yes, he said nodding.

There's nothing for hiccups.

The other pharmacist gave her something before that helped. The man . . .

For hiccups?

Yes, for hiccups.

Well, do you know what he gave her? Because as far as I'm concerned there's no such thing for treating hiccups.

No, but she swore by it.

I had to work hard to stop my eyes from rolling in their sockets. Maybe if she just holds her breath . . . Some people say you should try to sing your favourite song. Anyway, it's not something that requires medical treatment.

She needs something.

They'll just go away. If she's worried, tell her to come and see me herself but . . . I trailed off suddenly, my gaze shifting to the soldier with the birthmark peering through the artificial windows again. What now? I shouted, spreading my hands apart in exasperation. What?

The boy turned to see what had caught my attention. The soldier turned away but I just kept staring after him.

So, the boy said, what are you going to give her?

I focused my attention on the boy. Piss off, I said.

Excuse me?

Just piss off, I hissed, and he must have thought I was demented because he did so without protest.

Levitt touched my back and I flinched. Are you sure you're OK? she said. Eleanor was still sleeping soundly, her thin wisps of hair poking up.

I just . . . I was already pacing towards the dispensary door. I need to go, but I'll be back soon, I said.

You can't leave me here, Levitt called out.

I'm sorry. I promise I'll be back soon.

I ran out into the corridor, trying to catch sight of the soldier, but he was gone. Was he headed for the lair? The noise of my gym shoes hitting the floor seemed to echo around me. I made it to the main chamber a little out of breath but there was no sign of him. Defeated, I made to return to the pharmacy before stopping; it occurred to me that Canavan might be back at the bunks expecting me to be on shift. And, sure enough, as I came and stood at the bottom of our row I could make out the bulk of him lying flat out on his bed.

I tiptoed quietly towards him. Are you avoiding me? I said, bringing my mouth close to his ear.

Startled, he sat up, turning on to his side. You look terrible, he said.

Thanks.

Why aren't you working?

I am. I'm meant to be . . . I'm going back now. I paused. Where were you this morning? I was worried.

He laughed. Did you think I'd been *dealt with*?

I was just worried.

He stared at me. I was taking care of some business.

I've something similar to be taking care of myself.

What's stopping you? he asked, seeming suddenly interested.

I swallowed. I just don't think I can do it. I've tried, but . . .

His eyes were bloodshot and he blinked as though he hadn't slept in days. Well, it gets easier each time, he said. You become more desensitised.

I focused on the temporary tattoos around his wrists, visualised the ink of the marker pen seeping into his skin. I'd read once about some people having green bones – forest-green – and I liked that idea. To never know you had green bones until surgeons cut into you and discovered the anomaly.

How's the baby? he said.

Why are you asking? It's not like you've taken any interest before . . .

He exhaled. I just think it's best not to get too attached, he said. Cooing over a baby won't help.

I disagree.

He rubbed at his face then, the stubble having grown into the beginnings of a wild beard. You care too much, he said. That's your problem. It does more harm than good.

Why would you say that? I whispered, a lump rising in my throat.

He paused. I'm sorry, Wolfe, I didn't mean that. I'm being cruel. I hate myself when I'm thinking about Thomas. Even just the thought of him feels too much right now.

Who's Thomas?

Thomas. My partner.

I fell silent before repeating his name, sounding it out in my mouth.

I never mentioned him before?

I shook my head. But I've never met a bad Thomas, I said.

I sold myself, Canavan replied. I sold myself to ND. I guess I was so desperate to live. But I never thought it through . . . There won't be anyone left to want me.

And I let his words sink a little deeper, let them create a new wound.

He said he loved my paintings . . . That's how it all started. He'd been a fan for a while and was buying up most of my collection. Then he started asking me to attend dinners so we could discuss the work further. One night, we sat alone and he placed his hand on my knee. He knew I had a partner and yet I didn't push his hand away. Canavan sniffed then, wiping his noise. We started spending more time together and it was like I couldn't go back once I'd started down this path. He told me that if I wished, with his help, I could become one of the greatest living artists.

He laughed then, as though it had finally dawned on him how ludicrous it all was.

What happened to Thomas? I asked.

He went for a walk and kissed me goodbye. I waited until I knew he was far enough away. And then I left. That was it. No note. Nothing.

I placed my hand on his head and he closed his eyes.

I need to go back to the pharmacy, I said. They'll be waiting for me.

Please, just stay a little while.

★   ★   ★

257

When I arrived back at the pharmacy there was a queue of people waiting. Locked in the dispensary, Levitt's voice was raised as she explained that no medication would be administered until my return. I pushed past the crowd and a familiar sensation swept over me – that feeling of guilt for having kept people waiting – being caught in traffic or having slept in, and patients growing agitated that even something as simple as getting paracetamol hinged on my being on the premises. I should have felt power over these people because they needed me, but it only brought a sense of resentment. I was chained to them.

Levitt looked relieved at my return and hurried to let me into the dispensary. Ignoring the queue of people, she placed her hand on my back. What's going on? she whispered. What happened?

Sorry I left you.

I thought about calling for Valentine.

Oh, God, the less he knows about this, the better.

She threw her arms around me then, and I was glad to have the weight of her pressing against me, Eleanor's little body so close to mine. Reluctantly I pulled away and turned to face the patients. Sorry about the delay, I said. It couldn't be avoided.

First in line was a woman requesting sanitary pads and I counted out her ration on the counter as though I were counting money. Next was a woman looking for her hormone replacement therapy and I asked Levitt to look those tablets out before passing them through the hatch. An older man was next. He looked familiar, as if he used to be someone important in his previous life – perhaps he had been famous, not that it mattered. The man leaned in close to the Perspex as though he didn't want anyone to hear. I've ... He hesitated, and it seemed to take him a moment to compose his thoughts. I've got this thick skin on my heels, he said. Thick calloused skin and it's sore to walk on.

I could feel my body inwardly shuddering.

I wish I could take a blade to it, he said, slice the layers away.

Well, I don't have any blades, but I do have a pumice stone that you could use.

Could I show it to you? he said. The skin around the heels has cracked as a result. Honestly, I've persevered for an immeasurable amount of time.

OK, give me a second, I replied. If you take a seat by the curtain I'll be with you shortly.

He nodded. As he turned he made a show of hobbling over to the waiting seat, and I couldn't decide if this was put on for my benefit or if he truly was in agony. I ushered the next patient forward and it was a quick transaction of medication. Levitt passed me the measuring cup – two green and yellow capsules rolling around next to each other – and I suspected our stock of tramadol would be depleted soon. I handed the woman her capsules and she swallowed them quickly. She didn't even need water.

When I looked up, Glass was standing behind her, smiling at me. I realised I was smiling back. I wanted to enter his mind and read his thoughts; I wanted to convince myself he was worth sacrificing. He gave me his ID number. Just the usual for me today, he said, letting a laugh sneak through his nostrils.

I pulled out his drug chart and held the marker pen poised in my hand.

What do you need? Levitt said, her hand already on a drawer, awaiting further instruction.

It's OK, I'll get this one, I said. Can you deal with the next patient?

She shrugged, and I moved back from the counter to let her in. I was hypersensitive, moving almost in slow motion. There was the noise of metal scratching as I pulled open the first drawer. I placed the plastic measuring cup down beside some of the medicine packets and reached for the atenolol – popping one orange tablet out and watching as it landed in the cup. I closed the drawer and moved to another one, alphabetised F to H. The drawer pulled open without a noise and I stared once again at the furosemide water tablets I was meant to be dispensing, and then at the box of gliclazide for lowering blood sugar. Both identical in size – white and round, with a scoring line for halving. The markings were slightly different – F40 verses 08. I reminded myself that dispensing errors happened all the time. The excess fluid on his lungs would be retained, while his blood sugar began to drop, dangerously low, until potential hypoglycaemic death if allowed to remain unnoticed. And I suspected, having looked into gliclazide's side effects, that his malnutrition from our limited diet might enhance the tablet's ability to destroy his liver, a full-on attack of its function.

My hand traced over the box of furosemide before it settled on the gliclazide. As if it wasn't even me any more, I watched my hand open the box with real purpose and pop two perfectly round tablets into the measuring cup.

I slipped his tablets through the hatch and the smile was still evident on Glass's face; he never doubted the cup's contents. His trust was fully with me and he threw the tablets into his mouth, right to the back of his throat. He took the smallest sip of water before passing the empty measuring cup back through, and opened his mouth wide. I nodded.

Thanks as always, he said before turning, and I stood there, rooted to the spot, watching the sway of his shoulders as he walked away. The measuring cup was still in my hand and I was squeezing it, harder and harder, hoping for the plastic to give way in my palm.

Levitt placed her hand over mine. Let go, she said. You're hurting yourself.

I came to and looked up at her. Sorry.

Can you check this medication before I give it to the patient?

I glanced from the written description of the tablet to the cup that Levitt held out. I was nodding, as though I was actually checking its contents but I had no idea what was inside.

Do you want me to show you the boxes they came from? she said.

No, it's fine. I recognise the tablets.

She handed the cup through the hatch and I remembered the patient with the cracked heels who was waiting to see me. I pocketed a pumice stone and left the dispensary, not bothering to lock the door behind me. I made my way to the patient and as he pulled off his gym shoe the elastic on the front stretched and I wondered when it would finally give way. I decided he had been famous in a previous life.

He brought what must have been his worst foot up and rested it across his opposite knee. The skin was thick and calloused, and had a strange tinge of yellow. It was as though the skin had solidified and become wax-like. I removed the stone from my pocket and got on to my knees. With my left hand I held his ankle and with my right I started rubbing the skin with the stone, furiously thrusting my hand backwards and forwards as if the foot could be thinned down to something that resembled flesh if I just kept going. You don't have to ... he was saying, but I stopped listening, I kept pushing, and if I was hurting him I was oblivious. Skin, like flakes of soap, started to fall on to the floor around my knees and I couldn't stop. This was what I was worthy of now. I could hear myself silently chanting, praying for forgiveness, but I sensed it was already too late.

My hand suddenly grew tired and I dropped the pumice stone to the floor.

Will I need to do it as hard as that? he asked.

I looked up at him. Probably not.

What about a cream?

I shrugged, my hand still holding his ankle. I'm so tired, I said.

He picked up his gym shoe and carefully slid his foot back inside. Thank you, he said, and collected the stone from the floor, placing it in the pocket of his boiler suit.

# 18

For weeks Glass kept walking through the pharmacy door, healthy and alert. I didn't really know what I was expecting. Was I naïve to think that it would have happened sooner? That he'd just go to bed and immediately fall into a dreamless hypoglycemic coma?

I popped gliclazide into the measuring cup while still holding a conversation with him. He was telling me about a telephone box in Japan where people would go to make phone calls to their deceased loved ones. He talked about one woman who went every week to speak to her husband – a fisherman lost at sea. People said that drowning was one of the best ways to die, that it might even be euphoric, but I couldn't accept that. Drowning terrified me.

Who would you speak to, he said, if you were to visit the phone box?

I . . . I started shaking my head. I don't know.

He smacked himself across the forehead. I'm sorry. I don't know why I asked that.

It's fine, I said, but it didn't feel fine.

He left, and I rested my hands on the counter. Levitt's baby let out this little noise, like a happy thought, her body draped over Levitt's shoulder. I tried to tell myself I was doing this for her, helping make the world she lived in a safer place. So why, after so much loss and sacrifice, was I still not convinced we could offer this little baby a better existence?

Levitt began rubbing Eleanor's back, a familiar tap-tap in a circular motion, and I looked on, mesmerised. Did someone show you how to comfort her? I asked. Or does it all just come naturally?

She looked down at Eleanor before responding. My mum has shown me quite a lot. As for the rest, I'm just trying to work stuff out as I go.

Some of it comes naturally, though, doesn't it?

It's not all perfect, if that's what you think. It's not like the old TV shows that make everything look easy. She paused. What's going to happen when she gets older?

What do you mean?

It's fine me working here now when she's so small and I can carry her about, but what happens when she gets bigger, begins to walk . . .

Well, do you want to leave? I said.

No. In this dispensary, with you, this is where I feel most safe. No one can reach us here. I don't ever want to give that up.

Well, we'll just make it work, I said. I don't want you guys leaving me either.

I was date-checking the I–K drug drawer when the alarm started sounding out over the speaker system. I had been thinking about my mum, about our trip to Cairo – we'd stood in a museum reading information plaques and I'd asked her somewhat flippantly if she read the signs in Arabic or English. She laughed as if I'd asked her something ridiculous. English, of course, she said. It would take me too long to read the Arabic now. I wondered when the switch had taken place in her mind. When did you begin to think and dream in a language that hadn't initially been yours?

Levitt turned to look at me, the noise continuing to sound out. That time already? she said.

I shrugged, opening the dispensary door and waiting while she fixed her wrap and placed Eleanor back inside.

As we made our way to the main chamber people seemed to be filtering out from all directions. When we turned the last corner there was a mass of people and I had this sense of already being lost among the crowd. I forced my way to the boundary line with Levitt holding my hand. I edged my toes over the yellow-dashed paint before taking a step back, feeling secure that I was firmly on my side of the bunker. People congregated in lines, waving across to one another, and it felt no different from the times before. I shuffled along a little further, glancing in both directions, trying to identify people I knew. My eyes locked on Stirling a few rows back, and we nodded our acknowledgment of one another.

Levitt made to leave, squeezing my hand in farewell, but I found myself clinging to her. Don't go, I said. Please . . .

I'll be right back.

But I still wouldn't let go.

My parents will be waiting for us. Look, I can see them, she said, pointing to a couple. They always stay close to the line.

Do your parents love her? I said.

She paused. Yes. They do.

Then why didn't you want your father to know?

Look, she said, trying to pull away from my grip, let's talk about this later.

Just tell me. Why couldn't they know?

She was anxious, flinching at the intensified beeping. It wasn't him I was trying to hide it from, OK?

I just . . . I think you should stay here. I can't explain it, but I don't like the idea of you being over there.

She stared at me, hesitating, before rolling her eyes and stretching to stand on her tiptoes, trying to grab the attention of her father in the thickening crowd. She waved, blowing kisses to her mother. I'll just be right here, she shouted, her hand gesturing to where we stood, but her voice caught in the air and I doubted those she loved were able to hear her. They were shaking their heads, growing quickly nervous and agitated at her decision to remain where she was.

I stared out again at the sea of bobbing heads but couldn't see Canavan. The beeps of the alarm were coming more frequently now and my eyes were suddenly drawn to little Baxter, who for some reason was across the line. He was standing next to a girl of similar age. She was holding a stuffed toy dog and Baxter was gripping it by the legs. I started looking for his mother but couldn't see her anywhere and panic began to rise within me. I heard her call his name and recognised the fear in her voice. Baxter? she shouted. Baxter? I sensed the wave of bodies moving as she fought to get to the front. The beeps were too close together.

I darted across the line. Baxter's hands were still firmly gripping the legs of the dog and I cupped my arm around his waist, lifting him, as if I was carrying a ladder. He started kicking against me, pleading for the dog. It's mine, he screamed. She stole it.

I forced the dog from his grip and thrust it towards the girl, thinking that would be the quickest and easiest way to separate them. He was sobbing, his arms still stretched out towards the dog. The wall was moving, coming down and I ran, gripping him. I ducked as the wall descended further but kept running, until I was falling into the people on the other side and Baxter's mum was taking him from me. I could hear her crying but the noise didn't register as anything to do with me, like watching a foreign film and relying on the subtitles to understand the story.

Have you lost your mind? someone said, pulling me to my feet. You and the boy could have been crushed. Are you OK? someone else said, but suddenly people were shouting and I couldn't understand why. Levitt found me among the crowd and gripped me by the arms, shaking me. *How did you know?* she said. Did *he* tell you?

Know what?

She turned me in the direction of the wall. Too much time has passed, she shouted, causing her baby to cry. It's not coming up.

People began to crowd the wall, banging their fists against the metal. They were screaming the names of people I didn't know – people's first names – and it felt so strange – the sheer variety. Baxter's mum came and stared at me before pulling me into an embrace. The tears streamed down her cheeks while she held Baxter's face next to her hip, cupping his chin.

I would have lost him, she said. I wouldn't have reached him in time.

Stirling was beside me now. He planted one hand on my shoulder and I couldn't move under his weight. He looked me straight in the eye. Are you OK?

I stared at him, dazed. People ask me that all the time . . .

Did you hurt yourself?

I'm fine, I said. The boy's OK, isn't he?

The boy's fine. He brought his face close to mine and I could feel his breath warm on my cheeks. Did the leader warn you about this?

No, I said, frantically shaking my head.

Promise me.

I didn't know. I swear.

He pulled away from me and nodded. Please don't do that to me again, he said. I thought I was going to lose you.

I surveyed the scene, taking in the full scale of the grief that surrounded me. People were still banging their fists and hips against the steel wall, pushing forward to gain an inch of space, and I feared there would be trampling. Levitt was silent, her feet rooted to the spot, and Stirling was talking to her. She nodded mechanically – a glazed expression with nothing behind the eyes. I backed away and traced the wall from one end to the other as though somehow I'd find a gap through which to reach the other side. I pushed past people who were screaming their loved ones' names and planted my palm on the cool metal. Where was Canavan?

Slowly the noise died down until there was only the echo of whispers and whimpers. It was sickly – the eerie quiet of shock – exactly like when we were first placed inside and weren't yet used to this being our reality. I gravitated back towards Levitt, who sat slumped on the ground with her shoulders pressed against one of the cast iron radiators, one arm protectively wrapped around Eleanor's body. Her eyes were dry, but not in a way that told me she was thinking logically.

I sat down opposite, crossing my legs. I didn't know, Levitt . . . I grabbed the toe of her gym shoe and squeezed it a little. Please, you have to believe me.

She began to trace figures of eight with her index finger across the floor. I think you would have let me cross if I'd given you my baby, she said.

No.

I see the way you look at her. I see the way they all look at her. People don't care about me, do they? Only her . . .

I shook my head. That's not true.

My family . . . Her voice was hoarse and the speed of her index finger intensified.

I'm sorry I held you back.

Who's diseased? Is it this side or the other? She was still figuring eights. Am I some sort of carrier now that I'm here?

What?

Isn't that the point of the wall?

Stirling would have heard something, I said. He'd have heard if there was a bug or virus and he would have told us . . .

Stirling will know fuck all, she said. Nobody does. She brought her hand up and traced the back of Eleanor's head. What am I going to do, Wolfe?

On entering the surgery's waiting room there was hardly space to move. The room was awash with men speaking in hushed and confused tones. Stirling was leaning on Nurse Appleby's desk, his foot pressed up against a drawer, and he glanced up before shaking his head, warning me to leave.

Back in the main chamber the soldiers were out in force, lining themselves along the wall, their guns pointing forward, their fingers resting on the triggers.

Something's really wrong, Levitt said. Everything's charged, hostile . . .

Let's get out of here, I replied, trying to move us forward.

But Levitt kept glancing back. Wolfe, if there's a virus or something, might they just kill us all?

Stop talking like that.

We walked the corridors until we reached the recreation room. Inside, people were clustered in groups and a woman was standing on a chair, waving her hands for attention. If you are missing people from your party can you please keep to the left? she said. We need to figure out some way of accounting for everyone on this side.

My husband is over there, a woman cried.

My boy. He's only fourteen, a man shouted.

We need to remain calm, the woman replied. We aren't sure yet what brought the wall down. It might just be a technical glitch and could perhaps be rectified by the day's end. The main thing is that we remain calm. I'm sure there will be an announcement soon.

I saw two figures hunched between some of the bookshelves and circled round, inspecting them from the end of the row. There was the top of Webb's head and the shifting shoulders of Foer. Wait here, I said.

Levitt gripped my arm. No, don't leave us.

She clung to the back of my boiler suit as I crept forward. Foer and Webb looked up, with the spine of a guidebook resting between their legs. Wolfe, Foer called out. And the baby!

How marvellous to see you all, Webb said. Are you joining us on our next adventure?

We're just getting ready to leave for Rome, Foer said before suddenly stopping. Although I'm not sure how baby-friendly it will be . . .

It's OK, I said, staring at the stain that remained on the floor after Levitt gave birth. We won't be coming on this occasion.

They nodded in unison. There was something manic about the way they were sitting together, moving in sync. Webb turned down the page of the guidebook and showed me the cover. We're going to visit the Colosseum first, then stop for pizza. Probably Vatican City after lunch. I was aware of Levitt staring at them, eyebrows furrowed in confusion. Webb stared back at her before he said, We can't go to Africa as we'd planned now that they've closed the airport.

I turned my attention to Foer. Where's Mr Foer?

She was quiet for a moment. He's overseas . . . Some banking business to take care of.

I crouched down to her level, my feet planted firmly on the ground, my knees bent as far as they would go – the way my niece used to sit. I'd always been envious of her soft and flexible joints. I looked straight at Foer and forced her to make eye contact. Is he on the other side of the wall? Is that what you mean?

She smiled, showing her teeth, and when I glanced at Webb he too was smiling in the same way. Yes, she finally said. He's on the other side.

Are you sure?

I watched him go.

We'd better leave, Webb said. There'll be a queue for the Colosseum already.

I swivelled, still balanced in my crouched position, and faced him. Do you understand what's happening? I spoke slowly and clearly. Do you understand that they've brought the boundary wall down between us and we don't know if they're going to bring it back up again?

He paused. We'll end up missing the Pope addressing his people if we don't leave now.

I stared at him. I tried to see behind his eyes and imagine the impulses firing off in the distance, the neurons carrying those messages to his brain. He stared back, his face content and happy – the same happiness I'd experienced after we took our first fictional trip together, but it dawned on me then that it had never been fictional to him. I rose slowly, finding my balance, my legs weak underneath me. Levitt held my elbow, steadying me as I continued to stare at Foer and Webb tucked in beside their travel books. Maybe they were the ones who had it right; maybe they'd had it right this whole time.

OK, well, enjoy yourselves, I said.

We turned back towards the crowds. People had divided themselves on either side of the ping-pong table, the worn bats resting on top beside a ball that had been crushed, making it impossible to play.

Levitt and I found a square of carpet unoccupied and sat down. We huddled together, our shoulders touching, and she gently brought Eleanor out of the wrap, struggling one-handed to open a few strips of Velcro to breastfeed.

I can hold her if you need help, I said.

No, it's OK, she replied, managing to align Eleanor to her chest.

This carpet reminds me of my old school, I said, pulling at the coarse fibres.

Levitt's body was rocking backwards and forwards as she fed, but it didn't seem to soothe anyone and I wished she would stop.

We had a really bad winter once, I said. You probably weren't even born then. I remember my dad tunnelling us out of our driveway, labouring for hours just to get us out of the house and towards supplies. It felt like the world could really, well you know . . . End. We managed to reach my high school, which was only along the road. Inside, there were hundreds of people and camp beds set up, and there was hot food too. I still remember the steam rising from the urns of hot water as these little old ladies poured cups of tea . . . As I spoke I realised I was now moving, my shoulders rocking backwards and forwards in time to Levitt's. They had so many hot water bottles, I said, all with little knitted covers on them.

Levitt just stared off into the distance.

Did your mum ever put your underwear on the radiator in the morning to keep it warm? I asked.

We had underfloor heating, she said, and, as her words lingered there, I imagined catching them and placing them in my pocket, keeping them warm.

Are you hungry? I said.

She shrugged, unresponsive, and I wanted to shake her back to life.

Let's go to the pharmacy, I said. The pouches are there.

She very carefully placed Eleanor inside the wrap and we traced our way out of the recreation room, walking the corridors back in the direction of the pharmacy. I unlocked the door but kept the *We Are Closed* sign facing out.

Get behind the dispensary and keep low in case anyone sees you, I said, locking the door behind me.

I gathered some of the patients' drug charts and laid them down, hoping to create some sort of paper bed and pillows, and then I brought the blankets and the food pouches over. Levitt placed her head on a pile of charts and lay flat out across the floor, curling her body protectively around Eleanor. Once they were settled I joined them, pulling the blankets over and tucking them in around us.

What's your preference? I said, holding a few food pouches out at arm's length.

I don't care, she said, jittering slightly from the cold.

We've got banana, apricot, Thai chicken curry, lamb and potatoes, strawberries, or rhubarb crumble.

She was slow to answer. Can I have the rhubarb one?

I passed it over and her fingers were ice-cold. This probably isn't the warmest place for a baby, I said. And suddenly I had an idea. There were empty plastic one-litre bottles from the paediatric paracetamol we'd given out over time. I'd rinsed them but hadn't known what to do with them afterwards. I got to my feet and started collecting the bottles, unscrewing the caps while letting the tap run.

What are you doing? Levitt said.

I ran my hand under the tap and it was slightly beyond lukewarm, almost reaching toasty. I started filling the bottles to the brim, screwing the caps on as I went, until there were six full bottles.

I gathered them in my arms and brought them down to Levitt. Quick, put these under the blankets before they go cold.

Wolfe . . .

I was already lying down, placing a couple of the bottles around me, letting their mediocre warmth touch my body. Not quite a hot water bottle but the next best thing, I said.

Levitt's hand fished around until she found mine, and she clasped my palm to hers. Thank you, she said. And it was perfect, to be huddled together, little Eleanor's gentle breath between us.

Eat your crumble. And then you'll need to move on to something savoury, but you can have both the banana and apricot pouches after.

Stop giving me your food.

You need to eat more. You have a little person who needs you to eat more.

I don't think that's how it works . . .

I brought my strawberry pouch to my lips.

Is it love, she asked, with Stirling? I'm just curious.

I inched closer towards Eleanor, all the while still gripping Levitt's hand. Eat your pouch. You're not getting out of it.

I think it is love, she said, seeming sure of herself.

What about you? I said. And Eleanor's father . . . Was it love?

No, she replied, almost laughing. It was definitely *not* love.

Where is he?

She hesitated. He's not on this side of the bunker, if that's what you mean . . .

Did you ever tell him?

She shook her head, sucking on her pouch before turning to face me. But I suspect he knows. There's no hiding it now. And then she too inched closer.

Levitt, who is Eleanor's father? You don't need to tell me if you don't want to – it's just . . .

Our eyes met and she tried to smile. You must already know, Wolfe.

No, Levitt, I don't.

She paused. It's him. Our leader. ND.

My breath was knocked from me, winded, and I tried to straighten. I couldn't comprehend her words, yet instantly knew them to be true.

Are you sure? I said, spluttering strawberry purée.

There's been no one else. She paused, squeezed my hand tighter. I can't imagine not seeing my mum, she said and finally the tears came. And she gripped me, her face pressing into my neck and shoulder, arching herself further around Eleanor. I could feel the tears running down my skin, and she cried with such pain that I thought she might never stop.

It's going to be OK. You will see them again, I whispered, but there was little conviction in my voice. Foer's husband is on the other side now, I added. You can sleep in his bed until the wall comes up.

All our things are over there. Everything.

We'll figure it out, I said.

OK. She nodded, trying to stop her tears. Thank you.

# 19

In the pharmacy, rumours were spreading like wildfire. An extreme strand of E. coli was plaguing the other side. Or was it Ebola? The leader himself was a sufferer, perhaps even dying. With each patient came more questions: Will they test us all? Couldn't the new inhabitants already be carriers? Is it in the water? Are the food pouches contaminated? It's airborne, isn't it? It wasn't clear yet how many people we'd lost and gained but new faces were starting to filter through. I'd hardly seen Stirling; the doctors were working flat out to accommodate the new people and determine their needs. Nurse Appleby had already been through twice to deliver a stack of new prescriptions.

In the chaos of it all Glass still arrived for his medication. So many patients were missing their doses but he was yet to surrender. I wanted to scream at him, tell him to leave and understand that his life was being shortened. Sometimes I imagined myself just coming out and saying it: *Why am I killing you?* But instead I continued popping the wrong tablets into a measuring cup and sliding them through the hatch.

He swallowed them before pouring himself some water with a slight tremor to his hand. As he passed the cup and paper cone back I decided he was finally starting to look ill, his eyes bloodshot, tinged yellow and seeming to bulge from their sockets. Are you feeling OK? I said.

He bobbed his head, perspiration gathering on his temples. Yes, I'll be fine. Just a little breathless. Hopefully I'll turn a corner soon. Don't want to bother the doctors when they're so busy. He bit down on the tip of his tongue.

Are the ulcers still bothering you?

He nodded. They won't go away.

I hesitated, the urge to confess pulsing through me. Well, remember to stay hydrated, I said.

He smiled this strange and sad smile. Have you lost anyone to the other side?

No, I replied, I'm alone here, but I know people who have.

We shall pray for them and hope to be reunited soon.

Yes. Indeed.

I watched him walk away, my fingers gripping the edge of the counter. I thought I was being punished, having to witness his deterioration.

What is it about him? Levitt said, interrupting my thoughts. What?

I don't know . . . You just seem to have taken a particular shine to him. You won't let me near him when he comes in.

I sat down next to her in one of the plastic chairs, trying to peer into the folds of her wrap to see Eleanor's sleeping face. I guess he reminds me of someone.

The door was opening again but this time it was Nurse Appleby returning. She slid another bundle of prescriptions through the hatch. Sorry, ladies, she said. More paperwork for you to write up.

That's OK. I licked my finger, flicking through the pile of new names and ID numbers.

Expect these patients any time, she said.

How are the numbers looking? Are things settling down?

She shrugged. How long is a piece of string? Some come

willingly, wanting to be acknowledged, but there are others and we've no means of accounting for everyone. We can't even determine yet whether we need to reduce the food rations . . . The doctors are saying that the soldiers may need to do another bunk count.

I wonder what they're doing now, Levitt said.

Who? Appleby asked.

My parents. Everyone on the other side.

Appleby hesitated. Of course . . .

A man was approaching us. He reached the division and bobbed his head forward, his shoulders tense, aggression seeping from his pores. I'd been dealing with men like him my whole career. He was already setting me up to fail. He rattled his knuckles on the Perspex and somehow I managed a smile. Surname and ID number, please.

There must be a better system than this. Don't you people have some sort of internal record? I was asked this every fucking day on the other side and it's wearing thin.

Well, do you know my ID number?

No.

Then don't assume I know yours, I said.

1972. Coats. I was told the nurse was sending my prescription through.

That'll be me, Appleby replied in a sickly-sweet tone. And fear not, I can assure you that your prescription has made it here safely. You're not easy to forget, she added before turning on her heel.

I flicked my finger through the ever-growing pile of new prescriptions. His was second from the last. I pulled a blank drug chart from the drawer below and started writing his name in black ink.

What do you need? Levitt said.

I slid the prescription along the counter to her and she glanced at it before opening the drawers. There was the rattle of tablets and capsules landing in the cup: pregabalin for neuropathic pain, clonazepam for anxiety, carbocisteine for mucus on the lungs and blood-thinning aspirin. I took the cup from her hand and glanced at the contents inside before passing it through the hatch. Coats thrust them towards his mouth but his aim was off and the pregabalin capsule fell to the floor.

He picked it up and slid it along the counter back towards me. I'll need a new one, he said.

Sorry. Limited supply.

But it's been on the floor.

I've already marked your dose up. Sorry.

He flicked the capsule back through the hatch. Do you feel God-like behind this thing? he said, pressing his index finger up against the screen.

In my previous life there had been a man of similar build – thin and gangly, and angry at the world. He had this mangy dog that he used to chain up outside the pharmacy and the thing would growl at anyone who passed. The last time I saw him, he walked into the pharmacy shouting at one of our other patients whom he suspected of being a drug addict. I can't fucking stand junkies, he shouted. They should all be shot. The previous pharmacist had banned him but I didn't have the conviction to confront him in the same manner. He thrust a torn and folded prescription towards me. It was for high-dose oral morphine and antibiotics for a skin infection. I handed him a pen to sign the back of his prescription and as he leant over to do so I saw the bandages wrapped around his wrists.

A few weeks later his neighbour told us he'd committed suicide – he'd lived in her block and this time he'd done the job properly. And I remembered being grateful I wouldn't have to see him again. It angered me that a stranger could make me feel so anxious and nervous that I'd need to evacuate my bowels – that my breathing would change and I'd feel my heart nervously tapping my insides. Coats, ID number 1972, made me feel this exact same way. There was a part of me wishing it had been him I'd been asked to poison instead of Glass. Maybe then it wouldn't have been so hard.

I was aware of people shifting in their bunks – blankets moving, hinges creaking – and I glanced up, momentarily expecting to see Canavan. But my eyes fixed on the canvas and its sagging emptiness. Climbing down I glanced at Foer, and then Levitt and the baby below her. Levitt's back was to me, her face towards the wall, and I could tell from her breathing that she was still asleep.

I weaved through the narrow rows of bunks until I reached the opening of floor space. My shoes made a squelching noise, the air seeming to pocket and pop under the soles of my feet. I stopped, slipping them off, the cold of the concrete almost unbearable yet strangely satisfying. But, as I continued on, my feet grew only numb. I walked the corridors with the confidence of someone who'd walked them a thousand times over but on entering the main chamber I stalled. All familiarity disappeared on seeing the sudden division of space.

I forced my way through a small, sleepless crowd of mourners until I was facing two soldiers and the entrance to ND's lair. The grip on their rifles was tight but that meant nothing. People had robbed banks before with bananas in their pockets.

I want to see him, I said.

That isn't possible.

Tell him it's Wolfe, ID number 0377.

The soldiers exchanged a glance. One shifted his footing and his gun bobbed with the motion. We're under strict instructions not to disturb him.

I too shifted my posture, trying my best to seem relaxed and friendly, dissociating myself from the weeping crowd. Look, you know me, I said, focusing on soldier number two. Clearly you must understand that I'm brought in and out of here for a particular reason.

The soldier swallowed and I watched the movement of his Adam's apple churn, sharp and jagged rather than bulbous. He seemed to contemplate something before he addressed the walkie-talkie clipped to his shoulder. Wolfe, ID number 0377. Awaiting further instruction.

I glanced up at the spy-hole camera. I had this sudden urge to wave but refrained. A voice was speaking back through the walkie-talkie but it was riddled in code. The soldier turned and tapped something out on the door that resembled Morse code and there was the noise of the lever turning on the other side. People pushed behind me but two more soldiers stepped out from the bulkhead door with their rifles aimed at faces and I could feel someone's grip pulling me forward.

The door closed behind me and I considered the idea that I might never emerge from this lair again. I should have told Stirling or Levitt, because I couldn't bear the idea of them thinking I'd abandoned them. And it dawned on me then that I'd chosen to abandon my own family. I'd never really thought about it like that before; always focused on the loss they'd left me with. I'd stayed over at my brother's house on that last weekend, an unannounced but welcomed visitor

– we drank whisky in the garden with the fire-pit roaring, pretending we knew something about star constellations. I broke one of their crystal glasses, shards of it slipping through the gaps in the decking. They said they didn't mind – that accidents happened. There was my niece's sandpit lid upturned and toy golf clubs scattered across the overgrown lawn. They had no idea I was leaving them behind to die. Like a coward I agreed to their plans for the future: a weekend of babysitting so they could go on a romantic child-free overnight trip somewhere scenic.

The soldier marched me into ND's kitchen and ordered me to sit on one of the breakfast bar stools. Then he turned on his heel and left me alone. On the counter sat boxes of cereal and bowls covered in clingfilm. I peered into one bowl and discovered tinned pineapple rings swimming in their juices. Glancing behind me, I peeled the clingfilm back, the rings of pineapple glinting in the dim kitchen light. I scooped one ring on to my finger and brought it to my nose. It smelled of sugar. I sucked on it and let its juice soak through my cheeks before biting down on the flesh.

I was midway through my second ring when ND walked in wearing pyjamas and his expensive silk robe. He looked gaunt, had physically aged in the weeks since I'd seen him last. But there was something else – a sadness, or was it worry, etched into the creases of his face?

This better be good, Wolfe.

I chewed away my mouthful before speaking. I've been poisoning Glass.

Yet he still stands.

It's taking longer than I thought.

So you've come in the middle of the night to tell me what exactly?

That I'm dealing with it.

Finish your pineapple and go . . .

Why is the wall down? I said. Why are you dividing us?

It's too late to have a coherent conversation with you, he said. Couldn't this have waited until morning?

Where is Canavan? I said. He's been missing since the wall came down.

How do you expect me to know? Canavan is his own man.

But are we ill? I said, raising my voice. You've separated families, are you aware of that? My hands were stretched out to my sides, and I wanted to shake him. I wanted to harm him. You don't seem to have any understanding of what's going on out there.

You think I have no understanding . . .

Are you bringing the wall back up?

He didn't respond.

If we're not ill then what's going on? These are our lives . . . I came close to where he was standing. There was the scent of menthol coming from his robe or maybe his skin. And as I looked at him I saw the liver spots and the skin tags that gathered around his neck. There was a greying of the eyes, hollow and near lifeless. He disgusted me; the idea of him even touching Levitt made me want to vomit. Look at you, I said.

Excuse me?

Look what's happened to you.

He grabbed me then, stronger than I thought he was capable of, gripping his right hand around my neck and pressing his thumb into the underside of my chin. He brought his lips close to my ear and whispered, I could do anything I pleased with you. I could get one of the soldiers to hold you while I took you right here across this counter and there wouldn't be a soul who would dare interrupt me. His lips curled into a smile. Do you think the doctor would still love you then?

I pulled away from his grip. Your breath is foul.

He started laughing, and his laugh grew louder as he walked to the door. But as he stopped at the threshold his face changed. How is the miracle baby? he asked.

I stared at him, unable to answer.

Tell her she won't have a sibling to play with any more. He paused, swallowed. I say to my wife that it wasn't meant to be. That it was not part of God's plan.

For the briefest of moments I thought he was at risk of crying.

I stood paralysed, listening to his stride as he walked down the hall. I stared at the cream cupboards, ran my hand along the countertops. So strange that such ordinary objects would find themselves in this environment. And I couldn't understand how I had come to find myself here either. I should have stayed with my family – I was so clear on that now. I brought my hand up to my chin and felt for the throbbing where ND's thumb had been. It would no doubt bruise and then there would be something of him left on me. I scratched the underside of my chin, until there was the warmth of blood on my fingers. When I looked down it was the most beautiful shade of red I thought I'd ever seen. I brought it to my lips and sucked on it, letting it mix with my saliva, hoping it would make its way back into my system.

I went for Stirling. We huddled in the shower cubicle and despite the warm water hitting my skin a chill travelled through my body, concentrating around the arch of my back. Stirling wrapped his arms around me, a vein bulging slightly in his upper arm as he reached out to kiss me.

Do you know anything? I asked. About the wall . . .

He paused. Supposedly there's a threat of tuberculosis on the other side. That's why the wall came down.

But nothing's been confirmed?

Nothing. And we've no contact whatsoever with the other side.

Do you believe it is TB? I said.

He shook his head.

No, me neither.

The doctors, we're nervous, he said. We don't know what's coming . . . what the leader is likely to do.

I saw him, I said. There's something wrong with him.

What do you mean?

I think he was mourning. He seemed vulnerable, if that's at all possible.

People are spouting claims that he's gone full-blown paranoid, he said. Developed a psychosis from his isolation. What do you make of that?

I shrugged. I couldn't understand why but I found myself guarding ND's privacy, the way I should have been guarding my patients' confidentiality – I didn't know which answers were right and wrong any more. Do you think maybe this bunker is just a good way to get rid of the worst of us? I finally said.

He turned his chin up towards the shower head, gathering water in his mouth before spitting it out. I don't think like that.

More often than not I like to imagine I'm right, I said, that the rest of the world is carrying on. Flourishing without us.

What, and we're the casualties of an experiment?

Perhaps we deserve what we get. We were willing to leave everyone else behind, weren't we? Did you think to offer your space up to someone else? Because I certainly didn't. I exhaled. I don't know, maybe it's just my wishful thinking.

He lowered his head until our foreheads were touching, water running down our cheeks. We're going to get out of here, he said. I really believe that.

My bunkmate Canavan is gone, I said. I'm worried something's happened to him.

Stirling rubbed his wet face, his fingers pruning. I looked at my own fingers and discovered they were pruning too. I'm sure he's OK, he whispered, holding me tighter. He's probably on the other side of the bunker, getting on just fine.

Maybe.

We'd better go, he said, pulling me to my feet. People will be starting their day.

Our boiler suits were only half on when the washroom door opened. We stood there, not daring to move, while one of the taps started running. Whoever was using it was pressing the water button repeatedly and there was the noise of a toothbrush inside a mouth. It sounded aggressive and forceful and I had an urge to discover who was brushing their teeth in such a way. The tap stopped running. Footsteps were moving towards the shower cubicles. My fingers lightly touched the curtain. Stirling looked straight ahead. Somewhere in the washroom there was the sound of a slow drip. Whoever was there stepped into the cubicle next to us, and started running the shower. I could hear their curtain being pulled over, saw the motion of a boiler suit being thrown over the top of the rail.

I think we just make a run for it, Stirling mouthed. You go left, he pointed, and I'll go right.

I nodded.

One. Two. Three, and we ran, thrusting the door open.

But Levitt was blocking our path.

I jumped back, but Stirling's grip was still on the door.

You left us, Levitt said. You said you wouldn't leave. She waited for Stirling to move his hand before stepping over the threshold of the washroom. I hate the nights here, she said. I can't handle them.

I'm sorry, I said, following her out. Instinctively I wanted to offer her reassurance, promise that it wouldn't happen again, but I couldn't. I would take any opportunity to see Stirling – our altered circumstances only allowed for snatched moments. And I needed to see him; it was desperation, his touch cathartic, his voice soothing.

Levitt and I walked the corridors until we reached the boundary wall. The middle clock read 6.52 a.m. Levitt rested her cheek against the metal, cupping her ear. I try to listen every day, she said. Somehow it feels like it'll help, you know? I like to think that my mum is standing right here on the other side, waiting, and we've got our ears pressed to the exact same spot.

I stared out at the same soldiers guarding ND's lair.

Levitt brought her cheek away from the wall, pink spreading across her skin like a suction mark or a slap. We set off on another loop, and as we walked I was surprised to see so many others walking aimlessly too.

We joined the kitchen queue and waited for our pouches. Levitt held her options out, inspecting them with her lip curled under.

What's wrong? Bad selection?

No. It's just ... Aren't you hungry? I'm starving ... She paused, trying to manoeuvre an irritable Eleanor in her wrap. *He* used to give me real food, she said. Like, actual solid food.

In the pharmacy, before we opened, I walked to one of the shelves, picking up a green plastic bowl – it was salad-bowl-sized and looked as if it had been part of a picnic set before making its way in here. I rinsed it out with water and brought it to her.

What do you want me to do with this?

I reached into one of the pockets of my boiler suit and removed a small carton of long-life milk and then, from a different pocket, a miniature-sized box of Rice Krispies. They'd always reminded me of visiting my grandparents as a child – they'd buy me the whole selection – eight varieties of cereal but I'd always leave the Rice Krispies and corn-flakes. Levitt silently stared on as I opened the box of cereal, tipping its contents into the green bowl and pouring the milk on top. The little grains of puffed rice bobbed to the surface, and there was this familiar noise of crackling. I collected two 5ml measuring spoons and handed one to her.

It's not much, but it's something, I said.

Where did you get this? she asked suspiciously, the spoon poised in her hand.

Where do you think? I pulled a chair up close to her and dipped my spoon into the bowl, scooping up Krispies and watery milk. Quick, I said. Eat them before they go soggy.

She took a spoonful, seeming to savour the texture before swallowing. He gave me chocolate cake once, she said. I think it was just one of those mixes that come from a packet, but still . . .

I stared at Eleanor, as though I was hypnotised, stretching out to briefly touch her little cheek. Why him, Levitt? I found myself saying. You could probably have had anyone you wanted . . .

Oh, come on, Wolfe, we can claim to be principled but where does that get us in here? You can either refuse his advances and feel his wrath, or accept it and take the small pleasures on offer – listening to a favourite song, drinking a beer . . . It all adds up, doesn't it? Makes it all a little more bearable. You just close your eyes when he's on you and focus on something else.

I wouldn't know about that part.

Are you telling me you've *never* slept with him?

No. I haven't.

A fleeting smile appeared and she shrugged. For a while I wondered if he'd moved on to you – if that was why he wouldn't let me back into the lair. She paused. Well, you're maybe not sleeping with him but you're doing something for him. And really, isn't it all just the same?

Maybe it's worse, I wanted to say, but the words only circled the inside of my mouth.

Levitt dipped her spoon into the bowl again and didn't stop until she'd scooped out the last of the milk, bringing the bowl to her lips.

# 20

I was providing a woman with an oral capsule for thrush when Glass arrived in the pharmacy. He came close to the Perspex and cupped his mouth.

I've been sick, he said before glancing over his shoulder to see if anyone was approaching. There's blood in it. I can't stop retching . . .

I lowered my voice to a whisper. I'm going to give you a mask to wear, OK?

He nodded. OK.

And it's probably best you give your medication a miss today.

His eyes seemed to plead with me. Are you sure?

One day won't make any difference to your heart, but it may help settle your stomach.

I tried to see a doctor but no one is free.

I hesitated. Do you want me to contact one for you?

Do you think I need one?

Go back to your bunk and sleep. I could check on you later . . . if you'd like?

He nodded before giving me his bunk location.

I'll come once I've finished my shift, OK?

He shuffled out of the pharmacy but held the door open for a woman entering and a wave of affection washed over me to the point that I almost wanted to hug him. The woman had been in many times before and it was always something trivial: *my nose is running, my left eye is twitching, it's been more than three days since I've had a bowel movement.* She faced up to the Perspex and inhaled before speaking. It's sore when I pee. I keep wanting to go but then hardly anything comes out when I do.

It sounds like you have a urine infection, I said. I can give you something, but I'll need to check what other medication you're on.

I swear I think it's to do with there never being enough toilet paper.

I saw a queue slowly building behind her. Levitt came to the counter but the next patient also wanted to speak to me. When you have a moment, Levitt said, this patient wants you to look at their finger.

I nodded.

So, what can you give me? I tried to see the doctors but they're all too busy with the new people.

I can give you an antibiotic. It's one of the few things I can prescribe myself, but you'll have to answer a patient questionnaire . . .

Wolfe, Levitt said, another patient is wondering if you can look at a rash on their neck after you've finished with the others.

I was aware of a woman joining the back of the queue. I hadn't seen her before and as she shuffled forward she swayed like a sail in the breeze and then, as I glanced up again, she keeled over, thumping to the floor. People stared on, perhaps too paranoid to touch her, but I ran out of the dispensary and crouched down. I placed my hand on the ground beside her. What's happened to you? I said.

Her mouth was slow to open and she seemed to struggle to find the words. The bruising, she said, trying to tug at her sleeve. The bruising is spreading.

I began to roll up one sleeve of her boiler suit and as I curled the fabric around her wrist I immediately saw the bruising. It was blotched and rising up the length of her arm. Is there bruising elsewhere? I said.

She nodded.

Someone call for the doctors, I shouted. Get someone now. She's haemorrhaging.

I gently took hold of her hand, aware that every touch I made would mark itself with a bruise. I visualised my niece's doodle pad and how the ink under the board would blotch out and leak with only the slightest touch of my thumb. Don't move, I said to the woman. Stay perfectly still. Her eyes focused on the ceiling and the bright fluorescent lights that shone down. When did the bruising start? I asked.

Her breathing was short and laboured, her ribcage rising and falling under the weight of her boiler suit. I'm not sure. I rarely take the suit off . . .

Have you had a fall? Did you hurt yourself?

She nodded again, closing her eyes.

What's your ID number? I need to check your records.

0068, she whispered. Harper.

I was repeating the digits and name in my mind when Dr Hays and his nurse arrived. He crouched down and I got to my feet, standing in line with the other observers, forever grateful I wasn't a doctor. Even when we'd be sitting on a plane, I'd sink further into my seat when a member of the cabin crew would ask over their speaker system if there was a doctor or a medical professional on board. Daniel used to nudge me in my side, his headphones pulled from his ears. They mean doctors or nurses, I'd say. Not a pharmacist.

Dr Hays called for men to help carry Harper into the surgery and within minutes all evidence of her lying on the floor of the pharmacy was gone. But as I went back into the dispensary I was still reciting her digits and wondering who she was. To have one of the first ID numbers in the bunker must have meant something.

I wasn't expecting to find a drug chart for her, assuming she'd come from the other side, but as my fingers moved quickly through the files I found her alphabetised under H, the ID number matching. I stared at it for a moment before pulling the file out. Her details were scribbled in Valentine's handwriting and as I looked through it I could see his initials signed next to each of her daily dosages. She had been prescribed warfarin for blood-thinning. It was recommended that the dose of warfarin always be taken in the evening so it made sense that she would come during Valentine's shift. She was prescribed 1mg and 3mg tablets in various altering but relatively low-strength combinations – a common practice, to be modified according to her INR readings. I kept being drawn back to the image of the bruising on her arm, the thought of the doctors removing her boiler suit to no doubt discover it elsewhere, like a new skin colour, a new shade of pigmentation. The strengths prescribed shouldn't have been capable of causing her such harm, but, even so, there would have been warning signs to raise an alarm with Valentine. This woman was going to die, most likely from a haemorrhage to the brain – her blood unable to clot, literally leaking out of her cavities.

What's happening to her? Levitt said, a protective arm resting over Eleanor's body.

I closed the drug chart over. She's bleeding, internally.

Is she going to be all right?

I turned to look at Levitt. It might be better if you just finish up now, I said.

She hesitated.

Please, I think you should go . . .

I was expecting some form of mild protest but she nodded, reaching for her blankets. She's not going to be OK, is she?

I'll see you back at the bunks, I replied.

There was a tap on the Perspex, bringing me back to reality. Are you still going to give me something for my urine infection? my waiting patient asked.

When Valentine arrived in the pharmacy he looked terrible. But then I couldn't comment – I made a point not to look at myself in the mirror any more. He shuffled his way across the shop floor and knocked on the dispensary door, despite me already standing there to let him in.

How are things looking? he said, his teeth yellow with plaque.

It's the end of times. Anyone who has the slightest cold is sure they're in the throes of death.

He tried to smile. I assume this is not something that concerns you.

Does it concern you? I said.

I don't think we're dying of a plague, if that's what you mean.

I paused. There was a woman who collapsed in here earlier.

Valentine shifted.

Bruising all over her body.

He nodded. Yes, I heard. The doctors were trying to save her but I think it's over now.

I pushed her drug chart towards him. Do you know anything about her?

He looked at me, narrowing his eyes. Tread carefully, he said.

If I were to drug someone to death, warfarin would be a pretty good way to go about it . . .

He was quiet. I would think so, he finally said.

They'd be so used to their dose being altered, they'd never notice an increase, I said.

We stared at each other; an understanding settling between us.

Giving gliclazide to a non-diabetic patient might be another way to go, though . . . I added.

He paused, his eyes narrowing. So we both want to be on the winning side.

We do what we need to survive, don't we?

Quite the romantic approach, he said.

What if he starts to play us off against one another? I asked, and as the words came out I realised it was more of a statement than a question.

He shrugged. If the time comes, I'll do what I have to do. And you should too.

I leant forward then and found myself embracing him, his arms slowly coming round too and resting on my back.

Do you have a family, Valentine? I've never thought to ask you.

He shook his head. I had a wife and son once but they died years ago in a car crash. He exhaled. I don't know why I came here, to be honest. I should have stayed behind. Perhaps I could have been reunited with them.

Afterwards, he handed me two packets of dextrose sugar tablets for Glass. Perhaps there was a chance they could reverse the hypoglycaemic damage I'd inflicted, but I suspected it was too late for that.

I walked past the doctors' surgery and lingered in the corridor. I saw one of the nurses open the door and for a brief moment caught a glimpse of Stirling, his shoulders, the collar of his white coat upturned. I decided that if the entire male population of the bunker were to congregate in one space with their backs turned to me, I would most certainly be able to identify Stirling among the throng. I used to think I could do the same with Daniel. I took pleasure in studying their profiles, their hairlines, the necks, anything that helped me feel as though that person somehow belonged to me.

I turned the corner, eyes cast down, wrapping my arms around myself as I inched closer towards the sleeping quarters. When I looked up, Holden was approaching from the opposite direction. I toyed with the idea of just turning and walking away but he'd already tilted his head in some sort of acknowledgement.

Hello, he said, coming to a stop in front of me.

Hello.

Haven't seen you in a while.

No, I said. How are you?

We're OK. How are you? How's the doctor?

Word certainly travels fast, I said.

Some kids came running past and Holden pulled me further towards the wall, out of their path. I stared down at my gym shoes. There was a smudge curled around the right toe, as if I'd stepped in a puddle, except there were no puddles to step in.

I suppose I should thank you, I said. I know the lengths you went to, to secure a place for me here.

Well, it was Stirling who signed your documents.

Why did you bother? Wouldn't it have been easier for you without me here?

He began to shake his head. Wolfe, it wasn't like I was going on holiday. You would have perished.

I looked up at him, trying to remember what it was like to be with him: his arms, our naked bodies, his laugh, the inside jokes. But I couldn't properly visualise it any more. There were memories but they were vague, like a film I'd seen but couldn't quite recall. The only memory that was clear was the one of me confessing I wasn't able to have children – the relief at having said the words aloud and it bearing no signi-ficance for him. If he wanted children he would be having them with his wife. It dawned on me then how deep-rooted and truly toxic my self-loathing had become. The only person consumed by my infertility was me. And I was suddenly so sad because I'd somehow ignored the moments of happiness – had forgotten the good that had taken place in my previous life.

Well, thank you anyway, I said. I appreciate the effort you made. But I spoke in a tone that suggested I was merely thanking a stranger for holding open a door.

He held his palms up towards me, perhaps offering some sort of truce. You are OK, though, aren't you?

No, not really.

In the sleeping quarters, I stared at Glass's bunk co-ordinates etched out in permanent marker on the palm of my hand. Halfway down one row I got confused, thinking that perhaps I'd missed a number. I stopped and counted, sensing I'd gone too far. Several people were curled up on bunks, their blankets pulled over their heads, and I stared at them, trying to decide if one of them was Glass. Then it occurred to me that he might already be dead and I'd left it too late.

I turned myself around in a circle. The white elastic strap of the face mask I'd given him caught my eye as it protruded from the blanket. Would the elastic strap be tight enough to asphyxiate? I heard myself laugh. What did it matter when you were already actively trying to kill someone?

I tapped him on the shoulder. He shifted and I relaxed. I tapped him again. Glass?

He began to stir, opening his eyes. He pulled down the mask from his mouth. I had this dream that you played the violin. But you don't play the violin, do you, Marla?

I'm not Marla. I'm Wolfe. The pharmacist. Remember?

He let his eyes come into focus. You came, he said.

I knelt beside him. How are you feeling? Have you been sick again?

He shook his head. I'm so weak . . . Is it my heart? It feels like it's beating too quickly . . .

Here, I said, handing him the dextrose tablets. I think you should take these. It will help.

He pushed my hand away with his frail fingers. No. I can't.

I hesitated, still kneeling with my heels raised off the floor. Can I sit next to you? I said.

He curled into the foetal position. He had the bottom bunk of his column and it was easy enough to hop on at the end, pushing my back against the frame and letting my feet dangle.

Are you sure it's OK if I sit here? I don't want to impose.

It's fine.

Where are your family? I asked.

His shoulders seemed to let out a shudder then, as if they'd been holding something in. They're on the other side. My son and his kids were located there and my wife was with them when the wall came down. It's better this way. It's better she's with them.

So you're alone now?

Do you think they'll be OK over there?

I think they'll be fine. I'm still confident the wall will be brought up soon.

You didn't have to come and check on me, he said. That's not your job.

I clasped my hands together. The skin on my fingers looked pale and dry and I had the urge to lick them, if only to try to offer them some source of moisture. The skin between my thumbs and index fingers had always felt so soft and gentle, but now it looked eroded and scaly. I could see the tips of my gym shoes bobbing in the air. I had accepted the slight webbing of my middle toes but now when I took off my shoes my feet somehow appeared worse, as though I was actually mutating with radiation.

I want to ask you something, and I need you to be honest with me.

He nodded. OK.

What did you do?

What do you mean? He started to wheeze, struggling to catch his breath.

I'm killing you, I said. I've been doing it slowly and deliberately and I need to find a reason to stop. The way you're feeling – it's all because of me.

He tried to sit up a little, placing his palm against his cheek. He looked me in the eye, his nostrils flaring. Please, let me be, he said.

I was told to drug you. I didn't really have any choice in the matter. But now I'm looking for a choice. Why does our leader want you dead?

He gasped, particles of blood-splattered saliva landing on his blanket. So be it, he said. What life is this for anyone?

It's the guilt, I said. It's eating my insides.

That's your problem, not mine.

So you're a good person and I've got it wrong. I've been killing a good man . . .

None of us is innocent. I'm not innocent. You're not innocent. There is no one in here who has the innocence of a newborn. Just look at your friend's baby – she's all the perfection that's left in the world, and she won't stay like that for long.

Please tell me why he wants you dead. I need to know.

A silent laugh escaped from his lips. The same way he'll probably want you dead next. For questioning him, I suppose, or doubting him. For daring to think there might be a better way . . . He took a breath. People do terrible things when they're trying to cling to power. I'd likely do the same. Wouldn't you?

How do we get rid of him?

He tried to laugh again but the effort it took caused him pain and he winced, wiping his mouth. I'm supposed to say: the same way every Western power defeats the last – democracy.

So now what?

I don't have all the answers, he said, and he shrugged, closing his eyes.

I placed my hand on his back, desperate for him to provide me with something more, all the while aware of his lungs inflating and deflating slowly. At what point could I have stopped and corrected my error? Reversible one day, terminal the next.

I wasn't sure how long I sat there with my hand resting against his back. I was thinking about one of those computer games I used to play as a kid when I realised, despite his warmth, that his chest was still and lifeless. Slowly, I reached for his wrist and checked his pulse but there was none. I'd lost full days to playing that game – simulating life, building houses, finding love, a salary from work. When the false life had got too tough and my character had yearned for another lover I'd realised that if you put the existing husband or wife in the swimming pool and removed the ladders they'd swim and swim until they died from exhaustion. And little happened to my character – she'd move on to another lover and swim around the gravestone as though it were nothing. I envied those characters and their ability to move on with little remorse for the past. Would we all behave in this manner if we thought there were no consequences to our actions? That probably depressed me more than anything else – this notion that the only driving force in conducting ourselves morally rested on our fear of how we were seen and perceived. How could that be explained when you believed in having a conscience, in having a soul?

I edged off Glass's bunk, checking the row for people before removing his face mask and leaving. I wondered how many hours would pass before someone else realised he was dead. But I suspected his bunkmates would go to bed none the wiser.

# 21

They came for me in my sleep. I'd been swallowing nitraze-
pam in a bid to block everything out but still they reached
me through the fog. A soldier shook me with his rifle resting
next to his chest, the barrel at my eye level, and I blinked,
thinking I was imagining it in my stupor. He helped me down
from my bunk, while Levitt and Foer silently watched on,
and I was struck by how soft his touch was, more like guiding an elderly patient than forcing someone against their
will. Not that I was resisting; I was resigned to whatever
awaited me.

The heat coming from ND's lair hit my face as the soldiers
opened the chamber doors. It pricked my skin like an open
fire and pulled me in further. And there, sitting in an embroidered chair while a guard stood over him, was Canavan. The
lamp on the sideboard flickered before it surged with power
and cut out, but Canavan didn't seem to notice. His hands
cupped his knees and I could see the beginnings of words
and drawings creeping out from his cuffs.

I stopped in front of him. I've been looking for you, I said
with affection in my voice.

He leant forward and stared at me intently, pursing his
lips, before pressing back into the fabric of his seat and shifting his gaze to the soldier standing guard. Why are we here?
he said, lifting his head upwards.

You know better than anyone that's not how it works, the soldier replied.

Canavan shrugged. He pointed the toe of his gym shoe to the carpet. He swivelled his ankle in a circular motion until it looked as if it might snap, and I flinched, shifting my gaze back to the sideboard and its broken lamp. The vase of silk flowers still sat in the middle, their buds open-mouthed and bright. There was also an empty fruit bowl and an old-fashioned rotary telephone. I couldn't remember the last time I'd used a landline phone; I had stopped answering them long before we came to the bunker. There was the memory then of my grandfather answering the telephone and repeating his home number before the caller even had a chance to tell him who it was.

Without being fully conscious of my actions, I found myself making my way to the telephone. The soldier was talking to me but I couldn't hear what he was saying. I lifted the receiver from its cradle and brought it to my ear. There was no dialling tone. Had I been expecting one? I started reciting the only number I knew – the telephone number of my childhood home – the one my parents had shared before divorcing.

Hello. 862 356. Hello 862 356. Hello?

The soldier's hand was on my arm and it hurt. What do you think you're doing?

I brought the phone down from my ear. I don't know . . .

He grabbed the receiver from my hand and planted it back on the cradle harder than was necessary. Sit down, he spat, pushing me, and I had to work hard to keep my balance. You'll get us all crucified, if we're not already, he said, with what sounded like real hatred. But for some reason his tone encouraged me, bringing me to life in a way that felt light and playful.

I smiled at the soldier and took my seat opposite Canavan. I tried to catch his eye, willing him to come to life too, but he kept shifting his gaze, focusing on the floor.

The soldier was standing close, the tips of his shoes pointing towards me. I could have reached out and touched his rifle, and I laughed then.

The soldier shook his head, gripping the rifle tighter when the kitchen door opened and out stepped the new Alison. He'll see you both together, she said.

Canavan and I glanced at one another.

Move it, the soldier said and we slowly rose from our seats. But, as we made to pass, the soldier thrust the butt of his rifle into Canavan's side, causing him to buckle.

That's enough, the new Alison said.

Why would you do that? I shouted, crouching next to Canavan.

The soldier sniffed phlegm up his nose. The likes of you deserve worse, you fag, he said, moving slowly backwards, raising his hands in a mocking gesture of peace.

The new Alison was still standing by the door. We don't have all day, she said, and I helped Canavan back on to his feet before we were ushered into the kitchen.

The cream gloss cupboards and wooden worktops were spotless. It really was like walking into IKEA, admiring a life I would have liked to lead. Facing us, perched on one of the high-legged stools around the breakfast bar, was ND. He was wearing a short-sleeved polo shirt with his usual embroidered initials and he was eating a slice of pepperoni pizza. There was a smear of grease resting above his top lip, his face appearing more gaunt than ever before. He threw his slice on to the plate and wiped his mouth, but the grease stain remained.

He was still chewing when he spoke. It's nice when I bring people together, isn't it?

Neither of us replied.

Don't you agree?

We reluctantly nodded in unison.

He nodded too, and for a moment nothing more was said.

So where do we stand, Canavan?

Canavan paused. It's not an instant thing. Gaining someone's trust takes time . . .

ND brought up his hand to silence him. All you have is time, he said. You've had an abundance of it. Clearly, Canavan, your powers of persuasion are not what you claim. That, or you're enjoying yourself more than you wish to confess.

Canavan took a step towards the counter and ND didn't stop him. Look, you know my loyalty to you is unquestionable. But there could perhaps be a small chance that this place is making you a little paranoid. It's happening to us all. He took another step towards the counter. Maybe if you visited the main chambers again, you'd see we are still with you.

Paranoid? Are you a doctor now? He started laughing. Wolfe, what do you make of Ralf's diagnosis? Do you agree?

I . . . I think you're not looking quite yourself.

ND stared at me, taking another bite and chewing with his mouth open. Finally some good news with regard to Glass. It took you long enough, however.

I could feel Canavan's eyes upon me now.

ND exhaled. It's like St Basil's Cathedral all over again.

Sorry? I said. What?

That's why I ask of you the difficult things required. I am

treated like the architects of that cathedral. I create something pure and beautiful and once it's nearing completion they want to destroy me. Take my eyes . . . Fearful that I will surpass my abilities if left in charge.

There was a pause. Are you referring, Canavan said, with what I thought was scepticism – are you essentially saying that you think the bunker's inhabitants are behaving like Ivan the Terrible?

Exactly, ND said, very sure of himself. The things I've done for our brothers and sisters . . .

One of ND's dogs came padding into the kitchen, followed by the other – spaniels or something similarly yappy – those dogs that seemed to have too much energy. They were sniffing around, their tails wagging frantically from side to side, and I had no idea how they hadn't gone mad in this confined space. One of them bounded over to where I was standing. It started licking my hand and suddenly I was petting it, rubbing it behind the ears.

Do you have to touch everything that belongs to me? ND said, before clicking his fingers and calling out, Claude. And immediately the dog came to his side, sitting obediently. Did you ever go to SeaWorld and meet those great big killer whales? he asked.

No one answered.

A piece of pepperoni had fallen off his pizza slice and he placed it back on, mashing it down with his palm before gathering the slice and taking another bite. They were incredible creatures, he said. A shame about their captivity, but still something marvellous to see. He held the pizza slice in his right hand and waved it about as he spoke. Their trainers had this ingenious way of teaching the new whales tricks. They'd pair a new whale with an experienced one and when the new one wouldn't do the trick both whales were punished. Isn't that clever? The trained whale would get so annoyed that it would start raking the skin of the new whale. Do you know what raking is?

I shook my head but Canavan didn't move.

Imagine Ralf here clawing your skin with his nails until the skin breaks and begins to bleed. I guess it would feel something like that, but on blubber.

He turned to smile at his dogs before throwing the crust on to the floor for them. The dogs fought, until one of them managed to gulp it down.

You see, before long the new whale was doing every trick in the book and all the whales began to live in harmony. The other dog was now licking the floor where a few crumbs must have remained. You are now my two little whales, linked together, and together you will allow harmony to be restored. He nodded to himself, seeming pleased. When one of my whales does not achieve what is needed, both will feel the consequences.

Canavan and I looked at each other.

There's no need to drag Wolfe any further into this, Canavan said. I'll do what you want me to do.

ND raised his hand to silence him. I lie awake at night listening to my wife struggle through her grief. And then, last night, when I thought I could take no more, I had an epiphany. He smiled. Your face appeared before me, Wolfe, and I realised it was fate. I finally understood exactly why you were brought into my life. What divine act you would be able to play.

I started shaking my head. I don't understand . . .

You're going to enable my wife to fulfil her greatest calling in life. Won't that be something? Won't that be incredible?

A shiver ran down the back of my neck, but I resisted flinching and remained completely still.

You will bring the baby to me, he said. The child, *my* child, deserves a better existence than the one Levitt can offer her.

My head began to shake as I absorbed his words.

She will be happier here.

I won't do it, I said, propelling myself forward as though I was ready to attack, but Canavan gripped me, pulling me back.

ND stared at me, amused. Why would you deny that baby a better life?

I won't take Levitt's baby away from her, I said. I'd rather die . . .

And Ralf too? He laughed. Or, perhaps more importantly from your perspective, Stirling . . . He smiled. Yes, Stirling. How long would he last if we placed him inside an airlock chamber? A few days, a week? I suspect Stirling would be quite inventive, under the circumstances, don't you think?

I could feel my throat constricting and I ran my hand along my neckline. Please . . . I begged. Please, don't make me take the baby.

ND rose from his stool and patted one of the dogs. His hand ran around the underside of the dog's ear and continued to stroke it tenderly. You can go now, he said, nodding to me. But Ralf, you might as well stay for a while and make yourself useful. Since you're here . . .

I stared at Canavan, hesitating, wanting to reach out and take him with me. If we really were tied to one another, then it didn't seem right to be leaving him behind.

Wolfe, just go, Canavan said. It's OK. I'll be OK.

But still, I lingered a moment longer. And tell your

boyfriend to prescribe me more of my pills, ND said. All of them.

I turned and walked out of the kitchen, as compliant as one of his dogs.

The new Alison was waiting for me but there was no sign of the soldiers. As she made to usher me down the hall I turned and asked, What *did* happen to Alison?

She brought her hand up to silence me. What does it matter? I get to be here now.

In the main chamber I stood staring at other inhabitants trying to go about their lives, doing their best to ignore the great divide. Were we to accept that the wall might never come up? I'd listened once to a podcast that suggested the only reason humans survived was due to our deep-rooted resilience. We were like cockroaches – you could try to kill us off, but we'd still somehow filter through. I wasn't sure if any other creature would survive, but I was confident that cockroaches were most likely scuttling about somewhere, perhaps evolving into larger creatures – finally the Biblical scale from the book of Revelation.

I really wanted to know what the outside world looked like. Would ash still be falling like grey snow from the sky, destroying everything it touched? The podcast had said that even when dealt immeasurable grief – a grief we could not perhaps have ever contemplated – we still came through it and survived. And some part of me understood that, was able to relate to the logic. When I had found my mum after her suicide she had looked like herself, but what about the rest of my loved ones? What did nuclear fallout do to a person's body, to their bones, to their skin? I thought about my niece's cheeks, the sallowness and cluster of freckles. Would they have peeled away? Did it melt extremities, fingers and toes falling off? There were people who exhumed the bodies of their loved ones once all flesh had rotted away – they'd leave socks or shoes on the dead to keep all the little bones intact. But I hoped there was nothing left of the ones I loved. Dying inside an airlock chamber was probably nothing compared to what they'd endured.

I stared at the different time-zoned clocks and tried to pretend I was somewhere else in the world. I wanted to see Stirling, wanted to tell him about my predicament, that I somehow had to choose between him and Eleanor. But what could he possibly say to alter the situation? I supposed I was worried that he'd try to be selfless – tell me under no circumstances to take the baby away from Levitt – that he would bear the consequences. But I couldn't contemplate that; couldn't consider the possibility of him not being in my life. And maybe ND had a point – perhaps Eleanor would thrive better in the lair.

So instead of heading to the surgery I aimlessly made my way towards the dining hall. There was the familiar smell that repulsed me – a suffocating odour that had nowhere to escape. I stopped at the water fountain. I let the water run for a second before bringing my mouth to the spout. I'd never been good at drinking from a water fountain; it was as if I was scared to get too close. I didn't like the sensation of the water blocking my mouth, of swallowing and struggling for breath.

I took a seat at the end of a bench and pulled a food pouch out from my pocket. I had no desire to eat but it didn't seem right to be sitting there empty-handed. I unscrewed the cap of my pomegranate-flavoured pouch and brought the rim to my lips, immediately aware of someone sitting down on the bench opposite me. Baxter's mother half-smiled, already opening her own pouch. She was child-free and I glanced around, checking if the hall was at full capacity, needing to know if she'd had no other option but to sit near me.

Aside from the obvious, like people, what else do you miss? She spoke with broken, sloshing words as the puréed mush circled her mouth.

I was quiet for a moment, wanting to give her question real consideration. I miss going to the pub, or going to a coffee shop. Running outside. I should probably have a more meaningful answer. But that's what I miss.

She smiled.

What about you? I asked.

She took in a breath. I miss opening windows. I miss the exchange of money, of using a bank card. I miss swimming . . . I even miss soft play, if that's at all possible.

I miss holding a knife and fork, I said, and as I spoke I realised my hands were forming the shape they would have held if there had been cutlery in them. I miss that feeling of climbing into a freshly made bed.

I miss walking in the woods, she said. Or sitting out in the garden. I really loved my garden. She took another mouthful of her pouch, her cheeks momentarily puffing out.

How is little Baxter? I asked.

Fine. He's with his father. She paused. I've been meaning to talk to you, actually. Thank you properly for what you did when the wall came down.

I shrugged. It was nothing . . .

She paused. But I also wanted to apologise . . . She swallowed another mouthful. You've tried to help me on a number

of occasions, and on one particular occasion I was less than
gracious.

Honestly, please don't . . .

No, let me just say what I want to say. She lowered her
voice to a whisper. You were right, about *him*, the leader.
There is growing consensus among many that he is no longer
fit to lead. His mind . . . She paused. The tide is beginning to
turn. It's slow, but it is turning.

I see.

However, in changing circumstances, some see you as an
informant.

Sorry?

I've tried to explain . . . She took another sharp intake of
breath. But . . . I just want you to be careful.

I closed my eyes and tried to think of something calming.
I focused on the magic lamp in my grandmother's lounge. A
floor lamp, emitting a glow across her sofa and armchair. It
had had a shade like an antique window – stained glass
curved in segments with lead, a copper-beaded cord dangling
from its base. I used to count to three and command the
lamp to turn off with the power of my mind, just when my
grandfather would be reaching for the switch on the plug.
They were lucky to have missed this – to be buried together,
dying with the knowledge that the world could still be a good
place.

I'm on the same side as you, I whispered. I'm not like
him . . .

I know that, she said. I just worry for you, OK?

I paused, closing and opening my eyes. A slow-turning tide
is no use, I said. It's not fast enough. It will change nothing.

Suddenly someone started screaming from the bottom
of the hall and my head jolted in its direction. A woman

stood on top of a bench, hysterical, and pointed towards one of the waste buckets on the ground. People began to move closer, collectively alert, and I followed, pushing through until I was near the front, the waste bucket in my line of vision.

What's wrong? someone was asking.

The woman kept shaking her head, her hand now covering her mouth, as if she had to physically contain her voice from escaping.

I took another step towards the bucket and peered inside. A few of the men had come forward too, our heads nearly touching. There was a noise coming from inside the bucket, like a rustling of sorts, faint and barely audible but there was something.

Those of us who had ventured close enough glanced at each other, cautious and confused. The rustling noise was intensifying.

One of the men, a patient I recognised, without warning kicked the bucket over on to its side. A mouse ran out – a baby mouse but it was there and alive, panicked and scurrying across the floor.

The room erupted with noise, people jumping, some running after the mouse or on to the benches. The little thing had no idea where to go and one man raised his foot, attempting to stamp the life out of it.

Stop, I screamed. Don't kill it.

The mouse dodged the feet of those that followed it and disappeared.

And then silence fell over us, this strange, unfamiliar silence.

Baxter came to where I was standing. A mouse . . . she said. How on earth?

I stared out in the direction of where it had disappeared. Was it possible that the world above could be healing, capable once again of hosting life? Alternatively, perhaps the best of the world was indeed continuing, as though a coup had rid it of the rotten apples. Or maybe it was nothing. What did I know about mice? There had probably been mice in here before we were. Regardless, it was a much-needed distraction from the fact I was coming around to the idea of taking a child away from her mother.

# 22

It was around midnight and Levitt and Eleanor were sleeping, Mrs Foer too, above them. Eleanor whimpered and I watched the flickering of her eyelids, the skin still so thin and transparent. What did babies dream of? Milk? I reached down and placed my hands around her tiny torso, cupping her body. As I slowly brought her towards me Levitt stirred, smiling, before suddenly becoming alert. I brought the baby to my chest and clung to her, taking in her smell as I began to retreat.

Wolfe ... Levitt said, cautiously, not yet pleading. What are you doing? You know I don't like people holding her.

Eleanor began to cry and I gripped her tightly. I'm sorry, I said. I don't think I have a choice any more. I knew I sounded manic. I *was* manic; a woman deranged.

She straightened up on her bunk. I watched her nostrils inflate and deflate as a means of trying to remain calm. Please, she said. Give me back my baby.

I can't ... And I started crying. I'm sorry, I repeated, before breaking into a sprint.

I was aware of Levitt behind me, her bare feet making a painful slapping noise. As I rounded the corner Eleanor's head bobbed mid-air and I gripped her little skull between my fingers, terrified of hurting her. Levitt gained on me – a sharp and inconceivable noise that attracted the attention of everyone we passed. The door to the lair was already open and two soldiers pulled me forward into their embrace. I lost one of my gym shoes but there was no time to stop and retrieve it. Behind me they restrained a now hysterical Levitt, who tried to claw her way forward. Her cries were like the raw howls of an animal – instinctual and uncontrollable. And I couldn't believe, didn't want to accept, that I was the source of such pain.

ND was waiting for me with his wife in their lounge. It was painted a teal colour, with a mock fireplace and artificial flames burning bright on the far wall. His wife sat with her ankles crossed, a smart, dignified outfit on while she waited like an expectant mother. There was a nervousness to her smile but her eyes were tired and weary, as though she'd only recently stopped crying.

She came forward and extended her hands to take Eleanor from me, but instinctively I turned away, unwilling to let go.

Sarah, hand the baby over, ND said.

With his wife's hands still extended she came closer, gently prising Eleanor from me. She immediately brought the baby to her chest, distancing herself from me before making this cooing noise that had the potential to send anyone to sleep.

Good girl, ND said, and I looked up, unsure whether he was speaking to me or Eleanor.

You can see the nursery if you like, his wife said, glancing over her shoulder. I think you'll like it. We've got it looking beautiful for her.

OK, I whispered. My throat felt jagged, like broken glass and there didn't seem to be any point in refusing.

The nursery was painted in the shade of yellow sunshine. I stood over the threshold and stared at the contents of the room: a wooden cot and chest of drawers, a small rug on the floor. A hot-air-balloon mobile bobbed in the air, suspended from the ceiling, and felt cloud bunting was tacked to the walls. It was like something from a catalogue. And as I took in the room I allowed myself to believe that ND did indeed have the right intentions. Who wouldn't enjoy sleeping in this room?

You can go in, if you like, she said, and I hesitated before entering, running my hand across the cot's frame, tapping a finger on one of the paper hot-air balloons.

We packed for all eventualities, she said, with Eleanor sleeping in her arms, eyes closed to her new environment.

Beautiful, isn't it? ND said, now standing behind me.

Yes, I said. It is.

We're going to call her Eve, he said.

I flinched. She already has a name . . .

She'll have a good life here, he replied, I promise you. He placed his hand on my shoulder but it seemed as though it was to steady himself more than anything else. In the end, you'll be glad of what you did.

His wife tilted her head slightly, glancing at us. You must be tired. We should show you to your room.

Sorry?

It's all ready for you, ND said. It's next door to Ralf's.

I should go back . . .

ND smiled this pitiful smile and I thought he was about to embrace me in a fatherly hug. People will be angry, he said, his tone a gentle lull. It'll be like a lynch mob. They'll take your eyes out. They won't understand yet, so we must give them time to accept. Eventually, they'll come to appreciate we were acting in Eve's best interests.

I shook my head. I've left Levitt on her own. I promised I wouldn't do that.

Shhhh, ND said, bringing his index finger up to his lips and nodding towards the baby.

His wife was still staring at me. You only have one shoe. You're not going to manage much with only one shoe. And we'll need to get you out of that filthy suit. Perhaps a wash . . . She took a cautious step closer. Joanne can help you.

Suddenly I felt so confused that I had to close my eyes. Who's Joanne? I asked.

You know, Joanne, ND replied. She's our personal assistant. The one who replaced Alison after the whole Christmas tree débâcle.

Joanne shepherded me into a bathroom with antique-style ceramic tiles, a porcelain suite and a towel rail with expensive looking white towels hanging from it. The shower was separate from the bath, and Joanne turned it on, testing the water's temperature as it fell from a pan head. Are you capable of washing yourself? she asked, and I thought she was joking but there was no hint of humour in her face.

I can wash myself, I replied.

OK, good.

I stepped towards the toilet and on lifting the lid saw ND's initials branded on the porcelain. I began to pull my suit open, desperate for the toilet, but Joanne was still standing there, watching over me.

I can manage from here, I said.

Well, if you need anything I'm never too far away.

I think I'll be OK.

She paused. There's some lamb stew leftovers in the kitchen if you're hungry.

Unable to hold it in any longer, I was already sitting on the toilet seat, emptying my bladder. I don't have any clothes, I said.

You can put on a robe, she replied, pointing to one hanging on a chrome hook. But I'll be sure to leave clothes in your room for you.

Where is my room?

I've left the door open so you'll see it easily enough.

Alone, my bowels exploded over the porcelain toilet pan, such was the guilt and anxiety that festered inside me. I closed my eyes for a moment but it did nothing to clear my mind of Levitt's expression when she'd realised I was taking her baby away from her. Down the hall Eleanor had begun to cry, and it occurred to me then that I'd barely heard her cry when she was with her mother.

I walked into the kitchen wearing the robe and hotel slippers, my coarse and damaged hair wrapped up in one of the pristine white towels. The down-lighters under the kitchen cupboards were on, so that a soft glow filled the room. Alistair was closing the fridge and seemed startled to see me. He had a bottle of sparkling water in his hand, and he broke the seal before speaking.

How are you settling in? he asked.

I shrugged.

Are you hungry?

Warily, I nodded.

He spread his hands out as if he wanted me to take in the great expanse of the kitchen. Well, I'm off duty, but I'm sure you've already been told you can help yourself to anything in the fridge or the snack cupboards, he said, pointing to them. He paused. I'd prefer you didn't go into my larder or the freezers – it's difficult to plan meals and measure rations if others are interfering.

OK, I said. Thank you.

He nodded, looking me up and down. You can relax, he said. You've done it.

Done what?

Made it. Not many people make it this far.

Do you like it here? I asked.

I've nothing else to compare it to.

What do you do all day?

I keep myself busy in the kitchen . . . There's a gym, the cinema . . . Your friend's in there now, actually. He arrived not long before you.

Only once Alistair was gone did I dare look inside the fridge. It was stacked to the brim with bottles of water and packets of mostly defrosting food. One whole shelf was dedicated to chocolate and I found it bizarre that some people chose to keep their chocolate in the fridge. On the cooker, I lifted the casserole lid of the lamb stew but it smelled too strong. Instead I opened the fridge again and found a packet of chocolate-covered mini pretzels, ripping them open and forcing them into my mouth. Glancing around, I wondered how it was at all possible to keep a kitchen like this so well stocked. What quantities must they have had to bring? To be able to freely help yourself was a foreign concept. Before I was even aware of it, I'd finished all the pretzels and was placing the foil packet in the bin.

I stood in the hall and tried to decipher which door led to the cinema. I'd sat in this hall so many times, yet each door was now unrecognisable to me. I thought the cinema room was the last door on the right, but then doubted myself, thinking I'd never actually been to the end of the corridor before. I gripped the handle of the door, hesitating before turning it. Inside, there was the bright white light of the projector, but the volume had been turned down to almost silent. I stopped at a sofa now positioned in the front row, heaped with duvets. Tufts of Canavan's wild hair poked out from the top. There could have been at least three duvets over him, spreading out and on to the carpet.

He must have sensed my presence, because he turned and stared up at me with eyes as wild as his hair. Slowly, he sat up, the projector casting a shadow over half of his face. It was something of a sensory overload and I shielded my eyes before slumping on to the end of the sofa, landing on his feet under the parachute of duvets.

Imagine meeting you here, I said.

You could have dressed for the occasion, he replied, reaching down to the floor and bringing a bowl up with him. He scooped up a piece of meat and forced it into his mouth, his fingers sticky with sauce.

I stared at him. What are you watching?

A Western. As he chewed he tried to pull something from his mouth, sliding his thumbnail in between his bottom two front teeth. He offered me the bowl but I shook my head and he slumped back into his mass of duvets, continuing to fidget with what must have been a particularly fibrous strand of meat.

How's the little one settling in? he said. She's noisy, isn't she?

Tell me I did the right thing . . .

I don't think I'm the best person to ask, he said, forcing his hand further into his mouth, reaching towards the molars. Did you get the full tour?

No, not really.

Well, you must get him to show you the new portrait I did. It's hanging in the boardroom.

Whose portrait?

His gaze was fixed on the screen, a grin spreading across his face. Of him. It's my greatest work actually. But I don't think he even understands it . . .

Canavan, I feel this sickness. Like I'm rotting from the inside out.

We've sold our souls, he said, and he started laughing, the noise escaping from his nostrils. And for what? He bent his legs, his giant knees looking like two mountains under snowy duvets. Really, tell me – for what? I need to know?

I looked at his face. There was no glint at all left in his eyes. It was gone; stamped out.

He took the remote that was resting on the arm of the sofa and turned the volume up to an almost unbearable pitch. I got close to a person again, he said. A good man who cared for me when I thought no one else would . . . He exhaled. But I killed him. Just like that. As if it was nothing.

Who was he?

An advisor. Someone important. He shrugged. Sometimes I think we're all on a list and he's just working his way down until it's only himself left. He paused. Do you want to know how I did it?

No.

I strangled him in the shower while we were together. And he didn't even put up a fight. Can you believe that? I'm meant to make them look like an accident, or suicide, so the soldiers don't raise too many questions, but I couldn't do that with him. I can't sleep now, you see. I keep trying but my eyes won't go blank when I close them. Do people die from sleep deprivation? Is that a thing? Do you have any tablets that will help me sleep . . . ?

I shook my head.

It probably wouldn't be enough anyway to ensure I didn't wake up again.

Please don't say that, Canavan.

He sat up a little. I wrote some poems, he said pulling up a sleeve of his boiler suit. There's only room for haikus now.

| | |
|---|---|
| *Only salt for miles* | *The little spider* |
| *The flats so warm in the sun* | *My finger hovering high* |
| *Deathly cold at night* | *A slow change of heart* |

Eventually I said: I hate Westerns. Can I change it?

Pick something light-hearted, he whispered, shifting slightly in his seat before closing his eyes. Stay with me for a little while. I sleep better when you're here.

I scrolled through the *classics* film selection and landed on *Three Men and a Baby.* And as the opening credits played out to numerous women leaving an expensive New York apartment, Canavan slept with his cheek pressed into the sofa.

I hovered over the threshold to my room. Inside it was quite pretty, like something from a farmhouse – plain white walls with a cast-iron double bed and wooden chairs for bedside tables. Lying down, I discovered the duvet was made of goose feathers. Resting on top of a pillow was a stack of sweaters, joggers and five pairs of clean white pants. On one of the bedside tables lay a toothbrush and miniature tube of toothpaste like the ones I used to take on holiday. I lay my head down on the empty pillow and closed my eyes but the horror on Levitt's face was still there, etched into my mind. I opened my eyes quickly, my breathing heavy and erratic. I could hear Eleanor crying again down the corridor. It escalated into hysterical wails – a momentary pause where she must have been trying to catch her breath before the crippling cycle repeated.

At some point in the early hours I went and stood in the floral hallway, inching closer to the nursery and the noise of Eleanor. I could hear ND's wife singing a lullaby and I rested my head against the wall, willing Eleanor and myself to fall asleep to the hushed tones.

Joanne came marching out from the kitchen with a bottle of formula milk in her hands. On seeing me, she jumped, causing little droplets to fall on to the carpet. What are you doing up? she whispered.

I couldn't sleep.

She nodded. I'm sorry about the noise. She's refusing to take a bottle. I've been told to try a different teat. A latex one . . .

Do you need help?

Wolfe . . . She hesitated. You're not allowed to see the baby. Did no one make that clear to you?

But she knows me.

Joanne reached out, awkwardly attempting to place her hand on my arm. I'm not trying to be cruel. I'm just following my orders.

I swallowed. She'll be looking for her mother's milk, I whispered. I don't know how you'll get her to take a bottle.

She paused. I suppose that wasn't exactly taken into consideration . . .

ND's wife began shouting for the bottle and Joanne hurried away.

\* \* \*

By lunchtime ND's wife was growing frantic at Eleanor's refusal to feed from a bottle. The child was screaming from hunger and they had little choice but to summon Levitt to the lair, referring to her as the *wet nurse*. I edged out of my room, fearful of encountering her in the hallway and ran to the bathroom. Despite the shower the previous day I didn't feel clean.

I perched on the side of the bathtub and added copious amounts of expensive-looking bubble bath. It must have taken at least twenty minutes to fill, and for the entire duration there was a peaceful silence throughout the lair. I stripped off and edged my toes into the water. It burnt, pinpricking my skin, but I didn't stop until my body was submerged, the bubbles clinging to my collarbone. I felt faint, and rested my head against the back of the tub, wondering how easy it would be to simply pass out and drown under the water. Hadn't a number of celebrities accidentally drowned from overdosing in the bath? The thought was appealing.

When I opened my eyes, ND was standing over me. How are you settling in? he asked.

The bubbles covered my body but still I felt completely exposed, and squirmed a little, causing the water to slosh back and forth. OK, I replied.

Completely undeterred, he slowly, almost painfully lowered himself on to the lid of the toilet, lifting one knee over the other until he was facing me with his legs crossed. It's not exactly been smooth sailing, has it? he said, pointing towards the hall. But the little one is fed now, which is the main thing. We'll have ourselves in a nice routine soon enough.

Can I ask you something?

Yes, of course.

Why was there never really any music or radio played over the speaker system?

Why do you ask? he said.

It's just . . . it might have helped morale.

And you think morale is low?

I nodded.

Music evokes emotion and memories from the past, does it not? What good is that to the people out there, in the main chambers? He shrugged, as though it was all theoretical.

But . . . doesn't our sadness bother you?

He paused. Every leader has to make difficult decisions. We'd get nowhere if I only did what was popular. Popular doesn't mean right.

If it weren't me in here, I said, it would be someone else.

There's always someone else in everything you do. There will always be a queue behind you. He rubbed his palms together, staring at me as the bubbles began to disperse. Remind me to let you try some of these homeopathic bath salts we have, he said. They really help with any aches and pains. He laughed. Do you buy into that sort of thing? Maybe you don't, being a woman of science.

# 23

I watched old sitcom re-runs in my room with no real sense of time. Hours merged into days, days into weeks. No one, including ND, disturbed me, so I did my best to stay within my walls, feeling somewhat safe and secure. There was something numbing about watching old sitcoms – no real concentration was required but equally it stopped me from fully engaging with my own thoughts. I liked the canned laughter – pretended I had company, sometimes laughing along too, glancing from side to side in acknowledgement of my imaginary peers. It was the only way I managed to lull myself into any form of sleep. But the more hours I spent continuously watching, the more I realised these characters and their lives were completely unrelatable to me. I'd spent my youth aspiring to be these people, had grown preoccupied with fitting in, never wanting to be seen as something different. Perhaps that was why I'd slipped through the net in the bunker, years of practice finally coming into fruition. What would my mum have said to me now? Would she have lectured me on this being a classic textbook exercise – a means of eliminating any form of diversity?

There was a knock on my door and I shifted, startled, forcing a plate with pizza crusts under the bed.

May I come in? Joanne said.

I opened the door a fraction. What is it?

It's Canavan, she said. We're not quite sure what we should do with him . . . Can you come? She bustled me straight down the corridor towards the cinema room, hovering her fingers over the handle. You're quite close, yes? Previous bunkmates?

I nodded. He had the top bunk . . .

Is he likely to listen to you? she said.

What's going on?

He's refusing to leave the cinema room. He requested a bucket . . . I thought he was using it to clean or something but I believe he's actually using it now as a toilet. And when I try to go near him he threatens me with its contents.

I could feel my face creasing into a smile – an awkward trait.

She took a deep breath, letting her shoulders slump. We don't want to have to resort to the soldiers . . .

OK, I replied. Let me see him.

She opened the door before jumping back, as if she was trying to distance herself from the air of the room. I stepped over the threshold and the smell immediately hit me, acidic and catching at the back of my throat. The bucket she'd given him was bright orange and I found this amusing, familiar. Why did they make buckets orange?

I couldn't quite bring myself to sit next to him on the sofa so I settled down in one of the embroidered cinema seats in the row behind him. There was another Western film flashing across the screen, perhaps the same one as before.

We must have sat for twenty or thirty minutes in silence, staring at the cowboys and Indians shooting one another. The bang and smoke of the guns was comical but the horses were majestic, galloping across the land. I wondered how long it would take for a horse to succumb to radiation. I suspected they would last longer than humans and for a brief moment I liked the image of them roaming the land freely, feeling that they were unhindered.

I think we've seen this film before, I said.

Canavan's voice was gruff and he barked some sort of response from under his duvets.

What's going to happen once you've filled that bucket? I asked.

He brought the duvet down from his chin and tucked it under his arms. I'm still a while off. I'll think of something by then.

The film continued to flash across the screen but the sound cut out.

So, what is this you're doing here, then? Some sort of demonstration?

He shrugged. Perhaps this is my attempt at a dirty protest.

And is it a success?

ND has no desire to come near me, so it must be working.

Canavan . . .

Do you think it's summer yet? he said, interrupting me. I can't stand myself in spring.

The smell must have settled under my nostrils because it didn't seem to bother me any more. Canavan, I can't take the guilt. It's making me physically sick. You're the same. I can see it.

He turned his head to look at me over his shoulder. What are you suggesting?

I shrugged. What if Levitt took my place? Maybe that would be more bearable for her? At least she'd get to stay near her child and see her more . . .

He started laughing. You're joking? You really think the leader's wife is going to let the teenager her husband knocked up live here? What, play one big happy family? I don't know much but I'll tell you something – as soon as that baby doesn't need her mother's milk, Levitt will have nothing more to do with her.

I looked at him; his attention was completely focused back on the screen.

I don't think I can live like this, then, I said. I can't detach myself.

What's the alternative? Give this all up? he said, raising his hands to showcase our environment.

Maybe, I said. Yeah, maybe. I got to my feet and positioned myself directly in front of him, blocking his view of the screen. Nothing good will come from you sitting here, surrounded by your own shit.

I don't know, maybe I'll manage to spread some sort of faecal disease and wipe out the entire top tier. A smile spread across his face then. Now that really would be worth the self-sacrifice, don't you think? Maybe ask your doctor his advice on that one.

I'm going to go back, I said, suddenly sure of myself. But I want you to come with me. We're tied together, aren't we? And I think . . . I don't know, maybe we can reverse this in some way if we go back.

My marker pen has dried up, he said.

I'll get you a new one.

A tear fell and ran down his cheek. I thought my bucket . . . I thought that might be the only way to say something again.

Please come back with me, I said. And I extended my hand for him to take.

He hesitated, before slowly placing his hand in mine. I helped him up on to his feet and he seemed to sway as he stood, his height towering above me. If he had toppled over, I wasn't sure I would have found my feet again.

Out in the hall Joanne was waiting, relieved to see Canavan standing behind me. Excellent, she said. Let's get you settled back into your room.

I linked my arm through Canavan's and we took deliberate steps forward.

We're going back to the main chamber, I said.

She skipped to get ahead of us. I have it on strict authority that you both stay here in these quarters.

Canavan broke away from me then and came up close to her. I thought she was about to gag as she took a step back.

Mr Canavan, I strongly suggest you wait and we can discuss this with the leader himself.

If he wants us back, no doubt he'll see to it that we return, he said. But for now we're going to our own bunks. Maybe then we'll get some fucking sleep. Or redemption, or whatever.

She wavered, but as we reached the first chamber door she signalled for the soldiers to let us through. Slowly, they began to part ways.

Wait, she called back. You can't return to the main chamber in your leisure clothes. Hold on, she said, walking away. And she returned almost immediately with two new grey boiler suits in clear plastic packaging, and two pairs of pristine white gym shoes. You'll need to put these on. Now.

I gripped the sleeves of my hoodie, a space in the fabric for my thumbs to fit through, reluctant to part with the soft, fluffy lined cotton.

Strip, one of the soldiers said.

Here? Canavan asked.

I'm not wearing any underwear, I said.

The same soldier shrugged.

Only once we were naked did Joanne throw the boiler suit bags to our feet, gathering our discarded clothes, keeping them at arm's length.

There was a familiarity to the boiler suits but this brought no comfort. Once the Velcro strips were fixed in place, I sat on the floor and slipped my gym shoes on, their interiors feeling cold and harsh compared to the slippers I'd taken off.

The soldier escorted us through the first chamber door. When we reached the last door from the inside we were handed to a different soldier. Glancing up, I realised it was my soldier with the birthmark on his forehead. He regarded me with a smile, quietly reaching into the chest pocket of his boiler suit and removing a small, folded piece of paper. He placed it inside my chest pocket and patted the fabric. Holding my eye, he brought his index finger up to his lips. I stared at him, vacant, no strength left in me to fight off ND's control.

He turned the handle of the door and then we were thrust out. I could see the dividing wall and its dwindling mourners. The shock of the environment was overwhelming. It couldn't have been that long, yet seeing it once again brought the horror of our daily existence back to the surface.

Canavan darted towards the divided space, bringing his body up close to the metal, and I followed him. I looked at his hands – filth under his fingernails, dark grit shaped into thin moons – grazes on his knuckles. There was real bulk to them, but they were so clearly the hands of an artist.

He turned to look at me. I want to go back, he said. This was a mistake.

I tilted my head, as if I'd misheard him. What? You can't . . .

I don't want to be here. I want to go back. You shouldn't have talked me into this.

I placed my hand as high up his arm as I could reach, thinking my touch might calm or soothe him in some way. A scratch on his neck looked infected.

He pushed me. I doubted he meant to be so forceful but that was how it came off and I stumbled, losing my footing. I thrust my arms out but I was falling and the back of my head struck one of the cast-iron radiators. I was aware of a screeching from the soles of Canavan's shoes and then footsteps running towards us. The soldiers must have been watching and they circled us, their guns pointed at Canavan.

Hands in the air, one shouted.

Another was crouched beside me, pinning me down, but all I wanted to do was get to my feet.

A crowd of inhabitants slowly began to gather and the soldiers shifted their gaze from us to them. One soldier spoke into his walkie-talkie but it was numbers and codes and nothing tangible.

Why did he attack you? the man pinning me down asked.

It wasn't like that, I said. Just an accident. I stumbled.

The back of my scalp felt warm and I brought my hand up to meet the sensation. When I lowered my fingers they were sticky and smeared with red.

I'm fine, I said, trying again to get to my feet. Honestly, there's nothing wrong.

I'm not sure about that, he said, tightening his hold on me.

Hands up, the same soldier from before shouted.

Canavan slowly raised his hands in the air, showcasing their true size. From the inside of his cuff crept a doodle of a baby's carriage and an obvious outline of ND pushing it. Across the wrist of his other arm was the word *shoelace* written in bold capital letters and underlined – a title – but the rest of the writing was hidden.

One of the soldiers took a step closer to Canavan, the rifle aimed at his chest. The crowd encircled us and Canavan's giant frame looked as if it was about to crumple to the floor. The soldier took another step towards him.

Canavan's eyes grew wild and I knew a change had taken place – like a dog turning against its owner. He turned and smiled at me. I'm sorry, Wolfe. I tried. And then he leapt forward, grabbing the barrel of the rifle with the soldier still attached to it, and brought its aim to his own cheek. He started screaming; no words, just noise. It was piercing, and my ears seemed to be set to its frequency. The soldier's face morphed into confusion or perhaps panic. I called out to Canavan but it was hopeless. I wanted to remind him there was no point, that the gun might as well have been a toy. His hands were wrapped tightly around the barrel, his screams intensifying until we were suddenly silenced by the rifle's one shot. The noise radiated through the walls, breaking sound waves and causing my hands to instinctively cup my ears.

Canavan lay still on the floor, except for one finger that flickered a few times. And blood began to flow from the hole in his right cheek. He looked as though he was awake, just staring up at the ceiling. The soldier who gripped me let go and I scrambled to Canavan. I cupped his hand in mine and could see his shoelace poem clearly now.

*Straggling, trailing lace*
*Then forward under his shoe*
*Dancing to catch me out.*
*I have to cross the road*
*Eyes straight ahead.*

Scrawled across his forearm was a step-by-step drawing of the knot required to tie a shoelace. And it was as if I needed that image, because what if I did forget and Canavan was my only proof of knowledge.

Feet moved and arms pulled me away from him. Stirling was there, cupping my face with his hands and talking to me, but his words made no sound. The noise of the bullet still reverberated in my ears. I stared at his lips – parting and smacking back together. I wished I could lip-read because I didn't think I'd ever hear again. He kept bringing my head closer to him and then moving it back and I felt myself resisting, desperate for my head not to be held in place. Where I'd been numb there was now a stabbing pain. It was sourcing from the back of my skull and my hand found itself on the source again, thinking somehow I could force the pain back inside.

Stirling and someone I didn't know placed their hands around my back and lifted my arms over their shoulders. My feet barely touched the ground and it felt nice, as if I was floating. They carried me to the surgery. Nurse Appleby was rushing around and they sat me down in one of the plastic waiting chairs. I still couldn't decipher what it was they were trying to say but from the way they paused I assumed they were asking me questions and I kept replying: Yes. Yeah. Nodding my head. Yes.

Stirling's hands moved across my scalp, parting my hair

in places, and I was irrationally irritated that he'd see so many of my grey hairs – white at the shafts, having fully lost their pigmentation – why did everyone refer to it as grey hair rather than white? Perhaps the blood would cover them. There was the noise of electric clippers, the volume getting louder as they were brought to my head, and I was pleased because at last I could hear something. There was the sensation of the clippers gliding through my hair and it was oddly therapeutic. Clumps of blood-matted hair fell on to my lap and I gripped them, winding the strands around my fingers. The room seemed deathly quiet again once the clippers were turned off but Stirling's hands were still moving across my scalp, pinching skin together, and Nurse Appleby was handing him a tube of something that resembled superglue. And then his hands grew still and he brought them down, pressing them against the chest of his lab coat.

He crouched in front of me so we were of similar height and placed his hands on my knees. And he was staring at me, Nurse Appleby too, and it was as though they were waiting for me to do something. He removed a little torch from his chest pocket and started flashing it in my eyes. Suddenly I jolted forward as if he'd brought me back to life. I was panting, my breath running away from me, and I clutched my chest, rocking backwards and forwards in my seat. And he gripped my knees, trying to steady me. The tears came out in waves then and I let them run.

You're safe, he said. You're safe. He said it over and over, and I started breathing to the rhythm of his words, silently chanting them, letting them escape through my nostrils.

When I grew still again he listened to my chest. You're in shock, he said. He turned to Appleby – Can you get me a damp cloth or something to wipe her face? – and she nodded, scurrying off. He kept staring at me and I wondered what I must look like. Do you feel sleepy? he asked.

I nodded.

You have a concussion. We have to keep you awake.

Is he dead?

Yes, he said. I'm so sorry.

# 24

The first night I stayed in Stirling's surgery, lying out on his examination bed with his blankets trying to warm me back to life. Stirling sat slumped in his chair and I watched his eyes droop, his head briefly flopping to one side as though his neck had been snapped, before stirring and straightening himself in his seat.

I was only aware of it being morning from the noise outside his surgery – of the nurses arriving, of the other doctors getting organised for their patients and clinics.

How do you feel? Stirling asked, rubbing his face.

I shrugged, still lying flat, staring up at the ceiling.

Your head will be sore for quite some time.

Did anyone ever catch the mouse? I asked, turning to look at him.

He nodded. One of the kids managed to coax it with the dregs of a fruit pouch.

Did they hurt it?

Of course not, he said. The kids adore the little thing. There's a rota in the recreation room for who looks after it. It lives in a box from the pharmacy.

Is it healthy?

It appears to be.

I closed my eyes for a moment. I've been retaining this belief that everything I assume to be true might be wrong, I said. Like the mouse, and where it has come from . . . But with Canavan, I know he can't return.

I thought you wouldn't come back, Stirling said.

A tear trickled down my face. I'm here.

But for how long?

Do you hate me? I said.

Why'd you do it, Wolfe? Why'd you take her?

Because . . . I paused, struggling to find the words. It made sense to me at the time. Or I thought it did . . . But I'm not so sure any more. I reached up and ran my fingers across the bald patch on my head. There was a bristled texture and the unfamiliar feeling of the adhesive that held my wound closed.

Stirling came to my side and tugged my hand down from my head, holding it in his own hands. Wolfe, you need to get up now.

Will you lie next to me for a minute?

No, Wolfe, sorry.

Is this how it will be now?

He shrugged. I don't know. I'm not sure what I feel any more.

OK . . . I said, nodding, unsteadily trying to sit up.

He helped me on to my feet. I can walk with you, he said. Shall I take you to your bunk?

Can you take me to the pharmacy?

Do you think you're up to that? he said.

No point putting off the inevitable.

We followed the all-too-familiar route back. Perhaps I was paranoid but I was convinced a whispering crowd had begun to form behind us, people joining with each step we took. When we came to a stop outside the door, I peered in through the artificial windows to see Valentine dealing with a queue of patients, while Levitt faced the sink, her shoulders slumped, the fabric of her boiler suit hanging from her frame.

Stirling opened the door and stepped aside, allowing me to enter.

Valentine's head shot up, his face displaying something that resembled relief. His patient was still speaking but it was clear he wasn't paying her any more attention. And then Levitt turned.

I walked across the front shop, stopping at the dispensary door, and Valentine let me in, while Stirling nodded with the satisfaction of someone who had finally delivered a package to the right address, before retreating.

Valentine looked me up and down. I was beginning to think they'd killed you, he said before turning to Levitt. Aren't you going to say hello?

She just stared at me. Everything about her, from behind the eyes to the posture of her body, was mechanical and near lifeless.

Levitt . . . But my words trailed off. I had no idea what I could possibly say.

She returned to the sink, turning the tap back on to rinse out beakers and cups.

Well, Valentine said. I'm not sure everyone will agree but I'm certainly glad to see you again. Regardless of what's happened, people still need their medication. I can't run this place on my own and, in case you've forgotten, you do happen to be a pharmacist. You have a responsibility to your patients. And she, he added, pointing towards Levitt, is worse than useless now. He returned his attention to the waiting patient and dispensed her medication, inspecting her empty mouth before nodding her off.

How long have I been away? I asked.

What, you don't know?

I shook my head.

He glanced at Levitt before answering. Five weeks, give or take.

What do you want me to do? I asked.

You can deal with the rest of them today, he said, gathering his things.

What if I can't do it?

You'll be fine. It's just like riding a bike.

The next patient was another woman. I recognised her but couldn't recall her name. She offered it to me, and her ID number, but everything was hazy and I was slow in remembering my role, in finding her drug chart and popping out her tablets. I passed them through the hatch. She stared at me while she placed the tablets inside her mouth. She tossed the empty plastic cup back towards me and it landed on its side. She sipped some water, opened her mouth and stuck out her tongue.

Thank you, I said.

She shook her head in disgust. You should be fucking ashamed of yourself.

Afterwards, Levitt turned to me, hesitating, and I braced myself for what she was about to say. I'm sorry about your friend, she finally said. Canavan . . .

And I stared at her, unable to comprehend how she was able to say something so gracious and kind. She should have clawed my eyes out as ND had predicted. It was the least I deserved.

I nodded, and did everything I could to hold back my tears.

She continued with her task, set back on autopilot.

I returned to my bunk to find all the beds in my column empty except for Mrs Foer's. I knew without having to ask that Levitt was sleeping elsewhere. Perhaps she stayed with Stirling now. Foer was wrapped in her blankets, a book close to her nose, and I expected to be either ignored or sneered at, but on noticing me she sat up a little and smiled.

You're back, my dear, she said. It's lovely to see you.

Is it?

It's always nice to have you home.

What are you reading? I asked.

A book on Stockholm. I'm visiting there next. Have you ever heard of this thing called Stockholm Syndrome? It's fascinating . . .

I nodded, climbing up on to my bunk. My blankets were still there – apparently no one wanted the belongings of a traitor. Lying flat, I pulled a blanket over my face and let the coarse fabric absorb the tears I'd been holding in. And only then did I remember the little piece of paper handed to me by my soldier with the birthmark, folded up into a square and sitting in my chest pocket. I didn't think I had the energy to look, to take in another order, the claustrophobia of ND's control too much to bear. But I couldn't stop myself. I pulled the blanket down and unfolded the note. The paper was cheap, recycled, and written in pencil. It read: *Stay strong. Soon. You will be needed.*

After staring at it for what must have been minutes I started tearing it into pieces, like confetti, before swallowing them one by one. I had no idea what it meant. Was it offering salvation or calling me back? I repeated the words from the note in my head, like a mantra, like a message from God. I wanted to trust its author completely.

In the pharmacy I witnessed Levitt being called to the lair. She instinctively pressed her hand up against her breasts, as if she was checking they were still capable of holding milk. The soldiers didn't have to manhandle her; she obeyed without uttering a word, mechanical once again in her walk. When she returned, forty minutes or so later, she simply continued as though nothing had happened, crossing her legs on the floor and date-checking the M–N drawer.

Levitt . . . How is she?

We can't speak about her, OK? She's off limits.

I'm sorry, I whispered. I know that doesn't mean much . . .

She was quiet for a moment. I asked Stirling to sedate me, she said, without turning to face me. Because I just want to be numb, even for a little while. But he won't. It'll pass into my milk supply, supposedly.

And for the rest of our shift we worked in silence, the hours punctuated by Levitt's comings and goings from the lair until I told her she could finish early. Being left alone in the pharmacy didn't feel like the worst thing in the world any more.

I was tidying drawers, preparing for Valentine's handover, when a soldier ran in. He was one of the younger ones, serious and diligent in his job. He came close to the Perspex and passed through the hatch an official piece of paper, thick with the texture of expensive card.

It's urgent, he said. An emergency.

On the card it said: *Naloxone. Now. Bring Wolfe.*

It was written in pencil and in what I suspected was the same hand from the note I'd been given before. I cast my mind back to those days in my previous life, of substance misusers and confined consultation rooms – my eyes always being drawn to the naloxone leaflets while trying to make small talk. None of them ever asked for a naloxone kit; never considered their potential need. One of them did ask me once how it worked and I wasn't even sure – *an opioid antag-onist, reversing and blocking the effects of an overdose if admin-istered in time* was as much of a summary as I could offer.

I stared at the note. I don't have any, I said. The injections are kept with the doctors.

When I looked up, panic was shaking through his face and he gripped his rifle. Come with me, he said. Now. And before I could do anything I was being escorted down the corridor towards the doctors' surgery.

He hurled me through the door and towards Appleby's desk. She stared up at us, surprised yet simultaneously put out by our arrival.

He won't see you, she said.

It's an emergency, the soldier replied, marching me by the elbow towards Stirling's room.

He's with a patient, Appleby shouted behind us.

But the soldier flung the door open regardless and Stirling looked up, startled from where he stood, a male patient's abdomen on display.

What are you doing? Stirling said.

Leave, the soldier demanded, pointing from the patient to the door, and the man quickly got to his feet, pulling his boiler suit back on as he departed.

You can't barge in here when I'm with a patient . . .

Get what you need, the soldier said to me. We can't wait.

I showed the piece of paper to Stirling, staring at his face as he took in the message. For the leader? he said.

I nodded.

No, Stirling said. Not unless I can assess him.

The young soldier was really beside himself with panic now. Perhaps he felt his life too was on the line. Only Wolfe, he shouted. That's my orders.

Stirling shrugged.

The soldier raised his gun, pointing it at Stirling's face. I don't have time for this shit. Give her the injection so we can be on our way.

Or you'll shoot me? Stirling said.

I took a step towards Stirling, desperate to touch him. It's OK, I said.

No, it's not OK. Every time you go to him I lose more of you, he whispered. You're almost entirely gone. I don't even know you any more.

I stared at him, this broken man. Please, give me what he's asking for.

He paused, growling in anger, before walking to the medicine cabinet above the sink and unlocking it. He handed me a box with two injections.

The soldier once again gripped my arm, tugging me out of the door. And I turned, wanting to tell Stirling that I loved him, because I didn't think I'd see him again. But the words didn't come and he wouldn't have believed them anyway. They carried such little weight.

The soldier sprinted with me in his grip and I struggled to keep up, the soles of my gym shoes slapping off the concrete. At the entrance to the lair the doors were already open and I was thrust through, the soldiers parting ways to make room for me. In the floral hall, by a door I'd never entered before, Joanne waited for me.

Do you have what's been requested? she said.

I held up the box, before offering it to the soldier.

No, no, not him, Joanne said, taking the box and ushering the young soldier away, much to his obvious relief. I'll administer it, she said, looking down at the box with uncertainty.

Do you know what you're doing? I said.

She shrugged. I've done my first aid course . . .

I paused. Well, if you're not sure, I could do it.

You?

I used to give flu vaccines. Hundreds of them.

She hesitated, indecisive, before passing the box back to me. Will it take long to work? she asked.

I don't know . . .

But it will work? she pressed.

I don't know . . .

She fell quiet. Maybe I should wait in the kitchen, then. Give you some space.

Where's his wife? I asked.

In the nursery. She lowered her voice. She doesn't know anything about this.

OK, I said. I'll come for you when I'm done.

Inside, a bedside lamp shone dimly and I could see the outline of ND's body under the duvet. As my eyes darted around I acknowledged how beautiful a room it was – Arts and Crafts wallpaper and classic furniture. I took a step closer but his eyes were closed and he didn't seem to be aware of my presence. He looked fragile. Deathly.

I cleared my throat. His eyes opened slowly and he stared at me, all recognition momentarily lost. He blinked. I'm glad you're here.

You look terrible, I said. Have you seen a doctor?

He managed a smile. His breathing was heavy and desperate, the way the oxycodone had intended it to be. I tried to imagine the tolerance his body must have endured, finally buckling under the weight of abuse. Had he expected to defy his addiction? Was it denial? Naloxone was his only chance of reversing the respiratory depression, of stopping those opiate receptors from binding further. And I was to be his saviour – how odd that it should be me he had to trust.

I came close and took in the creases of his face. He tried to reach out and touch me, but struggled. I pulled back the duvet, revealing his branded silk pyjamas.

Do it now, he whispered.

I removed one naloxone injection from its packaging and pulled the cap off the needle. I brought it close to his thigh and stopped. Why me? I asked.

His eyes were wide, willing me on. Why not you? he said, panting for breath.

I paused. But why is it always me? You have so many others . . .

He spluttered, small particles of saliva resting on his bottom lip. Because you don't think you deserve to be here. You'll do what's expected because you're grateful, even if you don't know it . . . He trailed off, struggling, and I imagined his lungs labouring with each inflation.

I brought the injection upright, remembering Canavan's painting of the nurse with the tricorn hat and the purple injection. Suddenly, as though this too was inevitable, I placed the injection down on the bedside table, clearly in his line of vision.

What are you doing? he whispered.

It gets easier each time, I said.

He closed his eyes before slowly opening them. And he tried to laugh, the reality of it all dawning on him. My portrait . . . he whispered. Canavan will still be laughing, wherever he lands.

I sat down on the edge of the bed, before deciding to lie next to him. We lay there for a moment, staring at each other, before I reached out and clasped his hand. I doubt it will be painful, I said.

He gripped my hand tighter. And I could see he was scared, but he knew more than anyone that there were worse ways to die.

I stayed with him, as I had with Glass, watching his chest move up and down, before he finally took his last breath. His eyes and mouth were open and I closed them so he looked as if he was sleeping. There was a calmness in his expression that I hadn't expected. It was almost beautiful.

The floral corridor was empty and I walked towards the nursery. Inside, there was no sign of ND's wife, just Eleanor sleeping soundly in her cot, the hot-air-balloon mobile bobbing above her. Instinctively I gathered her in my arms and she smelled wonderful – maybe it was baby powder or maybe it was just her smell. With her eyes still closed, she puckered her lips and I rested her head over my shoulder, bringing my hand up to the back of her scalp. It was as if I was in a trance, almost floating back down the corridor towards the soldiers and the entrance to the bunker's main chamber. I was aware of two sets of hands trying to take hold of me, rifles bobbing next to their hips, but it didn't matter. I was willing to die before letting go of this child. My path was blocked but still I tried to continue moving, not listening to their aggravated tones. And then one of them came forward – the one with the droplet birthmark – and he ordered the others to step aside. With his palm resting gently on my back, he escorted us through the doors until we were once again facing the familiar concrete of the main chamber, and its dividing wall.

I turned to him and he smiled this odd, comforting smile. I told you you'd be needed, he whispered.

ND is dead, I said. I—

But he cut me off. I know, he replied. But at least his heart attack was instant. We can take comfort from that. Everything's going to be OK.

He waved me forward as if he was freeing a wild animal, willing me to find my way back. And I walked, one step and then another, the crowd gathering and growing, following me until I was facing Levitt, handing her baby back to her.

I retained few memories of the days that followed. I spent most of my time lying on my bunk, sleeping or staring up at the empty Canavan-shaped canvas above. Mrs Foer delivered food pouches, holding them to my lips while I gulped down what I could. Occasionally I'd wake confused, expecting Canavan's face to appear, before having to remind myself of the reality. I was so tired, an exhaustion that overwhelmed my bones. Something irreplaceable had been depleted from within me.

I had expected someone to come – soldiers or an unidentified ally of ND's – and I was OK about it, had made peace with the prospect. Eleanor was back with her mother so I reasoned that perhaps it was time for me to return to mine. I wanted to cling to my memories of the past, let happy thoughts be on my mind when it all ended. There wouldn't have been a better way to go. It was all just a waiting game. But as it turned out no one ever did come for me. ND's death was announced over the speaker system, with Dr Bishop's dulcet tones confirming it had been from natural causes, like all the others. There was to be a period of mourning, while two soldiers rather unceremoniously removed his body in a black bag. He was placed inside the airlock chamber on our side – no military service, or plaque, his body rotting with everyone else's, only bones to be stepped over on our release. No better than the rest of us.

They brought the wall back up and I heard that Levitt was reunited with her family, not that I ever considered venturing across. Whatever ND's reasons were for bringing the wall down, they had died with him. And all the previous hierarchies appeared to be dying too. An election was organised. Some of ND's appointed advisors considered themselves candidates but there was fresh blood too: a young twenty-something woman who spoke with compassion and empathy was gaining ground. The schoolteacher also considered his chances, his slogan being: *Regardless, the children will be OK*. And I supposed he had a point. After all, the sun was only halfway through its life cycle, so maybe there was reason to plan for a future. Everything seemed to happen in a circular motion, trends of time and moods continuously repeating on a loop. Perhaps we were now approaching the best part in the cycle, where we were allowed to be hopeful again.

I didn't know what had happened to my soldier with the birthmark, or what would become of ND's lair now he was gone. Maybe nothing. Would the next leader take it, despite their promises, and settle into a better life? We were so fixed on teaching the children how to share what limited supplies we had, but it was tokenistic and superficial. In this world or the one above ground, who really wanted to share anything?

But I tried not to dwell too much, or live inside my own head. Instead, I made my way to the recreation room, eyed Stirling from behind the bookshelves, and considered if there was still something there worth salvaging.

# ACKNOWLEDGEMENTS

There are many people who helped this book become a reality. Still, I continue to be overwhelmed by their time, encouragement and generosity. Thank you.

To Eve Hall, for taking a chance on this book and being the editor of my dreams; to Joanne Dickinson for your unwavering support and guidance; to Sorcha Rose for your editorial assistance and patience; and to the whole team at Hodder & Stoughton for championing me and my writing. I could not have asked for a better home for *The Pharmacist*.

To my wonder of a literary agent Cathryn Summerhayes, as well as Jess Molloy and everyone at Curtis Brown. I will be forever grateful for all that you do.

To Lynsey Rogers, Caitrin Armstrong and everyone at the Scottish Book Trust. Your dedication to championing new writers knows no bounds. Receiving a New Writers Award was monumental in my development as a writer.

To Wayne Price and Alan Spence who so kindly offered me their wisdom and encouragement during my time at the University of Aberdeen; to Alan McMunnigall and everyone I was lucky enough to meet through those legendary Tuesday night writing classes. Without you all I wouldn't be a writer.

To Rebecca Smith, Shane Strachan and Gavin Gilmour for giving up their time to read early drafts of this book and for offering such insightful feedback; and to Zoë Strachan and Helen Sedgwick, I owe you both a great deal.

To my parents, thank you for your love and belief in my ability even when I couldn't see it myself; to my family and friends, thank you for your endless support and enthusiasm. Truly, I'd be lost without you.

To the pharmacists, and pharmacy teams I've had the pleasure of working with – you're heroes and the hardest working people I know. Carry on the good fight.

To Fraser and Phoebe, I hope to make you proud. And finally to Angus, for everything.

# READING QUESTIONS

- How does the setting of the bunker affect the characters' actions?
- As a pharmacist, do you think Wolfe has an easier life than some of the other residents of the bunker?
- Did you miss not having another point of view during the novel?
- Do you feel sorry for Wolfe? If the novel was not from her point of view would you feel differently about her actions?
- 'The literature had been carefully censored: children's books, light romance, travel and craft magazines made up the bulk' – why do you think there was this much control over the bunker's library?
- Wolfe explains that she left her family behind without saying goodbye in order to move into the bunker. How does that make you feel towards her?
- How does Wolfe's previous personal and family relationships influence her behaviour in the bunker?
- The pharmacy becomes a microcosm of the bunker and the people who live within it. Did anything surprise you about the patients Wolfe helped or the situations she faced?
- When the two sides of the bunker compete by decorating Christmas trees, were you surprised by the reaction?

- Do you think the characters who have family with them in the bunker compared to those who do not have a different experience? If so, in what ways?
- At one point in the novel, Wolfe stops Levitt from going back over to her side of the bunker when the alarm sounds. How does this change the direction of the novel?
- Which character in the text is the most innately good? Why do you think this?
- What do you think of Wolfe and Stirling's relationship? Do you think they should be together?
- At the end of the novel, did you agree with Wolfe's actions?
- What do you imagine unfolds after the final scene of the novel?

# THIRSTY ANIMALS

**The world is running out of water.**

Aida is forced back home to live on the farm with her mum. For now, they are safe with enough to get by.

But Aida's life continues to change. The service station she works at grows emptier with each day, and suspicious strangers arrive on the farm who are beginning to overstay their welcome. And with the horrific scenes she witnessed at the border – between those with water and those without – she wonders how it could get any worse.

**And then their taps are turned off.**

Everything Aida and her disjointed family have been preparing for, and Aida thought impossible, is happening. Now they must try and survive long enough for the rain to come.

HODDER